THE SCARLET LETTER IS NOW A "V."

A vampire who feeds on something far more intimate than blood.
A revenge as perfect as true love.
A Japanese vampire who burns with passion — literally.
A legendary sexual dismemberment performed on stage.
A boy introduced to the sweetest pleasures of Hell.
A vampire who finds fulfillment on the last night of her life.

—⚕—

VAMPIRIC EROTICA BY

Charles de Lint • Jessica Amanda Salmonson • Gene Wolfe •
Kathe Koja and Barry N. Malzberg • Christa Faust • Steve Rasnic Tem
and Melanie Tem • Norman Partridge • Ian McDowell •
Nancy Holder • David B. Silva • Douglas Clegg •
Wilum H. Pugmire • Brian Hodge • Mike Baker • A. R. Morlan •
Elizabeth Engstrom • Danielle Willis • Robert Devereaux •
Thomas F. Monteleone • Wayne Allen Sallee

LOVE in VEIN

TWENTY ORIGINAL TALES OF VAMPIRIC EROTICA

Edited by
POPPY Z. BRITE

HarperPrism
An Imprint of HarperPaperbacks

This anthology owes much to the assistance of Martin Greenberg and Richard Gilliam. Thanks to them and the authors who did the real work.

—P.Z.B.

HarperPaperbacks *A Division of* HarperCollins*Publishers*
10 East 53rd Street, New York, N.Y. 10022

Library of Congress Cataloging-in-Publication Data

Love in vein: twenty original tales of vampiric erotica / edited by Poppy Z. Brite.
    p.   cm.
   ISBN 0-06-105312-0 : $11.99
   1. Erotic stories, American. 2. Vampires—Fiction. I. Brite, Poppy Z.
PS648.E7L68 1994
813'.01083538—dc20   94-29901
                                CIP

❖ 10 9 8 7 6 5 4 3 2 1

Introduction

The vampire is everything we love about sex and the night and the dark dream-side of ourselves: adventure on the edge of pain, the thrill to be had from breaking taboos. In editing *Love In Vein*, I hoped for the chance to see what some of my favorite writers would make of an endlessly versatile creature that had, after all, been kind to me.

I wanted stories exploring the visceral connection between vampirism and eroticism, the attraction we feel to a creature who requires our lifeblood (and sometimes more) for eternal sustenance. I wanted stories that ventured into a world where the mutant can be considered beautiful even as it is feared; where the bizarre is something to be sought and treasured, not destroyed; where the drinking of blood does not necessarily make one a monster.

I selected the stories by sending out guidelines to several of my favorite writers in horror and related genres. I would have liked to ask even more, but I only had one volume to fill, and stories by *all* the writers I admire would have required at least twenty. Some of the writers had too many other deadlines to meet, a fate I understand all too well. Some were attracted by the idea and agreed to write stories.

And a few heard about it through the grapevine.

Love In Vein was a more-or-less invitational anthology, which meant I didn't put out a general call for stories, but I did read anything that came in over the transom. Of these, I think I ended up taking three. A few others I would have liked to use came in after the book was already full. The interest in this project reinforced my belief that most horror writers enjoy trying their hand at the traditional tropes—the vampire tale, the ghost story—sooner or later, perhaps because the familiar canvas can show off one's individual flourishes so well.

In my guidelines I asked the authors to explore all types of vampirism and sexuality. They have done so more thoroughly than I dared hope. Though blood is drunk in some of these stories, you won't find many fanged guys with capes and cruciphobias here. Yet all the stories in *Love In Vein* are vampire tales of one sort or another, in that they deal with creatures who feed off others' vital forces in some way.

My first novel, *Lost Souls*, was begun when I was nineteen but not published until I was twenty-five. *Lost Souls* is a homoerotic, Southern Gothic rock 'n' roll vampire tale set partly in New Orleans and partly in my fictitious town of Missing Mile, North Carolina. I had never been especially fascinated with vampires before this book. I chose to write about them because it was 1987 and I was interested in and involved with the Gothic subculture—the beliefs distilled from dark music and darker emotion, the black lace and torn velvet, the affinity for graveyards, the bloodletting. That was what I wanted to write about, and vampires are an essential icon of that culture. Those kids are beautiful, alienated, at once craving wild experience and romanticizing death. Is it any wonder they identify with vampires?

By the time the novel was published, my outlook had changed somewhat, mostly because the eighties were over and I was still alive. You can only maintain an intensely Gothic frame of mind for so long before either killing yourself or starting to feel like a bit of a

Introduction

poser, and neither alternative appealed to me.[1] But now that I had said all I ever wanted to say about vampires, I was asked to talk about them in interviews, solicited to write ever more about them, even accosted at parties and signings by people who claimed to be them. The vampire is not only perennially popular, he is the only supernatural creature who has become a role model.

After *Lost Souls* sold to Delacorte Abyss, I heard that another publisher had declined to bid in the auction because an editor found the story "amoral." That editor was right. Attempting to cram the fun-loving, sensuous vampire into the tired old dichotomy of good versus evil denies all that is potentially appealing, even useful about him. To impose morals on him is to deny his erotic decadence, or to imply that erotic decadence itself is somehow without morals. This is insulting to anyone who enjoys sex. Most people do not consider their pleasures or their loves amoral, and do not appreciate being lectured on how wrongly they are conducting their private affairs.

The most famous and enduring vampire tales—from Bram Stoker's *Dracula* and Sheridan Le Fanu's "Carmilla" to Anne Rice's *Vampire Chronicles*—are almost invariably shot through with a strong vein of eroticism. And eroticism in fiction—meaning the exploration and enjoyment of sex in all its forms—is often subversive. It can be openly so, as in Flaubert's *Madame Bovary* or Burroughs's *Naked Lunch*; it can be subtly so, as in "Carmilla." This nineteenth-century lesbian vampire love story contains no explicit sex, yet it disturbed many critics so deeply that they all but rewrote the story to prove that Le Fanu's obviously female narrator was a boy!

The vampire is a subversive creature in every way, and I think this accounts for much of his appeal. In an age where moralists use the fact that sex is dangerous to "prove" that sex is bad, the vampire

---

1. Heather Bricks, editor and publisher of Chicago gone zine *The Web*, made me rethink this by pointing out that many participants in the Gothic subculture do not worship or court death. They simply refuse to fear it, and they stop themselves from fearing it by exploring it, becoming intimate with it. I suspect Heather's perception will strike a chord with any number of horror readers and writers.

Introduction

points out that sex has *always* been dangerous. These days, if you wish to make love to someone without a layer of latex separating your most sensitive membranes, it becomes necessary to ask yourself, "Would I be willing to die a slow, lingering death for this person?" The answer may be yes—but for the vampire, it's not even an issue. He laughs in the face of safe sex, and he lives forever.

Since I write about gay male characters and include explicit sex in my work, I am often suspected of Trying To Make A Statement. An interviewer for a gay/lesbian newspaper in Colorado recently said to me:

> *One gay friend of mine thought you were trying to capture an aura of decadence. I thought you were simply presenting [homosexuality] as a norm of youth counterculture. Or perhaps you're just trying to turn mainstream conventions upside down . . .*

The answer could be all of the above, but truly it is none of the above. I don't feel that one genital configuration is inherently more decadent than another; I'm not aware that youth counterculture *has* any norms; and I care about my characters far too much to put them on soapboxes and make them rail against mainstream conventions. Like most writers of erotic fiction, I simply write about what turns me on, what I love. If a gay reader finds courage in my words—if a conservative reader is bothered or, dare I hope, swayed by them—I am ecstatic. But I couldn't make it true on the page if it wasn't true inside me.

I believe the authors of these stories have found erotic truth inside themselves and put it on the page for you to read. From this point on, *Love In Vein* is their book. I hope you enjoy it.

Poppy Z. Brite
New Orleans, November 1994

Table of Contents

—⁓—

Do Not Hasten to Bid Me Adieu

by
Norman Partridge

One

He was done up all mysterious-like—black bandanna covering half his face, black duster, black boots and hat. Traveling incognito, just like that coachman who picked up Harker at the Borgo Pass.

Yeah. As a red man might figure it, that was many moons ago . . . at the beginning of the story. Stoker's story, anyway. But that tale of mannered woe and stiff-upper-lip bravado was as crazy as the lies Texans told about Crockett and his Alamo bunch. Harker didn't exist. Leastways, the man in black had never met him.

Nobody argued sweet-told lies, though. Nobody in England, any-how. Especially with Stoker tying things up so neat and proper, and the count gone to dust and dirt and all.

A grin wrinkled the masked man's face as he remembered the vampire crumbling to nothing finger-snap quick, like the remnants of a cow-flop campfire worried by an unbridled prairie wind. Son of a bitch must have been *mucho* old. Count Dracula had departed this vale of tears, gone off to suckle the devil's own tit . . . though the man in black doubted that Dracula's scientific turn of mind would allow him to believe in Old Scratch.

You could slice it fine or thick—ultimately, the fate of Count Dracula didn't make no nevermind. The man in black was one hell of a long way from Whitby, and his dealings with the count seemed about as unreal as Stoker's scribblings. Leastways, that business was behind him. This was to be *his* story. And he was just about to slap the ribbons to it.

Slap the ribbons he did, and the horses picked up the pace. The wagon bucked over ruts, creaking like an arthritic dinosaur. Big black box jostling in the back. Tired horses sweating steam up front. West Texas sky a quilt for the night, patched blood red and bruise purple and shot through with blue-pink streaks, same color as the meat that lines a woman's heart.

And black. Thick black squares in that quilt, too. More coming every second. Awful soon, there'd be nothing but those black squares and a round white moon.

Not yet, though. The man could still see the faint outline of a town on the horizon. There was Morrisville, up ahead, waiting in the red and purple and blue-pink shadows.

He wondered what she'd make of Morrisville. It was about as far from the stone manors of Whitby as one could possibly get. No vine-covered mysteries here. No cool salt breezes whispering from the green sea, blanketing emerald lawns, traveling lush garden paths. Not much of anything green at all. No crumbling Carfax estate, either. And no swirling fog to mask the night—everything right out in the open, just as plain as the nose on your face. A West Texas shit-splat. Cattle business, mostly. A matchstick kind of town. Wooden buildings—wind-dried, sun-bleached—that weren't much more than tinder dreading the match.

The people who lived there were the same way.

But it wasn't the town that made this place. He'd told her that. It was that big blanket of a sky, an eternal wave threatening to break

4

over the dead dry husk of the prairie, fading darker with each turn of the wagon wheels—cresting, cresting—ready to smother the earth like a hungry thing.

Not a bigger, blacker night anywhere on the planet. When that nightwave broke, as it did all too rarely—wide and mean and full-up with mad lightning and thunder—it was something to see.

He'd promised her that. He'd promised to show her the heart of a wild Texas night, the way she'd shown him the shadows of Whitby.

Not that he always kept his promises. But this one was a promise to himself as much as it was a promise to her.

He'd hidden from it for a while. Sure. In the wake of all that horror, he'd run. But finally he'd returned to Whitby, and to her. He'd returned to keep his promise.

And now he was coming home.

"Not another place like it anywhere, Miss Lucy. Damn sure not on this side of the pond, anyhow."

She didn't fake a blush or get all offended by his language, like so many of the English missies did, and he liked that. She played right with him, like she knew the game. Not just knew it, but thrived on it. "No," she said. "Nothing here could possibly resemble your Texas, Quincey P. Morris. Because no one here resembles you."

She took him by the lapels and kissed him like she was so hungry for it, like she couldn't wait another moment, and then he had her in his arms and they were moving together, off the terrace, away from the house and the party and the dry rattle of polite conversation. He was pulling her and she was pushing him and together they were going back, back into the shadows of Whitby, deep into the garden where fog settled like velvet and the air carried what for him would always be the green scent of England.

And then they were alone. The party sounds were a world away. But those sounds were nothing worth hearing—they were dead sounds compared to the music secret lovers could make. Matched with the rustle of her skirts, and the whisper of his fingers on her tender thighs, and the sweet duet of hungry lips, the sounds locked up in the big stone house were as sad and empty as the cries of the damned souls in Dr. Seward's loony bin, and he drew her away from them, and she pushed him away from them, and together they entered another world where strange shadows met, cloaking them like fringed buckskin, like gathered satin.

Buckskin and satin. It wasn't what you'd call a likely match. They'd been dancing around it for months. But now the dancing was over.

"God, I want you," he said.

She didn't say anything. There was really nothing more to say.

She gave. She took. And he did the same.

He reined in the horses just short of town. Everything was black but that one circle of white hanging high in the sky.

He stepped down from the driver's box and stretched. He drew the night air deep into his lungs. The air was dry and dusty, and there wasn't anything in it that was pleasant.

He was tired. He lay down on top of the big black box in the back of the wagon and thought of her. His fingers traveled wood warped in the leaky cargo hold of a British ship. Splinters fought his callused hands, lost the battle. But he lost the war, because the dissonant rasp of rough fingers on warped wood was nothing like the music the same rough fingers could make when exploring a young woman's thighs.

He didn't give up easy, though. He searched for the memory of the green scent of England, and the music he'd made there, and shadows of satin and buckskin. He searched for the perfume of her hair, and her skin. The ready, eager perfume of her sex.

His hands traveled the wood. Scurrying like scorpions. Damn things just wouldn't give up, and he couldn't help laughing.

Raindrops beaded on the box. The nightwave was breaking.

No. Not raindrops at all. Only his tears.

The sky was empty. No clouds. No rain.

No lightning.

But there was lightning in his eyes.

Two

—◊—

The morning sunlight couldn't penetrate the filthy jailhouse window. That didn't bother the man in black. He had grown to appreciate the darkness.

Sheriff Josh Muller scratched his head. "This is the damnedest thing, Quincey. You got to admit that that Stoker fella made it pretty plain in his book."

Quincey smiled. "You believe the lies that Buntline wrote about Buffalo Bill, too?"

"Shit no, Quince. But, hell, that Stoker is an Englishman. I thought they was different and all—"

"I used to think that. Until I got to know a few of the bastards, that is."

"Well," the sheriff said, "that may be . . . but the way it was, was . . . we all thought that you had been killed by them Transylvanian gypsies, like you was in the book."

"I've been some places, before and since. But we never got to Transylvania. Not one of us. And I ain't even feelin' poorly."

"But in the book—"

"Just how stupid are you, Josh? You believe in vampires, too? Your bowels get loose thinkin' about Count Dracula?"

"Hell, no, of course not, but—"

"Shit, Josh, I didn't mean that like a question you were supposed to answer."

"Huh?"

Quincey sighed. "Let's toss this on the fire and watch it sizzle. It's

7

real simple—I *ain't* dead. I'm *back*. Things are gonna be just like they used to be. We can start with this here window."

Quincey Morris shot a thumb over his shoulder. The sheriff looked up and saw how dirty the window was. He grabbed a rag from his desk. "I'll take care of it, Quince."

"You don't get it," the man in black said.

"Huh?"

Again, Quincey sighed. "I *ain't* dead. I'm *back*. Things are gonna be just like they used to be. And this *is* Morrisville, right?"

The sheriff squinted at the words painted on the window. He wasn't a particularly fast reader—he'd been four months reading the Stoker book, and that was with his son doing most of the reading out loud. On top of that, he had to read this backwards. He started in, reading right to left: O-W-E-N-S-V-I-L-L . . .

That was as far as he got. Quincey Morris picked up a chair and sent it flying through the glass, and then the word wasn't there anymore.

Morris stepped through the opening and started toward his wagon. He stopped in the street, which was like a river of sunlight, turned, and squinted at the sheriff. "Get that window fixed," he said. "Before I come back."

"Where are you headed?" The words were out of Josh Muller's mouth before he could stop himself, and he flinched at the grin Morris gave him in return.

"I'm goin' home," was all he said.

There in the shadows, none of it mattered, because it was only the two of them. Two creatures from different worlds, but with hearts that were the same.

He'd come one hell of a long way to find this. Searched the world over. He'd known that he'd find it, once he went looking, same as he'd known that it was something he had to go out and find if he wanted to keep on living. His gut told him, *Find it, or put a bullet in your brainpan.* But he hadn't known it would feel like this. It never had before. But this time, with this person . . . she filled him up like no one else. And he figured it was the same with her.

"I want you."

"I think you just had me, Mr. Morris."

Her laughter tickled his neck, warm breath washing a cool patch traced by her tongue, drawn by her lips. Just a bruise, but as sure and real as a brand. He belonged to her. He knew that. But he didn't know—

The words slipped out before he could think them through. "I want you, forever."

That about said it, all right.

He felt her shiver, and then her lips found his.

"Forever is a long time," she said.

They laughed about that, embracing in the shadows.

They actually laughed.

She came running out of the big house as soon as he turned in from the road. Seeing her, he didn't feel a thing. That made him happy, because in England, in the midst of everything else, he'd thought about her a lot. He'd wondered just what kind of fuel made her belly burn, and why she wasn't more honest about it, in the way of the count. He wondered why she'd never gone ahead and torn open his jugular, the way a vampire would, because she sure as hell had torn open his heart.

Leonora ran through the blowing dust, her hair a blond tangle, and she was up on the driver's box sitting next to him before he could slow the horses—her arms around him, her lips on his cheek, her little flute of a voice all happy. "Quince! Oh, Quince! It *is* you! We thought you were dead!"

He shook his head. His eyes were on the big house. It hadn't changed. Not in the looks department, anyway. The occupants . . . now that was a different story.

"Miss me?" he asked, and his tone of voice was not a pleasant thing.

"I'm sorry." She said it like she'd done something silly, like maybe she'd spilled some salt at the supper table or something. "I'm glad you came back." She hugged him. "It'll be different now. We've both had a chance to grow up."

He chuckled at that one, and she got it crossed up. "Oh, Quince, we'll work it out . . . you'll see. We both made mistakes. But it's not too late to straighten them out." She leaned over and kissed his neck, her tongue working between her lips.

Quincey flushed with anger and embarrassment. The bitch. And with the box right there, behind them, in plain view. With him dressed head to toe in black. God, Leonora had the perceptive abilities of a blind armadillo.

He shoved her, hard. She tumbled off the driver's box. Her skirts caught on the seat, tearing as she fell. She landed in the dirt, petticoats bunched up around her waist.

She cussed him real good. But he didn't hear her at all, because suddenly he could see everything so clearly. The golden wedding band on her finger didn't mean much. Not to her it didn't, so it didn't mean anything to him. But the fist-sized bruises on her legs did.

He'd seen enough. He'd drawn a couple conclusions. Hal Owens hadn't changed. Looking at those bruises, that was for damn sure. And it was misery that filled up Leonora's belly—that had to be the answer which had eluded him for so long—and at present it seemed that she was having to make do with her own. Knowing Leonora as he did, he figured that she was probably about ready for a change of menu, and he wanted to make it real clear that he wasn't going to be the next course.

"You bastard!" she yelled. "You're finished around here! You can't just come walkin' back into town, big as you please! This ain't Morrisville, anymore, Quincey! It's Owensville! And Hal's gonna kill you! I'm his wife, dammit! And when I tell him what you did to me, he's gonna flat-out kill you!" She scooped up fistfuls of dirt, threw them at him. "You don't belong here anymore, you bastard!"

She was right about that. He didn't belong here anymore. This wasn't his world. His world was contained in a big black box. That was the only place for him anymore. Anywhere else there was only trouble.

Didn't matter where he went these days, folks were always threatening him.

Threats seemed to be his lot in life.

Take Arthur Holmwood, for instance. He was a big one for threats. The morning after the Westenras' party, he'd visited Quincey's lodgings, bringing with him Dr. Seward and a varnished box with brass hinges.

"I demand satisfaction," he'd said, opening the box and setting it on the table.

Quincey stared down at the pistols. Flintlocks. Real pioneer stuff. "Hell, Art," he said, snatching his Peacemaker from beneath his breakfast napkin (Texas habits died hard, after all), "let's you and me get real satisfied, then."

The doctor went ahead and pissed in the pot. "Look here, Morris. You're in England now. A man does things in a certain way here. A gentleman, I should say."

Quincey was sufficiently cowed to table his Peacemaker. "Maybe I am a fish out of water, like you say, Doc." He examined one of the dueling pistols. "But ain't these a little old-fashioned, even for England? I thought this kind of thing went out with powdered wigs and such."

"A concession to you." Holmwood sneered. "We understand that in your Texas, men duel in the streets quite regularly."

Quincey grinned. "That's kind of an exaggeration."

"The fact remains that you compromised Miss Lucy's honor."

"Who says?"

Seward straightened. "I myself observed the way you thrust yourself upon her last night, on the terrace. And I saw Miss Lucy leave the party in your charge."

"You get a real good look, Doc?" Quincey's eyes narrowed. "You get a right proper fly-on-a-dung-pile close-up view, or are you just telling tales out of school?"

Holmwood's hand darted out. Fisted, but he did his business with a pair of kid gloves knotted in his grip. The gloves slapped the Texan's left cheek and came back for his right, at which time Quincey Morris exploded from his chair and kneed Arthur Holmwood in the balls.

Holmwood was a tall man. He seemed to go down in sections. Doctor Seward trembled as Quincey retrieved his Peacemaker, and he didn't calm down at all when the Texan holstered the weapon.

Quincey didn't see any point to stretching things out, not when there was serious fence-mending to do at the Westenras' house. "I hope you boys will think on this real seriously," he said as he stepped over Holmwood and made for the door.

There was a Mexican kid pretending to do some work behind the big house. Quincey gave him a nickel and took him around front.

The kid wasn't happy to see the box. He crossed himself several times. Then he spit on his palms and took one end, delighted to find that the box wasn't as heavy as it looked.

They set it in the parlor. Quincey had to take a chair and catch his breath. After all that time on the ship, and then more time sitting on his butt slapping reins to a pair of swaybacks, he wasn't much good. Of course, this wasn't as tough as when he'd had to haul the box from the Westenra family tomb, all by his lonesome, but it was bad enough. By the time he remembered to thank the kid, the kid had already gone.

Nothing for it, then.

Nothing, but to do it.

The words came back to him, echoing in his head. And it wasn't the voice of some European doctor, like in Stoker's book. It was Seward's voice. *"One moment's courage, and it is done."*

He shook those words away. He was alone here. The parlor hadn't changed much since the day he'd left to tour the world. The curtains were heavy and dark, and the deep shadows seemed to brush his cheek, one moment buckskin-rough, next moment satin-smooth.

Like the shadows in the Westenras' garden. The shadows where he'd held Lucy to him. Held her so close.

No. He wouldn't think of that. Not now. He had work to do. He couldn't start thinking about how it had been, because then he'd certainly start thinking about how it might be, again . . .

One moment's courage, and it is done.

God, how he wanted to laugh, but he kept it inside.

His big bowie knife was in his hand. He didn't know quite how it had gotten there. He went to work on the lid of the box, first removing brass screws, then removing the hinges.

One moment's courage . . .

The lid crashed heavily to the floor, but he never heard it. His horror was too great for that. After all this time, the stink of garlic burned his nostrils, scorched his lungs. But that wasn't the hell of it.

The hell of it was that she had moved.

Oh, *she* hadn't moved. He knew that. He could see the stake spearing her poor breast, the breast that he had teased between his own lips. She couldn't move. Not with the stake there.

But the churning Atlantic had rocked a sailing ship, and that had moved her. And a bucking wagon had jostled over the rutted roads of Texas, and that had moved her. And now her poor head, her poor severed head with all that dark and beautiful hair, was trapped between her own sweet legs, nestled between her own tender thighs, just as his head had been.

Once. A long time ago.

Maybe, once again . . .

No. He wouldn't start thinking like that. He stared at her head, knowing he'd have to touch it. There was no sign of decay, no stink of corruption. But he could see the buds of garlic jammed into the open hole of her throat, the ragged gashes and severed muscles, the dangling ropes of flesh.

In his mind's eye, he saw Seward standing stiff and straight with a scalpel in his bloodstained grip.

And that bastard called himself a doctor.

There were shadows, of course, in their secret place in the West-enra garden. And he held her, as he had before. But now she never stopped shaking.

"You shouldn't have done it," she said. "Arthur is behaving like one of Seward's lunatics. You must be careful."

"You're the one has to be careful, Lucy," he said.

"No." She laughed. "Mother has disregarded the entire episode. Well, nearly so. She's convinced that I behaved quite recklessly— and this judging from one kiss on the terrace. I had to assure her that we did nothing more than tour the garden in search of a better view of the moon. I said that was the custom in Texas. I'm not certain that she accepted my story, but. . . " She kissed him, very quickly. "I've feigned illness for her benefit, and she believes that I am in the grip of a rare and exotic fever. Seward has convinced her of this, I think. Once I'm pronounced fit, I'm certain that she will forgive your imagined indiscretion."

"Now, Miss Lucy, I don't think that was my *imagination*," he joked.

She laughed, trembling laughter there in his arms. "Seward has consulted a specialist. A European fellow. He's said to be an expert in fevers of the blood. I'm to see him tomorrow. That ought to put an end to the charade."

He wanted to say it. More than anything, he wanted to say, *Forget tomorrow. Let's leave here, tonight.* But he didn't say it, because she was trembling so.

"You English," he said. "You do love your charades."

Moonlight washed the shadows. He caught the wild look in her eye. A twin to the fearful look a colt gets just before it's broken.

He kept his silence. He *was* imagining things. He held her.

It was the last time he would hold her, alive.

Three

—m—

Quincey pushed through the double doors of the saloon and was surprised to find it deserted except for a sleepy-eyed man who was polishing the piano.

"You the piano player?" Quincey asked.

"Sure," the fellow said.

Quincey brought out the Peacemaker. "Can you play 'Red River Valley'?"

"S-sure." The man sat down, rolled up his sleeves.

"Not here," Quincey said.

"H-huh?"

"I got a big house on the edge of town."

The man swallowed hard. "You mean Mr. Owens's place?"

"No. I mean my place."

"H-huh?"

"Anyway, you go on up there, and you wait for me."

The man rose from the piano stool, both eyes on the Peacemaker, and started toward the double doors.

"Wait a minute," Quincey said. "You're forgetting something."

"W-what?"

"Well, I don't have a piano up at the house."

"Y-you don't?"

"Nope."

"Well . . . Hell, mister, what do you want me to do?"

Quincey cocked the Peacemaker. "I guess you'd better start push-ing."

"You mean . . . you want me to take the piano with me?"

Quincey nodded. "Now, I'll be home in a couple hours or so. You put the piano in the parlor, then you help yourself to a glass of whiskey. But don't linger in the parlor, hear?"

The man nodded. He seemed to catch on pretty quick. Had to be that he was a stranger in these parts.

Quincey moved on. He stopped off at Murphy's laundry, asked a few questions about garlic, received a few expansive answers detailing the amazing restorative power of Mrs. Murphy's soap, after which he set a gunnysack on the counter. He set it down real gentle-like, and the rough material settled over something kind of round, and, seeing this, Mr. Murphy excused himself and made a beeline for the saloon.

Next Quincey stopped off at the church with a bottle of whiskey for the preacher. They chatted a bit, and Quincey had a snort before moving on, just to be sociable.

He had just stepped into the home of Mrs. Danvers, the best seamstress in town, when he glanced through the window and spotted Hal Owens coming his way, two men in tow, one of them being the sheriff.

Things were never quite so plain in England. Oh, they were just as dangerous, that was for sure. But, with the exception of lunatics like Arthur Holmwood, the upper crust of Whitby cloaked their confrontational behavior in a veil of politeness.

Three nights running, Quincey stood alone in the garden, just waiting. Finally, he went to Lucy's mother in the light of day, hat literally in hand. He inquired as to Lucy's health. Mrs. Westenra said that Lucy was convalescing. Three similar visits, and his testiness began to show through.

So did Mrs. Westenra's. She blamed Quincey for her daughter's poor health. He wanted to tell her that the whole thing was melodrama, and for her benefit, too, but he held off.

And that was when the old woman slipped up. Or maybe she didn't, because her voice was as sharp as his bowie, and it was plain that she intended to do damage with it. "Lucy's condition is quite serious," she said. "Her behavior of late, which Dr. Seward has

16

described in no small detail ... Well, I mean to tell you that Lucy has shown little consideration for her family or her station, and there is no doubt that she is quite ill. We have placed her in hospital, under the care of Dr. Seward and his associates."

Mrs. Westenra had torn away the veil. He would not keep silent now. He made it as plain as plain could be. "You want to break her. You want to pocket her, heart and soul."

She seemed to consider her answer very carefully. Finally, she said, "We only do what we must."

"Nobody wants you here," Owens said.

Quincey grinned. Funny that Owens should say that. Those were the same words that had spilled from Seward's lips when Quincey confronted him at the asylum.

Of course, that had happened an ocean away, and Dr. Seward hadn't had a gun. But he'd had a needle, and that had done the job for him right proper.

Quincey stared down at Mrs. Danvers's sewing table. There were needles here, too. Sharp ones, little slivers of metal. But these needles weren't attached to syringes. They weren't like Dr. Seward's needles at all.

Something pressed against Quincey's stomach. He blinked several times, but he couldn't decide who was standing in front of him. Owens, or Seward, or ...

Someone said, "Get out of town, or I'll make you wish you was dead." There was a sharp click. The pressure on Quincey's belly increased, and a heavy hand dropped onto his shoulder.

The hand of Count Dracula. A European nobleman and scientist. Stoker had split him into two characters—a kindly doctor and a hell-born monster. But Quincey knew that the truth was somewhere in between.

"Start movin', Quince. Otherwise, I'll spill your innards all over the floor."

The count had only held him. He didn't make idle threats. He didn't use his teeth. He didn't spill a single drop of Quincey's blood. He let Seward do all the work, jabbing Quincey's arm with the needle, day after day, week after week.

That wasn't how the count handled Lucy, though. He had a special way with Dr. Seward's most combative patient, a method that brought real results. He emptied her bit by bit, draining her blood, and with it the strength that so disturbed Lucy's mother and the independent spirit that so troubled unsuccessful suitors such as Seward and Holmwood. The blind fools had been so happy at first, until they realized that they'd been suckered by another outsider, a Transylvanian bastard with good manners who was much worse than anything that had ever come out of Texas.

They'd come to him, of course. The stranger with the wild gleam in his eyes. Told him the whole awful tale. Cut him out of the straitjacket with his own bowie, placed the Peacemaker in one hand. A silver crucifix and an iron stake jammed in a cricketing bag filled the other.

"You make your play, Quince," Owens said. "I'm not goin' to give you forever."

"Forever is a long time."

"You ain't listenin' to me, Quince."

"One moment's courage, and it is done."

Count Dracula, waiting for him in the ruins of the chapel at Carfax. His fangs gleaming in the dark . . . fangs that could take everything . . .

The pistol bucked against Quincey's belly. The slug ripped straight through him, shattered the window behind. Blood spilled out of him, running down his leg. Lucy's blood on the count's lips, spilling from her neck as he took and took and took some more. Quincey could see it from the depths of Seward's hell, he could see the garden and the shadows and their love flowing in Lucy's blood. Her strength, her dreams, her spirit . . .

"This is my town," Owens said, his hand still heavy on Quincey's shoulder. "I took it, and I mean to keep it."

Do Not Hasten to Bid Me Adieu

Quincey opened his mouth. A gout of blood bubbled over his lips. He couldn't find words. Only blood, rushing away, running down his leg, spilling over his lips. It seemed his blood was everywhere, rushing wild, like once-still waters escaping the rubble of a collapsed dam.

He sagged against Owens. The big man laughed.

And then the big man screamed.

Quincey's teeth were at Owens's neck. He ripped through flesh, tore muscle and artery. Blood filled his mouth, and the Peacemaker thundered again and again in his hand, and then Owens was nothing but a leaking mess there in his arms, a husk of a man puddling red, washing away to nothing so fast, spurting red rich blood one second, then stagnant-pool dead the next.

Quincey's gun was empty. He fumbled for his bowie, arming himself against Owens's compadres.

There was no need.

Mrs. Danvers stood over them, a smoking shotgun in her hands.

Quincey released Owens's corpse. Watched it drop to the floor.

"Let me get a look at you," Mrs. Danvers said.

"There ain't no time for that," he said.

Dracula chuckled. "I can't believe it is you they sent. The American cowboy. The romantic."

Quincey studied the count's amused grin. Unnatural canines gleamed in the moonlight. In the ruined wasteland of Carfax, Dracula seemed strangely alive.

"Make your play," Quincey offered.

Icy laughter rode the shadows. "There is no need for such melodrama, Mr. Morris. I only wanted the blood. Nothing else. And I have taken that."

"That ain't what Seward says." Quincey squinted, his eyes adjusting to the darkness. "He claims you're after Miss Lucy's soul."

Again, the laughter. "I am a man of science, Mr. Morris. I accept my condition, and my biological need. Disease, and the transmission of disease, make for interesting study. I am more skeptical concerning the mythology of my kind. Fairy stories bore me. Certainly, powers exist which I cannot explain. But I cannot explain the moon and the stars, yet I know that these things exist because I see them in the night sky. It is the same with my special abilities—they exist, I use them, hence I believe in them. As for the human soul, I cannot see any evidence of such a thing. What I cannot see, I refuse to believe."

But Quincey could see. He could see Dracula, clearer every second. The narrow outline of his jaw. The eyes burning beneath his heavy brow. The long, thin line of his lips hiding jaws that could gape so wide.

"You don't want her," Quincey said. "That's what you're saying."

"I only want a full belly, Mr. Morris. That is the way of it." He stepped forward, his eyes like coals. "I only take the blood. Your kind is different. You want everything. The flesh, the heart, the . . . soul, which of course has a certain tangibility fueled by *your* belief. You take it all. In comparison, I demand very little—"

"We take. But we give, too."

"That is what your kind would have me believe. I have seen little evidence that this is the truth." Red eyes swam in the darkness. "Think about it, Mr. Morris. They have sent you here to kill me. They have told you how evil I am. But who are they—these men who brought me to your Miss Lucy? What do they want?" He did not blink; he only advanced. "Think on it, Mr. Morris. Examine the needs of these men, Seward and Holmwood. Look into your own heart. Examine your needs."

And now Quincey smiled. "Maybe I ain't as smart as you, Count." He stepped forward. "Maybe you could take a look for me . . . let me know just what you see."

Their eyes met.

The vampire stumbled backward. He had looked into Quincey Morris's eyes. Seen a pair of empty green wells. Bottomless green pits. Something was alive there, undying, something that had known pain and hurt, and, very briefly, ecstasy.

Very suddenly, the vampire realized that he had never known real hunger at all.

The vampire tried to steady himself, but his voice trembled. "What I can see . . . . I believe."

Quincey Morris did not blink.

He took the stake from Seward's bag.

"I want you to know that this ain't something I take lightly," he said.

Four

He'd drawn a sash around his belly, but it hadn't done much good. His jeans were stiff with blood, and his left boot seemed to be swimming with the stuff. That was his guess, anyway—there wasn't much more than a tingle of feeling in his left foot, and he wasn't going to stoop low and investigate.

Seeing himself in the mirror was bad enough. His face was so white. Almost like the count's.

Almost like her face, in death.

Mrs. Danvers stepped away from the coffin, tucking a pair of scissors into a carpetbag. "I did the best I could," she said.

"I'm much obliged, ma'am." Quincey leaned against the lip of the box, numb fingers brushing the yellow ribbon that circled Lucy's neck.

"You can't see them stitches at all," the whiskey-breathed preacher said, and the seamstress cut him off with a glance.

"You did a fine job, Mrs. Danvers." Quincey tried to smile. "You can go on home now."

"If you don't mind, I think I'd like to stay."

"That'll be fine," Quincey said.

He turned to the preacher, but he didn't look at him. Instead, he stared through the parlor window. Outside, the sky was going to blood red and bruise purple.

He reached into the box. His fingers were cold, clumsy. Lucy's delicate hand almost seemed warm by comparison.

Quincey nodded at the preacher. "Let's get on with it."

The preacher started in. Quincey had heard the words many times. He'd seen people stand up to them, and he'd seen people totter under their weight, and he'd seen plenty who didn't care a damn for them at all.

But this time it was him hearing those words. Him answering them. And when the preacher got to the part about taking . . . *do you take this woman* . . . Quincey said, "Right now I just want to give."

That's what the count couldn't understand, him with all the emotion of a tick. Seward and Holmwood, even Lucy's mother, they weren't much better. But Quincey understood. Now more than ever. He held tight to Lucy's hand.

"If you've a mind to, you can go ahead and kiss her now," the preacher said.

Quincey bent low. His lips brushed hers, ever so gently. He caught a faint whiff of Mrs. Murphy's soap, no trace of garlic at all.

With some effort, he straightened. It seemed some time had passed, because the preacher was gone, and the evening sky was veined with blue-pink streaks.

The piano player just sat there, his eyes closed tight, his hands fisted in his lap. "You can play it now," Quincey said, and the man got right to it, fingers light and shaky on the keys, voice no more than a whisper:

> Come and sit by my side if you love me,
> Do not hasten to bid me adieu,
> But remember the Red River Valley,
> And the cowboy who loved you so true.

Do Not Hasten to Bid Me Adieu

Quincey listened to the words, holding Lucy's hand, watching the night. The sky was going black now, blacker every second. There was no blood left in it at all.

Just like you, you damn fool, he thought.

He pulled his bowie from its sheath. Seward's words rang in his ears: *"One moment's courage, and it is done."*

But Seward hadn't been talking to Quincey when he'd said those words. Those words were for Holmwood. And Quincey had heard them, but he'd been about ten steps short of doing something about them. If he hadn't taken the time to discuss philosophy with Count Dracula, that might have been different. As it was, Holmwood had had plenty of time to use the stake, while Seward had done his business with a scalpel.

For too many moments, Quincey had watched them, too stunned to move. But when he did move, there was no stopping him.

He used the bowie, and he left Whitby that night.

He ran out. He wasn't proud of that. And all the time he was running, he'd thought, *So much blood, all spilled for no good reason. Dracula, with the needs of a tick. Holmwood and Seward, who wanted to be masters or nothing at all.*

He ran out. Sure. But he came back. Because he knew that there was more to the blood, more than just the taking.

One moment's courage . . .

Quincey stared down at the stake jammed through his beloved's heart, the cold shaft spearing the blue-pink muscle that had thundered at the touch of his fingers. The bowie shook in his hand. The piano man sang:

> There never could be such a longing,
> In the heart of a poor cowboy's breast,
> As dwells in this heart you are breaking,
> While I wait in my home in the West.

Outside, the sky was black. Every square in the quilt. No moon tonight.

Thunder rumbled, rattling the windows.

Quincey put the bowie to his neck. Lightning flashed, and white spiderwebs of brightness danced on Lucy's flesh. The shadows receded for the briefest moment, then flooded the parlor once more, and Quincey was lost in them. Lost in shadows he'd brought home from Whitby.

One moment's courage . . .

He sliced his neck, praying that there was some red left in him. A thin line of blood welled from the wound, overflowing the spot where Lucy had branded him with eager kisses.

He sagged against the box. Pressed his neck to her lips.

He dropped the bowie. His hand closed around the stake.

One moment's courage . . .

He tore the wooden shaft from her heart, and waited.

Minutes passed. He closed his eyes. Buried his face in her dark hair. His hands were scorpions, scurrying everywhere, dancing to the music of her tender thighs.

Her breast did not rise, did not fall. She did not breathe.

She would never breathe again.

But her lips parted. Her fangs gleamed. And she drank.

Together, they welcomed the night.

Geraldine

by
Ian McDowell

"And Christabel saw the lady's eye,
And nothing else saw she thereby,"

—*Coleridge*

Chris woke from a dream about her father's penis to feel Joey fucking her from behind, his hips thrusting against her buttocks and hands gripping tightly at her waist. She often had difficulty sleeping with another person in the bed, but he'd gotten surly when she suggested he go home, so she'd doped herself with Actifed in order not to be kept awake by his tossing and turning. Now, her brain still clouded by antihistamine, she decided it would be less trouble to pretend to be asleep and let him finish, so she lay there on her side, listening to the creaking bedsprings and staring blearily at a cracked patch of moonlit wall.

Hurry up, she thought; *come and be done with it*. Of course, he might not be able to. Joey claimed rubbers made it difficult for him, and sometimes he never managed at all, or would lie there whining until she peeled off the condom, smeared K-Y on his penis, and took it between her breasts or against her stomach, rubbing it on her lubricated flesh until he ejaculated. He also disliked blow jobs almost as much as she did, although, thank God, he didn't mind going down on her.

This time he came quickly, and when she felt him do so, she realized he wasn't wearing a rubber. "You fucker!" she yelled as she twisted away from him, completely awake now. Chris had long since given up the pill, hating how it played havoc with her mood swings and inflated her already large breasts to Russ Meyer proportions. Her one abortion since then had made the "no glove, no love" cliché an ironclad rule.

She sat up and turned on the light, pulling the sheet over herself for psychological protection. Joey continued to lie there on his side, his face flushed and his smooth upper torso pale and glistening, his long brown hair a tangled mess. "Hi," he said softly, giving her a sheepish grin.

The grin, the cheekbones, the blue eyes; none of it would work this time. "Hi, nothing. Get your clothes on and get out."

He sat up then, shaking hair out of his eyes. "What?"

"You heard me. Get out."

His smile wilted like his cock. "Oh, come on! Why?"

She reached over and grabbed his penis, stifling the urge to twist or squeeze. "This is why. It's bad enough that you started fucking me while I was out cold from Actifed, but you didn't even have the courtesy to use a condom."

He gave her that shamefaced little boy look that she immediately decided she never wanted to see again, not on anyone. "Oh. I'm sorry. I was kind of asleep myself."

His penis was slick with more than just their own secretions; the tube of K-Y lay depressed and uncapped beside the lamp on the nightstand. "Bullshit, Joey. You were awake enough to get it all greased up so it could slide in easy. Now get out of here before I tear it off." She did squeeze then, just briefly before letting go, and the flash of terror in his eyes was immensely gratifying.

He pulled his skinny hairless legs protectively up to his thin chest and stared at her over his knees, his face all eyes and hair. "Look," he finally stammered. "Can't we talk about this tomorrow?"

"Go," she said coldly. She was newly glad of her preference for delicate, small-boned boys, the opposite of strapping bruisers like her father. She had an inch of height on him and maybe twenty pounds, little of it fat, and felt confident she could eject him physically if she had to. "Get. Out. Now."

They locked eyes for a long moment, and then he looked away. Sliding over to the side of the bed, he found his clothes and began dressing, keeping his back to her and muttering to himself. She stared at the ceiling and tried not to hear him. *It's probably not wise to end on this note*, she thought. Supposing, God forbid, she was pregnant, making him pay for the abortion would be less difficult if they were still speaking to each other. For now, however, she couldn't form any words. It was easier to keep quiet and let him leave. In another minute, he did.

"Jesus," she said to the ceiling. "Jesus fucking Christ. It's girls from now on."

Chris had been bisexual since her senior year in high school, and in the five years since then her relationships with other women had generally been the more satisfying ones, although not by much. Despite her man problems, she'd never let herself become exclusively lesbian. For one thing, she hated clichés, and the idea of being driven into the arms of her own gender by what her father had done to her when she was little was more than she could stand. If she went out with someone, it was because she liked that person, not because daddy had soured her on anybody with a dick. She wasn't going to give him that much power over her.

Who are you kidding, she thought. *You were dreaming about him when Joey stuck it in you.* "Fuck it," she said out loud. Fuck it, fuck it, fuck it. When she rubbed her eyes, she found them wet.

The rest of the week was a depressed haze. It was bad enough, worrying that she might be pregnant, but shame and anger at what

Joey had done gnawed at her like a canker. And Jesus, to think she'd just lain there, not caring, waiting for him to finish. But then again, she'd just lain there for a lot of men, pretty, long-haired boys who used her, or expected her to be their mommy, who stole from her and mooched off her and treated her like furniture. Fuck them all, but fuck her for settling for them.

Such feelings might be easier to deal with if she were still employed, but the educational workbook company she'd been with for the last year had recently hired a very expensive vice president away from their major competitor, and consequently cut expenses by laying off all their associate editors. She hadn't liked the job very much; the blueline proofs drove her allergies crazy and the bosses were a pair of annoyingly perky ex–grade school teachers, the sort of women who set her teeth on edge. Still, it had kept her occupied during the day. Fortunately, she qualified for unemployment, and the benefits would cover her rent and basic groceries for a couple of months. The problem was, that made it so much easier to lie around the apartment and mope.

Mostly, she slept. She had several more dreams about her father, which were unpleasant but not unexpected, for she always suffered those dreams in times of stress. But she also dreamed about Joey, and that, if possible, bothered her even more. He wasn't worth it; the little bastard hadn't been that big a part of her life. Hell, they'd only been going out for four months. Was her life really so empty that she needed to obsess on him?

By Thursday, she still didn't feel like looking for a new job, but she decided she was tired of the stereo and the TV and her limited selection of movies on cassette. She wanted sunlight, and people around her. She still lived a couple of blocks away from the UNCG campus, and it would be nice to just sit under a tree and read, the way she used to when she was a student. None of her books looked appealing, but she decided to go to the bookstore and spring for the new Anne Rice in hardcover, limited finances or no. By God, she'd come out of this funk if it killed her.

• • •

Geraldine

Chris had to look up to meet the gaze of the gorgeous brunette behind the counter at News 'N' Novels, not a familiar sensation when it came to other women. Big green eyes, high cheekbones, pale triangular face framed by a shaggy bob of shiny black hair, a good two inches taller than Chris's five-eleven and slender where Chris was zaftig; it was hard for Chris not to drool, much less stare. Instead, she put *The Tale of the Body Thief* on the counter and got out her checkbook.

The tall brunette looked at her purchase. "You've heard the news about Tom Cruise playing Lestat?" Her voice was very deep, another point in her favor.

"Yeah. That sucks, but I can't get too worked up about it. I'm not the real vampire junkie I was during my first two years in college." Chris twirled a copper bang and surprised herself by laughing, not something she'd been doing much of lately. "I dyed my hair black, slapped makeup over the freckles, listened to Bauhaus, smoked clove cigarettes, all that Goth stuff. I'm mainly buying this out of nostalgia. Now that I've been in the real world a while, I'm pining for my youth."

The other woman laughed, too. "Come on, you can't be more than twenty-five."

"Twenty-three and feeling like fifty. It's not been a good week." Chris handed her the check, wondering if she'd be impressed by the artwork reproduced on it.

The brunette woman looked at it for a long moment. "Münch's *The Scream*. God, that's certainly how *I* feel each time I write a check. I'd love to have these when I'm paying my bills."

Chris was glad she'd seen the ad in *Spy* and ordered the special checks. The admiring grin on this goddess's face was worth the twenty bucks. The tall clerk initialed the check and put it in the cash register. "Christabel Annette Brown. Christabel's a pretty name."

Chris surprised herself by blushing. "My mom was an English teacher. It's from something by Coleridge."

"I know the poem. By a funny coincidence, my name's Geraldine."

Chris didn't immediately get the reference, though she felt as if she should. "Pleased to meet you, Geraldine. What coincidence?"

"You know, in the poem. It's all very allusive and mysterious, but Lady Geraldine seems to be some sort of vampire or lamia. She bewitches Christabel, then her father."

Chris remembered, vaguely. "You're welcome to my father."

Geraldine's face was unreadable. "It's not him I'm interested in," she said softly.

This can't be happening, thought Chris, *it can't be this easy. Gee, God, are you trying to make up for what Joey did last Saturday?* She made no move to pick her book up off the counter. Fortunately, there was nobody in line behind her, or even in sight, much less earshot. Geraldine's eyes were very green. Well, ask her out, stupid.

"*The Hunger* is on cable tonight. I'd rather not watch it alone." That sounded cheesy, but she didn't care.

Geraldine grinned and shook her head. "Lesbians have *got* to find another first date movie, don't you think? Or aren't you sick of that one yet?"

For the first time since before she met Joey, Chris found herself laughing hard and loud. "Well, there's *Fried Green Tomatoes*, but while Mary Stuart Masterson is a doll, Mary-Louise Parker bugs me, the way she curls her lip and rolls her eyes around, and the stuff with Kathy Bates and Jessica Tandy just gets in the way. You got any suggestions?"

Geraldine wrote something on a Post-it note. "Why don't we have dinner and talk about it then? I get off at six. Here's my number." She stuck the Post-it on Chris's book. "Would you like a bag with that, ma'am?"

"No, this is fine. I'll call you tonight."

"Please do."

On the way out, she felt Geraldine's eyes on her back, but repressed the urge to turn around. Before going home, she decided to stop by the library and check out the collected Coleridge.

•   •   •

Geraldine

It had been a long time since Chris had read "Christabel," despite her late mother's alleged fondness for the heroine's name. What the Hell was that bit at the end about the "little child, a limber elf/Singing, dancing to itself"? What happened with Christabel, her father, and Lady Geraldine? Was it supposed to be unfinished, like "Kubla Khan"? All in all, she much preferred Keats.

The doorbell rang. Chris paused to look at herself in a mirror. She was wearing her newest jeans and a Tori Amos T-shirt, her red hair tied back with a ribbon. Not fancy, but Geraldine had told her not to dress up. "I'm bringing the dinner," she'd said; "it will be good but messy. I hope you like seafood." Chris loved seafood, but she wondered why Geraldine had wanted to go to the trouble of bringing it here, rather than cooking it at her place. Did she live with someone? Oh well, this was too early in any prospective relationship to be asking why.

Chris opened the door, Geraldine stood there, looking taller than ever, holding a covered wok. She wore a similar ensemble of jeans and black T-shirt, and two bottles of red wine stuck out of her matching black shoulder bag. "You've got to invite me over the threshold before I can enter," she said with a grin.

Chris returned the grin, hands on hips. "Oh, really?"

"No." Geraldine stepped forward and kissed her full on the mouth. "Where's your kitchen?"

Dazed but pleased, Chris pointed. "Through there. Don't let Roscoe wind around your feet and trip you." Roscoe was her sixteen-pound neutered tomcat, an affectionate but inordinately stupid animal who thought anyone going into the kitchen intended to feed him. Shutting the door, she followed Geraldine,

Geraldine put the wok down on the stove. When she uncovered it, Chris saw that it was full of blue-black shellfish. "Live freshwater mussels," said Geraldine. "They're $3.99 for a two-pound bag at Kroger's."

Chris was impressed. "I love oysters and clams but I've never had mussels. How do you cook them?"

LOVE IN VEIN

Geraldine put her shoulder bag on the counter and took out the wine and a small Tupperware container that held a stick of butter and a jar of minced garlic. "You scrub the mussels with an old toothbrush, pull their beards off, and run cold water over them. Any open ones that don't close up, you throw away. I've already done all that. Then, you take a bottle of cheap red wine and pour it over them." She took a corkscrew out of her bag and attacked one of the bottles. "Trakia Bull's Blood, $4.99 at Kroger's." Opening it, she poured it over the mussels. "You also throw in a stick of butter and as much minced garlic as you can stand. Then you turn the heat up, cover the wok or bowl, and let everything simmer until the mussels open up. Eight minutes, maybe."

"Wow."

Geraldine put the lid on the wok and turned back toward her. "The best thing is, you have to eat them by candlelight, sitting on the floor and using your fingers to get them out of the shell. It's very sensuous. Or do I mean sensual?"

"Sensuous, I think." Chris stepped closer and kissed her.

Geraldine returned it for a long moment, then pulled away. "Later. If we get distracted, the mussels will turn to rubber. You want to give me the grand tour of your apartment?"

Chris showed her around while the smell of garlic and red wine wafted in the from the kitchen. Geraldine expressed proper appreciation for the hardwood floors, the Klimt prints, and the Persian rug that once belonged to her grandmother. She even said polite things about the much-abused sofa and armchairs, and pretended not to notice the claw marks and the cat hair. Surprisingly, Roscoe himself did not appear to wrap himself around their feet while making the crying baby sound that was the only sign of his Siamese ancestry. He usually liked women, although he tended to hide from strange men, unless they were really sweaty or otherwise enticingly smelly. He'd loved Joey's Doc Martens.

The mussels were soon ready, and Geraldine ladled them out into Chris's largest bowl. They did indeed eat by candlelight, sitting on

Geraldine

the living room floor and sipping the other wine Geraldine had brought, a Black Opal Chardonnay, from a matched pair of "What Really Killed the Dinosaurs" *Far Side* mugs. "Presents from two separate people on two separate birthdays," explained Chris. "I used to be a heavy smoker."

Geraldine showed her how to eat the mussels, picking them up and using her fingers to pluck out the dark purplish morsels, then discarding the shells in an empty coffee tin. They were delicious, somewhere between oysters and wild mushrooms, heavy with the taste of garlic and red wine. Geraldine had forgotten to bring bread, but Chris had half a baguette from the discount shelf at Harris Teeter, which she warmed in the oven and they dipped in the savory purple liquor at the bottom of the bowl.

For a tall, lanky girl, Geraldine was as graceful as a cat, rather more graceful than the absent Roscoe, as she folded herself upon the bare floor and took mussels from the bowl with pale swooping hands, her eyes focused all the time on Chris, her face an alabaster mask framed by the darkness of her hair and shirt. Chris had deliberately restrained the urge to put on one of her favorite CDs, since she didn't own anything instrumental and wanted to facilitate conversation. Instead, she'd selected the local NPR channel, explaining it was easier to talk over when Geraldine asked her if she was a big classical music fan.

Despite this, they didn't do much talking, just stared at each other, and sipped wine and ate mussels and licked the juice off their fingers, then off each other's fingers, until Geraldine sidled closer, a sudden flowing movement that should have been a crablike scuttle, and they were actively sucking each other's fingers, nuzzling each other's wrists and hands, tasting the food they'd just eaten and the salt of each other's arousal. Then they were kissing, licking the last of the supper off each other's faces, joining mouths and tongues, fumbling with buttons. At some point, Roscoe emerged from where he'd been hiding and stalked in a tense circle around them, huge eyes locked on Geraldine and his tail big around as Chris's upper arm, but she had no attention to spare for his strange behavior.

Sometime later they lay in Chris's bed, where she was very grateful she'd just changed her sheets to the black silk ones she'd found on sale at Cocoon, the candle from the living room flickering in the breeze from the open window, Nina Simone whispering and growling from the box atop the bookcase. It was there that they finally talked, or rather that Chris talked and Geraldine listened. She told her about important things and trivial things; about the job she'd been laid off from and the books she liked to read; about Joey and what he'd done to her; about David Pugh, whom she'd beat up in the fifth grade, and Josephine Hoffman, whom she'd french-kissed in the twelfth; about being six years old and not understanding why her mother wouldn't be coming back from Duke hospital; about growing up in a town of soldiers and red-light districts and pawnshops; about passions like Snickers bars and E. Nesbit and Tori Amos and Cyd Charisse and Stamey's barbecue and Neil Gaiman; about the morose iguana she'd owned when she was fourteen, whose favorite food was Domino's pizza; about the bad relationships, the users, men and women both, the long nights staring at the ceiling; about playing pool in a redneck bar; about the red fox she'd seen behind her apartment building last week; about how she loved the idea of islands, any islands, Nags Head or Mykonos or the Hebrides, and wanted to live surrounded by water; a host of unrelated things, a murmuring flow that left her drained but content, entwined with the taller woman as a breeze lifted her frayed curtains and the candle guttered out. She did not, however, mention her father, although she meant to; it was always the next thing she was going to talk about. Maybe that's why, later, when they drowsed in each other's arms, she dreamed about him.

She seemed very small, though she couldn't have been that young; surely he didn't start this before her mother died, yet in the dream he was huge, a colossus looming in his armchair over the plain of the living room carpet like a symbolist painting she'd once seen, *Resistance: the Black Idol.* "Come on, sweetheart," his voice boomed, trying to be soothing, "crawl to daddy," and so she did, creeping like a soldier through enemy country, then sidling up the khaki columns of his legs, over the hill of his knees, toward his waiting penis, a pink-and-lilac minaret, thrusting up from the folds of his open pants and the sweaty thatch of coppery red pubic hair. Her mouth seemed tiny and his organ very big, but she got the former round the latter, after licking it the way he'd taught her, and she sucked and sucked, until he spasmed, and she would have pulled away, but big rough hands were clasped behind her head, holding her face down until she swallowed.

She woke up with a lurch, gasping for air and shaking. Geraldine stirred beside her and held her tight without a word, and after a minute she could no longer hear her own heart pounding.

"My father," she said finally, forcing herself to speak slowly and softy. "After my mom died, before I left home when I was seventeen, he . . . " She caught herself, not wanting to say he sexually abused her, thinking that sounded clinical, so clichéd. "He made me go down on him. He taught me how when I was seven. For the next ten years, I did it maybe twice a month, maybe not that often. Never anything else, just clumsy fellatio, though sometimes he'd talk about putting it in me when I was old enough, whatever 'old enough' meant."

Geraldine hugged her tighter. Those long white arms, corded with muscle beneath the soft skin, felt stronger than any man's arms she'd ever lain in, so strong she thought of the time she'd held the python at the Natural Science Center. "Most of the time, it didn't even bother me that much. Not then, I mean. It was just something unpleasant I had to do, like cleaning my room or mowing the lawn."

Geraldine stroked her head, long fingers gentle in her hair. Chris never thought that having her head stroked could feel so good, could understand Roscoe's look of imbecilic pleasure when she did it to him. "This isn't something I've remembered under hypnosis, or any of that crap. There's a lot of bullshit about sexual abuse going around; it's practically trendy these days to say you were diddled by daddy. But this is no neurotic fantasy; it isn't something I ever repressed; it was just another unpleasant part of growing up, like high school, only a little more degrading. Most of the time, I don't think about it, except when I'm stressed out. I guess what Joey did messed me up more than I thought, not just at the end, but the whole fucked-up relationship itself. That, and worrying about whether or not I'm pregnant. Jesus, I can't afford an abortion."

Suddenly, she wanted to be more than cuddled. In her mouth was the memory of something she'd not tasted in six years, and to wipe out that sensation she kissed Geraldine, gnawed her lip, probed with her tongue, and Geraldine kissed and bit and probed back. The next thing she knew, the dream had receded, become just a dream, as she lay on her back and felt the tickle of Geraldine's hair as her caressing mouth traveled down Chris's breasts, over her stomach, to her damp crotch.

Geraldine was an indistinct shape crouched at the foot of the bed, pale arms and shoulders, dark downturned head, her tongue lapping in Chris's juices. Then there was a new sensation, a prick or stab, something sharp nipping delicately at soft tissue. Chris felt something hot surge through her, a fiery douche, then a spasm like the worst menstrual cramp in the world. She would have screamed, it was so sudden and stabbing, but then somehow it receded without going away, she was outside of herself, still aware of the surging waves of pain yet not really feeling them. There was a final splattery gush, accompanied by an absolutely incongruous burst of orgasmic pleasure, then nothing, just a returning awareness of her own body, sweat pooling in her navel and the small of her back, the sheets sticking to her buttocks and shoulders.

After a while she had the strength to lift her arm and turn on the light. Geraldine looked up from her crotch, dark stains on the lower part of her pale, indistinct face, and wiped her mouth clean with fingers which she then licked. "Don't be frightened, Chris," she said in a voice of apologetic sorrow. "Everything's okay."

"I'm not frightened," said Chris weakly. She smelled her own blood, the stink of menstruation. But it was too soon for that, surely. "What happened?"

Geraldine scrunched forward to lie beside her, yet kept a certain distance between them. "You were pregnant. Now you're not."

Chris replayed this in her head several times until she was sure she'd heard it correctly. Then she shifted to her side and thought for a long time about what it meant. It was amazing that she could think so clearly. Stupidly, she found herself wondering if her good sheets were ruined. "I had a miscarriage," she said finally.

"Yes, in a sense."

In a sense? What sense? Nothing made any sense, least of all what she was thinking.

"You did something, I don't know how, but you made it happen."

A long pause. "Yes."

"How?"

"Chris, I don't think. . . "

She wasn't frightened or angry; instead, Chris wasn't sure what she felt. She looked at Geraldine.

"Show me how."

Geraldine flicked on the light and lay back. Her lips were pursed. Something emerged from between them, something long and thin, like a tentacle, or a python's tongue, although it wasn't forked. Its tip was dull black and sharp-looking, and it was striped with glossier black, red, and yellow bands, like a coral snake. It twisted in the air for a few seconds, glistening six inches above Geraldine's face, then was gone.

Chris knew it was true, then, that the tall girl beside her wasn't really human. She clutched the sheet beneath her, feeling its crumpled texture, its damp reality. "So. You made it happen. And then you ate it."

"Drank it, really," answered Geraldine. "I can eat other food, but this is what I need to live. I have to do it every couple of months. Things aren't as tidy for me as they are for the Vampire Lestat."

Chris didn't flinch when Geraldine touched her, although from the tentative nature of the caress, she could tell Geraldine expected her to. Why did she find this so easy to believe? Was she crazy? Go with it, then. "Boy, the pro-lifers would love you." She even managed a dry laugh at her joke. "Tell me more."

"It has to be within a week or two of conception," said Geraldine. "That's the physical part. There's the psychic component, also."

"Psychic?" Some part of her thought mordantly that this was just her luck. Geraldine couldn't be a nice normal horny lesbian or bisexual bookstore clerk. No, she had to be some sort of vampire that fed on miscarriages. *You sure can pick 'em, Chris.*

"I subsist on more than just a few pints of blood and a scrap of tissue," said Geraldine gently. "Try to think about Joey, what he did to you. Envision him doing it."

Chris found that she couldn't. Oh, she knew it intellectually, could remember it happening, but it no longer seemed to have happened *to her*. "There's nothing there. No feelings, I mean."

"That's right," said Geraldine. "Think about your entire relationship with him. Try to recall any specific moment of it, good, bad, or trivial. Not the facts, not what happened, but how you felt."

She couldn't. It was all secondhand, the experience of someone else, someone who'd told her every detail and helped her memorize them, but that was all it was, details. No pain, anger, shame, any of that. No joy or lust, either. She could remember the blue of Joey's eyes, but not her reaction the first time she saw them glancing at her over the used CD bin at Schoolkids. She remembered the tone of his voice when he asked her for a loan to help pay his rent, but not what went on in her head when he spent the money on a quarter bag. She remembered the tactile sensation of him coming inside her, but not the mental sensations that followed. It was as though the whole emotional tape of their relationship had been erased.

"Oh my God. What are you?"

Geraldine sat up. She ran one finger along the back of Chris's right hand. "I don't know. There aren't many of us, and we're all women, although we're able to mate with human men. My mother told me a little, eighty years ago, when I was younger than you. No, we're not immortal, but we age at a slower rate. My mother said that on the Russian steppes, unmarried village girls were brought to our kind when they'd been raped or seduced. We could not literally restore their virginity, but the peasants considered what we did a cleansing act. Later, opinions must have changed, for we were hunted as monsters. Now we're forgotten, more or less. Some faint echo of us survives in the lamia and vampire, but not much."

Chris ached down below, but only slightly. Whatever Geraldine had done, it hadn't racked her up as much as an ordinary miscarriage would have. Still, she felt nasty down there, and she longed to shower and douche, but she was still too weak to sit up. Instead, she finally held the hand that was touching hers. "Thank you, I guess." It sounded dumb, but it was all she could think of to say. "I did say I was pining for my youth, when I was into vampires. Never thought I'd be dating one."

Geraldine's pale face looked so sad, like a sentimental painting of a brokenhearted clown. "We're not dating, Christabel. I could take this memory from you, but I won't. I want you to remember me the way I remember you, as someone who came to me freely, rather than under a glamour. I could have made you want me."

"You didn't need to." Chris barely recognized her own voice.

"No. And more importantly, I was lonely. I can't have a normal *relationship*, so I tried for a normal date. But just one. You can't get pregnant every couple of months, just to feed me, and I doubt you'd like sitting back and watching me find others."

"I wouldn't mind."

Geraldine stroked her cheek. "Come on, you're better than that. Don't become a cliché obsessive psycho-lesbian on me, okay?" She bent to kiss her. Chris forced her own hands to remain at her sides, wouldn't let them grasp at Geraldine. She lay there stiffly, silently, not watching Geraldine dress. Sometime later, she heard her rattling around in the kitchen, collecting her things. She never heard the door, but when Roscoe jumped upside her and butted her head, purring, she knew that Geraldine was gone.

Chris spent almost three weeks trying to convince herself it hadn't happened. She applied for fourteen jobs, even though she didn't qualify for any of them, just so she could send the necessary cards to the Employment Security Commission. She avoided Anne Rice, but sat on campus and read a *Sandman* comic, the new Sylvia Plath biography, and about ten pages of Anaïs Nin, the last for the umpteenth time, as she always forgot how much Nin's stuff irritated her until she tried to plow through it. She went to a typically cheesy Stephen King movie and a bombastic Spanish art film at the Janus, where several of the employees knew her and let her in for free during matinees. She watched *The Wages of Fear* and *Sorcerer* back-to-back on Cinemax and five straight hours of *The Real World* on MTV. She went to New York Pizza on Pitcher Night with her buddy Jamie and his boyfriend Doug and to College Hill Sundries on cheap draft night with her neighbors Elise and Sarah. She spent several hours at the end of each day trying to get to sleep and several more at the beginning of the next trying to get up.

Finally, she went to see Geraldine. She was getting off work at News 'N' Novels. Chris was waiting for her outside, loitering in front of Radio Shack, hands in the pockets of her baggy overalls. "Hi," she said, trying to sound casual. "Obviously, sunlight doesn't bother you."

Geraldine looked at her with an unreadable expression. "Or garlic or silver or the crucifix or any of that. I live in a studio apartment, not a grave, and I travel around in a Honda Civic, not on bat wings. What's your point?'

"I miss you."

"You don't know me." Something that might have been yearning flickered across that smooth white face.

"I want to."

Geraldine just stood there. She wore black slacks and a black-

Geraldine

and-white blouse with a pattern like interlocking Ëscher lizards. A gust of wind tousled her short hair, which she didn't bother to fix. She blinked, and Chris saw a wet glimmer in the corner of each eye.

"You said you were lonely," said Chris. "Can you really look straight at me and tell me you don't want me, that you want to go on being alone?"

Geraldine rubbed her eyes. Instead of answering, she reached into her purse and put on a pair of narrow black sunglasses. "Wait here," she finally said in a tiny voice.

"What?"

"Just wait." She was already off, long legs carrying her briskly across the parking lot, heading straight toward the Mirage Entertainment Complex. This was an upscale titty bar, the sort that proudly advertised itself as having the Triad's only VIP shower stage, whatever that was. Only recently opened in Kroger Plaza, it had proved a less-than-welcome addition to the complex, nestled as it was between a grocery store and a Tons O' Toys. Most afternoons there'd be a small group of Baptists and other family-values types picketing in front of it, although never at night, when it was actually open. Today there were four of them, two nondescript housewives in stirrup pants, a skinny, pop-eyed man in a bow tie who could have been a balding Don Knotts, and a plump woman wearing a baggy flowered dress and green and orange curlers in her hair. Geraldine talked to the skinny man and the woman in curlers for less than a minute, and when she turned around and walked back toward Chris, they put their signs down and came with her, the remaining picketers staring dumbly after them.

"What's this?" said Chris, uncomfortably aware of the lack of any recognizable expression on the faces of Geraldine's two companions.

"A demonstration. Which is your car?"

Nonplussed, Chris pointed mutely at her battered yellow Volvo.

"It'll hold four more easily than mine, so we'll take it. Come on; here's your chance to learn where I live."

Geraldine sat up front with Chris, the fat woman and thin man riding silently in back. Trying to ignore them, keeping her questions to herself, Chris concentrated on Geraldine's directions. *Okay*, she thought, *play it all mysterious*; she was game for anything Geraldine could throw at her. At least, she hoped she was.

The apartment turned out to be in the College Hill Historical District, less than three blocks from Chris's building, although Chris couldn't recall ever seeing her in the neighborhood. They parked in a gravel lot and walked up a rear fire escape, the fat woman wheezing on the stairs.

The apartment was smaller than Chris's, but better furnished, decorated with lots of books and CDs and several incongruous floppy stuffed animals. Chris didn't ask about these. "Sit on the couch and wait," said Geraldine to the two protesters, neither of whom had yet said a word. "What kind of drink do you want?" she asked Chris. "You'll need one, with what I'm about to show you. I've got Rolling Rock, scotch, and Cuervo."

"A shot of Cuervo is fine," said Chris, finally making herself take a long look at the man and woman on the couch. "You've hypnotized them, haven't you? This must be what you call your glamour."

"Yes," said Geraldine from the kitchen. "They won't be aware of any of this." She returned from the kitchen with two shot glasses, handed one to Chris, and downed the other. "Sorry, but I don't have any limes. Now keep quiet and watch. After it's over, we'll talk about whether or not you want to know me." She turned to the protesters. "Okay, start fucking."

The plump woman pulled down her pantyhose and hiked up her dress, her eyes calm and empty. The skinny man stood up and dropped his pants. Chris was amused to see he wore bright red bikini underwear, of all things, which he also pulled down, exposing a thin, wrinkled penis which became erect like stop-motion footage of a plant wilting in reverse. He turned clumsily around, hobbled as he was by the pants and underwear at his ankles, and flopped awkwardly on top of the woman. They fumbled for a bit, him staring intently at the sofa cushion beside her head and her gaping glassily up at the ceiling, but they apparently got it in, because his pale, wrinkled butt started plunging up and down, his slight paunch slapping meatily into her massive one. It didn't last long. When he came, he farted.

"Thank God they managed the first time." said Geraldine. "I'd hate to have to sit here until he could try again."

Chris knew what was going to happen, and couldn't decide whether she was amused or repulsed. "How long will you have to wait? And how do you know it worked?"

"It worked," said Geraldine. "I can sense when conception has occurred, and when I'm controlling both parties, I can even help things along a bit. And no, I don't have to wait. The moment the egg's fertilized, I can feed."

At her command, the skinny man went and stood by the door, his pants and underwear still down around his ankles, his penis dangling limp and wet, nothing at all in his eyes. The woman lay on the couch, her fat legs bent at the knees, her round red face looking up at the ceiling. Bending over her, Geraldine held her heavy thighs apart and, dipping her head without preamble, began rooting sloppily in the woman's crotch with none of the seductive grace she'd shown with Chris. This went on for several minutes. The woman's thighs quivered like Jell-O and her mouth opened in a spit-flecked "O." She began to shake all over, the seismic convulsions dislodging an orange curler from her head. The sounds Geraldine was making became progressively wet and bubbly, not so much licking or nuzzling as slurping. Then Geraldine sat up, giving Chris a dripping red grimace. "Still want me?"

Chris had been cool with it up to now, even priding herself on how well she was taking it, but this was too much. She bolted for what she thought was the john, but which turned out to be closet, choked back her bile and stumbled down the hall until she found the real bathroom, lurched into it, and threw up the Taco Bell Grande she'd had for lunch. Once her heaving subsided, she flushed and sat down on the toilet seat to collect herself. *Damn it, Geraldine*, she thought to herself, *you don't win that easily*. She could deal with this. Hell, she'd dealt with worse.

After a while, Geraldine came in without knocking. She gave Chris a sympathetic look, but didn't say anything. Instead, she washed her face and gargled with Listerine.

Her shocked nausea passed; Chris thought about her deeper feelings. "It didn't work," she said finally.

Geraldine spit out the mouthwash and rubbed her face with a fluffy black towel. "Excuse me?"

"It didn't work. I still want you. I know you wanted to shock me, and you did, and it got to me for a moment, but I still want you." Chris also found herself wanting a cigarette. "God help me, but that's how I feel."

Geraldine knelt beside her. "Yeah, you do, don't you? Jesus." She tentatively stroked Chris's brow. "I'm sorry I put you through that."

Chris reached out and fiddled with the black plastic shower curtain. "Yeah, me too." She tore off a ply of toilet paper and blew her nose on it. "What did you do with those two?"

"Sent them away. Told them to forget what happened. They'll come to their senses while walking home. The woman looked like a long walk would do her good."

Chris thought about this for a while. "Walking sounds good to me, actually. Can we go for one? I need fresh air."

They ended up in the little park beside College Hill Sundries on Spring Garden Street, where they climbed onto the wooden platform beside the monkey bars and lay on their backs, watching the sky darken through the branches of the elms and maples overhead. Once she was sure they couldn't be seen from the road, Chris fumbled in her purse and found the fatty her friend Jamie had rolled for her, the one she'd meant to save until her cramps kicked in again. She shared it with Geraldine. It was a while before either of them spoke.

"I'm sorry I got grossed out," said Chris finally. "Was that good for you?

"Not really," said Geraldine, coughing from the pot. "It's very artificial, casting a glamour over two people and making them conceive like that. The result is a bit like airline food. Neither tasty nor nourishing."

Chris thought about this and took another drag on the joint. "You said you feed on more than just blood and the fertilized egg. You take the emotions, too."

Geraldine killed the joint. "Yes, all the emotions the woman ever felt toward the man who fertilized that egg. I've destroyed marriages that way, emptying a newlywed bride of her love for her husband along with her ovum. I've also healed rape victims of their trauma, taking away the pain and fear and sense of violation. I can be a monster or a saint."

At some point, Chris wasn't sure when, they'd started holding hands. She shouldn't be feeling so damned content, not barely an hour after her shocked nausea, but she was. Everybody had their secrets; everyone was something of a monster inside. At least Geraldine's secret was such a *material* one. She did what she had to do to live, that was all. It's not like there was anything worse that Chris could find out about her.

"If I was a more charitable sort, that would be all I did," continued Geraldine. "I'd work at a Rape Crisis Center and become a regular angel of mercy."

"Why don't you?"

"Because I'm a sybaritic bitch. I need variety, pain *and* joy. I hope you liked my mussels, but could the best cause in the world make you eat nothing but them all your life?"

Instead of answering, Chris leaned into Geraldine and kissed her. "You must have seen a lot," she said when their lips parted. "Over all the years, I mean. Just how old are you?"

"Old enough."

The evasion didn't bother Chris. "Ever meet anybody famous?"

"Dorothy Parker, once. She had a great horsey laugh, and made a joke about my height. I saw Billie Holiday perform. A few decades later, I was in Judy Collins's apartment when Leonard Cohen played

'Suzanne' for the first time." Geraldine sang a couple of bars in a lilting contralto.

When she stopped, Chris imagined that the rustling branches continued whispering the tune. "Why did you come here?"

"To be somewhere else. New York isn't what it once was. There was that article, couple of years back, that listed Greensboro as one of the best places in the country to live."

Chris snickered. "Lots of locals were smug about that. The rest of us had a good laugh."

She stroked Geraldine's face and Geraldine kissed her hand. She touched Chris's finger with her tongue, then with something that slid out from beneath that tongue, something long and prehensile, that coiled around Chris's index finger like one of the worm snakes she sometimes rescued from Roscoe's jaws. Unlike a snake, it was warm and wet.

"You can't scare me," said Chris. "Not anymore."

They lay back together, and Geraldine began massaging Chris's hand, gently kneading the knuckles with her fingers, working the palm with her thumb, and Chris felt her body relaxing by inches, the tension gradually draining from her hand, her arm, her shoulder. She lay on the rough wood, warm and pitted and too soft for splinters, and looked up at the branch-screened sky through narrowed lids. Cicadas were singing around them, trilling their mechanical trill, and if she listened intently, she could also hear crickets and katydids and, somewhere farther off, the baritone lullaby of frogs. Some sort of beetle crawled across her ankle, but that was okay, bugs didn't bother her. Fireflies flashed their mating beacons in the trees overhead, like tiny novas in the sighing branches.

Stoned, content, yielding to the night's chorus and Geraldine's soothing touch, she never heard the man approach. He'd crept up through the park behind them, rather than sliding down the hill from the sidewalk where the streetlights flickered. The monkey bars groaned and rattled and there he was, a dark shape pulling himself up into view, stinking of dirty clothes and fortified wine.

"Don't scream," he hissed. "I got a gun."

Geraldine

Something glinted in his hand, sure enough. Before Chris could even consider how to react, Geraldine lashed out. The weapon dropped onto Chris's foot, landing heavily enough that she knew it was real, and the man's hand *crunched* in Geraldine's grip. He made a gurgling sound until Geraldine cut him off, shushing him like a child.

"Sssh," she said, almost gently. "Now it's your turn not to scream."

Oh Christ, it had been so fast, and this on top of everything else! Chris fumbled for her Zippo, flicked it, finally got it lighted. The flickering light revealed a dirty, gnarled face framed by a dirtier brown beard and faded red bandanna. She recognized the man as one of the regular panhandlers on Tate Street, the rat-faced little cracker who could usually be found drinking Scorpio from a paper bag in front of Ben and Jerry's. His bloodshot eyes were glassy, his features frozen in a grimace of pain and surprise, and his breath whistled through the gaps where his teeth were missing.

Geraldine let go of his hand, which definitely looked broken. "You got a knife on you?"

"Yeah," he said tonelessly, eyes fixed above and beyond them.

"Good. Once we're gone, use it to cut off every toe on your left foot. When you're done, I want you to eat them. Wait until we're out of the park."

Geraldine vaulted lightly off the platform. "Come on, Chris; let's leave this creep to his meal. If he'd hurt you, he'd be eating his dick." Chris wished she was frightened by what happened, by the tone in Geraldine's voice, but no, even this she could accept. Was she that obsessed? Had Caryl Anne Fugate felt this way about Charlie Starkweather? It didn't matter. As she backed away from their would-be assailant, who still clung to the side of the platform like a monkey, her foot touched his gun. She was familiar with pistols, had once practiced at the shooting range for the better part of a summer. Acting on impulse, she picked it up, checked the safety, and put it in her purse. Then she jumped off the opposite side of the platform, not landing as lightly as Geraldine.

Geraldine helped her to her feet and brushed leaves off her. "Don't worry. He won't start cutting until we're gone." She seemed to be able to see in the dark, for she led Chris back up the grassy hill to the lighted sidewalk, steering her around holes and roots.

"Did you take the gun because you thought you might need protection from me?"

Chris looked back down into the darkness, where their would-be mugger (or rapist) was just a dim shape on top of the shadowy platform. She wondered how hard it was to cut off a toe with a pocketknife or switchblade, especially when not using your best hand, and if you could a swallow a big toe without choking. "No. It's given me an idea, though."

"Which is?"

She wondered if Geraldine could read her mind. "I'll tell you next time you need to feed."

Five weeks later, they took Geraldine's Honda down I-40 to Fayetteville. Geraldine had the entire Mary Poppins soundtrack on cassette, and they listened to it as they drove, singing "It's a Jolly Holiday with Mary" and "Spoonful of Sugar" together, with Chris soloing on "Tuppence in the Bank" and Geraldine on "Feed the Birds." They stopped at a Stuckey's on the way, where they had meatloaf and fried chicken, and Chris grossed Geraldine out by buying a Pecan Log and a bag of the orange-marshmallow atrocities called Circus Peanuts. Coming through Fort Bragg, some GIs in a Jeep made predictably crude remarks, and Geraldine later said she thought about putting a glamour on them to make them go form a daisy chain on the parade grounds, but the light changed too soon.

Chris's father still lived just the other side of the base, right off Bragg Boulevard, a garish ten-mile avenue of Putt-Putts, pawnshops, strip clubs, and used car dealerships, all of them even tackier than such establishments normally are. She'd checked Directory Assistance, then called and gotten his answering machine. But she'd not left a message; the visit was meant to be a surprise. "I doubt he's changed the lock," she said, "not in the six years since I left. If he's not home, we can wait for him."

The yard was more overgrown than she remembered it, the house smaller, the piss-yellow paint flaked and peeling. Someone had knocked the head off the lawn jockey, and the dogwoods were in sorry shape. The porch swing looked as if its warped slats would break if you sat on it, if its rusted chain didn't. There was a *Sports Illustrated*, a Southern Bell phone bill, and a *Reader's Digest* stuffed into the small mailbox, and she rang twice without getting a response. Maybe he wasn't in.

She was fumbling in her purse for the old key when the door opened. Her father stood there in paint-splattered shorts and a dirty, tobacco-stained T-shirt. His sagging man-tits and beer belly were far more prominent than they'd been when she left home, and his hair was much receded, the red peppered now with gray. His smile exposed nicotine-stained teeth.

"You girls selling something? I don't mind, when you're both so pretty."

"No, Dad, we're not selling anything." Recognition had already dawned in his eyes before she opened her mouth, before he'd quite finished speaking. His smile died. "Chris."

"Yeah, it's me. This is Geraldine."

He wasn't as tall as she remembered, certainly not as tall as Geraldine, whom he didn't even look at. "I don't know why you're here, Chris, but I don't want you in my house. Not after what you did."

During her last year at home, Chris's father had been dating Peggy Jo, a divorced RN from the local VA hospital. The month before Chris walked out the door, he'd even proposed to her. Peggy Jo had a five-year-old daughter cursed with the name of Cissy, and Chris didn't want the child to endure any worse hardships. Before running off to Greensboro to live with her maternal Aunts Selma and Anne, she'd written Peggy Jo a long, detailed letter. She later heard the engagement was called off.

"Still bitter about Peggy Jo, huh?"

He looked like he'd been slapped, and his right hand balled up into a fist, but he didn't raise it. He'd seldom ever raised his hand to her when she lived at home. "Get out of here," he said through clenched yellow teeth. "You got something to talk about, you can call me on the phone." He started to close the door, but Geraldine casually put out her arm and stopped it.

His face was very red until he saw the gun in Chris's hand, and then it went white. Chris knew that Geraldine could have controlled him, but she wanted to do it this way.

"Invite us inside, Dad."

"You come to rob me, Christabel? You'll be disappointed. I don't own shit anymore. Hell, I'm about to lose this house."

Geraldine put her other arm around Chris, who leaned into her. "I don't care about your troubles, Dad. Invite me and my girlfriend in or I'll blow your brains out right here on the stoop." Thankfully, no neighbors were in sight. If he proved obstinate, she might have to let Geraldine take over after all.

That wasn't necessary. With an exhalation that might have been a sigh, might have been a mumbled prayer, he backed down the hall, letting them inside. Chris locked the door after them.

The living room was rearranged, and the old goosedown couch was replaced by a sagging vinyl one, brown foam showing through where its cushions were split. The mounted smallmouth bass still hung over the mantel, dust heavy on its glass eyes. The old stereo, a deluxe sixties hi-fi system with huge speakers, was gone, and from the crummy picture on the TV she could tell the cable was disconnected. The big armchair was still there.

"Take your pants off and sit in the chair," Chris said quietly.

"Are you crazy?"

Geraldine watched, cool and distant, her face impassive. "It might be easier if I took over."

Chris shook her head. "Not yet. Do as I say, Dad, or you're dead." She put a bullet in the sofa to emphasize her point.

Geraldine

The little .25 was loud in the dark living room, if not so loud as guns in the movies. Fortunately, the nearest houses weren't close enough for her to be worried about the neighbors hearing anything. Her ears rang and the room stank of gunpowder, drowning out the odor of beer and mildew.

Chris's father stood there, his eyes bugging out, his mouth open as wide as that of the varnished bass on the mantel. A big blue vein had appeared in his temple, one Chris could not remember ever seeing before. Although his face was still deathly pale, his ears had gone bright red.

"You crazy bitch!"

"Next one goes into you, Dad. Now take off your pants and sit down."

He did. Unlike the protester last month, he wore respectable boxer shorts. At Chris's order, these came off, too.

Chris handed the gun to Geraldine. "Shoot him if he moves a muscle." She knew Geraldine could handle this with less fuss, would probably have to cast a glamour over him soon, but she wanted him good and scared first. People under Geraldine's control were too calm.

Chris undid her belt and kicked off her jeans, then wiggled out of her panties. She pulled her T-shirt over her head and unhooked her bra. "Like what you see, Dad?"

"Please Chrissie, I got a heart condition . . . "

The familiar "Chrissie" spurred her into action, snarling in anger. Grabbing him by the ankles, she pulled him bodily out of the chair, so that he landed with a thump on the floor. She looked down at him, flat on his fat ass, his hands thrown up for protection. "Okay," she said to Geraldine. "Give him an erection."

The tumescent penis also looked smaller than she remembered it. His eyes had gone glassy, but she thought she could still read something in them. *Let him stay aware of this*, she thought.

"Can you make him stay like that, even if we leave the room?"

Geraldine nodded, neither approval nor disapproval on her alabaster face. Chris took her by the hand and led her down the hall to her father's bedroom, where she pulled the dingy sheets off the mattress. "Okay," she said. "Get me good and wet."

It took a while, under those conditions, but eventually Geraldine's tongue worked its spell. "I'm sorry you have to watch this," said Chris as she got up. "If I could do it without your help, I would."

"That's okay," said Geraldine, wiping her lips with a tissue. "I made you watch once."

Back in the living room, Chris's father still lay on his back, penis pointing at the ceiling. Still lubricated by passion, Chris slid on top of it and began moving up and down. "Pick up the gun," she said to Geraldine. "Come close and hold it on him, but give him control of himself again."

"Oh God," mumbled her father on the floor. "Oh God oh God oh God." His erection, however, remained firm.

"She's going to kill you as soon as you come," said Chris through gritted teeth. "You wanted this all these years, to be inside me. Now you are. How long can you keep from coming?"

His eyes were rolled back to the whites, sweat streaming in rivulets down his red-and-white face. His lips moved, but all that came out of his mouth was spittle and a long, blubbery groan.

Chris bounced up and down, urging him on, snarling, pushing on his flabby chest, his doughy, sweat-matted male breasts yielding beneath her stiffened palms. She went dry almost at once, gritting her teeth against the rough friction of his penis, hoping he wouldn't lose the erection. Just when she thought he'd never be able to come, that he'd go soft inside her, she felt him spurt. His mouth was open wider than ever, roped with spittle, big blood vessels flaring in his forehead and smaller ones in his eyes. A wet rattling sound was coming out of his mouth, which began filling with blood from his bitten tongue.

"Jesus!" said Chris, shooting backwards off him, scuttling into Geraldine's steady legs. "Shit, is he dying?"

His body arched, his head and heels thumped into the thin, dirty carpet, then he was still. There was one wet, wheezing breath, a second, then no more. Chris heard nothing but her own heart, her own breath.

Geraldine

Geraldine walked to him and checked his pulse. "Even if we dared call an ambulance, I don't think it would be on time."

Chris pulled on her pants and shirt, stuffed her underwear into her purse, fumbled for her shoes. "Tell me it worked, please, just tell me it worked, that I won't be stuck with this!"

Geraldine knelt beside her. "Easy, honey. Easy. It worked."

All fortitude gone, Chris clutched her leg like a child, her face suddenly wet and stinging. "Take me out of here, please," she whispered, ashamed of her own weakness.

Geraldine helped her up. "It'll be over, soon. No more bad dreams."

Chris struggled to regain something of herself. "I hope not. I didn't want him dead." Taking a deep breath, she found she could stand, could walk. The worst was done, the worst of all worsts; only the final purification remained, and that could be done somewhere else, away from this place of the dead.

The weather had changed while they were inside; the horizon pregnant with rain, thunder booming somewhere beyond Fort Bragg. "Great," said Chris sourly, pointing at the sky. "It'll be a long drive in this."

Geraldine opened the car door for her. "That's okay. We can stop at a motel and listen to the storm. There I'll make it all better."

An hour later they were in bed in an Econolodge in Sanford, making fierce love on the cheap but clean motel sheets, Chris's back arching and her hands clenching sweatily as Geraldine's mouth whispered secret words inside her, thunder rolling outside, lightning flashing through the blinds. The power went out, but that was okay, there in the cool darkness where nothing existed but the two of them, Chris's cunt and Geraldine's mouth, the touch, the tremors, the stirring deep inside, the purging flood. As before, there was pain, but also as before, it quickly receded, and the rush of pleasure was stronger this time, a torrent of what William Blake might have meant by Crimson Joy. Her blood was the Blood of the Lamb, absolving all as it flowed out of her into Geraldine.

"I want to be the only one who feeds you," said Chris when she could talk. "The only one. Sweet blood and tender tissue, and emotions you never tasted before."

Geraldine kissed her and Chris probed with her tongue, tasting her own fluids in Geraldine's mouth. They lay like that for some time, the pale thin girl and the ruddy voluptuous one, one sticky at the crotch, the other at the mouth, their arms and legs entwined, listening to the storm's roar and murmur. The thunder rolled past, fading in the distance, and then they could hear only the rain falling, hammering the motel roof, rattling the window frame and the housing of the air-conditioning unit, washing the world clean.

In the Greenhouse

by
Kathe Koja and Barry N. Malzberg

S tamen, anvil, pistil, stem:
Lying in something approaching state, slow moist respiration, slower thud and rhythms of her heart causing only the most silken of movement, slight, slight the motion of her lungs and of her dampened breasts; she could be dead, she *is* all but dead, lying within the greenhouse her rooms have become. Flowers surround her: plants, foliage, bonsai and bouquets, staggered floor to ceiling, wall to wall, heaped like coverlets upon and beside the refuge bed; their exhalation is gigantic in the room, their scent the smell of anguish and desire.

Lucia lies quietly amidst the flowers, each bouquet—roses and orchids, baby's breath, iris and bonsai—bearing an impossibly white card and the name of a donor, some inscribed with messages in a private lovers' argot, others blank of words and bearing only the impressed image of heart or lips, the delicate signature of origin. Once she had been able to look at those cards, had if only haphaz-

59

ardly matched the flowers with their givers but that was a long time ago, the early days when the first tentative rustlings had begun, the flung, crushed orchids, mute roses slipped under the door, the riotous gladioli like some boyfriend in a cheap new suit; then as her life seemed to open, split like a seed to fill rapid with flowers as if in time-lapse, bud to bloom in panting moments, she lost as well as the illusion of command all ability to evoke the identity of the givers: men and men, name and name and what did any of that mean, what could any of that mean to her now?

On the bed, her nostrils and respiration steaming in the slow, baked odor of the flowers, some dying, some dead, some just achieving their first fine putrescence, she feels as if it might be possible to recall her life against the screen of her consciousness and in so doing achieve if not meaning then at least a *reason*: but in another, firmer part of mind knows that this is impossible; she is suffocating under the flowers, subsiding into the heaving rattle of Cheyne-Stokes. The flowers smell like flesh, flesh like sex, sex like love but it is the love she cannot precisely recall, cannot retrieve as she tries to rise to that screen of memory: and failing falls, falling fails, shifts under the heaped flowers a hundred times as the stink and the sweat move like animals across and over her motionless flesh. Lucia: our lady of the flowers, of the Bronx and Staten Island too, our lady of the greater and lesser boroughs, our lady queen of the night. Against the apartment door drifts in static rhythm the jungle burst of philodendron, of dour English ivy and other, less identifiable vines and farther off, through some odd chink of light in the green, some dazzled version of the Willets Point bridge, twisted akimbo in the dying light, the bridge of chain, recollection, desire and darkness.

Lucia, my lady of light: "Lucia, my lady of light," he says and leans against her, tilts her against the wall, gives her a long, slow, openmouthed kiss as her hips nudge his, deliberation and encouragement as she feels the pathetic shadow of his rising, the insistent press of his little genitals against her. "Oh," he says, "oh, oh," and

In the Greenhouse

attempts timorously to put his hand on her breast, clumsy and she shrugs and the hand droops away without protest as again she eases into the kiss, then as easily back and away.

"We can't stay here," she says, "it's too cold. Let's go."

"When," he says, "when—" and he wants, she knows, to say *When do we make love* but he cannot properly articulate his wants, cannot say what he means and so how is that her problem? "When is when," she says, taking his hand to move him farther from her, as the petal lies far from the stem, the lovely bloom from the stiff extending root.

Walking then, and then another wall, less his impetus than hers now and she allows him to achieve a long, slow, heaving motion, coaxing him along in the winking darkness, traffic murmur to the left and right of them and just as he seems to have yearned himself into some growing rhythm which approaches the arc of true completion she breaks from him, pushes him back and away: away, get away, get lost.

"No," she says, "no, no, what do you think you're doing? What do you think you're *doing?*" Staring at her, moist mouth a little open and in the darkness she can sense his panic, his confusion and his flight. "Just take me home," she says. "Take me home right now." Hearing the arch, the ragged edge of his breathing she understands without articulation the skittering thunder of his heart, his hands unsteady as they press random down his shirt, smoothing and straightening, hands without touch and "Take me *home*," she says, "right *now* or I'll—"

"No," he says, "no, Lucia, don't," and tries to take her arm but she steps away from him, back and away in the secret arc of the smile he will not see and now his walk uncertain, motion tentative and dry and she imagines for an alien moment the pain he must be feeling, inside and out, in his timid heart and aching balls; she no longer bothers even to smile; is it her problem? His wrist is thin and glazed in her grasp as she leads him along and after a while she drops it to let him follow her stuporously like a dog, like a mendicant blessed by no favors, a broken stalk trailing the senseless ground but she is not interested anymore, she knows now how it has all come out, the ending. The climax.

He sends her daffodils and jonquils, one rose a day then several, then bouquets, then at last the emptied contents of the bonsai store. In the onrush and annealment of his pain he leans toward pretty bonsai and a multicolored field of flowers, flowers to loop and strangle, their fuses clambering toward her throat and into her thighs, the stink refracted, the secret folding and unfolding of petals and of lips.

He begins with mixed bouquets: She marries at last because quite simply there is nothing else to do that year, no way around being twenty-nine years old in a foolish, dead summer and he is rich or at least says he is coming into some money and that was the summer that her two best friends married the men with whom they lived and left her feeling sullen and vaguely cheated. She keeps her side of the bargain, wifey-wife and even lets him try to get her pregnant (pistil and stem; seed and blossom) but one Saturday morning, emerging from a hangover and no fun at all in August's Saratoga she knows that it is all over, that she cannot bear any more of him and so, because she prides herself on being honest, because she has never lied to men unless she had to, she tells him that things between them are finished and she wants a divorce as quickly as possible. Alimony is not a permanent consideration, but some rehabilitative settlement is definitely in order.

He looks at her from the rustle of dry blankets, the weeping finished, eyes wide as if now poison must come past tears. "Lucia, oh God Lucia, how can you do this to me, how can you dismiss me like this? You lied, didn't you? That's all you ever did. You lied."

She does not know what to say to this and so says nothing, only watches him as he gathers the bedclothes, wraps them like gauze for the wounded, wraps them around his stricken groin. Lied? How so? She has never pretended to great passion, deep feeling, a heart to break or burst; it is not her way, that way, not her style at all. After a few moments, attenuated so profoundly that even she is made uncomfortable by their racklike stretch, she turns to leave the bedroom, to leave the apartment; to leave him there in his crouch and his fresh weeping until such time as the papers are readied, are finally prepared; when she needs him again.

But he surprises her, he is resourceful and cunning and so he begins with mixed bouquets of gladioli, chrysanthemums, the usual prom stuff, two or three of them a day and then moves on to potted plants and cacti, in the coda of their conjoinment he sends her pots and bags and prickly, extinguished vegetable things which glow in the dark and smell round and huge, which seem to pant secretly as dogs in the empty places of the apartment. And meanwhile, meanwhile, fecundity ferox and flowers and flowers, more and more but even as the bouquets pour in, hungry as kudzu, flagrant as base gold from a hundred men it is the peculiarly meaty and ugly aspects of *his* plants, *his* flowers, the steaming lumpy stink of their stems which seems somehow to wrack her the most; she is not sure why this should be. Perhaps because he was her only husband, the only one to whom she made the promise formal; perhaps it is for reasons she in her honesty cannot guess as she slips and tumbles, moving gracelessly, relentlessly down the walls of consciousness as a tear runs down a cheek, as blood runs down a window: as the silent water of rain runs down the broad green leaves of a plant.

Pistil, anvil, stamen, stem: She does not know why they hate her so, or seem to hate her; once they had seemed to love her, and who is dishonest now? Who are the real liars, the ones who groan and weep, clutch and cry Lucia Lucia as if she were an opera, as if she were some movie they had seen as teenagers, horny boys falling open-mouthed in love with some larger-than-life representation, some skyscraper tit, some vast enormous smile; and what does any of that have to do with her? She is the one, the real one, the real woman; she is the one at the end of these glowerings and tears, these rages, these pathetic cards and notes; these flowers, helpless as a victim on her bed turned now to funeral slab, narrowed to coffin confines by the creeping encroachment of green and white, pink and yellow, life and death and if she could have screamed, fled, attacked or attempted to attack that time is over, past, she had somehow let it get away from her—the flowers perhaps had done that too, had stripped her attention, had robbed with visions of the past any hope for the future, any possibility or engine for escape. But I didn't love them, she wants to cry, wants to shout not as apology but defense, I didn't love any of them, I never wanted to love any of them at all! Is it my fault? How is it my fault that they loved me?

Now in silence or perhaps on the most delicate cusp, the balanceless tip of death she lies: in the redemptive and carnivorous, the plangent and murmurous, the devouring and incarcerating stink of her admirers' bouquets, their plants, their buds, all of them most fully and finally prepaid, all of them looming over her. Dwindled then in the darkness they impose, the heavy indoor green of their stance and last, most last and final approach Lucia takes herself through the growth of meaning to *be* a plant, a vegeaceous being brought now through rot and stink, through mulch and agony to a new and primordial consciousness. The flowers, the stiff and crackling stems continue to arrive, ribboned and carded, ferocious and unknown they flood the apartment, they stream through the windows, heave and batter from beneath the floorboards like an earthquake, a steaming riot of unstoppable growth; pour in and pour in, the flower of the hour club, embracing and smothering and at last, pistil, anvil, stamen, stem, the submerged cognizant Lucia begins in growth to move slowly, slowly under the earth: herself to sprout, to bloom, to bring forth the faint green shoots of redemption from that pope's staff of herself, all forgiveness, all prayer in the warm and loamless chancel of the night.

Cafe Endless: Spring Rain

by
Nancy Holder

—ɯ—

It was spring in Yoyogi Park, and not a rain, exactly. Cool mist floated in the air, drawn to the heat of the thousand milling bodies, clinging to all the things that lived: girl groups dressed in black lace and garters, thirty young boys dressed up as James Dean, pompadours and chains and black leather jackets. The perennial hippies in black velvet hats and tie-dyed dusters. Ointen Rose, the most popular Sunday street band in Harajuku, their pride and joy a black bass player who was actually quite good.

It would have been a perfect day to go to the empress's iris garden in the Meiji Shrine complex. If you stood still long enough and stared across the fish pond in a tranquil state, you could see Her Majesty's spirit shimmering in the mist that was not mist but gentle spring rain. But Satoshi's charge for the day was Buchner-san, the American agent for Nippon Kokusai Sangyo, and she had asked to be shown the famous street-dancing kids of Harajuku.

She had made the request boldly, knowing it wasn't the polite Japanese thing to do. That was no problem; no one in Ni-Koku-Sangyo expected Buchner-san to act Japanese, and they would never have hired her if she had. She was their American, their contact with the States, and they wanted her as bold and brassy and utterly unsubtle as she was.

"These are great! This is great!" she kept exclaiming as they traversed the closed-off boulevard. As they did each Sunday, the groups had set up as far apart as possible, which was not very far at all; and the din was so great that you couldn't hear the generators that powered their electric guitars. Satoshi had never heard the generators.

The fan clubs of the more popular groups invented gestures and little dances to accompany the songs of their heroes, and as they shouted and pointed and shoo-whopped, Buchner-san shouted in his ear, "It's like *Rocky Horror*! Do you know about *Rocky Horror*?"

"Oh, yes," he said politely. With the arrogance of her countrymen, which he found so charming, she always assumed his ignorance. That there was a fundamental lack in his country. In fact, he had seen the original stage play in London, and had owned a bootleg laser disc before Americans could even purchase laser disc players. "It is very interesting."

"I love Tim Curry." She flashed a smile at him. He was getting tired, but would never let her know. All the English, all her talking and questions. Her energetic curiosity. Not that he was complaining; he was happy to show her this amazing Tokyo phenomenon, and pleased if she enjoyed their Sunday afternoon together. He was Ni-Koku-Sangyo's representative today, and entertaining her was his responsibility. Satoshi was a Japanese man, and fulfilling responsibilities with good effort gave him a sense of pride and accomplishment.

After a while he steered her to the food booths and bought her some doughy snacks of octopus meat and a beer. When she discovered what she was eating, she laughed and said, "I'm eating octopus balls!" and Satoshi laughed back, although other Americans had made the same joke. He didn't mind. He never found their humor offensive or insulting, as some of his colleagues did. Americans to him were like puppies, eager, alert, bounding and fun. Although not to be dismissed as unintelligent or lacking in shrewdness. They were tough businessmen. Business *people*.

"Do you believe in ghosts, Buchner-san?" he asked her after they finished their snack.

"Hmm. Do I believe in ghosts." She looked at him askance. "Why do you ask?"

"If you look across the iris garden at the Meiji Shrine, you can see a ghost."

"If you're Japanese." She grinned at him. "I'm afraid I'm far too earthbound for that, Nagai-san."

"No. Anyone can see it. Because it's there. No special abilities— or genetic traits—are required."

"Then let's go see it."

He inclined his head. "Unfortunately, it is now closed. But you must come back if you have free time before you go. Tell the taxi *Meiji-jingu*."

"And the subway stop?"

How he admired these American women! "*Meiji-jingu-mae*."

"Got it." She was writing it down. Abruptly she frowned and looked up. "God, it's raining harder."

Perhaps that was her way of hinting that she would like to go, and not an indirect rebuke that he had not thought to warn her that it might rain, or to bring umbrellas. Or neither; Americans didn't think like that. It might simply be a comment about the weather.

"Shall I take you to Roppongi? The Hard Rock Cafe is there." She had made mention to Satoshi's boss, Iwasawa-san, that she would like to buy a Tokyo Hard Rock Cafe T-shirt for her nephew. Although she was almost forty, she was not married. Iwasawa privately called her "Big Mama." Satoshi thought that was hilarious.

"Oh, the Hard Rock! That'd be great. I want to buy my nephew a souvenir." Obviously she had forgotten she'd told Iwasawa. A Japanese would not have. He—she—would have taken it for granted that the request had been made, and now was about to be fulfilled. And a small notch on the chart of indebtedness was now made in favor of Ni-Koku-Sangyo, to be be paid at the proper time.

They walked back down the boulevard, taking one last look at the bands. The rain was falling not harder, but more like gentle rain now than mist. Perhaps the Harajuku kids would have to shut down; all that electricity could not be safe.

He began to hail a cab, but she asked to take the subway "if it's not too much trouble." Then she would know how to come back if she had time to "visit his ghost." He acquiesced, content to do as she wished, although he was a little disappointed. While with her he was on his expense account, and he far preferred cabs to crowded subways.

He showed her how to walk to the station, pointing out landmarks, and explained how to buy a ticket. In Japan there was no stigma attached to ignorance, only to not trying one's best. They went to the trains and he explained how she could tell she was boarding the correct one. With a sense of fearless joy she absorbed all he said. He was very sorry she would not meet Tsukinosuke.

But of course, she would have quite happily informed him that she didn't believe in vampires, either.

The ride was not long but it was crowded. He could remember a time years ago when Japanese people stared at Americans and Japanese men groped American women on the trains as everyone stood netted together like fish. Now it was Tokyo, London, New York, the three big cities of the world, and such days of primitive behavior were over.

As they ascended the Roppongi station, the rain was falling like strands of spiderwebs catching dew. Satoshi's chest tightened. He took measured steps as they turned the corner past the big coffeehouse, Almond, pretending he was scanning for umbrellas.

Cafe Endless: Spring Rain

Resourceful Roppongi merchants kept supplies of cheap umbrellas on hand for sudden thundershowers.

People hurried into Almond, jamming the pink-and-white foyer and cramming into booths for hot coffee and pastries. Hordes of young Japanese girls, giggling and beautifully dressed. No other women on earth dressed with as much fashion and taste as Tokyoites. Although Satoshi was almost thirty, he was not married, either. He imagined his reasons were more compelling than Buchner-san's.

As they passed the windows resplendent with bright pink booths, he had to force himself not to look to the right and up to the leaded-glass windows on the third floor of the building. Still, he saw in his mind their exquisite, ancient beauty and his heart began to pound, much as he imagined Buchner-san's heart would if she saw the empress's ghost. The throbbing traveled through his veins and arteries to his groin, a journey often taken in this vicinity.

Ignoring the growing, biting pleasure, Satoshi began to lead his American charge down the main street. Halfway between here and Tokyo Tower was the Hard Rock Cafe. Beers there currently went for eight hundred yen, about eight dollars. That would give her something to talk about back home.

His back was to the windows, but he felt the sudden heat of the spring rain, and he struggled not to turn around.

Buchner-san touched his arm, and he almost shouted. "Wait, Nagai-san, please. What's that place?"

Of course it had drawn her. How could it not? He replied, as evenly as he could, "Oh, that's Cafe Endless."

"Those windows are beautiful!"

As indeed they were, even in the gray light of spring rain: turquoise and emerald and ruby blood; lapis and onyx. There were no designs, no patterns, but one responded to the intention: enticement, seduction, promise.

She said, "I wish I had my camera."

Immediately Satoshi began to scan for instant cameras as well as umbrellas. Buchner-san had no idea he was doing so. She was staring at the windows, unaware that washes of color were shifting over her face. Hypnosis; Satoshi felt only a fleeting pang of jealousy, for he was secure in his love.

And his need.

"Let's go there." She jabbed her finger toward the windows as if he might not know where she meant. "We could get some coffee."

He smiled. If that was what she wanted to do, that was what they would do. "As you wish."

"Oh. That is, if you have time." Now she looked concerned. She checked her watch. Americans were so unbelievably direct, yet they constantly put others in the most awkward of positions. How could he ever admit that yes, he was in a bit of a rush? For now he was beginning to sweat, so close were they to Cafe Endless. The scars on his neck burned; on his chest, burned; on his penis and testicles. Burned up.

"Of course we have plenty of time." He gestured for her to go first, although it made more sense for him to lead the way. She smiled at him, happy puppy, and with his guidance behind her, led the way to the plain gray elevator that opened onto the street.

They got in and he punched the button for the third floor. The doors open and he shepherded her out, very politely. There was no sign, although it was not a private club.

"Do you think they'll have cappuccino?" she asked over her shoulder. So far they had not been able to find cappuccino for her. He had a feeling they called it something else in Japanese, although he didn't know what. That could have been a cause for embarrassment, but since she was American, it was simply an amusing puzzle for them to solve.

"Perhaps they will," he said. Before he opened the swirling Art Nouveau doors of carved wood flowers and etched pastel glass, he smelled the blood that was for him the essence of Cafe Endless. He breathed in and dreamed of pain, and of *her*.

Cafe Endless.

He had first seen her in the winter, in a *kabuki* play, which was outrageous: even in ultramodern Japan, women did not perform

72

kabuki. It was the province of men, men playing men and men playing women and men believing in the women and men believing themselves to be women, so strong was their commitment and talent.

He had ducked into the *kabuki* theater only to get out of a driving winter rain. It was so odd, the streets icy, the sky liquid. It seemed that as soon as the rain hit the earth, it froze. He was loaded with parcels from his shopping expedition: this was the Ginza, the famous shopping district of Tokyo, and he was buying himself a new suit to celebrate his promotion. But he was loaded down, and it was rush hour; so he thought to buy a standing-room-only ticket for one act of *kabuki* until things calmed down.

Inexplicably (to this day), there had been plenty of seats, and he had been able to settle in and relax. The scrim had lifted; the musicians began to play.

Marvel.

She danced of a snow ghost, traveling sadly through a landscape of white. Shimmering white and blue, a figure of distinct and profound loneliness, a creature of tragedy.

And then a bride: moment of joy! Flashing snowflake instant!

And then a heron, a bird of majesty and delicacy. To him, a winged picture of fidelity and forbearance that flew away,

away,

over the snow.

Silence had blanketed the theater, then applause so overwhelming that Satoshi absorbed it as if for himself, and wept. Backstage he tried to find the actor, billed as *Tsukinosuke*. But no one saw *Tsukinosuke* then, nor ever again.

In that winter rain he had stumbled out of the theater, bereft. He was in love with that dancing creature. His new clothes, his promotion, his being were meaningless beside the beauty of that dance. As never before, he understood the vitality of tradition, the dignity of the worship of what had existed before one's own self had come into being. There was no shame in awe; there was exaltation.

The wonder was that *she* believed that, too.

Now, with Buchner-san, he sat at a wrought iron table of leaves and sexual flowers topped with glass. After some discussion the waiter brought Satoshi some absinthe and—voilà!—what they called *café au lait* in Japan, but in America was *cappuccino*.

"It's like finding the Holy Grail," Satoshi said as the waiter set the cup down before his charge. "I feel that I can die now." Buchner-san laughed long and hard and told him he was a card.

As they sipped their beverages, he couldn't help but look past her toward the doors on the other side of the cafe. She wasn't there; he would feel it if she were. But there was exquisite pain in the longing that made his body tight and hot and breathless.

And then:

Marvel.

As the weak sun began to sink and the windows washed orange, crimson, blood, blood red, the Chinese scarlet of dying birds. Voluptuous and ostentatious, free of restraint, smears and pools of red that transformed the rooms of Cafe Endless into the chambers of a beating heart.

"Oh," Buchner-san murmured, "look." She pointed at a mirror, and for a moment he panicked. Slowly he swiveled his head, and saw his reflection. And he knew in that moment that he did not fully trust *her*, and he was ashamed. Quickly he recovered himself and said nothing, waiting for a cue to reveal what Buchner-san was talking about.

"I look like I'm bleeding." She made a little face. "I look terrible!"

"Never." Satoshi picked up his absinthe and sipped the bitter liqueur. Discreetly he held it in his mouth so that the taste would linger when she kissed him.

"Oh, you're so gallant." She smiled at him and turned her head this way and that. "It's ghoulish."

"No, very lovely. Very *kabuki*."

She struck a pose, tilting her head and crossing her eyes. "*Banzai!*"

He liked her so very much. For a moment he considered sharing his situation with her, not in the sense of telling her about it but of

74

inviting her to participate. But as she said, she was far too earth-bound for that. And he was too selfish.

Then it was dark. "Jesus, we've been here for over an hour!" she said, glancing at her watch. "It seems like we just got here." She drained her cup. "I've got to get going." Satoshi let the last few drops of absinthe slide down his throat and signaled for the check. "No, no, you stay. I'll grab a cab."

"Your Hard Rock T-shirts. It will only take a minute," he said, and then: Marvel. Waves of pleasure, excitement, desire. The blood in his veins warmed, literally; he began to sweat, his organs to warm. Warm, endlessly warm, heat melting away the last snow, the first endless spring rain. His nipples hardened, his penis stiffened and throbbed, his testicles contracted and pulsated with semen.

"I'll have to get them later," she said breathlessly. "I have a dinner tonight."

"Oh, I'm so sorry." It was natural to apologize. He hadn't asked how long she could stay out. His forehead beaded with perspiration and he put his hands in his lap because they were shaking. If he left Cafe Endless now, he would probably fall to his knees in the street, reeling.

He got to his feet. "I'll take you back to your hotel."

"No, no, I'll grab a taxi." She held out a hand. "Don't worry about it, Nagai-san. It's really no problem."

The waiter silently glided over to their glass and metal table. Satoshi signed for the drinks. Moving cautiously, he got to his feet. His mouth was filled with absinthe and the memory of blood. His scars ached and burned. He daubed his forehead with his handkerchief and put it back in his pocket.

"You really don't have to bother," Buchner-san assured him as they went to the elevator. "I'll just grab a cab on the street."

They got to the ground floor. Satoshi felt as if his penis were being pulled through the ceiling of the elevator and back to Cafe Endless, back to the rooms above Cafe Endless. She was there. She was there, and she was waiting, his blue snow goddess.

Buchner-san cried, "Look, there's one!" and waved her hand. Instantly a cab pulled over. Satoshi had been to New York many times, and realized that he would probably never see that loud, raucous place again.

"Thank you so much," Buchner-san told him as she climbed into the cab. Satoshi smiled and told the driver in Japanese exactly where her hotel was. "It's been so nice to see you. I'm really sorry I have to dash off like this."

"Oh, please excuse me," Satoshi replied. His English was beginning to go. "It was nothing." He would order a number of T-shirts from the Hard Rock and have them sent to her hotel. Different sizes and the two choices, white or black. But not too many to overwhelm her. Just enough to impress her and perhaps—if it were possible to so affect this brassy American lady—to make her feel indebted to him and, therefore, to Nippon Kokusai Sangyo.

"*Ciao!*" she cried gaily, and the taxi took off, weaving her into the traffic and fabric of Roppongi.

He stumbled, wiping his forehead, and lurched back to the elevator. No one else was inside; he fell against the wall and closed his eyes, his penis fiery, found the buttons and hit the one not for the third floor and Cafe Endless, but for the fourth floor, where she was waiting.

He saw her as he opened the door, as she often appeared to him: *Tsukinosuke*, *kabuki* master in a *kimono* of ice blue, snowy white and golden herons whose embroidered wings were the long, floor-length sleeves of the fabulous gown. She twirled slowly in a circle, her face chalk white as if with *kabuki* makeup, her eyes black and liquid. Her hair, a long tail of smoke that reached her hips. Her mouth, tiny red flame. In her hands she held two white fans that she moved like heron's wings. The room was Japanese, spare and beautiful and natural, with paper *shoji* walls and straw *tatami* floors. Two pen and ink drawings of irises flanked her as she stood against the black-night window, the curtains pulled back.

"Good evening," he said, locking the door. She regarded him. She rarely spoke. Slowly she waved the fans, as if teasing the flames in his blood to rise.

He pulled off his shoes and clothes and went to her, facing her. She moved her fans over him. He opened his mouth and she flicked one of the fans shut and held it sideways. He accepted it into his mouth. She pulled from the folds of her *kimono* sleeve white silk sashes, came behind him, and tied one to the ends of the fan, brought it around, tied the other ends behind his head so that he was gagged with the fan. His eyes watered as if from smoke. His body quivered.

A slice across his buttocks. He almost ejaculated.

A slice over the nether part of his testicles. A pearl of semen blossomed on the tip of his penis as he moaned.

The blood, trickling.

Holding his penis, stroking with her frigid hands and long nails, she sliced his neck.

Drinking, drinking as he became a bonfire, taking more, draining more, and more and more as he began to suspect with mounting ecstasy that this was the night, tonight it was the fulfillment, and he groaned louder, fighting not to come.

Too late, almost too late, they fell to the *futon* that, when he touched it, became a field of snow through which tiny iris buds shot. Her long black hair swirled like waves against the moon. She threw open her legs and Satoshi thrust himself into the iciness. From his penis rose steam that was not steam but spring mist.

Oh, he loved her, he loved her; and he filled her as she gave a hoarse growl deep in her chest. And still coming as she came, he reached under the *futon* for the stake and pressed it between her breasts until droplets of blood burbled hot around the tip. Her eyes were wild with pleasure and fear; she threw back her head and convulsed around him. He pushed harder than he ever had before, piercing the skin. She gasped and reached out her hands to stop him.

He captured one of her arms and slipped the black velvet

77

restraint around her white, cold wrist. Pulled on the rope through the hook in the wooden brace of the wall, taking up all the slack until she was stretched, hard. Restrained her other arm. She sobbed once, and he could see the question in her eyes as well: *Tonight?*

He looked past her eyes and into her hair that swirled and moved and made him see ghosts. Then he rose and went to the phone beside the alcove where he prayed to his ancestors. Chrysanthemums, not irises, stood in a black bowl. A scroll of a heron flapped gently against the wall.

He took the gag out of his mouth and called the Hard Rock Cafe and ordered the T-shirts, giving them the number of his Nippon Kokusai Sangyo Enterprises Visa card. Buchner-san's hotel address.

The joy of being Japanese was that each action existed for itself, and fulfillment was possible in infinite, discrete moments. He had been a good representative of Nippon Kokusai Sangyo. He had been a good host. He had been a good man.

He would be a good vampire.

"Satoshi," she whispered, and his heart seized inside him as if she were boiling the blood into a heart attack. Silently he returned to her. She was still bound, and she writhed. Opening her mouth, she beckoned him toward her. He covered her, closing his eyes, bracing himself.

Fire, fire and pain; he felt the blood stripped from his veins and arteries like gunpowder trails. Her white face beneath his as he hardened again and thrust inside her while she sucked and sucked. He wasn't afraid, and he was terrified.

Then it was happening, not as she had ever said it would, because she had never told him what it would be like. But his soul rose into the sky like a vapor and hovered with the stars above Cafe Endless. He had a sense that she was with him; together they soared through the exquisite night sky of Tokyo, lights and clouds and moon and spring rain dropping on umbrellas and upturned faces, the wings of herons.

On the roof garden of the New Otani Hotel, where Buchner-san lay.

Cafe Endless: Spring Rain

In through her window. She stirred and moaned. Soft from a bath, and fragrant, and searing to his touch. She slept naked. Satoshi glided over her burning breasts and parted her burning legs. She protested mildly, asleep or enthralled; he bent over her. He was very, very cold and she was hot enough to melt metal. Where he touched her, steam rose. And smoke.

Then the vapor that was *she* guided him to Buchner-san's neck. Tears slid down his face and became sparkling icicles. He bent, and drank.

Ecstasy! Lava into his freezing loins, his penis, his heart. Warm candle wax, boiling *miso* soup. A bath among steaming rocks and bubbling hot springs. And pleasure of the most sensuous nature, hard and soft, pliant and conquering. It would be his last gift to Buchner-san, whom he admired greatly.

And *she* with him, taking also, then sharing with him, her hands on his body, inside his body.

Ecstasy! Beyond all imagining; the fulfillment of the dance she had promised short months before, indescribable wonder that set him to weeping.

And then:

On top of her body, on the *futon*, as she pulled her teeth from his neck and swallowed the last pearly drops. His eyes barely able to open. He whispered, "Was it just a dream?"

Her black eyes answered, "Wasn't it all just a dream?" And Satoshi was sorrowful for everything left behind, for this discrete, infinite moment that he would lose and for all the other moments that had been his life.

They regarded one another.

She whispered, in her real voice, "It will be soon. Hold me very tightly."

He did, arms around hers, legs around hers. He fought to keep his eyes open. Hers were drooping as well. He had thought they would be aware together.

Moments passed. As he drowsed, he listened to the rain.

Then he felt the heat on his shoulder first. He gasped and his eyes popped open. Beneath him, she took a sharp breath and tensed, and looked at him.

"I'm not afraid," he whispered. And truly as never before, he understood the vitality of tradition, the dignity of the worship of what had existed before one's own self had come into being. There was no shame in awe; there was exaltation.

"Nor I," she said. "Nor am I afraid."

Then at once he ignited. Flames and smoke; he heard the choked cry in his throat but then had no throat to express it. Hair, skin, bone, but no blood as the weak sun began to rise and the window washed orange, crimson, blood, blood red, the Chinese scarlet of dying birds. Forgiving and enduring, free of restraint, crackles and washes of red that transformed the rooms above Cafe Endless into the chambers of a burning, stilling heart.

And then, as she caught fire as well, a moment of joy! Flashing snowflake instant!

Writhing, they danced of ghosts traveling gloriously through a landscape of white. *Kabuki* masters, transcendent beings shimmering white and blue, figures of distinct and profound companionship, creatures of triumph.

And then, two simple herons, birds of majesty and delicacy. A winged picture of fidelity and forbearance that flew away,

away,

into the spring rain that was not rain exactly, but tears of exquisite emotion,

to the empress's iris garden, where the ghosts of other herons lived.

Empty
Vessels

by
David B. Silva

—⚏—

First off, I guess I should let you know right up front that my mother was not a woman you'd consider for sainthood. When I was a boy, she referred to herself as a lady of the evening. It wasn't until the fifth grade, when Paul Whittaker called her a whore, that I first began to understand the true meaning of her self-reference. I had always assumed that the night was her playground, that she liked the full moon and the darkness and the dim streetlights, that she was like a cat, nocturnal in her nature, sleeping during the day, out prowling at night. And all that was true, I suppose. Just not in the way that I understood it.

But Paul Whittaker straightened me out.

Whore.

My mother the whore.

I never could bring myself to use that word—*whore*. It was not the way I would have described her. Though looking back now, I doubt I would have described her as a *lady of the evening*, either. She was neither of those, and she was both of them.

Beyond the semantics, though, was this: there wasn't an eleven-year-old alive who wanted to hear that his mother was a whore. Or that his father was a stranger, a man who had driven out of the night in an old pickup, done his business, then disappeared again, never to return. Or that as much as his mother loved him, he had been a surprise to her. Given the choice, she would have preferred not to have been a mother at all.

My mother did love me, though, as much as she could, and I confess I would have liked to have had more time with her.

I was eleven—going on thirty-three, as she liked to say—the night my mother's soul was taken. It was a school night. I had gone to bed around nine, after finishing my homework and watching an hour or so of television. Mom had been "out"—something else she liked to say. Exactly when she had returned, I'm not sure, but it was a little after eleven when something stirred me out of my sleep. I sat up, listening intently, feeling the cool night air against my skin. Outside, there was the soft whistle of wind through the branches of the walnut tree in the backyard. Inside, it was as if the house were holding its breath; everything had fallen under the spell of a hush.

"Mom?"

It had been raining on and off for several days. Through the curtains, I saw the sky above the tenement across the way light up with a flash of lightning. The darkness in my bedroom scurried back under the bed and into the corners, and I found myself counting out the seconds—almost five—before the thunder hit. It hit with the crack of a whip, followed closely by a long, low grumbling noise that sounded a little like Grandpa Edmonds when he was fussing about a salesclerk or a waitress.

And then I heard a cry.

It was like nothing I had ever heard before. Not a shriek or a scream, but a whimper that sounded oddly submissive. And it had come from my mother's room.

Empty Vessels

I had heard noises from that end of the house before, strange sounds that I had mostly chosen to ignore. I guess I'd always had a general idea of what was going on when she brought men home, though maybe not the specifics. Maybe not the reasons why. But I knew it was something to be kept behind closed doors, away from a young boy's curiosity. My mother might have brought home lots of guys, but she had never been ugly about it. She had always been discreet. She had always tried to shield me.

But this was different.

"Mom?"

It came again—softer this time—as I made my way down the hall. Outside her door, I pressed my ear against the cool surface and held my breath. It was quiet on the other side, so quiet I could hear my heart pounding in my chest. It was something I had never done before, but finally I reached out and tried the knob. My hands were shaking. The latch slipped. The door swung silently open an inch, maybe two, and suddenly there was just enough of an opening that I could see into the darkness.

There was a soft glow pouring in through the window from a streetlight. I could see the blocklike silhouette of my mother's bed, the sheets rumpled, the pillows out of place. For a moment, I thought she hadn't come home yet. Everything was dark and perfectly still. Then a flash of lightning exploded outside. The room brightened, and I saw the pale gray form of a man rise up off the bed. He arched his back, threw back his head, and drew in a huge uninterrupted breath.

I shrank back.

"Jesus, Blaine."

That was my mother, talking to the stranger. There was a mix of anger and unease in her voice, something I had heard only once before, after she had come home all swollen and bleeding from a beating some john had given her. She had kept the curtains drawn, the house dark, for nearly a week after that. And for a while longer, she had even insisted that she'd finally had enough, that she was ready to make some major changes in her life. She had said that before and, like all the other times, there had been no change, things had continued merrily on their way. And now, as I listened, it sounded faintly as if they had brought her back full circle.

The stranger whispered something in response, something I couldn't quite hear, then he lowered himself back into the shadows of the bed. My mother moaned, not unpleasantly. I sat back, toying with the idea of going back to bed. It wasn't the first time she had brought someone home, and I was sure it wouldn't be the last. Maybe I had been wrong. Maybe what I had heard in her voice hadn't been unease at all. Though something *did* seem different.

If I *had* gone back to bed, I suppose it wouldn't have made any difference. Nothing would have changed. Except that I wouldn't have been a witness then, and maybe it would have been easier to put it all away without the nightmares.

But I didn't go back to bed.

I stayed and watched and eventually saw the outline of my mother in the Picasso of shadows and light. She was lying on her back, a soft glow of outside light falling across her breasts. I had seen her naked once before, when I was five or six and had walked in while she was bathing. To be honest, I didn't remember the occasion. But my mother liked to tease me about it when she got together with her sisters. "He started to unbutton his shirt," she would say. "And I asked him what he was doing, and he said, 'You look lonely, mommy.' He was all set to climb right in with me." She had always thought that was hilarious, though I had never been able to find the humor in it myself.

Now, she was lying perfectly still, her eyes closed, her mouth slightly open.

The stranger, who was lying on top of her, gazed darkly into her eyes as if he were trying to catch a glimpse of her soul. "What makes you happy?" he asked suddenly. His voice was low and smooth, and I thought how easy it would be to believe in the words spoken by a voice like his.

"You do," my mother said disingenuously. "You make me happy."

"No. The truth."

Empty Vessels

"Honest," she whispered, running her hand across his chest.

"No, you don't understand, Eve. I'm not looking for a compliment. I'm looking for the truth. I want you to tell me what makes you happy. Truly happy."

My mother's hand fell away from his chest, and though I couldn't read her expression, I imagined by the tone of her voice that she had been surprised by his question. "Me?"

"Yes, you."

She turned her head away from me, staring thoughtfully out the window. "My boy, Marshall. He makes me happy."

The stranger nodded with apparent satisfaction. Then he took in another deep, uninterrupted breath, as if he thought he could inhale her happiness. "Ah . . . yes," he said, lowering himself again. I could see the glisten of sweat on his bare back, and I heard my mother let out a soft, muffled cry.

There's no pleasure in that *sound*, I remember thinking. I glanced back down the hall at my open bedroom door. I had left the light on. My pillow was rumpled. The sheets on the bed were pulled back. That room seemed a thousand miles away now. I had left it in innocence, but I would go back . . .

There was another cry from my mother.

They had begun to work themselves into an uneasy rhythm now, two strangers trying to get to know one another. Their movements became oddly choreographed, as if they were both mechanically rehearsing a dance they had learned a long time ago and were waiting for it to overtake them.

Another flash of lightning swept into the room. I saw the man run the tip of his tongue across her belly. He licked his lips, savoring the taste, then continued up her body, between her breasts and along her neckline.

"Easy," he said.

A thrust, deeper.

She moaned.

The stranger's face twisted into an ugly grin, and then I witnessed something, something that I still don't fully understand. He opened his mouth as if he were going to yawn, his jaw nearly coming unhinged, and he began to draw the breath from my mother's mouth. It came from her in the form of a long, greenish gold stream of light that lifted her several inches off the bed. What it was . . . to be honest, I didn't know what it was. Her spirit. Her love. Whatever it is that makes a person real and alive. He took it all in, like a man taking a hit from some fine Jamaican weed, and when he was done, my mother fell emptily back into the mattress.

The stranger shuddered, and caught his breath.

I think I might have shuddered, too. I wasn't sure exactly what it was that I had witnessed. Something horrible, it seemed. Though at eleven, the world was still full of mysteries, and for all I knew, this was just one more of those things that would someday make perfect sense to me. I wanted to believe that, but I think I shuddered anyway.

I don't know what happened in the room after that. I had seen enough. I had seen more than enough. So I left the door slightly ajar and scrambled back to my bedroom, where I turned off the light and buried myself under the covers. When you're eleven, you're supposed to be too old to believe in hiding under the covers. But that didn't matter, and in the end who really knows anyway? Maybe those covers were the only thing that kept me alive.

I stayed under them until my muscles ached from not moving. By then, a couple of hours had passed, maybe more. The house had long since fallen quiet.

It was still dark out. The rain had stopped. The night temperatures had left the room unseasonably cold. I didn't want to get up, but eventually I was able to scoot out from beneath the covers and cross the floor. I peered down the hallway. At the far end, there was a faint pattern of light forming a misshapen rectangle across the floor.

It was a while longer before I ventured down the hall again. I stopped and listened at my mother's door, heard nothing, then pushed it open until I was certain the stranger was no longer in the room. Unless, of course, he was hiding in the shadows, a possibility I thought unlikely. He was not a man who hid from anything, I imagined. Still, I fumbled quickly for the light switch.

I'm not sure exactly what I expected to find. That the stranger was gone, certainly. That my mother was sleeping peacefully and everything was all right, that was my hope. That she was dead . . . well, as much as I hate to admit it, that was the single worst thought I had allowed myself to consider.

And the stranger *was* gone.

And my mother was not dead. But she looked as if she had come back from the dead. She looked like one of those wax figures you see in museums, pasty and glassy-eyed and not quite right. Her cheeks, which had lost their fullness, resembled loose skin stretched across a crudely made drum. There was drool running down her chin, and her Adam's apple bobbed horridly as she tried to swallow.

The stranger had left the sheets pulled back. I could see her breathing was shallow, and embarrassed more than I should have been, I used a blanket to cover her breasts.

No, she wasn't dead.

But she wasn't alive, either.

It's been nearly thirty-five years since that night. My mother lives in a convalescent home on the south side. Physically, she functions just fine, though she doesn't get around as easily as she once did and her doctor told me last week that she's developing a cataract in one eye. Nothing out of the ordinary for a woman in her mid-sixties.

But it had never been her physical state that had troubled me.

After her encounter with Mr. Jeffries—that was his name, as I was eventually able to discover: Blaine Jeffries. Sounds a bit aristocratic, doesn't it? A man of royalty, maybe?—anyway, after her encounter, my mother had never been the same. He had left her alive and breathing and with a hole in her heart the size of the Grand Canyon. He had left her an autistic child, emotionally vacant, a woman who could only look past you, never directly at you.

The morning after was a strange timeless dream. I don't know exactly when I became aware of the fact that I was alone with my mother and that things had changed, that in the darkness of the night my world had been turned upside down like an hourglass and presently I was the parent and my mother was the child. Eventually, when I finally did make that realization, I called my aunt.

She called an ambulance.

The doctors at County General kept my mother for a couple of weeks. Her room was on the third floor at the end of the hall, with a window that overlooked the parking lot. I spent a good many hours standing at that window, peering down at the people climbing out of their cars. Even then, I had started looking for him, I guess.

There was a battery of tests, I remember. Mostly neurological and psychological, according to my aunt, who tried to explain things to me as they were happening. Neither one of us really understood, though. I'm not sure the doctors understood, either.

"Apoplexy," the doctor said, at the end of a long day of testing. "That's the best we can come up with."

My aunt stared at him, obviously not catching what he was saying.

"A stroke," he tried to clarify. "Apparently a blood vessel in the brain broke. When that happens, there's a sudden paralysis, a loss of consciousness, and sometimes a loss of feeling."

"A loss of feeling," my aunt repeated numbly.

"Yes."

I think it was then that she began to understand more than the doctors. It wasn't a loss of feeling my mother had experienced, like when you wake up in the middle of the night and your toes are all tingly and you realize your foot's asleep. It was more like waking up in the middle of the night and realizing that the world was an empty place and you didn't give a damn one way or the other, because you couldn't *feel* anything.

No love. No hate.

No joy. No sorrow.

Nothing.

That was my mother.

Empty Vessels

My aunt made the arrangements for the convalescent home. It was a nice place, run by an Italian couple who tried to keep things comfortable and homey. When I went to visit, usually on Sundays, there was always the fragrance of oregano and parmesan in the air. Nothing like the hospital mouthwashy odor I had come to hate so much after her stay at County General. I was grateful for that. I think my mother would have been grateful, too, if she were capable of being grateful.

Things never did return to what you might call normal.

I lived with my aunt, and I guess you could say gradually we worked ourselves into a comfortable routine together. It was a better life for a young boy. Someone always around. No late-night visitors with a few extra bucks and a long list of fantasies.

After I graduated from high school, I moved out and found myself a studio apartment in a neighboring town. I worked at a print shop during the day and attended community college at night, taking one class at a time until I was eventually able to earn an architectural engineering degree through the state university. At the Eleventh Annual Greenhaven Arts & Crafts Faire, I met Elizabeth Banner, a beautiful, joyful young woman who I eventually fell in love with and married. We had two children: Ben, who is now thirteen, bright, and plays a wicked game of tennis; and Julie, who is eleven and loves horses and just about any movie starring Corey Haim.

It's a long, long way from the world where I grew up.

But there isn't a day that goes by when my thoughts aren't drawn back to that dreadful night when Mr. Blaine Jeffries stole my mother's soul.

When I hit my mid-forties, I went through what a pop psychologist might call a hidden-trauma crisis. Over a period of several weeks, I was haunted by a recurring nightmare that took me back to that night outside my mother's bedroom. I was kneeling, trying to catch a glimpse through the crack in the door, when the door suddenly swung wide open. Jeffries, who was startled nearly as much as I, turned in my direction, his lips curled back, fangs exposed. He growled at me.

LOVE IN VEIN

"Too late," he said, the words coming from deep in his throat.

I fell back against the wall, the impact sending a sharp pain through my shoulder blades, a pain I hardly noticed at the time.

"There's nothing left for little boys."

He laughed, his voice gruff and irritating, and gradually I became aware of another voice, a soft soprano, joining in. It was my mother.

She sat up, using her sticklike arms as leverage against the bed. Her cheeks were sunken, her eyes distended, and she looked not just malnourished but like a flower, dry and near death. It was almost as if I could see her wilting right before my eyes.

"Nothing left," she said weakly. "Not even for you, Marshall."

And then I would wake up. I'd be drenched from a night sweat, and the dream would still be lingering in the fore of my mind. Sometimes I'd be able to close my eyes and fall back to sleep again, but most of the time I'd end up downstairs at the kitchen table, sipping coffee and trying to forget.

I knew what she meant when she said there was nothing left.

She meant she had no love left.

And that, I suppose, had been true enough.

After the nightmares, I hired a private detective. I told him my mother had been raped when I was a young boy, which was certainly closer to the truth than not. I told him that I had witnessed what had happened, which was also as close to the truth as you can come and still not be there. And I told him the time had now come when I felt I had to face the man who had done it.

He was a good detective, maybe because he believed in the case. It took him a little over three months, working part-time, with nothing more to go on than a vague description and the stranger's first name, which were all I had to offer. Then one night after Beth and the kids had gone to bed, I got a call to meet him at the local Denny's. He handed me a piece of paper across the table. Printed on one side in blue ink was: BLAINE JEFFRIES. 16289 TICONDEROGA. SARATOGA, CA.

Empty Vessels

"What are you going to do?" he asked with honest concern.

"I don't know," I said, just as honestly. I stared at the paper with the name on it, then folded it in fourths and stuck it in my shirt pocket. "Visit him, I suppose."

And eventually that's what I ended up doing.

"Mr. Jeffries? Blaine Jeffries?"

He stood in the doorway, beneath an entry light, and I realized this was the first time I had seen this man out of the shadows. His eyes were dark and weary, the eyes of an old dog that knows its better times are far behind it now. That realization seemed to have settled deeply into many of Mr. Jeffries's features. By his coloring, I gathered he had not been out under the sun in a good long time. His face was lined. His sagging jowls reminded me more of fresh bread dough than the fleshly face of an old man. And beneath it all, there was a sense that here was a man who was near the end of his life.

"I know you," he said, after a good look. "A long time ago, wasn't it? A little boy in a little no-name town on the outskirts of Sacramento."

"Greenhaven," I said. "The name of the town was Greenhaven."

He nodded. "I remember." It seemed almost as if he had surprised himself, remembering such a little thing from so long ago. "You hid in the shadows, outside the bedroom door. I . . . don't recall your name, but you were a young man then, a boy, with eyes much wiser than your years. And I see they still are."

"My name's Marshall," I said.

"Yes. And your mother was Eve. Yes, I remember."

I could barely find the restraint to stand there without lashing out at him. Hearing my mother's name spoken through this man's lips . . . it . . . it stirred a rage inside me that I could only assume had been there, waiting, for more than thirty-five years now. It may have settled there, this rage, like sediment to the bottom of a river, but suddenly it was kicking up again, and I was forced to swallow it down, because if I didn't, I was afraid I might very well lose all control.

"She was an exceptional woman," Jeffries said with admiration. He stepped away from the door like a butler inviting in a guest, proper and courteous. "Why don't you come in, Marshall. I'll try to explain the unexplainable; you try to listen and understand."

I hesitated, wondering why I had come here, and what I had expected to find beyond an old man still clinging fondly to his memories. There was a part of me, aside from the rage, that felt surprisingly sympathetic to the man.

"When you stop asking questions," he said, "the answers come naturally."

He raised his eyebrows questioningly. I didn't know if what he said were true or not. I had always asked questions. It was how I got along in the world. Sometimes the questions led to answers. Sometimes not. Maybe I had been asking the same questions for too long now.

I entered.

I think my mother would have described the house as uptown, or out of our league. It had an old European-family flavor. The floor was done in brown British quarry tile, the walls in some sort of imported stone. There was a dank, musty smell inside and I thought how much the house and its master resembled each other.

Jeffries, his feet doing an old man's shuffle across the tile floor, led me through a huge anteroom into an even larger room with a rustic stone fireplace that stood nearly as tall as I. Near the center of the room was a banquet table handcrafted from dark wood, perhaps mahogany. He motioned for me to sit, then sat across the table from me. I could feel the heat of the fire against the side of my face.

"You came to me," he said flatly. He steepled his fingers, patiently, apparently aware that he had all the time in the world and that I did not. And it was true: *I* had come to him, not he to me.

"I want you to explain the unexplainable," I said.

"Ah, my own words used against me." He smiled, with a touch of sadness, and it occurred to me that this was a lonely man sitting across the table. I wondered when he had last held a woman in his arms, when he had last conversed with a neighbor or a friend. It had been a long time, I imagined.

"Where to start?" he said. "Where to start?"

"How about with my mother?"

That smile again. Then he rested his chin atop the bridge of his hands and stared at me as if he could read my entire history with a single glance. His hands were pale and brown-spotted, the fingers thin and delicate. His fingernails were unmanicured and quite long, and, as strange as it was, I thought of Howard Hughes and reports of how long *his* nails had grown near the end of *his* life.

"She was chosen, you know," Jeffries said calmly. "Your mother was an exceptional woman. Most young ladies in her line of work, they've long since stopped feeling anything. They're dead inside. Maybe it's defensive, I don't know. Or maybe it's a form of self-punishment. Though I rather suspect it's probably a little of both, don't you?"

"I wouldn't know," I said evenly.

Jeffries grinned, a little self-satisfiedly, and I thought it was his hideous side creeping through. His teeth were the color of a dark urine stain against white Jockey shorts. I could see that something black and funguslike had begun to form pockets along the line of his gums, and it occurred to me that this man's teeth weren't going to last much longer.

"No?" he said. "I would have thought that you were intimately qualified to know such things."

"Then you would have thought wrong," I responded.

"Really?"

"Really."

"I see." He frowned and gazed hypnotically at the fire, and seemed to drift away in his thoughts. Apparently he was fond of where they had taken him, because he seemed suddenly peaceful and at ease with himself.

"I was born in 1887," he said at last. "In a small New England town called Willows Branch. My father was an industrialist, my mother a seamstress. I had two brothers and four sisters, and I was the youngest.

"In those days—much unlike these modern times of ours, I might add—children were expected to contribute to the finances of the family. We worked from a very young age. We did anything and everything just to bring home a few extra pennies."

He sighed, somewhat longingly, his gaze still fixed on the fire.

"And?" I prompted.

"I'm sorry. An old man's thoughts can wander at times. I'm learning that." He smiled dully, unaffectedly, then sighed again, and if I had taken a deep breath myself I have no doubt I would have inhaled a good deal of this man's loneliness. He was a creature who I suspected had always lived in solitude. And how sad that was.

"I worked for a carriage house," he continued. "As a stableboy. One day, when I was . . . oh, eleven or twelve, a woman came to town. She was a foreigner, with an accent that sounded like a mix of British upper class and Austrian, very different from anything I had ever heard before. I was a good stableboy, and she took a liking to me. And when she was ready to depart after her two week stay, she pulled me aside and asked me what I thought of the idea of immortality."

Jeffries paused and shook his head. "I had never heard the word before. So she had to explain it to me, and it was the kind of dream that sparks a young boy's imagination. The chance to live forever. Incredible. It was absolutely incredible.

"She offered it to me as a gift, though it wasn't a gift at all. Not with the price I had to pay. You see, in exchange for this thing called immortality, she wanted my innocence."

"Is that what you took from my mother?" I asked.

"Your mother had no innocence left," Jeffries said matter-of-factly.

"You killed her, you know."

"I did *not* kill her. I emptied her."

Emptied her. Now there was a polite way of putting it. Though it was true, she wasn't dead. She was sitting in a convalescent home, breathing and eating and getting around with a little help when she needed it, but she wasn't dead. *Emptied her.* I hated the way that sounded.

"Let me show you," Jeffries said, with tired resignation. He climbed, with some effort, out of his seat, and when I didn't follow immediately, he looked down at me. "You coming or not?"

He took me down a flight of stairs to the cellar.

At the bottom, there was a short tunnel leading off to the left. One side was a rubble and brickwork wall, damp and cool to the touch. The other side was a floor-to-ceiling wine rack. There must have been a thousand bottles doing their time here. Blaine lightly tapped one and said, "1910 Château d'Yquem." He beamed, like a little boy showing off his prized marble.

The end of the tunnel was blocked by a wood panel that drew back and opened into a small, dimly lighted room lined with shelves on both sides. It smelled musty here. I took a breath and felt as if I might cough myself silly. Somewhere in the distance I could hear the *plop-plop-plop* of dripping water.

Jeffries stepped into the shadows at the far end.

I stopped at the doorway.

"This is where I keep them," he said cryptically. Except I understood what he meant, the way a husband understands a half-finished thought from his wife. He meant that this was where he kept his *collection* of whatever it was that he had stolen from my mother and undoubtedly from others as well.

He flipped a light switch.

The room brightened.

And I knew immediately *this* was why I had come here. The shelves on both sides were lined with specimen jars: thick glass, maybe four liters in capacity. Each fell under the soft glow of an individual spotlight. Each was labeled with a brass plate, engraved in black.

I read the one nearest me on the right. It said, simply enough: JOY. Inside was a brightness nearly indescribable. I would suppose—not having experienced such a thing myself—it was something like the light at the end of the tunnel that people who have had a near-death experience often talk about. It was peaceful and serene and most of all it was what it was labeled to be: joyous.

Beneath that, one shelf down, was a jar labeled: ENVY. It was true, apparently, that old saying about turning green with envy. I didn't know where the saying had come from, but the stuff in the container—which resembled a thick, lumpy goo—was the grayish-green color of weathered copper. Green with envy.

"They're all here," Jeffries said.

"All?"

"The emotions. They're all here."

"These are what you took from my mother?" I asked. I was standing over a container labeled ANGER now. Inside was a roiling blackish cloud that seemed to be pressing against the inside of the glass. *It's going to break out someday*, I thought, and I stepped back a pace.

"No," Jeffries said. "Not these. Not specifically. Your mother's emotions . . . I used those up a long, long time ago."

He said it so matter-of-factly that he caught me completely off guard. And for the first time, I realized that something was terribly wrong here, something inside Jeffries was not only bankrupt, it was barren. No, this was not a well man. Not physically, and not emotionally. Where was the man's fear? And if he felt he had nothing to fear from me, then where was his joy or his anger or his—

In the glass jars, I thought. *They're all in the glass jars.*

"You on a diet, Jeffries?" I asked.

"Pardon?"

I nodded to the nearest container. "You aren't partaking, are you?"

He smiled again, and now I could see it clearly. It was a practiced smile, a smile without anything behind it at all. "No," he said solemnly. "Immortality is not all it's cracked up to be, as you might well have guessed already. It's a lonely life, my friend. A long, lonely life."

"And what happens if you don't. . . "

"Draw a breath every once in a while?" he said euphemistically. "I guess you could say my immortality would be shortened considerably."

"You'll die?"

"I'll die."

Empty Vessels

"And that's what you want?"

He inhaled deeply, exhaled slowly, thoughtfully. "It's not so much that I want to die," he said. "It's that I don't wish to be immortal any longer. I hope you can find the distinction there, because there is a difference. It is, perhaps, the difference between the time it takes to say yes and the time it takes to say no, but it is a difference."

I thought I understood what he was trying to say, at least as well as any mortal man can understand such a thing. "So, you're dying?"

"I am . . . aging. I haven't made the decision to die yet. I may not make that decision at all, and by not making the decision, I may die. Or perhaps the decision will be made for me. We shall see what we shall see."

He stared fondly at a nearby container, then ran his hand along the rim of it, like a hungry man staring at a pastrami sandwich that belongs to someone else. It was everything he could do not to empty it, I thought.

"We're all born that way," he said suddenly, as if he could read my thoughts. "Empty, you know. And when our mothers pick us up and hold us and lovingly coo at us, we breathe it all in. One breath after another. And when our fathers jingle the plastic keys in front of us and read us bedtime stories and playfully toss a ball in our direction, we breathe all that in as well. We breathe it in and it becomes part of us, part of who we are and how we see the world and what makes us laugh and what makes us yearn. We're all born empty. All of us."

"It's a little like an addiction, isn't it?" I asked.

"A little."

"And you're the addict?"

"We're all addicts."

And maybe we were. I didn't know for certain, of course, though I knew that it was an addiction that had brought me here, an addiction I had carried with me since the age of eleven. And I couldn't have said if I'd ever get over my addiction, regardless of what I was about to do. Maybe some addictions are never satisfied.

"It's got to stop somewhere," I said. "Don't you think?"

"Does it?" he asked. He said it in such a way that it wasn't a question as much as a prompt. It was what a father might say to his son who has come home crying after being picked on by the local bully. The words didn't matter. What mattered was what lay beneath the words, and that part went like this: *So what are you going to do about it?*

I hadn't come with anything specific in mind. I had come to see what this man looked like, to discover what this man was beneath his mask, but I had not come with the intent to do what I did. I looked at his face, and something erupted inside me, and without thought, I found myself crossing a line that I never thought I was capable of crossing.

"Yes," I said. "It's got to stop."

And I smashed the glass jar nearest me. It was the one labeled ENVY, and the glass shattered much more easily than I ever would have imagined. I hit it with the knuckles of my right hand, and when I pulled my hand out, it was covered in grayish-green slime. It felt cold. I snapped my wrist in an attempt to throw off as much of the substance as I could.

Jeffries didn't move an inch, didn't flinch, didn't smirk, didn't react at all. "Feel better?" he asked.

"No." I reached for the next container, this one label ANGER—and oh, how appropriate that was. No fist this time. I simply scooped it off the shelf and let it crash against the concrete floor. It shattered instantly. Glass shards exploded in every direction. For a moment, it looked like a miniature nuclear explosion, a little mushroom cloud expanding upward, black and malevolent.

I gasped and stepped back, and I'll admit without argument that it frightened me at first. But then I felt something inside me like I had never felt before. It was the most unambiguous, most primal passion I had ever experienced. I wanted this man dead. I wanted him dead so badly I could taste it, and I had never been so frightened of myself before.

Jeffries had backed away a step as well, maybe two, and he was pressed against the back wall, holding both hands over his mouth. It didn't occur to me at the time what he was doing—except cringing in a fear of his own—but later it became oh so obvious: Jeffries was making certain he didn't inhale any of the anger. What had he said? *Or perhaps the decision will be made for me.*

I slammed another container to the floor. I can't remember now which one it was. It doesn't matter, I suppose, because they all went, one after another, until the shelves were empty and a small portion of my anger had dissipated.

I leaned back against the doorjamb, bent over, nearly out of breath. Jeffries hadn't moved. "*Now* I feel better," I said triumphantly. Only it didn't feel triumphant at all. It felt a little sad, I suppose, a little like winning a race because you took a shortcut. Not a victory at all, but a hollow sick feeling because you know that you haven't accomplished much of anything.

"Done?" Jeffries said finally. For all my anger, he was completely unruffled.

I nodded, and straightened again, feeling my breath coming back. "You can rot here, for all I care," I said angrily. "My mother deserved better."

Then I headed back down the tunnel and up the stairs.

And I never looked back.

It was several weeks later, when I was reading the paper, that I came across an article with a slug that read simply enough: MAN FOUND DEAD IN CELLAR. It was about Jeffries. When the mail had begun to pile up in his box, his delivery man notified the authorities. They ended up breaking into the house, and after a thorough search upstairs, they made their way downstairs to the cellar.

Jeffries was found lying at the back of a small room, the floor covered with shards of broken glass. They were still trying to determine his age and how long it had been since someone had last seen him, because the man they found at the back of that room looked as if he might have died of malnutrition. There was plenty of food in the cupboards in the kitchen, and authorities were speculating that he had somehow gotten himself downstairs and was unable to get back up again. After all, the article mentioned, he appeared to be well over one hundred years old.

I took the article with me the next time I went to visit my mother. She was fighting a cold that day, and she was still in bed, so I pulled a chair up and read her the entire piece. At the end, I told her that this Mr. Jeffries was the same man who had *emptied* her.

How much of what I told her she actually absorbed, I guess I'll never know. But when she didn't react, not even with a blink or an attempt to raise a hand, I found myself leaning over her, screaming with a rage that seemed as if it had been boiling at the bottom of a volcano for centuries.

A nurse came rushing in before I could do anything crazy. She pulled me away and scolded me as if I were a little boy who had gotten into a scuffle out on the playground during recess. As she hovered over my mother, making sure I hadn't hurt her, I backed into the wall and suddenly became aware of what I had nearly done.

I had nearly struck her. I had wanted to strike her. I had wanted to knock her on the side of the head until she understood that Jeffries was dead and that I had helped make that decision for him.

I had wanted to hurt her.

Oh, my God.

It was the anger.

I didn't know why I would have walked out of Jeffries's cellar with his anger and only the anger. Maybe I hadn't been as susceptible to the other emotions. Maybe the anger was far more potent. Or maybe this was as much *my* anger as it was his.

I just didn't know.

All I knew was that it was my anger now, and I could feel whatever was left of it still churning inside me.

The
Final Fête
of Abba Adi

by
Jessica Amanda Salmonson

The Grizla triplets were famous, if not quite notorious, for their beauty and artistry. While they were not courtesans in any boasted sense, a mythology arose regarding their skill at arts of love, which was imagined to be three times greater than that of other women, which together made them nine times greater, an ecstasy no man could survive should the Grizlas come upon him in concert.

Giulia was a songstress, Ernesta an actress, and Carlotta a dancer. The only means by which they could be told one from the other was by their variegated talents. Now there were those who said Giulia had a miniscule mole in the recesses of her navel; that Ernesta had an equally small one hidden between the moons of her ass; and Carlotta's mole, likewise little, was tucked away midst her dark locks, high on her left temple. The belief in their discreet imperfections was promulgated by the Grizla sisters themselves, though it may have arisen only as a jest at a salon gathering. One or the other of them (who could tell which?) commented idly that by these differences they need have no fear of resting in a mismarked grave, for there was no reason that their corpses should be confused. While this long-remembered piece of offhand information may or may not have been meant seriously, the hidden moles nevertheless became as famous as were the purported bearers thereof.

They spoke often of corpses, in conversation and their varied arts, this being their one uncharming trait. In truth they frightened many people, for they were more than passing strange. Each was a similitude of the other, often laughing together as with a single tinkling voice—and their laughter was on occasion stunningly inappropriate. Or they would exclaim a thing together, for they were apt to have the same wickedly dark thought at exactly the same moment. Then again they might make a sudden motion this way or that way as though there were but one woman standing between mirrors. Every quirk of one was reduplicated in the others. There was thereby nothing about them that was unique, though nothing in this world was quite like them but themselves.

Ernesta, who was a dramaturge as well as actress, performed her own gloomy vignettes regarding such subjects as a princess languishing unto death awaiting each night the slowly murderous yet addictive embrace of a demon lover; or a young witch pining away of love for a celibate knight until, in her misguided affectionate desire, she transformed him irretrievably into an adoring puppet *sans* all the traits she had longed to possess. Giulia sang original compositions of tragic lovers' ghosts who had committed suicide rather than be parted, and afterward (in Giulia's successive verses) passed through level upon level of hellish places where suicides were condemned and lovers scoffed, places the singer comprehended in a singularly familiar manner. Carlotta, who choreographed her own ballets, sprang about the stage like a martyr in flames, a dance of sacred passion bordering on maniacal, so that her grace held each observer thrall to equal portions of awe and terror.

Now Ernesta married into a bourgeois family; at least in theory she had done so. Her husband was large, curly-haired, with a distinctly Arabic countenance, despite his pallid complexion. This was due to some Moorish ancestor—or possibly the sole indiscretion of his otherwise priggishly moralistic mother—and of this nameless ancestor he was inordinately proud. He was no longer young, indeed could have been the father of women as youthful as the Grizlas. But he had the stamina and naïveté of ten youths alongside the mellowing cynicism and gentle wisdom of his years. He had gorgeous, delicate hands; a girl would envy them. Although he no longer had the litheness of his youth, and in fact was grown somewhat lumpish around the middle, his arms and legs were long and very powerful so that for all his girth he was graceful in his stride.

He wore Arabic costumes to highlight his forbidden ancestry (or bastardy), including a turban, a broad mustache, golden earrings and bracelets, blossoming trousers, slippers of emerald sheen that turned up at the ends, and a fabulous silk cummerbund from which dangled a scimitar given to him during his travels, he maintained, by a sacred harlot at the Well of Zumzum, where he had gone to honor the black stone personified by the name of Kubaba the Hagaritess.

In all, he was like unto a genie in a children's book. Although nothing of his manner and appearance was the fashion, a few shirt-tail toadies imitated him. He was not handsome, but so eccentric and interesting in his appearance and speech that many a common Adonis regretted that his own looks were not more ruggedly bizarre.

He was known exclusively by his *nom de plume*, Abba Adi, to the relief of his bourgeois family, though it was said he was more embarrassed by their manner than they by his, and he missed only the cuffings he used to get from his mother. In his youth he had been a genius at poetry, and it was in those days he first acquired the habit of dwelling amidst musicians and courtesans and theater people. His choices in companions aggrieved his unforgiving family to such an extent that he was disowned by them.

Deprived of his family's support, he was forced away from his poems and into a lamentable journalistic career, reviewing theater and books, and commenting with an idle elegance on each week's raging fad soon to become passé, or favored personality soon to be forgotten. His opinion could make or break a theatrical performance or an author's sales, yet he was sufficiently tactful (and, it must be said, generous of spirit) that he had only a few enemies, and these of such miniscule talent that he could not restrain himself from bantering at their expense. By contrast he had many friends, a few of them sincere, which fact alone gives proof that he was not a journalist at heart but only of necessity.

At his despised journalistic tasks, he was gravely and moderately successful in the monetary sense. He personally hated every word he penned for the *Lantern*, spirited though that daily sheet could be. He lamented every day, nay, every hour, that he was no longer devoted to an art, but to the squib. Without these journalistic efforts which devoured the soul of his creative energies, he would have starved. But with such work, he was able to sustain Ernesta in sufficient luxury (she did not require excess) to allow her to leave off performing in the public theaters and become, instead, the darling of the most distinguished private salons.

It was said who married one of the Grizlas married them all, and while Abba Adi never boasted, he often smiled. Certainly the sisters were rarely parted from each other, and lived in the house Abba Adi had rented in the newspaper district (he could not afford a more fashionable neighborhood, but none complained of traveling to the edge of the Flauberg to attend his charming fêtes). The three girls traveled about town in a gold-emblazoned carriage Abba Adi had bought for them, drawn by three white mares whose manes were black.

These women had strange accents that none could place. Their advent in the city of Aispont, some three years prior, and two years before one of them married the poet-*cum*-journalist, was an unutterable mystery to all, as though they had popped upward out of the ground from a world of light unmanifest into an earthly realm of play, pausing en route to heaven. A few knowing and vainglorious travelers stated with grandiose certainty where, within the geography of this expansive planet, the Grizlas' manner of speech was common; their nationality or origin was thereby asserted to be no mystery at all, for the prettily indistinguishable Three were obviously from a certain country distantly placed and easily named. The trouble was that no two travelers gave out an identical assertion.

Their speech patterns were dramatic and musical; hence Giulia's success as a singer and Ernesta's in performing tragedies. Carlotta by comparison rarely spoke, except with motions of her body. Yet none doubted she could have sung or acted had she pleased, for it was supposed they had once drawn lots to see which arts they would separately dominate.

It was rumored they were Catholics, a rare sect of worshipers, for they spoke reverently of a Goddess called Meris, whose son was a tortured King of Summer who sang of his love for Dynamis the Female Power of the Universe. His limbs (all of them, as they explained) were lopped off one by one to be planted amidst the corn while virgins danced and lamented. Virtually everyone took Meris to be a mispronunciation (on account of the sisters' weirdly beautiful accents) of Mary, and her slain son was Logos, that dying God who had been chopped into little bits and sprinkled on the ever-shifting page of that small yet infinitely changing *Book of the Dreaming Aeons*.

Never mind that the Grizlas never spoke of any Logos per se, but only of a nameless paramour of Meris, slain for love of Her. The rumor of their Catholicism was taken for gospel, for rumor was as good as truth in Aispont, and often better. To confirm this general belief, it was noted that the three damosels had a look of Italia about them, commingled, it was true, with a touch of the Oriental in the flashing darkness of their sinister eyes and in their raven's-wing hair glimmering with night's rainbows.

Inexplicably (to those who were apolitical their whole lives) there was a bourgeois uprising, and the newspapers were taken over. Abba Adi besmeared his noble soul by ingratiating himself before men who were, in point of fact, his cousins. But they were unforgiving of his years of persistent tweaks at their hypocrisies, their petty obsessions, their unmerited self-importance. Indeed, he had made them squirm so many times, it was the *Lantern* they conquered first, to put an end to his quaint and lovely ravings. When they slung hot tar upon the pate of that newspaper's publisher and set his head afire, Abba Adi perceived he could expect nothing from his cousins beyond safe passage through the revolution, like a bit of flotsam too insignificant even to brush from the surface of the water.

From that moment on he lived in poverty. Months went by without a moment's relief from his increasingly penurious state. It was expected that at any moment aristocratic forces would unseat the new bourgeois establishment in order to reinstate elegance, decadence, and liberty—amusing though it was to consider noblemen the protectors thereof—or at least to restore the former pleasing chaos, wherein marvels and beauty flourished.

Nothing of the sort occurred. Pacts had been made between the bourgeoisie and aristocrats in order that the latter continue as the figureheads they practically constituted in any case. The precise intricacies and machinations would be too dull to recount herein. All that need be said is that these things would indeed come undone in their own good time, when the rounded bourgeoisie were pounded back into their square holes. In the meantime the arts were treated much as were houses of prostitution (which, perhaps, they indeed resembled). Both areas of endeavor were so heavily besieged as to have all but closed shop for the duration. A journalist not of the right persuasion could not expect to earn a sou.

Abba Adi could no longer maintain his spacious and comfortable rental in the wrong part of town. One day he was served notice to vacate within the week, for his landlord was greatly feeling his oats, being now a part of an empowered caste. It was instantly rumored that Abba Adi with his wife and her two sisters would depart—afoot, their carriage having been confiscated for use by a member of the present city government—for a boarded-up theater, in the dressing rooms of which they were to live meagerly.

The Final Fête of Abba Adi

In the meantime, invitations were sent out to all the cowed intelligentsia of Aispont, announcing the final fête. There was certainly nothing else happening in the city that was delightful, so the event was better attended than any previous (or subsequent) gathering in that house. It was fortunately large enough to hold a great number of people, and had its own theater room on the main floor. Many extra couches were crowded into that room for ease of lounging while devouring sweetmeats and pastries and exchanging witticisms and flatteries between performances on the stage.

During Abba Adi's final fête, many attendees remarked in whispers as regarded an unaccountable expression of serenity upon their host's visage, a look that belied his plight. His expression might have been carved in ivory, so ghostly pale and motionless was his untragic pose. He gave himself over to none of his usual verbosity and poignant observations, nor yet a single criticism of the present state of affairs. It was as though he had said all in his life that needed to be said, and could now rest in a comfortable quietude amidst his laurels.

On the other hand, there was something about his face that made it seem as though he might well be dead, that this was his death mask and not his head. But if this were so, he must have died without convulsions or terror, and, what is more, without sorrow or triumph, for there was neither regret nor glee upon that placidly satisfied expression.

The change was extraordinary and nevertheless subtle. It was as though he had obtained by magery the visage of a perfect saint of such humble disposition he sought never to reveal even his beatitude, but only this astonishing serenity, born of a secret certainty requiring no past, no present, no future. One would suspect he had not wept in his entire life, nor suffered for so much as an hour. No, he had not even wept when he was born, a time when we all have no capacity for anything other than to suck and to weep—and to swim, by the by, though we forget within a week or so.

His wife, Ernesta, remarked upon just such capacities and incapacities of newborns, saying, "In heaven we perpetually drink from the Mother's left breast of oil, and Her right breast of honey. We swim as do joyful careless dolphins in oceans of Her blood and milk, never suspecting Fisher Death is hooking us one by one. Therefore, finding ourselves gasping in the world of matter, the first thing we do is cry out in our tragic little agonies. We seek desperately for the breasts, settling for whatever first we find. When we've forgotten why it was we were anguished in our first moments of illusory existence, only then do we begin to learn to speak and laugh, and by degrees give up our pointless sucking."

Carlotta whirled by as Ernesta was speaking, a leaf caught in a pretended gale, rushing fantastically in and around the seats and couches. All the while, Giulia played wildly upon the harpsichord. The dance and instrumentation were together called "A Tempest." All eyes were riveted upon the flourishes of dance, all ears upon the startling glissades of melody, so that Ernesta's strange sermon came by way of a back door into the subconscious. Although her words were never to be forgotten in the realm of dreams, even so, no one present in the aftermath could quote a single word when asked.

"The serene man," she continued, in the love seat at her husband's side, placing her lithe fingers in the crook of his arm, "is like unto a thing of stone. He might indeed have been created without spirit, hence there is nothing he requires to forget, nothing which he misses, for he had not a before-life wherein he sucked and swam. This serenity we personify as Lucifer, King of Matter, not forgetting Lucifer was God's favorite. He is called Light-giver whose Light is Unmanifest and thus of the darkest pitch beneath the loam; and he is the Motherless One, who, being carved of rock, never sucked. Rather, observing acutely the beauty of materiality, he has *imagined* through his verse that this is a heavenly place worthy of his beautiful words.

"He is the Earth's foremost paramour, this stone of serenity, and his lover the Earth is none other than the Heavenly Mother descended to the material sphere in search of Her lost children, leaving Her perfect realm of spirit far behind, polluting Herself in order to regain those whom She loves.

The Final Fête of Abba Adi

"The arms of this Serene Man, this carven giant, are broken off, and rendered into alabaster dust and mixed with wine that She may drink and become giddy with delight. His toes and ankles and feet and legs and knees and thighs are taken in pieces to be placed according to ancient regulations in specific locations all about a field of corn. His final rigid member, that is petrified, stands outside Her shrine where worshipers may honor Her with orgasms astride the mounted olisbos that is symbolic of the whole of the Man of Serenity. His head is taken to Her island temple far away, where he awakens nightly to give oracular advice in exquisite rhyme, and to praise the Mother who adopted him, yes only him, this lowly and motherless savior whom She made to be reborn in the grain. As for his torso, this becomes the planet Jupiter, to rule in Her stead while She busily gives birth to all things of the world, sustains and suckles them, and afterward devours them whole."

As if this insinuating lecture were not alarming enough, it must be added that when someone asked Abba Adi to change the mood and to please recite one of his most beloved poems, he gave out that he had never written such a thing. He seemed quite surprised that anyone thought he had ever written a word in his life, let alone anything so precious and ridiculous as a poem.

Some few suspected he was having a nervous breakdown, but to observe the depths of his serenity they wished for some of that madness for themselves. Lines of verse were recited for his edification, in an effort to stimulate his memory, but he merely gazed about with a bewildering condescension, denying all knowledge of such trivialities.

Others chimed in with this or that example of his poetic prowess, each in disagreement as to which was *the* signal masterpiece of his youth, for all of them would certainly be sung in Aispont for centuries to come. How could he have forgotten that he wrote them? But Abba Adi continued to smile with such amazing benignity that he seemed no longer an Arabian genie, but a universal god. In the veritable gleam of that mildly condescending smile, many became instantly convinced he had, after all, never been a poet, nor even a journalist, but was, at least, divinely forgiving of their delusions regarding supposed and valueless achievements.

Now Carlotta danced into the place of Giulia, and played the harpsichord as Giulia stood to sing. It was a weird hymn in a language none had before heard, an ancient and liturgical language no doubt, for it sounded all mournful and malignant. The guests became uneasy, and wondered what caprice or practical joke was being perpetrated against them. Someone said to Abba Adi, "This is too monstrous! You must clear the air of this mockery at once. Can you not see your fête is no success?"

But if it were not successful, why then did no one rise to leave? They were riveted by the subtleness of the pageant, by their inability to ascertain jest from madness, malignancy from radiance, spectacle from tedium, insult from romance, or philosophy from foolishness. They were not certain what it was that held them in their seats, save the strange gorgeousness of the three women who wove about the gathering an invisible net, as well as the equally splendid (if mad) serenity of Abba Adi. None of this was reassuring, but it was undeniably captivating.

None wished to confess they, the bohemian intelligentsia of Aispont's most fashionable streets, lacked a sufficiency of wit to comprehend every subtlety placed before them. None would say they were bewildered, only that they were held rapt. All pretended to be privy to some stunt they dare not reveal until the moment it was made manifest to others.

Much wine was available to all. It smelled sweet. Someone remarked that it contained opium, though only enough to ease the bitterness of a concoction of wormwood, bay laurel, spores of exotic fungi, and extract of morning glory germination. It was a deadly brew, to be sure, but none reproved it, assuming its degree of poison was safely measured by a perversely expert chemist. They quaffed deeply for the sake of the promise of an hallucinatory revelation such as had already begun to invest the assembly with a kind of "quiet hysteria" from which they could not rouse themselves.

By stages they became convinced, by their own whisperings from mouth to ear, that they were beginning to share a mass illusion, to experience in congregate a stunning vision of Truth that, upon awakening, might well reveal itself as nothing whatsoever.

As the evening progressed, it was Ernesta's turn to entertain the gathering, who now sat as though within a stupefying and visionary vapor, a veritable cloud of unknowing. Upon their faces was something distantly resembling Abba Adi's serenity, though lacking his uncanny emptiness such as was wisdom's fullest purity. Indeed, they were filled to the brim with contradictive thoughts and explanations and half-formulated queries. They could neither express themselves nor expel from their brains the myriad of ideas pouring into them as from a ceaseless fount. Many composed, upon ephemeral pages in their minds, essays and verses such as might have brought about an eerie renaissance, save that every turn of phrase was instantly mislaid in the subconscious.

This very rampancy of thought meant they were no closer to nirvana today than they had been yesterday, though they mistook these flights of fancy and emotion for just that. They comprehended a deep profundity shared among themselves without requiring speech. One by one, they felt as though they had come to a very chasm of a dark imagining. Their eyes would momentarily penetrate the bleak abyss, where All's secrets were to be revealed.

Ernesta's drama started as a pantomime, which was surprising, as she was so famous for her voice and her emotive monologues. She seemed only a ghostly projection of herself by not speaking. When words were at length added to the tableau, it was not she who spake, but her husband, for he had joined her on the upraised stage. His voice was resonant and powerful and, it must be added, very masculinely beautiful, for which reason at every fête he had ever given, he was asked to recite those early poems he now denied were his.

At first it seemed as though Abba Adi was only expostulating on a common subject, more vigorously than was usual, with points well met. He said, "A belief in the divinity of poetry and the sacred calling of the poet is not egoism, but naïveté. When you are young and dream of writing a masterpiece, it is very well to live in a garret with a pack of excitable drunkards who have heard the divine call. But when your masterpiece is written, and so soon becomes a rare book collected by few; when your bones show signs of creaking, and still your famished stomach aches; then will you know what an awful lot of rubbish those youthful passions were, and true divinity lies elsewhere than in art. This is why the aged poet regrets never having started revolutions or torching a governor's palace. And if, ironically, the aged revolutionist wishes he had been a poet, it is only because each wishes to unlearn what each has learned."

He continued thus for some while, standing in front of an ornate chair, as Ernesta made incomprehensible preparations on the dais. She revealed a dancer's grace equal to that of Carlotta as she waved a peacock feather like a wand, wove mystic signs with her fingers, seemingly bestowing blessings or performing purification rites with a frightening intensity. By imperceptible degrees (and by what means no one quite observed) her smooth hair became wild and tangled. Her long garments, which were those of a priestess very neatly arranged, began to fling about her body in an otherwise unperceived gale. Her expression was that of an ecstatic hyena inconceivably possessed of grace.

What now was Abba Adi jabbering? The familiarity of his ideas became increasingly alien as he progressed, bounding toward themes either so advanced, or so irrational, little could be fathomed. He seemed more mesmerist than orator, and slowly the congregation began to sway from side to side in time with his intonations.

"No more bitterness, my friends. No more regrets, O my beloved companions of years ill spent; no anger, no more unhappiness, never again to feel yourself adrift and alone, cut away from some unknown greatness. I feel such pity, such pity; and I feel a love for you with an immensity I cannot express in any physical or speaking manner. The road to full expression is paved with blood, for mine is the road to Dissolution; I would give you my limbs, my eyes, this broad chest, my very mind, if by this means might you know all things I have come to know."

It was then that Carlotta stepped upon the stage with Abba Adi's famous scimitar and, without preamble or forewarning, severed his arm expertly, handing it behind to Ernesta. The audience, captured in the dream, did not so much as gasp, for what could this be, beyond harmless illusion? They turned their gazes stage left to see, as they suspected, if Giulia would appear. She did so, and received the bloodied scimitar from Carlotta. With a clean sweep the task was done, with such ease she might have done it a thousand times before. She caught the severed arm and handed it to Ernesta.

Blood gouted from Abba Adi's shoulders. In this twinned ablution, the ethereal white garments of Carlotta and Giulia were made heavy with crimson. Their master's expression was all this while blissful. He took two steps backward to the ornate chair, sat down heavily, and sighed not as with affliction, but with sweet pleasure. He was still speaking, but of what he spoke no one could quite hear, for it was as though they were striving to catch his meaning from an altogether different realm.

Such speech, insofar as they could make it out, was akin to a sermon heard in a dream, or a revelatory essay encountered in a book within the selfsame dream. Every word was recognized for its profundity, and yet, upon awakening, nothing could be recalled to mind, or, what little speck remained was nonsense. In days to follow, some recollections were compared among the guests of that night.

Some believed he had spoken of a spice. Was it frankincense? Why, no, he had spoken of myrrh, that's right! Or had he spoken of a woman called Myrrh? Oh, or he had declared himself a Catholic, that was it! No, no, that wasn't at all what he intended, but he *had* declared himself a savior, and promised to drag the bourgeoisie downward into dark regions, there to ponder their banal criminality until the time of Dissolution. Or, no, rather, he had spoken of a shooting star and of a dew-damp stalk of corn; of sheepfolds and a golden buckle (or was it an adamantine sickle?) and two great and wonderful pots, one of oil, one of honey, huge and round and sealed on top. Then, hadn't he given a little homily about his mother? They thought he had, and he spoke also of the nameless Arab who made of him a bastard. But then again no—he had claimed to be adopted, yes, that was it—that was why he looked like an Arab though his kin did not. Or was he speaking of a mother and a nameless father in another sense than they perceived?

Many other fragments of the speech were repostulated in feeble attempts at restoration. It was as though naught but an ineffable mist had emanated from his mouth. No one had gotten from it quite the same thing. Nothing was certain; none of it cohered into a meaning or purpose the conscious mind could fully grasp.

That which was most clearly recollected was not of mind or ear, but what the eye beheld, whereas it should have been the other way around, had they greater inward vision. Abba Adi spoke half-mystically, half-mundanely, of things that could be taken this way or that way or another way altogether. While he spoke thus in riddles, Carlotta and Giulia cut away his garments with a pair of scissors, until he sat with neither arms nor clothing. When his codpiece was discarded, his rigid member was revealed, poking upward, dare we say it, like a dew-damp stalk of corn.

Then with a pair of pincers Carlotta and Giulia by turns removed his toes one after the other, first a right toe, then a left, and so on until there were none left; and when this was done, they carved away his feet.

Then Ernesta handed over a matching pair of curved garden saws with which they pruned his legs at the knees.

Through all this he spoke as though he were unaffected by any misery or surprise, although it must be confessed his voice grew quieter and quieter as his blood decreased. The vermilion liquor of his arteries drained onto the floor and sluiced toward the front of the stage, where slow gobbets formed a little falls which oozed its way

The Final Fête of Abba Adi

thence amidst the motionless feet of the spectators.

Meanwhile Ernesta was performing increasingly incomprehensible acts with Abba Adi's various parts, arranging them on the dais, climbing upon the dais in order to roll amidst the severed pieces, painting herself with her husband's blood. She kissed his beloved arms that had so often held her near. She hugged his thighs, first one then the other. She selected a dainty from amidst the array of toes, licked it like a candy, and with it added color to her full pale lips.

She was groaning, but her groaning was a song, an erotic melody, as she lifted one of his splendid lithe hands and rubbed it around her face and along her breasts and between her thighs. She writhed upon her knees amidst the sundry portions of Abba Adi. When at last she received from the hand of Carlotta the thick and solid penis, she took it reverently. It was like a well-carved thing of figwood that never once throughout these horrible events failed to express its plain uprightness and delight. It did not bleed, but pulsed with life that could never be eradicated, and, if anything, grew increasingly rigid, void of flaccidity.

She held it upward and forth, showing it left and right, that all might see the splendor of her lover's organ. She blessed it, and took it into herself, calling it by the name of Osiris and Damuzi and Yesod and Dionysus and other mysterious personages who may or may not have had meaning to various of the observers. She spoke of it with adoration, as though it were not a part of a man, but a whole man, and more than a man, a god.

During this display, Giulia regained the scimitar, and Abba Adi finally spoke no more, for with one swipe of the blade his head was removed, and Carlotta had it by the curly locks. Giulia dipped her face to the stump of his neck and drank deeply of the blood that welled there, while Carlotta held the head face-forward for the audience to witness the unbroken serenity of Aba Addi's expression. His lips still moved with a silent prayer of gratitude, love, and benediction.

When Giulia stepped away from the torso, it did not topple from the seat, but was shining like a star. The three ensanguined women, chanting in unison, moving in unison, had each the same posture, save only that Ernesta was on her knees upon the dais with her wide, drooling vagina exposed to the audience.

As they sang, the shining torso of Abba Adi began to rise into the air. The least of magicians could do no less, yet the levitation impressed itself upon the congregation. The torso hovered above them, dripping on their faces. They gazed upward with mouths agape, droning mantrically the same weird tune of the three sisters, receiving from the drippings of the flying torso a sacrament of blood.

Since the audience had taken up the song, the women let off singing, but were devouring parts of the beloved Abba Adi, with tears clearing white tracks on their bloodstained cheeks. They seemed not ghouls, but goddesses, and who can say by what method divine beings must grieve? They feasted, blood and flesh and froth gorging their pretty mouths, filling out their cheeks.

The incredible scene set before Aispont's cleverest artists and sharpest thinkers—a scene which they could not afterward adequately penetrate in either their art or their thoughts—began to fade away into darkness. It was as though candles were being snuffed one by one, and night drew close around. But the light was not dimming; it was only the consciousness of the guests that was fading into slumber.

Sleep was a side effect of the drugged wine, or a safety device that assured them their sanity just at the point when they were beginning to suspect they shared not fanciful visions of revelation, but a cruel reality, whether or not divine. And so Light became again Unmanifest, to spare them further blasts of fiery enlightenment.

The looks upon their nodding faces, with eyes shut tight, were indeed blissful and serene, with a beauty spoiled only by the awkward drooping of their limp positions and the occasional individual who snored.

A few things may be said of the aftermath of the last fête of Abba Adi. Shortly after that gathering, the bourgeois revolution came to an abrupt close due to internal squabbling. Some few who had attended the fête though they recollected a fragment of Abba Adi's speech, but couldn't quite place the connection it might have with the thankful reverses in the power structure of the city.

Then, too, the price of grain plunged downward so that many farmers, bringing in record harvests of wheat and corn, were bankrupted by their success. Again someone recalled how Abba Adi *might* have said a thing or two about the sacredness of grain profaned by a profiteering motive such as required a few with money to be well fattened while the many starved.

However, it must be admitted that many easy fabrications were concocted after that sadistic night—a night attendees came more and more to think of as sacred although those who missed it (even those without religious convictions) considered that which had occurred to have been blasphemous.

No one was able to speculate forcefully on the meaning of the event, though many were inspired by the challenge, and strove, within the context of that night, toward a priestly avocation.

Founders or converts to the cult of Abba Adi, Poet of Splendor, ascribed many occurrences to the effects of the Night Macabre. His cult flourished for about fifteen years, at the end of which time a rival cult of thuggees began assassinating Abbiadites with such effectiveness that inside a few more months, not one such worshiper was to be found in all of Aispont or the surrounding countryside.

The three sisters were never seen again. Nor were quite all the separated pieces of Abba Adi recovered. His torso had simply vanished, as had his head. Fables held that the head had been transported by Mary's Tripartate to the Isle of Myrrh (the location of which was unknown) and placed in Her temple of sublime iniquities. At the same time, "Torso" became an epithet for the planet Jupiter, and remained so even after the sinister elimination of the Abbiadites.

Several of his lesser parts were gathered and preserved as relics. Some of these were used in planting and harvest rituals during the fifteen years of the cult's existence, and thereafter fell into the hands of private collectors and thaumaturgists. Among the magical texts of the latter, a decayed remnant of Abbiadite ritual has been preserved.

Abba Adi's most private part was, naturally enough, the best cherished of the short-lived cult's treasured relics. It had become petrified by what means none could surmise nor reduplicate in the imitative sacrifices that occurred on anniversaries of the key event. Though this relic had somewhat darkened in the unknown process of its preservation, it was otherwise unchanged from life, as a dozen converted harlots testified at Abbiadite rallies.

After the aforementioned demise of the Abbiadites, this valued relic was appropriately deposited in the temple of Cybele, which dominates the temple quarter of Aispont. By whose wise decision Cybele received it is unrecorded, but the priestesses knew its history and gladly accepted the treasure. This sacred emblem of the vanished Abbiadites can be viewed there to this day. For a suitable donation to the temple, the high priestess will unwrap the object from its case, and place it momentarily in your hands, should you wish to see for yourself this evidence of the verity of our tale.

Cherry

by
Christa Faust

Alex was a girl that night, back in the strange, hopeless summer of 1981. Deep in the churning entrails of New York City, the heat was thick and filthy, clogging the lungs of its parasitic denizens with grit and despair. The hot black sky was heavy with dead dreams and the ripe threat of nuclear annihilation. The concrete burned like fevered flesh. For Alex, it was business as usual.

Long, hungry body sheened with sweat and wrapped in gaudy silver lace, Alex labored over an anonymous cock in the cramped prison of a Japanese subcompact parked on Little West Twelfth street, across from London Meat Packing. The car stank of cigarettes and unclean flesh. An air freshener shaped like a bikini-clad woman hung from the rearview mirror, its vague, stale-candy odor unable to compete with the brutal effluvia of the car's owner.

The gearshift dug into Alex's ribs as he worked the tough-skinned erection with monotonous precision. The trick was close, he could feel it. Alex shifted in the seat, swaths of bare skin sticking to the warm vinyl, and concentrated on ending this irrelevant drama. A dozen heartbeats later, the guy came, grunting softly, fat fingers clutching the sticky dashboard. Alex sat up and spat discreetly into a crumpled tissue.

Back out on the street, Alex pulled a bottle of cheap whiskey from his snakeskin purse. He drew in a stinging mouthful, swishing the liquor over the abused and tender flesh inside his mouth. The slick jiz flavor eventually surrendered to the alcohol's smoky fire and he spat the tainted cocktail on the steaming cobblestone. He took another swig for keeps, letting the whiskey burn a trail of thin heat down to his belly while he fixed his lips, wiping them clean on the back of his hand and then slicking them candy-apple red. He studied his reflection in a car windshield to be sure they were even.

Such a pretty face. Sinful mouth. Delicate cheekbones. Feral eyes like polished amber peering from beneath tangled black hair whose obsidian gloss was only marginally dulled by too much hair spray and not enough shampoo. If he had been born a girl, such beauty would have been a blessing, a key to open all the doors. But for a little boy on the first day of third grade in a brand-new school, it had been a nightmare. Long, dark eyelashes and girlish hands were his curse, reason enough for any self-respecting bully to rub his pretty face in the dirt.

His father had been so ashamed. Alex had been the product of his rash youth, left behind by a passionate artist who could not tolerate the bondage of motherhood. Alone and brokenhearted, Alex's nineteen-year-old father had done the best he could to care for the strange and beautiful child who watched him with his lost love's eyes. As he settled down to start a new family with a plain but loyal woman, it became harder and harder to make room in his heart for Alex. With the birth of new children, all blond and ordinary, with smiling faces and simple problems, it became impossible. While his sisters and brothers were joining teams and winning awards, Alex was cutting himself to see what it felt like.

Cherry

As he grew older, the gap widened. The boisterious horde that surrounded him felt less like family than fellow prisoners too stupid to understand the nature of their incarceration. He used to imagine that his mother had lied about the father of her baby. He imagined who his real father might be, an artist, a rock star, some powerful man who reveled in his beauty and was not ashamed. A man whom no one would dare call "faggot" or "sissy." He would kill anyone who tried to rub his face in the dirt.

It wasn't long before these fantasies grew stale and childish. Puberty loomed and Alex's imaginings grew darker, tinged with inexplicable longing. But through all the swampy new feelings and aching, half-glimpsed desires, one image remained. The beautiful, dangerous man who would take him away and make him strong.

It was a sticky summer just like this one when Alex made two discoveries that would change his life. The first was the extraordinary sensations that flooded his young body when he touched himself a certain way. The second was a book from the big library. It was old and tattered and the title stamped on its dusty spine in fading gold letters was *Dracula*.

From that moment on, Alex read anything and everything on the subject of vampires. Here was the beautiful monster of his darkest fantasies, in all its sinister glory. Here beauty was deadly strength, not weakness. It was everything he ever wanted.

He stopped cutting his hair, stopped camouflaging his beauty with drab, ugly clothes. Instead, he chose clothing as black as his growing hair, clothing that hugged the contours of his narrow body. He avoided the sun, taking pride in his pallor. The boys who used to steal his lunch money and call him faggot now kept their distance, telling their pretty girlfriends that he worshipped the devil, that he sacrificed cats and drank their blood. He did nothing to discourage these rumors. When his father noticed the change, he asked his son if he was queer. Alex left home the next day. He was sixteen.

Headlights slid across Alex's reflection, obliterating his features in a sudden pale wash. He looked up, instinctual tropism drawing

him out into the street. His high-heeled shoes were unsteady on the
cobblestone as he hustled out to meet the slowing car. Drag was fairly
new to him, more a economic endeavor than a personal preference,
and though his face lent itself effortlessly to feminine fiction, his body
was still awkward with the strictures of modern fashion. Tricks found
it charmingly coltish, so he made no great effort to change.

Poised, waifish, and sweet in the blinding headlights, Alex
watched the car roll towards him, moving slowly, almost nonchalant.
As it came closer, a thin trickle of adrenaline constricted his throat
and he was filled with irrational anxiety. He felt like a cringing animal caught in the merciless glare.

As the car pulled up beside him, he saw that it was a Mercedes,
black and full of quiet power. The tinted window slid down with the
organic ease of an eye opening, revealing a face that stopped Alex's
heart.

Luminously smooth and aristocratic. Ageless and horribly beautiful. Eyes the color of cold steel. White hair slicked back on a
streamlined skull, tightly braided in a thick, slivery cable that hung
all the way to the leather seat. Immaculate charcoal suit, subtle tie,
manicured nails. Every aspect of this man spoke the whispered language of old money.

"You're not a real girl, are you?" the man asked, gray eyes
detatched and serious, a careful consumer. His rich voice was flavored with a hint of unnameable accent.

"I can be anything you like," Alex answered, hating the canned
sound of that overused phrase, wishing as soon as it passed his lips
that he had said something else instead.

Shame warmed his skin as the man's pale eyes skewered him like
a squirming insect. He felt suddenly desperate, an orphan aching to
be chosen, torn apart by doubt and fear.

"Let me see your cock," the man commanded, eyes unflinching.

Alex's heart clenched. His cheeks burned. Desire to please this
chilly beauty warred with the hard-earned knowledge that nothing is
free. His fingers drifted to his crotch and the man's gaze followed.

Cherry

He realized that he wanted very badly to obey. The tight panties that kept his penis securely tucked between his legs were suddenly a hellish constriction. He looked up, torn, and caught a flare of stealthy heat in the gray depths of the trick's eyes. This tiny spark filled Alex with momentary strength.

"No free show," he said.

Standing cold and fearful in the wake of his defiance, he was sure that the window would slide closed and he would be left to wait for yet another fat prick from Jersey with ten bucks and a hard-on.

But the man did not close the window. Instead, he smiled and everything changed.

The man's teeth were small and even, their smooth line interrupted by elongated canines that dug sharp points into his soft lower lip.

Alex's breath froze in his chest. Panic and unspeakable excitement churned in his belly. The newly cynical, streetwise part of him struggled violently against the ecstatic child who was already utterly in love, willing to do anything for this sudden manifestation of his dark dreams.

The man's carnivore smile vanished as if it had never been. He reached into his jacket and withdrew a sleek billfold. Arching a silver eyebrow, he extracted a hundred-dollar bill and let it drop to the hot cobblestone.

Alex scrabbled after it, gripping the bill in his grubby fist as if he were afraid it wasn't real. Suddenly ashamed to be groveling in the street like a desperate junkie, he stood, burning with contradictions.

"Show me," the man said, seemingly indifferent to Alex's inner struggle.

Struck with inexplicable shyness, Alex turned his face away. He had done much worse for much less, but there was something about exposing himself to such cold-eyed scrutiny that made him feel shamefully inadequate. He had to force his clumsy fingers to peel back the layers of fabric that hid the secret of his masculinity.

Once exposed, his penis did not shrink away from judgment.

129

Instead, it began a slow swell towards erection that astonished Alex.
His inability to control his rebellious flesh deepened his humiliation
and his shame fed the fire of his need. He knew then that he would
do anything for this man.

A thin sliver of a smile passed across the trick's lips, a shadow of
his earlier toothy display.

"Get in," he said.

The trick took Alex to a lush apartment deep in the gentrified
labyrinth of one-way streets that was the West Village. Like the
streets, the apartment was a complex network of narrow hallways
punctuated with curious asymmetrical rooms and exotic antiques.

"Don't steal anything," Alex's host had told him, disappearing
without explanation behind an unremarkable door.

Alex wandered aimlessly through the crooked rooms, fingers
returning again and again to the thick roll of hundreds tucked into
his glittery purple bra. He was terrified, ecstatic, filled with jangling
adrenaline and unfocused lust. Waiting was torture. Time passed
with lazy precision, unimpressed by Alex's impatience. He struggled
to distract himself from obsessive thoughts of blood and fucking. The
trick's warning echoed back to him and he made a game of guessing
which things might be worth stealing.

He turned a small jeweled knife over and over in his hands,
admiring its razor delicacy, trying to name the exotic-hued stones
covering the scabbard. A bright splash of fearful excitment filled his
body and he slid the knife under his corset. He wondered if hidden
cameras were filming his transgression. Maybe the trick would catch
him and punish him for his disobedience. Sweet fantasies of punishment and forgiveness played out on the eager screens of his closed
eyes. The knife lay cold and thrilling against his skin. He nearly
screamed when a soft voice spoke inches from his ear.

"Thirsty?"

Alex turned to face his host with blood pounding in his throat.

The man's pale feet were bare and his hair was loose around his exquisite face. His jacket and tie were gone, his custom-tailored shirt open at the neck. Alex fought against a sudden urge to kneel down and kiss his bare toes. There was something almost feminine in the angles of those smooth little feet. He held a dusty bottle in one long hand and a single stemmed glass in the other.

Alex took the offered glass like a sleepwalker, watching the splash of dark, murky liquid from the bottle's mouth. It smelled like medicine, like bitter licorice and potent alcohol.

"What is it?" he asked, raising the glass to his lips with the slow inevitability of a nightmare.

"Absinthe," the trick told him.

"Absinthe," Alex repeated, rolling the word around in his mouth as if it were the drink itself.

Feeling brave and romantic, Alex swallowed a daring mouthful. It was poisonously bitter, filling his belly with narcotic fire.

The trick watched him drink with reptile curiosity, steel eyes unblinking. Alex drained his glass, wondering if the man might try to drug him. The thought had no urgency in the warm glow that suffused his body. He held the empty glass out to the trick and, instead of taking it, the man filled it again.

"Don't you want any?" Alex asked, watching the dark liquid splashing in the curve of the glass. His mouth felt strange, rebellious.

"I don't drink," the trick said, eyes dancing with secret humor.

Alex burst out with a string of helpless giggles, splashing absinthe over his wrist and down the front of his tiny silver ballerina skirt. Potent drops of liquor clung to the lacy mesh and soaked through his panties. He raised his hand to his lips, licking the drops from his fingers.

"Well I do," he said, draining what was left in the glass.

He felt his entire body go suddenly soft and uncoordinated. His skin felt outrageously sensitive. The faint currents of dusty air caressed him like lover's fingers. The weave of the rug beneath him seemed fascinating and he wanted to press his cheek against it. He might have done just that if the trick's arms had not slid around him and held him like a child.

LOVE IN VEIN

Supported in this strong embrace, looking up into that cold and flawless face, Alex was gripped by powerful resurrection of his long-buried childhood fantasy. He wrapped his arms around the man's neck and buried his face in the curious fragrance of his white hair, crying helplessly. His ecstatic tears clung to the silver strands like the drops of absinthe on his five-dollar skirt.

Alex allowed himself to be led like a blind boy through hallways striped with light and dark shadow and into the unexplored territory behind the mysterious door.

"I love you," Alex said as the trick laid him down gently on a wide expanse of dove gray velvet. Four dark wooden posts rose above him, intricately carved with fruit and angels. The pillow beneath his cheek bore a tapestried lion, fierce and golden, its toothy red mouth gaping.

The trick touched Alex's tear-streaked face, catching the salty drops on his fingertips.

"Are you afraid?" he asked, touching a wet finger to his lips, pink tongue sneaking out to taste.

"No." Alex shook his head, the motion seeming to go on for far too long.

"Take your clothes off," the trick commanded.

Alex's fingers leapt to obey, but they found themselves thwarted by a thousand tiny hooks and buckles and fasteners. Frustration dug long nails into his heart. He began to tear furiously at the complex network of purple and silver that held him in such cruel bondage. The roll of hundreds tumbled, unnoticed, to the carpeted floor, beside the forgotten blade.

The trick watched this struggle with detached amusement that fed Alex's humiliation. He acknowledged the pilfered knife with an arched eyebrow and cryptic silence that terrified Alex, stealing away the last fragments of coordination.

Alex was ready to scream when the last scrap of clothing tore and gave and he collapsed gratefully into the bed's velvet embrace, resting his spinning head against the lion's warm golden flank. His pale body was crossed with angry red creases where restrictive elastic had bitten deep.

Docile as an infant, he allowed his wrists and ankles to be caught and locked in soft leather cuffs. The cuffs were attached to a strong silver chain trailing off to some unseen mooring. They gave him about three inches of free movement.

He looked up at his captor, obsessive eye roaming the pure contours of jaw and throat, of shoulder and hip. Again, a teasing slice of smile and again a stripper's flash of razor canines. Alex's heart was manic in the vault of his chest.

"Please. . . " Alex whispered, begging desperately with every ounce of his body and soul for a thousand things he could barely articulate. *Please be real. Please don't leave me. Take me with you. Make me like you. Love me. Keep me forever.*

Tears started again, blurring the image, white hair and white skin melting into a shimmering wash.

"Stop crying." A cold command, stinging deeply.

Alex fought shame and a fresh onslaught of hot tears. He forced them back and struggled to still his shaking body.

"There will be enough of that later," the trick said, teeth flashing.

A seed of fear burst to sudden life in Alex's chest. He had imagined this scenario and hundreds like it for years, but never once had he considered that his dream lover could just as easily kill him and leave the meat behind. In the hot grip of fantasy, such a mundane outcome had been unthinkable. Now, in the face of awesome reality, that self-centered naïveté could prove to be his undoing.

Alex closed his eyes, bringing the full weight of his will down against his fear. Death was not an option. He had dreamed too hard for too long. It was up to him to seduce his executioner, to show that he was not a mere lamb ripe for slaughter, but a rare lover worthy of the gift of eternal life.

When he opened his eyes, he turned to face his captor with new resolve. The man seemed to sense this change and Alex was sure that he saw a spark of renewed interest in the metallic depths of those cold eyes.

Long white fingers set themselves to the slow task of unbuttoning the expensive shirt. Alex's gaze followed them eagerly, his body flushed with need. To see this exquisite creature unveiled would be worth any pain. As the last button fell open and pale cloth slipped down over the sculpted angles of narrow shoulders, Alex's disbelieving eyes were treated to the subtle curve of small but unmistakable breasts, coral nipples high and hard above the rippled shadow of prominent ribs.

A confused rush of emotion drenched Alex's shivering body. Reality was untrustworthy. Anything could happen. He had never been with a woman before, and the prospect filled him with dread and fascination. This game was proving to be infinitely more complex than his adolescent dreams had ever imagined. The trick was watching him with icepick eyes.

"There are a lot of things that you don't know," she said.

She unfastened the trousers and let them fall, revealing smooth, shapely legs and angular hips, delicate bones sloping towards a silver-furred delta full of rich pink secrets.

So still and pale she was, pale eyes, pale hair, pale skin. Alex could almost believe she had never moved at all. He felt heavy and frozen as if he had been still forever too, and they were both the stone children of some forgetful sculptor.

When she spoke, it was shocking, a blunt hammer shattering the fragile moment.

"You can leave if you'd like," she said, her voice a soft whisper. The world was suddenly alive with possibilities. There was a shadow of vulnerability in her flawless face igniting fierce passion inside Alex, passion that clenched his fists and closed his throat. As the two-dimensional fiction of his childish fantasy crashed and burned, he found an astonishing new love in its ashes.

"No," he said, his voice cracking as if he had been silent for years. "I never want to leave. I want to be yours forever."

Cherry

She smiled at him and his body went weak and hot, shivering as her narrow hand reached out to touch his throat. Her fingers sought his pulse, tracing the path of his blood beneath the skin. She touched his mouth and he kissed her fingers, drawing them in and biting gently, teasing. Scolding with her eyes, she pulled them away and brought them to her lips, tasting his saliva. He strained against his bonds, aching to touch her.

Standing apart, she watched him struggle, her face cool and thoughtful. Then, without warning, she leapt up and straddled him with frightening grace.

The shock of her flesh against his, her thighs brushing his hips, the soft skin of her belly caressing his burning erection, incinerated any doubts and left only incandescent lust that allowed for nothing else. If she wanted his life, he would gladly give it, baring his throat to her with unflinching trust. He surrendered to her kiss with his whole heart, letting her tongue take him the way a man takes a woman, the sharp points of her teeth slashing his tender lips. Blood flowed hot, like his love.

She pulled away, eyes wild and hungry. All pretense of calm objectivity was gone.

"Tell me you love me," she said.

Alex was crying again, blood in his mouth.

"Yes," he sobbed. "Yes, I love you."

She moved like a snake striking, her teeth penetrating the skin of his throat as his cock penetrated the slick mystery of her silver delta. Pain and pleasure fell in love with each other inside of him, fusing together into a single living emotion. Alex lost himself in her, in the pure circuit of mutual need. Hunger and sustenance. Lust and fulfillment. Giving and taking in a balance as old as time. As Alex gave himself over to the little death, filling her with blood and semen and the heady liquor of his love, he felt himself falling away into glittering blackness, melting down into the distillate essence of himself. The last thing he felt before unconsciousness claimed him was the meaty withdrawal of her invading teeth and a swelling sense of emptiness and loss.

• • •

When Alex woke, the first thing he became aware of was pain. Not the glorious ecstasy of the night before, but an ugly throbbing ache that spread burning fingers across his jaw and down into his shoulder. His fingers flew to his throat and found oozing scab and bright new hurt. His wrists ached. His head rattled with broken glass as he peeled back sticky eyelids to reveal gray morning sunlight. Beside him, his lover lay curled in on herself, lost in uneasy dreams. The dirty illumination was not kind to her sleeping face. Her skin was fragile as paper, pulled too tightly over sharp bones. Pale makeup smeared her pillow, no longer hiding the pinstripes of face-lift scar beneath her chin.

She began to stir beneath his scrutiny, bloodshot gray eyes sliding open and then narrowing to indignant slits against the morning sun.

"Christ," she said, hands cradling her head. "You're still here?"

"Of course," Alex said, hurt and confusion creeping into his voice. "I thought. . . "

"Oh please." The trick cut him off with a tired gesture. She sat up slowly and spat something into her cupped hand. "Let's not have an unpleasant scene, ok?"

She opened her fingers, revealing an arch of plastic connecting a pair of hollow fang teeth.

Choking on raw disappointment, Alex turned his face away. A thousand black emotions fought like starving dogs inside his belly. The trusting child who had fallen so hard so fast was torn apart, his fragile body lacerated by shrapnel and jagged fragments of his rejected love. The darkly cynical street urchin whipped himself with razor-tipped I-told-you-so's, disgusted at having been so suckered. Shame bloomed like rot and in the hot furnace of his heart, the shame smelted into viscous anger.

She was digging through a bedside drawer, her back to him, dismissing him utterly. From a tiny box of gold and lapis, she shook out a candy-colored handful of pills, sorting through the shapes to select a chemical cocktail. As she raised them to her dry lips, Alex's anger boiled over and he grabbed her skinny wrist, turning her to face him. Pills tumbled to the carpet, rolling like pearls.

"Hey, what the fuck is your problem," she said, her voice harsh and shrewish.

"I believed in you." Alex was furious, his fingers tightening around her wrist.

If she had cursed at him and told him to fuck off, he might have just taken the money and slunk away, but instead she burst into nasty laughter that raked the tender meat of Alex's freshly broken heart.

"Oh please," she said. "Give me a break." She yanked her hand free from his grip. "You got what you wanted, I got what I wanted. What's the problem?"

She bent down to retrieve the lost pharmaceuticals as if there were nothing left to be said.

Watching her chasing after the pills the way he had chased that hundred-dollar bill in another lifetime, Alex was filled with rage and hate and other more obscure emotions that tore him in a thousand directions at once. He clenched his fists, still feeling her fragile bones grinding under his grip. Staring at the shivering curve of her spine, he was struck with a sudden contradictory desire. Something about her vulnerability, her humanity, brought saliva to his mouth and hot blood to his slow-blooming erection. Then his eyes fell on the jeweled knife.

He reached out and caressed the back of her head, twining his fingers in her hair. At first she was tense, wary, but soon he felt her relax against his touch. Kneeling behind her amid the scattered pills, he slid an arm around her waist and pressed against the length of her back. With his other hand, he walked his fingers across the carpet until they found the cool metal of the knife. Tightening his grip on her hair, he kissed her softly on the cheek and yanked her head back.

The edge of the blade bit deep into her scarred throat and she bucked frantically against him, scrambling away. Silent fury sang in his veins as he leapt after her, pinning her again and pulling her close. Belly to belly, he held her wrists and pressed his face to the welling blood, a hot baptism driven by the dying panic of her cruel heart. He opened the wound wider with his teeth, tongue probing deep in the living meat as she thrashed against him. The vital flavor of her life spilling down his throat was beyond ecstasy, nauseating and luxurious and unlike anything Alex had ever imagined. This was no romantic fantasy, this was brutal reality, pure and delicious.

When she began to tire, her body going limp and still in his embrace, he unlocked his jaws and his fists, looking down into her face.

Gray mortality spilled across her features and made a lie out of all her careful artifice. Alex studied her while she died, but there was no revelation at the last minute, no shining truth. Just a shaky exhalation and then the unremarkable spectacle of slowly cooling meat.

After a moment of thoughtful contemplation, he found the blood-slick blade and opened her belly, sawing through tough abdominal muscle and spreading the lips of the gash with curious fingers. Nothing but the mundane truth that lies behind all our skin, wet and stinking and utterly human.

It seemed he should hate her for her subtle lies and her mortality, but instead he felt a strange, nostalgic affection. He knew he would always remember her. He had given her his cherry, and in return she had made him into a real vampire, after all.

White Chapel

by
Douglas Clegg

"Oh! Ahab," cried Starbuck, "not too late is it, even now, the third day, to desist. See! Moby Dick seeks thee not. It is thou, thou, that madly seekest him!"

from Moby-Dick, or The Whale *by Herman Melville*

I

"You are a saint," *the leper said, reaching her hand out to clutch the saffron-dyed robe of the great man of Calcutta, known from his miracle workings in America to his world-fame as a holy man throughout the world. The sick woman said in perfect English, "My name is Jane. I need a miracle. I can't hold it any longer. It is eating away at me. They are." She labored to breathe with each word she spoke.*

"Who?" the man asked.

"The lovers. Oh, god, two years keeping them from escaping. Imprisoned inside me."

"You are possessed by demons?"

She smiled, and he saw a glimmer of humanity in the torn skin. "Chose me because I was good at it. At suffering. That is whom the gods choose. I escaped, but had no money, my friends were dead. Where could I go? I became a home for every manner of disease."

"My child," the saint said, leaning forward to draw the rags away from the leper's face. "May God shine His countenance upon you."

"Don't look upon me, then, my life is nearly over," the leper said, but the great man had already brought his face near hers. It was too late. Involuntarily, the leper pressed her face against the saint's, lips bursting with fire-heat. An attendant of the saint's came over and pulled the leper away, swatting her on the shoulder.

The great man drew back, wiping his lips with his sleeve.

The leper grinned, her teeth shiny with droplets of blood. "The taste of purity," she said, her dark hair falling to the side of her face. "Forgive me. I could not resist. The pain. Too much."

The saint continued down the narrow alley, back into the marketplace of what was called the City of Joy, as the smell of fires and dung and decay came up in dry gusts against the yellow sky.

The leper woman leaned against the stone wall, and began to ease out of the cage of her flesh. The memory of this body, like a book written upon the nerves and sinews, the pathways of blood and bone, opened for a moment, and the saint felt it, too, as the leper lay dying.

My name is Jane, a brief memory of identity, but with no other past to recall, her breath stopped,

the saint reached up to feel the edge of his lips, his face, and wondered what had touched him.

What could cause the arousal he felt.

II

—~m~—

"He rescued five children from the pit, only to flay them alive, slowly. They said he savored every moment, and kept them breathing for as long as he was able. He initialed them. Kept their faces." This was overheard at a party in London, five years before Jane Boone would ever go to White Chapel, but it aroused her journalist's curiosity for it was not spoken with a sense of dread, but with something approaching awe and wonder, too. The man of whom it was spoken had already become a legend.

Then, a few months before the entire idea sparked in her mind, she saw an item in the *Bangkok Post* about the woman whose face had been scraped off with what appeared to be a sort of makeshift scouring pad. Written upon her back, the name, *Meritt*. This woman also suffered from amnesia concerning everything that had occurred to her prior to losing the outer skin of her face; she was like a blank slate.

Jane had a friend in Thailand, a professor at the University, and she called him to find out if there was anything he could add to the story of the faceless woman. "Not much, I'm afraid," he said, aware of her passion for the bizarre story. "They sold tickets to see her, you know. I assume she's a fraud, playing off the myth of the white devil who traveled to India, collecting skins as he went. Don't waste your time on this one. Poor bastards are so desperate to eat, they'll do anything to themselves to put something in their stomachs. You know the most unbelievable part of her story?"

Jane was silent.

He continued, "This woman, face scraped off, nothing human left to her features, claimed that she was thankful that it had happened. She not only forgave him, she said, she blessed him. If it had really happened as she said, who would possibly bless this man? How could one find forgiveness for such a cruel act? And the other thing, too. Not in the papers. Her vagina, mutilated, as if he'd taken a machete to open her up. She didn't hold a grudge on that count, either."

In wartime, men will often commit atrocities they would cringe at in their everyday lives. Jane Boone knew about this dark side of the male animal, but she still weathered the journey to White Chapel because she wanted the whole story from the mouth of the very man who had committed what was known in the latter part of the century as the most unconscionable crime, without remorse. If the man did indeed live among the Khou-dali at the furthest point along the great dark river, it was said that perhaps he sought to atone for his past—White Chapel was neither white nor a chapel, but a brutal outpost which had been conquered and destroyed from one century to the next since before recorded history. Always to self-resurrect from its own ashes, only to be destroyed again. The British had anglicized the name at some sober point in their rule, although the original name, *Y-Cha-Pa* when translated, was Monkey God Night, referring to the ancient temple and celebration of the divine possession on certain nights of the dry season when the god needed to inhabit the faithful. The temple had mostly been reduced to ashes and fallen stone, although the ruins of its gates still stood to the southeast.

Jane was thirty-two and had already written a book about the camps to the north, with their starvation and torture, although she had not been well reviewed stateside. Still, she intended to follow the trail of Nathan Meritt, the man who had deserted his men at the height of the famous massacre. He had been a war hero who, by those court-martialed later, was said to have been the most vicious of torturers. The press had labeled him, in mocking Joseph Campbell's study *The Hero With A Thousand Faces*, "The Hero Who Skinned A Thousand Faces." The war had been over for a good twenty years, but Nathan was said to have fled to White Chapel. There were reports that he had taken on a Khou-dali wife and fathered several children over the two decades since his disappearance. Nathan Meritt had been the most decorated hero in the war—children in America had been named for him. And then the massacre, and the stories of his love of torture, of his rituals of skin and bone . . . it was the most fascinating story she had ever come across, and she was shocked that no other writer, other than one who couched the whole tale in a wide swath of fiction, had sought out this living myth. While Jane couldn't get any of her usual magazines to send her gratis, she had convinced a major publishing house to at least foot expenses until she could gather some solid information.

To get to White Chapel, one had to travel by boat down a brown river in intolerable heat. Mosquitoes were as plentiful as air, and the river stank of human waste. Jane kept the netting around her face at all times, and her boatman took to calling her Nettie. There were three other travelers with her: Rex, her photographer, and a British man and wife named Greer and Lucy. Rex was not faring well—he'd left Kathmandu in August, and had lost twenty pounds in just a few weeks. He looked like a balding scarecrow, with skin as pale as the moon, and eyes wise and weary like those of some old man. He was always complaining about how little money he had, which apparently compounded for him his physical miseries. She had known him for seven years, and had only recently come to understand his mood swings and fevers. Greer was fashionably unkempt, always in a tie and jacket, but mottled with sweat stains, and wrinkled; Lucy kept her hair up in a straw hat, and disliked all women. She also expressed a fear of water, which amazed one and all since every trip she took began with a journey across an ocean or down a river. Jane enjoyed talking with Greer as long as she didn't have to second-guess his inordinate interest in children. She found Lucy to be about as interesting as a toothache.

The boatman wanted to be called Jim because of a movie he had once seen, and so after morning coffee bought at a dock, Jane said, "Well, Jim, we're beyond help now, aren't we?"

Jim grinned, his small dark eyes sharp, his face wrinkled from too much sun. "We make White Chapel by night, Nettie. Very nice place to sleep, too. In town."

Greer brought out his book of quotes, and read, "'Of the things that are man's achievements, the greatest is suffering.'" He glanced to his wife and then to Jane, altogether skipping Rex, who lay against his pillows, moaning softly.

"I know," Lucy said, sipping from the bowl, "it's Churchill."

"No, dear, it's not. Jane, any idea?"

Jane thought a moment. The coffee tasted quite good, which was a constant surprise to her, as she had been told by those who had been through this region before that it was bitter. "I don't know. Maybe—Rousseau?"

Greer shook his head. "It's Hadriman the Third. The Scourge of Y-Cha."

"Who's Y-Cha?" Rex asked.

Jane said, "The Monkey God. The temple is in the jungles ahead. Hadriman the Third skinned every monkey he could get his hand on, and left them hanging around the original city to show his power over the great god. This subdued the locals, who believed their only guardian had been vanquished. The legend is that he took the skin of the god, too, so that it might not interfere in the affairs of men ever again. White Chapel has been the site of many scourges throughout history, but Hadriman was the only one to profane the temple."

Lucy put her hand to her mouth, in a feigned delicacy. "Is it . . . a decent place?" Greer and Lucy spent their lives mainly traveling, and Jane assumed it was because they had internal problems all their own which kept them seeking out the exotic, the foreign, rather than staying with anything too familiar. They were rich, too, the way that only an upper-class Brit of the Old School could be and not have that guilt about it: to have inherited lots of money and to be perfectly content to spend it as it pleased themselves without a care for the rest of mankind.

Greer had a particular problem which Jane recognized without being able to understand: he had a fascination with children, which she knew must be of the sexual variety, although she could've been wrong—it was just something about him, about the way he referred to children in his speech, even the way he looked at her sometimes which made her uncomfortable. She didn't fathom his marriage to Lucy at all, but she fathomed very few marriages. While Greer had witnessed the Bokai Ritual of Circumcision and the Resurrection Hut Fire in Calcutta, Lucy had been reading Joan Didion novels and painting portraits of women weaving baskets. They had money to burn, however, inherited on both sides, and when Greer had spoken by chance to Jane at the hotel, he had found her story of going to White Chapel fascinating; and he, in turn, was paying for the boat and boatman for the two-day trip.

Jane said, in response to Lucy, "White Chapel's decent enough. Remember, British rule, and then a little bit of France. Most of them can speak English, and there'll be a hotel that should meet your standards."

"I didn't tell you this," Greer said, to both Jane and Lucy, "but my grandfather was stationed in White Chapel for half a year. Taxes. Very unpopular job, as you can imagine."

"I'm starved," Lucy said, suddenly, as if there were nothing else to think of. "Do we still have some of those nice sandwiches? Jim?" She turned to the boatman, smiling. She had a way of looking about the boat, eyes partly downcast, which kept her from having to see the water—like a child pretending to be self-contained in her bed, not recognizing anything beyond her own small imagined world.

He nodded, and pointed toward the palm leaf basket.

While Lucy crawled across the boat—she was too unbalanced, Greer often said, to stand without tipping the whole thing and this was, coincidentally, her great terror—Greer leaned over to Jane and whispered, "Lucy doesn't know why you're going. She thinks it's for some kind of *National Geographic* article," but he had to stop himself for fear that his wife would hear.

Jane was thinking about the woman in Thailand who claimed to have forgiven the man who tore her face off. And the children from the massacre, not just murdered, but obliterated. She had seen the pictures in *Life. Faceless children. Skinned from ear to ear.*

She closed her eyes and tried to think of less unpleasant images.

All she remembered was her father looking down at her as she slept.

She opened her eyes, glancing about. The heat and smells revived her from dark memories. She said, "Rex, look, don't you think that would be a good one for a photo?" She pointed to one of the characteristic barges that floated about the river selling mostly rotting meat and stuffed lizards, although the twentieth century had intruded, for there were televisions on some of the rafts, and a Hibachi barbecue.

Rex lifted his Nikon up in response, but was overcome by a fit of coughing.

"Rex," Lucy said, leaning over to feel his forehead, "my god, you're burning up." Then, turning to her husband, "He's very sick."

"He's seen a doctor, dear," Greer said, but looked concerned.

"When we get there," Jane said, "we'll find another doctor. Rex? Should we turn around?"

"No, I'm feeling better. I have my pills." He laid his head back down on his pillow, and fanned mosquitoes back from his face with a palm frond.

"He survived malaria and dengue fever, Lucy, he'll survive the flu. He's not one to suffer greatly."

"So many viruses." Lucy shook her head, looking about the river. "Isn't this where AIDS began?"

"I think that may have been Africa," Greer said in such a way that it shut his wife up completely, and she ate her sandwich and watched the barges and the other boatmen as though she were watching a *National Geographic Special*.

"Are you dying on me?" Jane asked, flashing a smile through the mosquito net veil.

"I'm not gonna die," Rex said adamantly. His face took on an aspect of boyishness, and he managed the kind of grin she hadn't seen since they'd first started working together several years back— before he had discovered needles. "Jesus, I'm just down for a couple of days. Don't talk about me like that."

Jim, his scrawny arms turning the rudder as the river ran, said, "This is the River of Gods, no one die here. All live forever. The Great Pig God, he live in Kanaput, and the Snake God live in Jurukat. Protect people. No one die in paradise of Gods." Jim nodded towards points that lay ahead along the river.

"And what about the Monkey God?" Jane asked.

Jim smiled, showing surprisingly perfect teeth which he popped out for just a moment because he was so proud of the newly made dentures. When he had secured them onto his upper gum again, he said, "Monkey God trick all. Monkey God live where river go white. Have necklace of heads of childs. You die only once with Monkey God, and no come back. Jealous god, Monkey God. She not like other gods."

"Monkey God is female," Jane said. "I assumed she was a he. Well, good for her. I wonder what she's jealous of?"

Greer tried for a joke, "Oh, probably because we have skins, and hers got taken away. You know women."

Jane didn't even attempt to acknowledge this comment.

Jim shook his head. "Monkey God give blood at rainy times, then white river go red. But she in chains, no longer so bad, I think. She buried alive in White Chapel by mortal lover. Hear her screams, sometime, when monsoon come, when flood come. See her blood when mating season come."

"You know," Greer looked at the boatman quizzically, "you speak with a bit of an accent. Who did you learn English from?"

Jim said, "Dale Carnegie tapes, Mister Greer. *How To Win Friends And Influence People.*"

Jane was more exhilarated than exhausted by the time the boat docked in the little bay at White Chapel. There was the Colonial British influence to the port, with guard booths now mainly taken over by beggars, and an empty customs house. The place had fallen into beloved disrepair, for the great elephant statues given for the god Ganesh were overcome with vines and cracked in places, and the lilies had all but taken over the dock. Old petrol storage cans floated along the pylons, strung together with a net knotted between the cans: someone was out to catch eels or some shade-dwelling scavenger. A nervous man with a straw hat and a bright red cloth tied around his loins ran to the edge of the dock to greet them; he carried a long fat plank, which he swept over the water's edge to the boat, pulling it closer in. A ladder was lowered to them.

The company disembarked carefully. Rex, the weakest, had to be

pulled up by Jim and Jane both. Lucy proved the most difficult, however, because of her terror of water—Jim the boatman pushed her
from behind to get her up to the dock, which was only four rungs up
on the ladder. Then Jane didn't feel like haggling with anyone, and so
after she tipped Jim, she left the others to find their ways to the King
George Hotel by the one taxicab in White Chapel. She chose instead
to walk off her excitement, and perhaps get a feel for the place.

She knew from her previous explorations that there was a
serendipity to experience—she might, by pure chance, find what she
was looking for. But the walk proved futile, for the village—it was
not properly a town—was dark and silent, and except for the lights
from the King George, about a mile up the road, the place looked as
if no one lived there. Occasionally, she passed the open door to a hut
through which she saw the red embers of the fire, and smelled the
accompanying stench of the manure that was used to stoke the
flame. Birds, too; she imagined them to be crows, gathering around
huts, kicking up dirt and waste.

She saw the headlights of a car and stepped back against a stone
wall. It was the taxi taking the others to the hotel, and she didn't
want them to see her.

The light was on inside the taxi, and she saw Rex up front with the
driver, half-asleep. In back, Lucy, too, had her eyes closed; but,
Greer, however, was staring out into the night, as if searching for
something, perhaps even expecting something. His eyes were wide,
not with fear, but with a kind of feverish excitement.

He's here for a reason. He wants what White Chapel has to offer, she
thought, *like he's a hunter*. And what did it have to offer? Darkness,
superstition, jungle, disease, and a man who could tear the faces off
children. A man who had become a legend because of his monstrosity.

After the car passed, and was just two sets of red lights going up
the narrow street, she continued her journey up the hill.

When she got to the hotel, she went to the bar. Greer sat at one
end; he had changed into a lounging jacket that seemed to be right

out of the First World War. "The concierge gave it to me," Greer said, pulling at the sleeves, which were just short of his wrists. "I imagine they've had it since my grandfather's day." Then, looking at Jane, "You look dead to the world. Have a gin tonic."

Jane signaled to the barman. "Coca-Cola?" When she had her glass, she took a sip, and sighed. "I never thought I would cherish a Coke so much. Lucy's asleep?"

Greer nodded. "Like a baby. And I helped with Rex, too. His fever's come down."

"Good. It wasn't flu."

"I know. I can detect the D.T.'s at twenty paces. Was it morphine?"

Jane nodded. "That and other things. I brought him with me mainly because he needed someone to take him away from it. It's too easy to buy where he's from. As skinny as he is, he's actually gained some weight in the past few days. So, what about you?" She didn't mean for the question to be so fraught with unspoken meaning, but there it was: out there.

"You mean, why am I here?"

She could not hold her smile. There was something cold, almost reptilian about him now, as if, in the boat, he had worn a mask, and now had removed it to reveal rough skin and scales.

"Well, there aren't that many places in the world . . . quite so . . . "

"Open? Permissive?"

Greer looked at her, and she knew he understood. "It's been a few months. We all have habits that need to be overcome. You're very intuitive. Most women I know aren't. Lucy spends her hours denying that reality exists."

"If I had known when we started this trip . . . "

"I know. You wouldn't have let me join you, or even fund this expedition. You think I'm sick. I suppose I am—I've never been a man to delude himself. You're very—shall I say—*liberal* to allow me to come even now."

"It's just very hard for me to understand," she said. "I guess this continent caters to men like you more than Europe does. I understand for two pounds sterling you can buy a child at this end of the river. Maybe a few."

"You'd be surprised. Jane. I'm not proud of my interest. It just exists. Men are often entertained by perversity. I'm not saying it's right. It's one of the great mysteries—" He stopped midsentence, reached over, touching the side of her face.

She drew back from his fingers.

In his eyes, a fatherly kindness. "Yes," he said, "I knew. When we met. It's always in the eyes, my dear. I can find them in the streets, pick them out of a group, out of a school yard. Just like yours, those eyes."

Jane felt her face go red, and wished she had never met this man who had seemed so civil earlier.

"Was it a relative?" he asked. "Your father? An uncle?"

She didn't answer, but took another sip of Coke.

"It doesn't matter, though, does it? It's always the same pain," he said, reaching in the pockets of the jacket and coming up with a gold cigarette case. He opened it, offered her one, and then drew one out for himself. Before he lit it, with the match burning near his lips, he said, "I always see it in their faces, that pain, that hurt. And it's what attracts me to them, Jane. As difficult as it must be to understand, for I don't pretend to myself, it's that caged animal in the eyes that—how shall I say—excites me?"

She said, with regret, "You're very sick. I don't think this is a good place for you."

"Oh," he replied, the light flaring in his eyes, "but this is just the place for me. And for you, too. Two halves of the same coin, Jane. Without one, the other could not exist. I'm capable of inflicting pain, and you, you're capable of bearing a great deal of suffering, aren't you?"

"I don't want to stay here," she told Rex in the morning. They had just finished a breakfast of a spicy tea and *shuvai* with poached duck eggs on the side, and were walking in the direction of the village center.

"We have to go back?" Rex asked, combing his hands through what was left of his hair. "I—I don't think I'm ready, Janey, not yet. I'm starting to feel a little stronger. If I go back . . . and what about the book?"

"I mean, I don't want to stay at the hotel. Not with those people. He's a child molester. No, make that child rapist. He as much admitted it to me last night."

"Holy shit." Rex screwed his face up. "You sure?"

Jane looked at him, and he turned away. There was so much boy in Rex that still wasn't used to dealing with the complexities of the adult world—she almost hated to burst his bubble about people. They stopped at a market, and she went to the first stall, which offered up some sort of eely thing. Speaking a pidgin version of Khou-dali, or at least the northern dialect she had learned, Jane asked the vendor, "Is there another hotel? Not the English one, but maybe one run by Khou-dali?"

He directed her to the west, and said a few words. She grabbed Rex's hand, and whispered, "It may be some kind of whorehouse, but I can avoid Greer for at least one night. And that stupid wife of his."

Rex took photos of just about everyone and everything they passed, including the monkey stalls. He was feeling much better, and Jane was thrilled that he was standing tall, with color in his cheeks, no longer dependent on a drug to energize him. He took one of her with a dead monkey. "I thought these people worshiped monkeys."

Jane said, "I think it's the image of the monkey, not the animal itself." She set the dead animal back on the platform with several other carcasses. Without meaning to, she blurted, "Human beings are horrible."

"Smile when you say that." Rex snapped another picture.

"We kill, kill, kill. Flesh, spirit, whatever gets in our way. It's like our whole purpose is to extinguish life. And for those who live, there's memory, like a curse. We're such a mixture of frailty and cruelty."

The stooped-back woman who stood at the stall said, in perfect English, "Who is to say, miss, that our entire purpose here on Earth is not perhaps to perform such tasks? Frailty and cruelty are our gifts to the world. Who is to say that suffering is not the greatest of all gifts from the gods?"

Her Khou-dali name was long and unpronounceable, but her English name was Mary-Rose. Her grandmother had been British; her brothers had gone to London and married, while she, the only daughter, had remained behind to care for an ailing mother until the old woman's death. And then, she told them, she did not have any ambition for leaving her ancestral home. She had the roughened features of a young woman turned old by poverty and excessive labor and no vanity whatsoever about her. Probably from some embarrassment at hygiene, she kept her mouth fairly closed when she spoke. Her skin, rough as it was, possessed a kind of glow similar to the women Jane had seen who had face-lifts—although clearly, this was from living in White Chapel with its humidity. Something in her eyes approached real beauty, like sacred jewels pressed there. She had a vigor in her glance and speech; her face was otherwise expressionless, as if set in stone. She was wrapped in several cloths, each dyed clay red and wrapped from her shoulders down to her ankles; a purple cloth was wrapped about her head like a nun's wimple. It was so hot and steamy that Jane was surprised she didn't go as some of the local women did—with a certain discreet amount of nakedness. "If you are looking for a place, I can give you a room. Very cheap. Clean. Breakfast included." She named a low price, and Jane immediately took her up on it. "You help me with English, and I make coffee, too. None of this tea. We are all dizzy with tea. Good coffee. All the way from America, too. From Maxwell's house."

•   •   •

White Chapel

Mary-Rose lived beyond the village, just off the place where the river forked. She had a stream running beside her house, which was a two-room shack. It had been patched together from ancient stones from the ruined Y-Cha temple, and tarpaper coupled with hardened clay and straw was used to fill in the gaps. Rex didn't need to be told to get his camera ready: the temple stones had hieroglyphic-like images scrawled into them. He began snapping pictures as soon as he saw them.

"It's a story," Jane said, following stone to stone. "Some of it's missing."

"Yes," Mary-Rose said, "it tells of Y-Cha and her conquests, of her consorts. She fucked many mortals." Jane almost laughed when Rose said "fucked" because her speech seemed so refined up until that point. No doubt, whoever taught Rose to speak English had not bothered to separate out vulgarities. "When she fucks them, very painful, very hurting, but also very much pleasure. No one believes in her much no more. She is in exile. Skin stolen away. They say she could mount a believer and ride him for hours, but in the end, he dies, and she must withdraw. The White Devil, he keeps her locked up. All silly stories, of course, because Y-Cha is just so much lah-dee-dah."

Jane looked at Rex. She said nothing.

Rex turned the camera to take a picture of Mary-Rose, but she quickly hid her features with her shawl. "Please, no," she said.

He lowered the camera.

"Mary-Rose," Jane said, measuring her words, "do you know where the White Devil lives?"

Seeing that she was safe from being photographed, she lowered the cloth. Her hair spilled out from under it—pure white, almost dazzlingly so. Only the very old women in the village had hair even approaching gray. She smiled broadly, and her teeth were rotted and yellow. Tiny holes had been drilled into the front teeth. "White Devil, he cannot be found, I am afraid."

"He's dead, then. Or gone," Rex said.

"No, not that," she said, looking directly into Jane's eyes. "You can't find him. He finds you. And when he finds you, you are no longer who you are. You are no longer who you were. You become."

Jane spent the afternoon writing in her notebooks.

Nathan Meritt may be dead. He would be, what fifty? Could he have really survived here all this time? Wouldn't he self-destruct, given his proclivities? I want him to exist. I want to believe he is what the locals say he is. The White Devil. Destruction and Creation in mortal form. Supplanted the local goddess. Legend beyond what a human is capable of. The woman with the scoured face. The children without skins. The trail of stories that followed him through this wilderness. Settling in White Chapel, his spiritual home. Whitechapel—where Jack the Ripper killed the prostitutes in London. The name of a church. Y-Cha, the Monkey God, with her fury and fertility and her absolute weakness. White—they say the river runs white at times, like milk, it is part of Y-Cha. Whiteness. The white of bones strung along in her necklace. The white of the scoured woman—her featureless face white with infection.

Can any man exist who matches the implications of this?

The Hero Who Skinned A Thousand Faces.

And why?

What does he intend with this madness, if he does still exist, if the stories are true?

And why am I searching for him?

And then, she wrote:

Greer's eyes looking into me. Knowing about my father. Knowing because of a memory of hurt somehow etched into my own eyes.

The excitement when he was looking out from the taxi.

Like a bogeyman on holiday, a bag of sweeties in one hand, and the other, out to grab a child's hand.

Frailty and cruelty. Suffering as a gift.

White Chapel

What he said, Two halves of the same coin. Without one, the other could not exist. Capable of great suffering.

White Chapel and its surrounding wilderness came to life just after midnight. The extremes of its climate—chilly at dawn, steamy from ten in the morning till eight or nine at night, and then hot but less humid as darkness fell—led to a brain-fever siesta between noon and ten o'clock at night. Then families awoke and made the night meal, baths were taken, love was made—all in preparation for the more sociable and bearable hours of 1:00 A.M. to about six or seven when most physical labor, lit by torch and flare, was done, or the hunting of the precious monkey and other creatures more easily caught just before dawn. Jane was not surprised at this. Most of the nearby cultures followed a similar pattern based on climate and not daylight. What did impress her was the silence of the place while work and play began.

Mary-Rose had a small fire going just outside the doorway; the dull orange light of the slow-burning manure cast spinning shadows as Mary-Rose knelt beside it and stirred a pan. "Fried bread," she said, as Jane sat up from her mat. "Are you hungry?"

"How long did I sleep?"

"Five, six hours, maybe."

The frying dough smelled delicious. Mary-Rose had a jar of honey in one hand, which tipped, carefully, across the pan.

Jane glanced through the shadows, trying to see if Rex was in the corner on his mat.

"Your friend," Mary-Rose said, "he left. He said he wanted to catch some local color. That is precisely what he said."

"He left his equipment," Jane said.

"Yes, I can't tell you why. But," the other woman said, flipping the puffed-up circle of bread, and then dropping it onto a thin cloth, "I can tell you something about the village. There are certain entertainments forbidden to women which many men who come here desire. Men are like monkeys, do you not think so? They frolic, and fight, and even destroy, but if you can entertain them with pleasure, they will put other thoughts aside. A woman is different. A woman cannot be entertained by the forbidden."

"I don't believe that. I don't believe that things are forbidden to women, anyway."

Mary-Rose shrugged. "What I meant, Miss Boone, is that a woman is the forbidden. Man is monkey, but woman is Monkey God." She apparently didn't care what Jane thought one way or another. Jane had to suppress an urge to smile, because Mary-Rose seemed so set in her knowledge of life, and had only seen the jungles of Y-Cha. She brought the bread into the shack and set it down in front of Jane.

"Your friend, Rex, he is sick from some fever. But it is fever that drives a man. He went to find what would cool the fever. There is a man skilled with needles and medicines in the jungle. It is to this man that your friend has traveled tonight."

Jane said, "I don't believe you."

Mary-Rose grinned. The small holes in her teeth had been filled with tiny jewels. "What fever drives you, Miss Jane Boone?"

"I want to find him. Meritt. The White Devil."

"What intrigues you about him?"

Jane wasn't sure whether or not she should answer truthfully. "I want to do a book about him. If he really exists. I find the legend fascinating."

"Many legends are fascinating. Would someone travel as far as you have for fascination? I wonder."

"All right. There's more. I believe, if he exists, if he is the legend, that he is either some master sociopath, or something else. What I have found in my research of his travels is that the victims, the ones who have lived, are thankful for their torture and mutilation. It is as if they've been—I'm not sure—baptized or consecrated by the pain. Even the parents of those children—the ones who were skinned— even they forgave him. Why? Why would you forgive a man such unconscionable acts?" Jane tasted the fried bread; it was like a doughnut. The honey that dripped across its surface stung her lips—it wasn't honey at all, but had a bitter taste to it. *Some kind of herb mixed with sap?*

It felt as if fire ants were biting her lips, along her chin where the thick liquid dripped; her tongue felt large, clumsy, as if she'd been shot up with Novocain. She didn't immediately think that she had been drugged, only that she was, perhaps, allergic to this food. She managed to say, "I just want to meet him. Talk with him," before her mouth seemed inoperable, and she felt a stiffness to her throat.

Mary-Rose's eyes squinted, as if assessing this demand. She whispered, "Are you not sure that you do not seek him in order to know what he has known?" She leaned across to where the image of the household god sat on its wooden haunches—not a monkey, but some misshapen imp. Sunken into the head of this imp, something akin to a votive candle. Mary-Rose lit this with a match. The yellow-blue flame came up small, and she cupped the idol in her hand as if it were a delicate bird.

And then she reached up with her free hand, and touched the edges of her lips—it looked as if she were about to laugh.

"Miss Jane Boone. You look for what does not look for you. This is the essence of truth. And so you have found what you should run from; the hunter is become the hunted." She began tearing at the curve of her lip, peeling back the reddened skin, unrolling the flesh that covered her chin like parchment.

Beneath this, another face. Unraveling like skeins of thread through some imperfect tapestry, the sallow cheeks, the aquiline nose, the shriveled bags beneath the eyes, even the white hair came out strand by strand. The air around her grew acrid with the smoke from the candle as bits of ashen skin fluttered across its flame.

A young man of nineteen or twenty emerged from beneath the last of the skin of Mary-Rose. His lips and cheeks were slick with dark blood, as if he'd just pressed his face into wine. "I am the man," he said.

The burning yellow-blue flame wavered and hissed with snowflake-fine motes of flesh.

Jane Boone watched it, unmoving.

Paralyzed.

Her eyes grew heavy. As she closed them, she heard Nathan Meritt clap his hands and say to someone, "She is ready. Take her to *Sedri-Y-Cha-Sampon*. It is time for Y-Cha-Pa."

The last part she could translate: Monkey God Night.

She was passing out, but slowly. She could just feel someone's hands reaching beneath her armpits to lift her. *I am Jane Boone, an American citizen, a journalist, I am Jane Boone, you can't do this to me*, her feeble mind shouted while her lips remained silent.

III

———∿∿———

Two years later, the saint lay down in the evening, and tried to put the leper he had met that day out of his mind. The lips, so warm, drawing blood from his own without puncturing the skin.

Or had it been her *blood that he had drunk?*

Beside his simple cot was a basin and a ewer of water. He reached over, dipping his fingers into it, and brought the lukewarm droplets up to his face.

He was, perhaps, developing a fever.

The city was always hot in this season, though, so he could not be certain. He wondered if his fear of the leper woman was creating an illness within his flesh. But the saint did not believe that he could contract anything from these people. He was only in Calcutta to do good. Even Mother Teresa had recognized his purity of heart and soul; the Buddhist and Hindu monks, likewise, saw in him a great teacher.

The saint's forehead broke a sweat.

He reached for the ewer, but it slipped from his sweaty hands and shattered against the floor.

He sat up, and bent down to collect the pieces.

The darkness was growing around him.

He cut his finger on a porcelain shard.

He squeezed the blood, and wiped it across the oversized cotton blouse he wore to bed.

He held the shard in his hand.

There were times when even a saint held too much remembered pain within him.

Desires, once acted upon in days of innocence and childhood, now seemed dark and animal and howling.

He brought the shard up to his lips, his cheek, pressing.

In the reflecting glass of the window, a face he did not recognize, a hand he had not seen, scraping a broken piece of a pitcher up and down and up and down the way he had seen his father shaving himself when the saint was a little boy in Biloxi, the way he himself shaved, the way men could touch themselves with steel, leaning into mirrors to admire how close one could get to skin such as this. Had any ever gone so far beneath his skin?

The saint tasted his own blood.

His skin.

Began slicing clumsily at flesh.

IV

—⚍—

Jane Boone sensed movement.

She even felt the coolness of something upon her head—a damp towel?

She was looking up at a thin, interrupted line of slate gray sky emerging between the leaning trees and vines; she heard the cries of exotic birds; a creaking, as of wood on water.

I'm in a boat, she thought.

Someone came over to her, leaning forward. She saw his face. It was Jim, the boatman who had brought her from upriver. "Hello, Nettie," he said, calling her by the nickname they'd laughed about before, "you are seeing now, yes? Good. It is nearly the morning. Very warm. But very cool in temple. Very cool."

She tried to say something, but her mouth wasn't working; it hurt even to try to move her lips.

Jim said, apparently noticing the distress on her face, "No try to talk now. Later. We on sacred water. Y-Cha carry us in." Then, he moved away. She watched the sky above her grow darker; the farther the boat went on this river, the deeper the jungle.

She closed her eyes, feeling weak.

Ice-cold water splashed across her face.

"You go back to sleep, no," Jim said, standing above her again. "Trip is over." He poled the boat up against the muddy bank. When he had secured it, he returned to her, lifting her beneath her armpits. She felt as if every bone had been removed from her body. She barely felt her feet touch the ground as he dragged her up a narrow path. All she had the energy to do was watch the immense green darkness enfold about her, even while day burst with searing heat and light beyond them.

By the time she felt pins and needles coming into her legs and arms, she had been set down upon a round stone wheel, laid flat upon a smooth floor. Several candles were lit about the large room, all set upon the yellowed skulls of monkeys somehow attached to the walls. Alongside the skulls, small bits of leaf and paper taped or nailed or glued to the wall; scrawled across these, she knew from her experience in other similar temples, were petitions and prayers to the local god.

On one of the walls, written in a dark ink that could only have been blood, were words in the local dialect. Jane was not good at deciphering the language.

White Chapel

A man's voice, strong and pleasant, said, "'Flesh of my flesh, blood of my blood, I delight in your offering.' It's an incantation to the great one, the Y-Cha."

He emerged from the flickering darkness. Just as he had seemed beneath the skin of Mary-Rose, Nathan Meritt was young, but she recognized his face from his college photographs. He was not merely handsome, but had a radiance that came from beneath his skin, as if something fiery lit him. His eyes, blue and almost transparent, flamed. "She is not native to this land, you know. She was an import from Asia. Did battle in her own way with Kali, and won this small acre before the village came to be. Gods are not as we think in the West, Jane; they are creatures with desires and loves and weaknesses like you or me. They do not come to us, or reveal themselves to us. No, it is we who approach them, we who must entertain them with our lives. You are a woman, as is the Y-Cha. Feelings that you have, natural rhythms, all of these, she is prey to also."

Jane opened her mouth, but barely a sound emerged.

Meritt put his finger to his lips. "In a little while. They used to use it to stun the monkeys—what the bread was dipped in. It's called *hanu*, and does little harm, although you may experience a hangover. The reason for the secrecy? I needed to meet you, Miss Boone, before you met me. You are not the first person to come looking for me. But you are different from the others who have come."

He stepped farther into the light, and she saw that he was naked. His skin glistened with grease, and his body was clean-shaven except for his scalp, from which grew long dark hair.

Jane managed a whisper. "What about me? I don't understand. Different? Others?"

"Oh," he said, a smile growing on his face, "you are capable of much suffering, Miss Boone. That is a rare talent in human beings. Some are weak, and murder their souls and bodies, and some die too soon in pain. Your friend Rex—he suffers much, but his suffering is of the garden variety. I have already played with him—don't be upset. He had his needles and his drugs, and in return, he gave me

163

that rare gift, that"—Meritt's nostrils flared, inhaling, as if recalling some wonderful perfume—"moment of mastery. It's like nothing else, believe me. I used to skin children, you know, but they die too soon, they whine and cry, and they don't understand, and the pleasure they offer . . . "

"Please," Jane said. She felt strength seeping back into her muscles and joints. She knew she could run, but would not know to what exit, or where it would take her. She had heard about the temple having an underground labyrinth, and she didn't wish to lose herself within it.

But more than that, she didn't feel any physical threat from Nathan Meritt.

"You're so young," she said.

"Not really."

"You look like you're twenty. I never would've believed in magic, but . . . "

He laughed, and when he spoke, spoke in the measured cadences of Mary-Rose. "Skin? Flesh? It is our clothing, Miss Jane Boone, it is the tent that shelters us from the reality of life. This is not my skin, see." He reached up and drew back a section of his face from the left side of his nose to his left ear, and it came up like damp leaves, and beneath it, the chalk white of bone. "It may conform to my bones, but it is another's. It's what I learned from her, from the Y-Cha. Neither do I have blood, Miss Boone. When you prick me, I don't spill."

He seemed almost friendly; he came and sat beside her.

She shivered in spite of the familiarity.

"You mustn't be scared of me," he said in a rigid British accent. "We're two halves of the same coin."

Jane Boone looked in his eyes, and saw Greer there, a smiling, gentle Greer. The Greer who had funded her trip to White Chapel, the Greer who had politely revealed his interest in children.

"I met them in Tibet, Greer and Lucy," Meritt said, resuming his American accent. "He wanted children, we had that in common, although his interests, oddly enough, had more to do with mechanics than with intimacy. I got him his children, and the price he paid. Well, a pound or more of flesh. Two days of exquisite suffering, Jane, along the banks of a lovely river. I had some children with me—bought in Bangkok at one hundred dollars each—and I had them do the honors. Layers of skin, peeled back, like some exotic rind. The fruit within was for me. Then, the children, for they had already suffered much at Greer's own hands. I can't bear to watch children suffer more than a few hours. It's not yet an art for them; they're too natural."

"Lucy?"

He grinned. "She's still Lucy. I could crawl into Greer's skin; I was enjoying the game. She could not tell the difference because she didn't give a fuck, literally or figuratively. Our whole trip down the river, only Jim knew, but he's a believer. Sweet Lucy, the most dreadful woman from Manchester, and that's saying a lot. I'll dispose of her soon, though. But she won't be much fun. Her life is her torture—anything else is redundant."

Jane wasn't sure how much of this monologue to believe. She said, "And me? What do you intend to do?"

Unexpectedly, he leaned into her, brushing his lips against hers, but not kissing. His breath was like jasmine flowers floating on cool water. He looked into her eyes as if he needed something that only she could give him. He said, softly, "That will be up to you. You have come to me. I am your servant."

He pulled away, stood, turned his back to her. He went to the wall and lifted a monkey skull candle up. He held the light along the yellow wall. "You think from what I've done that I'm a monster, Miss Boone. You think I thrive on cruelty, but it's not that way. Even Greer, in his last moments, thanked me for what I did. Even the children, their life-force wavering and the stains along their scalps spreading darker juices over their eyes, whispered praise with their final breaths that I had led them to that place."

He held a light up to the papers stuck to the wall. His shadow seemed enormous and twisted as he moved the light in circles; he didn't look back at her, but moved from petition to petition. "Blessings and praises and prayers, all from the locals, the believers in Y-Cha. And I, Miss Boone, I am her sworn consort, and her keeper, too. For it is Nathan Meritt and no other, the Hero Who Skinned A Thousand Faces, who is her most beloved, and to whom she has submitted herself, my prisoner. Come, I will take you to the throne of Y-Cha."

A pool of water, a perfect circle filled with koi and turtles, was at the center of the chamber. Jane had followed Nathan down winding corridors whose walls seemed to be covered with dried animal skins and smelled of animal dung. The chamber itself was poorly lit, but there was a fire in a hearth at its far end; she thought she heard the sound of rushing water just beyond the walls.

"The river," Nathan said. "We're beneath it. She needs the moisture, always. She has not been well for hundreds of years." He went ahead of her, toward a small cot.

Jane followed, stepping around the thin bones which lay scattered across the stones.

There, on the bed, head resting on straw, was Lucy. Fruit had been stuffed into her mouth, and flowers in the empty sockets of her eyes. She was naked, and her skin had been brutally tattooed until the blood had caked around the lines: drawings of monkeys.

Jane opened her mouth to scream, and knew that she had, but could not even hear it. When she stopped, she managed, "You bastard, you said you hadn't hurt her. You said she was still alive."

He touched her arm, almost lovingly. "That's not what I told you. I didn't hurt her, Jane. She did this to herself. Even the flowers. She's not even dead, not yet. She's no longer Lucy." He squatted beside the cot and combed his fingers through her hair. "She's the prison of Y-Cha, at least as long as she breathes. Monkey God is a weak god in the flesh, and she needs it, she needs skin because she's not much different than you or me, Jane. She wants to experience life, feel blood, feel skin and bones and travel and love and kill, all the things animals take for granted, but the gods know, Jane. Oh, my baby," he pressed his face against the flowers, "the beauty, the sanctity of life, Jane, it's not in joy or happiness, it's in suffering in flesh."

He kissed the berry-stained lips, slipping his tongue into Lucy's mouth. With his left hand, he reached back and grasped Jane's hand before she could step away. His grip was tight, and he pulled her toward the cot, to her knees. He kissed from Lucy to her and back, and she tasted the berries and sweet pear. Jane could not resist—it was as if her flesh required her to do this, and she began to know what the others had known, the woman with the scraped face, the children, Greer, even Rex, all the worshipers of Y-Cha. Nathan's penis was erect and dripping, and she touched it with her hand, instinctively. The petals on the flower quivered; Nathan pressed his lips to Lucy's left nipple, and licked it like he was a pup suckling and playing; he turned to Jane, his face smeared with Lucy's blood, and kissed her, slipping a soaked tongue, copper taste, into the back of her throat; she felt the light pressure of his fingers exploring between her legs, and then watched as he brought her juices up to his mouth; he spread Lucy's legs apart, and applied a light pressure to the back of Jane's head.

For an instant, she tried to resist.

But the tattoos of monkeys played there, along the thatch of hair, like some unexplored patch of jungle, and she found herself wanting to lap at the small withered lips that Nathan parted with his fingers.

Beneath her mouth, the body began to move.

Slowly at first.

Then more swiftly, bucking against her lips, against her teeth. The monkey drawings chattered and spun.

She felt Nathan's teeth come down on her shoulder as she licked the woman.

He began shredding her skin, and the pain would have been unbearable except that she felt herself opening up below for him, for the trembling woman beneath her, and the pain slowed as she heard her flesh rip beneath Nathan's teeth. She was part of it, too, eating the dying woman who shook with orgasm, and the blood like a river.

A glimpse of her, not Lucy.

Not Lucy.

But Monkey God.

Y-Cha.

You suffer greatly. You suffer and do not die. Y-Cha may leave her prison.

She could not tell where Nathan left off and where she began, or whether it was her mouth or the dying woman's vagina which opened in a moan that was not pleasure, but was beyond the threshold of any pain she had ever imagined in the whole of creation.

She ripped flesh, devouring, blood coursing across her chin, down her breasts, Nathan inside her now, more than inside her, rocking within her, complete love through the flesh, through the blood, through the wilderness of frenzy, through the small hole between her legs, into the cavern of her body, and Y-Cha, united with her lover through the suffering of a woman whose identity as Jane Boone was quickly dissolving.

Her consciousness: taste, hurt, feel, spit, bite, love.

V

—⟶m⟶—

In the morning, the saint slept.

His attendant, Sunil, came through the entrance to the chamber with a plate of steamed vegetables. He set them down on the table, and went to get a broom to sweep up the broken ewer. When he returned, the saint awoke, and saw that the servant stared at his face as if seeing the most horrifying image ever in existence.

The saint took his hand to calm him, and placed his palm against the fresh wounds and newly formed scars.

White Chapel

The saint felt the servant's arousal. Sunil was a beautiful dark man, with piercing eyes, and the great man let his free hand slide down Sunil's back, beneath his shirt, to the curve of his buttocks.

Sunil gasped because he was trying to fight how good it felt, as all men did when they encountered Y-Cha.

The saint found his warmest place and stroked him there, like a pet. His mouth opened in a small O of pleasure.

He was moist and eager. Already, his body moved, he thrust, gently at first; he wanted to be consort to Y-Cha.

He would beg for what he feared most, he would cry out for pain beyond his imagining, just to spill his more personal pain, the pain of life in the flesh.

It was the greatest gift of humans, their flesh, their blood, their memories. Their suffering. It was all they had, in the end, to give, for all else was mere vanity.

Y-Cha pressed her finger into him, delighted in the sweet gasp of expectation from the beautiful man's mouth.

Words scrawled in human suffering on a yellow wall:

> Flesh of my flesh, blood of my blood
> I delight in your offering
> Make of your heart a lotus of burning
> Make of your loins a pleasure dome
> I will consecrate the bread of your bones
> And make of you a living temple to Monkey God.

The servant opened himself to the god, and the god enjoyed the flesh as she hadn't for many days, the flesh and the blood and the beauty—for it was known among the gods that a man was most beautiful as he lay dying.

The gift of suffering was offered slowly, with equal parts delight and torment, and as she watched his pain, she could not contain her jealousy for what the man possessed.

169

Delicious
Antique
Whore

by
Wilum H. Pugmire

I knelt beneath twilight and prayed to the depraved angel. My quivering lips had difficulty mouthing the arcane words that dreamed within my skullspace. I felt those words stir within the pit of my being, felt them ooze toward my mouth and linger on my dry tongue.

Trembling, I prayed. Shaky hands clasped elbows. Tearful eyes that had been kissed by inhuman mouths scanned the nighted sky. They watched the weird moon, saw how dark and hazy it seemed, how its outline ebbed and flowed as it sank slowly from the heavens.

Ah, no—it was not the moon.

Cool air chilled my naked flesh. I could smell the hunger of immortal lust. I closed my eyes as liquid tongues smoothed the surface of my throat. It kissed me there, and there; oh, and there. My lips found its single breast. I sucked. Its curdled nourishment dripped into my mouth and churned within my soul.

I tried once more to recall when I had first devoured this delicious decadence. But I could not remember. My other life was but a dim forgotten dream, gladly tossed away like useless skin. This angelic beast alone was my reality.

It drifted from me, whispered my name. My eyes opened. I beheld its swirling shapeless shadow, the blur of its endless wings, its halo of dark flowing blood. I gazed at the multitude of grinning mouths and wept as a chorus of the damned spoke my name with longing.

The creature bit into its tongues with perfect fangs. Its raining blood baptized my body. The scarlet dew sank hungrily into my numbing flesh, became a part of my substance. My mouth stretched wide, shaped newly in rebirth.

The beast seethed before my face. Lips that were strangely soft sucked the nectar from my eyes, eyes I could not close. I was blessed with nameless vision. I beheld myself surrounded by others of my kind. We were the chosen ones who writhed among the passion of celestial monsters. We lurked the darkness of night in search of soft human skin, sweet succulent blood. We celebrated our lust with wild abandon as we fucked among the shadows of gods.

Stinging orgasm returned me to my senses. The formless angel howled in dæmonic delight. I felt its fangs upon my throbbing throat.

"Drain me," I begged. And it did. O, so delicious. And I died, for a little while.

Triptych di Amore

by
Thomas F. Monteleone

I was here before the Great Temples at Luxor, the Colossus of Rhodes. I walked with Aeneas at Carthage, Alexander at Philippi. I saw the horror of Black Death, the joy of Polo's return. I heard the heresies of Galileo, watched the Sistine Chapel transformed. I am Helen to Menalaeus; I am Geraldine to Christabel; I am the Vlad of Desire. I am as old as the world is young.

—Inscription found on the underside of altar's capstone, village church, Scarpino, Sicily, 1944.

Vienna, 1791

One of his earliest memories was of his father, Papa Leopold, touching the keys of a harpsichord or a piano, demanding the instrument's pitch to within an eighth of a tone. Before he had learned to read German, he was reading music in his mind. Little Wolfgang's ears had been magically sensitive, his fingers lithe and almost supernaturally quick. Crystalline memories of being in the circle of astounded adults as he played, while his father beamed with pride.

But memories seemed to be all he had lately. If only he were not such a goddamnably bad businessman! If only his Constanze were not so sickly all the time! If only there were ways to protect and warrant the music he'd created!

If only the world were fair. . . .

Mozart laughed at this crazy little wish as he sat on the outdoor table of his favorite *Konditore*, a pastry shop on the Domgasse near his previous home. He had lived in the Figarohaus for three years, until it became too expensive for him and his fragile wife. How he had loved that woman, and now . . . how he sometimes despised her!

She was as devoted to him as a house pet, as helpless as a child, and less passionate than either. What with his home life being so miserable, his financial situation taking him to the edge of poverty itself, and a new emperor ascending to the throne, it was incredible, even to Mozart, that he could still continue to produce musical masterpieces with the precision and punctuality of a Swiss clock.

The war with the Turks had finally ended and the Viennese court was starting to pay more attention to frivolity and the arts again. The ten-year reign of Joseph II had just ended and Leopold II was now in the palace, but Wolfgang hated the man. He seemed to have no soul for music, and even less understanding of what it meant to *create* anything. Leopold II, despite being told by many esteemed men (even Haydn himself) that Mozart was a "national treasure," refused to issue him a royal stipend. Even though *Don Giovanni* proved to be the most popular opera in the history of the city, Mozart remained estranged from any of its profits—such had been the nature of his original agreement with the theater owners.

Almost destitute, Wolfgang had appealed to the Vienna magistrates, asking that he might be appointed as "humble assistant" to Kapellmeister Hoffman at Saint Stephen's Church. It was a grand ploy, except that the magistrates were so overwhelmed with such a modest petition, that Mozart was appointed to the post as an honorary employee without a salary.

Fuck them all! he thought viciously as he finished his pastry and coffee. It did not seem to matter anymore what happened to him. He had just nursed Constanze back to a fair simulation of good health, and perhaps she would have to take in sewing or laundry to pick up a few extra ducats.

And I will continue to give music lessons to the few in this city who can afford me, he thought as he downed the last of his linzertorte. Picking up his coffee cup, he drank down the final swallow, the rim almost touching his forehead, obscuring his vision.

He didn't see her until he put the cup down.

Then, he could not stop looking.

Shining blond hair enveloped her head like spun gold, and her long, aquiline face seemed like a piece of Greek sculpture, so perfect were its lines. She had eyes of the most penetrating green he had ever seen, and their gaze had him fixed like a butterfly on a pin. If she'd told him her name was Helen of Troy, he would have only smiled.

Suddenly she was sitting at his small table, having somehow slipped down in front of him, during the instant that he sipped the last of his coffee.

Astonishing!

He cleared his throat and tried to speak. "Yes?" The word fell off his lips hoarsely.

The woman smirked, her mouth glistening with the sensuous moisture of youth. "You are Wolfgang Amadeus Mozart?"

He nodded. "There is none other."

"Oh, I know . . . your music aspires to Olympus. Surely the gods themselves have never heard such strains." Her voice was even and refined, suggesting a maturity unexpected in one so young.

Mozart laughed nervously. "Well, I've never heard anyone express it quite like that, but, yes, I agree with you: my music *is* special."

The woman smiled openly this time, prompting him to continue.

"My father keeps telling me to write more simple stuff, so that more of the people can understand what I am doing. 'What is slight can still be great,' my father said, but that is not my style. I would first jump into the Danube before writing less than *my* music!"

"Good for you, my Amadeus. It is said that you are the world's foremost musical genius, and even upon first meeting you, I am already inclined to agree."

She stroked his ego so skillfully he did not even think to ask her name or her purpose in sitting at his table. By the cut of her

clothes, it was apparent she was an extremely wealthy woman—
the wife of a great landowner, or perhaps a duchess, maybe even
an emissary from the Court of Leopold II. It would be wise not to
be too arrogant with this woman until he knew more about her.

"Uh, thank you, madame . . . " he said more cautiously, as he
watched her breasts heave and swell above her bodice. It seemed
as though they had a life of their own, that they were straining to
break free of the constraining cloth. Finally, coming out of his
trance, he addressed her once again. "As much as I enjoy the
praise of strangers, I am compelled to ask if there is anything I
might do for you. . . ."

She reached out to touch his hands.

"These are the fingers which dance upon the piano keys with
such magic, are they not?"

"So I've been told, yes."

She stroked his fingers lightly, stirring passion in him that he
had not felt since his first times with Constanze. "I would have you
give me lessons, Mozart. . . ."

He was stunned! Surely she did not mean what she said. He had
never had a female student, and indeed, it was rare to hear of any
women studying under one of the masters in the city.

"What?" he asked politely, but not hiding his surprise. "You
wish to study the piano?"

"In a sense. More precisely, I wish to study you, Amadeus."

"Me? You mean my music?"

She tilted her head slightly as though considering her answer
carefully.

"Well, your music will make a good beginning. . . ."

And it did.

The woman introduced herself as the Countess Bellagio from
the city of Como in northern Italy. She had a large house on
Schullerstrasse, complete with servants and maids on every floor.
Although she was not Austrian by birth, she understood the Aus-

Triptych di Amore

trian concept of *Gemütlichkeit* very well: good living with charm
and graciousness. On every visit to her home, Mozart was treated
to the finest breads, cheeses, wines, and pastries.

And she took her music lessons very seriously for several
weeks, until the roles of teacher and pupil became reversed.

Wolfgang had been seated with her at the piano when it happened. She had been practicing a little rondo he had written especially for her lessons, when he became aware of what could only be
described as an overwhelming scent. It seemed to envelop him
like the snakes of Laocoön tugging at his consciousness, squeezing
off his powers of will and concentration.

It was a raw, pungent, animal smell. It was the aroma of rutting,
the heat-musk of desire. It was the scent of mating and release.
The music in his mind, in his ears, faded away like smoke. The
only thing he could concentrate upon was the ripe body of the
woman seated by him.

She stopped playing, turned to face him, and he could see an
inferno boiling like a volcano beneath the Sargasso green sea of
her eyes.

"Is there something wrong, maestro?" she asked, with a coy
upward turn of her lips.

"I, I don't know. . . ." was all that he could say.

She laughed with a suggestion of cruelty and stood up from the
bench they shared. The rustle of her skirts seemed loud and exag-
gerated, almost like a melody in itself. He sat transfixed, as though
under the influence of a powerful drug, and watched her unfasten
her gown. With a smooth, graceful motion, she peeled off the
pieces of clothing, which seemed to fall away from her like the layered dried husk of a butterfly's cocoon.

Golden light of early afternoon entered the conservatory window, bathing her flesh with a warm, vibrant light. She seemed to
surge with an inner energy, a sexual power that was unstoppable.
Wolfgang became as rigid as a maypole, feeling as though he
would burst from his britches, hurting himself from the wretched

codpiece. He tore at his clothes with a feverish joy, laughing and smiling, on the edge of hysteria.

The countess joined him in his merriment as she climbed up on the bench, spreading her legs over him as she let the final piece of underwear slip away from her. He had never seen a woman so free in her nakedness, so bold and so proud. In the middle of the day, with no shame! It fired his passion to the point of confusing him as though made drunk. His fingers became clumsy imitations of themselves and he fumbled free of his clothes like an awkward child just learning the task.

Taking his head in her hands, she guided his face into the golden triangle of her pubic hair, which was fine and wispy and soft as the down on a newborn chick. Her lips seemed to part magically as he raised his tongue to her. When he touched her, a galvanized current passed through his body. She was like an electrolyte, the heedless fire of an animal in heat. Her body odor was sweet and heavy. He had never imagined a woman could be so *clean.*

Pulling her from the bench, he threw this madwoman, this sex-creature, across the top of the piano. She landed with such force that the strings and hammers gave forth a single discordant sound, but she responded with laughter that was most musical in itself.

And so she became the instrument of his pleasure, atop what had always been the instrument of his pleasure. It was a glorious, hedonistic coupling, the likes of which he had never known. Compared to this woman, his wife was a cold slab of stone.

When she was finally finished with him, there was a brief, silent rest, and suddenly they were at each other again. Wolfgang had never known himself to be so full of sexual energy but here he was, standing at attention, and ready to cavort once more . . .

. . . and it was after dark by the time he stumbled away from her house, feeling as though he had just run a race through the Alps. His head was surprisingly clear for such an experience, and upon introspection he found it odd that he had been able to draw upon such boundless sexual reservoirs. He never had known himself to be much of an animal when it came to lusty adventures, and yet this Countess Bellagio had totally enflamed him, torched his very soul.

If only he could write music that could have such an effect on people! Then his immortality would be guaranteed, he thought with a sad smile.

The lessons continued for the next month. And the things she taught him were wondrous and dark and full of magic. He often fancied that she might indeed be some kind of witch or sorceress, but in the final analysis, he didn't give a damn what she might be.

His life was in a curious state of flux, and he was not sure how to deal with the strange brew of emotions and ideas which filled his mind and his soul. The countess had made him feel more alive than ever with her bedroom spells, but his health in general seemed to be on the decline. He had contracted the ague, and now it threatened to overtake him completely. His breath whistled in his lungs and he coughed up great gobbets of catarrh each morning, sometimes mixed with blood.

On the economic side, his finances seemed as if they might take a turn for the better. He was being paid a handsome fee by the countess for her "lessons," and of course there were the plans of Herr Schikaneder, the owner and manager of the Theater auf der Wieder.

Wolfgang did not care for Schikaneder as a person, even though he belonged to the order of the Freemasons. There was something oily about him, something which suggested a foulness, a despicable aspect. But the small, thin man had come to him with an offer that seemed attractive, an opportunity which would be hard to resist.

Herr Schikaneder had written the libretto to an opera called *The Magic Flute*, which showed surprising merit. Schickaneder wanted Wolfgang to compose the musical score for the opera, and they would share the profits. In spite of the man's horrible reputation, Wolfgang was attracted to the prospect of writing music for such a story: full of fairies and spirits and creatures of the night. It was a dark and magical tale that fitted his moods and his general outlook.

Even the countess encouraged him to embark upon *The Magic Flute*. She told him that it was a monumental project which would guarantee him a place in the pantheon of musical giants; she felt it would be a fitting use of his great mental energies.

Wolfgang was flattered by the words of Herr Schikaneder, but he was more inspired by the encouragement of Countess Bellagio. Before meeting her, he had been feeling so bereft of human feeling that he had been channeling all of his soul into his music. But now the woman was bringing him back to life! For the first time in many years, Mozart was beginning to feel happy again.

He began seeing her as often as time would permit, and gave her the nickname "Lyrica" because her presence in his life was the words to his music. Together, he felt, they captured the pure beauty of a *Lied*, a song.

He accepted Schikaneder's offer and began work on the musical score of *The Magic Flute*. The oleaginous theater owner was so overjoyed at this decision that he had a small pavilion built on the grounds, where Mozart could work without distraction or pause. At first Wolfgang thought this gesture was a magnificent demonstration of the esteem and regard of Herr Schikaneder, but he soon realized that the pavilion was more like a prison.

His meals were brought to him there, and he was not allowed to leave the premises until his daily work had been inspected by the theater owner each evening. The pavilion was hastily constructed and was therefore full of drafts—on rain-filled afternoons, Wolfgang would sit in the small confines of his musical jail wracked by a terrible chill. His illness progressed unchecked, and the coughing spasms became worse. He complained to his wife and his employer that his strength seemed to be leaving him and he began again to revel in thoughts of death.

Triptych di Amore

At one point he told Schikaneder that "death is the only worthwhile goal in life. It is our only real and devoted friend."

Schikaneder smiled and agreed with him, saying only that he should stay away from his friends until the opera had been completed.

Mozart managed to do this only because he had become obsessed with finishing the musical score. Lyrica would come to him in his tiny pavilion in early evening, and they would steal a few precious minutes of lovemaking from his work, and their encounters left him in a most curious state. During their bouts of love, he felt as vigorous and strong and full of life as he had ever in all his days . . . but when she had left him, he felt more drained and pale and weak than ever before.

The day finally arrived when the completion of the opera was in sight. Wolfgang had finished all but a few parts for a few instruments, and he could already hear the entire orchestra roaring in his mind. It was not good music, it was great music—even by his own high standards. He knew this in the depths of his soul, and he was pleased beyond measure.

He sat in the pavilion that evening, putting the finishing touches on the vellum sheets, when there was a soft knock on the door behind him. Turning and throwing up the latch, he watched a familiar figure enter. It was Lyrica wearing a black gown that made her seem thin and waspish.

Moving to him, she straddled his legs where he sat on the tiny stool, and lifted her skirts. He could smell the essence of her loins rise up and intoxicate him, and he was instantly ready for her. Lowering herself, she seemed to draw him up into her more deeply than ever before, and he felt as though he could not bear the sensation. But just as he was about to explode into her, she grabbed him with her secret muscles and shut him down, preserving the pleasure and the moment of final release. As she rode him wildly, he felt that she could play him like that indefinitely, and the pleasure crashed over him in ever-heightening waves, until the pleasure became a pain, a torturous thing from which he cried out for release.

Afterward, as she kissed him and prepared to leave, she paused and looked deeply into his eyes. "I have a surprise for you," she said in a soft whisper.

"Any more surprises from you, I don't think I can bear," he said only half in jest.

Reaching into her cloak, Lyrica produced a sealed envelope, which she handed to him. "Open it."

"What is it?"

"A commission."

His heart leaped wildly, and his hands began trembling. "What? From whom?"

"Please, open it."

Breaking the wax seal, Wolfgang tore away the parchment paper and began to read the document. It was indeed a commission naming a handsome sum of money to write a *Requiem*, a mass for the dead.

But it was unsigned . . .

Mozart looked up from the parchment to Lyrica. "Is this a joke?"

"No, of course not."

"But there is no signature. It is invalid."

Lyrica tilted her head, and her lip curled up in a slight, impish grin. "No, it is valid. The person who commissioned this piece wishes to remain anonymous, that is all. The commission will be paid through me, as I have been named the executor of the transaction. Everything is perfectly legal, maestro."

"But . . . he wants to be anonymous? I've never heard of such nonsense! I thought the nobility wanted it to be known that they were patrons of the arts?"

Lyrica smiled. "Some of the true nobility do not need such gratification."

Wolfgang sighed and slipped the commission and the promissory note into his blouse. "Very well, I shall begin it directly. The music for *The Magic Flute* will be completed on this very day, and I am already thinking of the dominant themes I might employ in this new *Requiem*."

"That is wonderful news, my Wolfgang." Lyrica turned to leave the pavilion.

"One more thing. . ." said Wolfgang. "For *whom* is this *Requiem* being written? Do you not think I should know this?"

For an instant, she looked grim and serious, but she banished the expression with a sultry smile. "No. Your patron would like that to be also a secret. . . ."

Wolfgang grinned. "Oh, he does, does he? Well, you tell him that I shall most likely discover his secrets, despite his silly wishes!"

Again she appeared serious as she took her leave. "Perhaps you will, Wolfgang . . . perhaps you will."

The Magic Flute was an incredible success. The opera played to full houses for more than two hundred successive performances. It was a record unequaled in the history of Viennese theater. Unfortunately, because of the wording of their contract, Wolfgang received very little of the profits, and Herr Schikaneder became impossibly wealthy at his expense.

The oily bastard was having a statue of himself erected while Mozart struggled to pay the rent on his small dwelling!

But this injustice was slight compared to the other slaps of Fate he had received. Constanze was again confined to her bed with the ague, and Wolfgang himself had been deteriorating badly, losing strength to the point that he could barely cut his meat at the table. His work on the great *Requiem* slowed because of his ebbing strength and spiritual energy. Despite his great musical achievements, he lived like a pauper, and he simply did not care any longer.

Even his noble wench, Lyrica, had been giving signs of deserting him.

LOVE IN VEIN

Not that he could blame her. She was so young and full of flame and breath! And he already seemed like such an old man. Their lovemaking was a pale and hollow shell of what it had once been, and he now felt so weak, so sickly, that he feared it would be impossible for him to perform.

As he lay in bed with a raging fever, his thoughts ripped about in his mind like sails in a storm. He shifted his concentration between the unfinished *Requiem* and his sweet Lyrica. He could not remember at what point the realization struck him, but he suddenly knew he would never recover from the terrible fever which consumed him.

He knew at that moment he was going to die.

Goddamn it all! Fuck them all! Nothing matters now . . . .

But he knew that was not true. There was much that mattered to him. He became angry and frustrated because his power and his life were slipping away.

He drifted off into a hazy dreamlike state, opening his eyes to discover that he was standing at the conductor's post in a large concert hall, which was filled to capacity. It was dark beyond the proscenium, but he could sense the presence of the audience—a large, tenebrous mass behind him. With a flourish, he guided the orchestra through the *finale* of his final composition, and listened to the building thunder of applause at his back. But there was something about the sound of their clapping that was wrong—it was too harsh, too sharp. It was a ratcheting sound like sticks of wood being struck together. Slowly, Wolfgang turned to face his audience and he saw the sea of bone white faces, the eyeless sockets and eternal grins. They called out to him with ghostly whispers of "Bravo!" and "Encore," and he finally understood for whom he had been composing his mighty *Requiem* . . . .

Arles 1899

There is a small antiquarian shop in the center of this French town of twenty thousand people. Situated close to the Rhône River

Triptych di Amore

and Port St. Louis on the Mediterranean, Arles caters to a fair share of international tourists and vacationers from the surrounding provinces. The antiquarian shop has become, therefore, something of a souvenir shop as well as a repository of things old and, most times, forgotten.

Its owner, an old man in his eighties, died two summers ago, and since there were no known heirs, the place and all its contents were put up for public auction. The shop seemed like the perfect diversion for a widow in her early forties who had inherited her husband's vast wealth after a boating accident. The sums from the insurance policies alone would allow her to live out her days in comfort, but she wished to have an idler's profession, and the purchase of the curiosity shop was just the ticket.

It was a small shop, but its interior seemed to defy the laws of physics, seemingly holding more in its numerous shelves and nooks and alcoves than would seem possible. The shop was truly a gestalt experience: a case of the sum of the parts being far greater than the whole. It was so jammed with junk and memorabilia of earlier times that no one could accurately detail all that was contained in it.

The prior owner had long ago stopped keeping track of his inventory, and the acquisition of old junk had merely become a part of his life as natural as eating and sleeping. The junk would come in, and some of it would go out. It was the natural order of things.

The new owner, the youngish widow, was not altogether interested in what might be found in her shop. She simply needed a profession, a place to go each day where she might have the chance to meet interesting people, to talk, and generally to enjoy herself with little pressure or insistence.

And so it was that she did not know of the thick leather-bound journal that rested in a far corner of the shop, buried halfway down a stack of old photograph albums and bound ledgers.

The book had been stolen by a housekeeper after its owner had committed suicide. In the confusion and shock that followed the man's death, no one missed the journal. The housekeeper had mistakenly thought it might be worth some money someday, but she died without making a franc. The journal was bound up with a stack of other old books, sold to a junk man, and eventually reached the dusty confines of the shop.

If anyone ever bought it, he would be in possession of one of the great artifacts of the art world—an additional look into the disturbed mind of a man who signed his tormented paintings with only his first name: Vincent.

December 12, 1888 — I have finally done it! I have left the drab cold landscapes of the north for the hot suns and bright days of the south of France. My friend, Paul Gauguin, has urged me to leave Paris and I have now believed him. He promises to meet me here and says we will share a studio together. That I will believe when it happens. Gauguin is such a bombastic, impulsive ass! And yet I admire him, as he admires me. We shall see if he is good to his word.

January 4, 1889 — I have just received another letter from Theo, wrapped about 150 francs. What a wonderful brother I have in Theo! No man could ever want a better sibling, that is for certain. His "allowance" to me keeps me alive. It is not crazy to imagine that once I begged him to quit his lucrative position at Goupil's Gallerie to become an artist with me!

Then the family would have had two starving wretches to worry about! At least Theo makes my father proud . . . while I, at the age of thirty-five, am still a problem child, still a crazy dreamer.

Speaking of dreamers, I am still waiting for Paul, yet a letter says that he is on the way as I write these lines. Somehow, I must confess to believing him. He claims to have a great need to be in the south for the colder months. He claims it is good for the soul, and I believe him. Arles is truly a beautiful place, where even in the winter there are flower gardens of crocus and daffodil, and greenhouses where there are blooms and flowers all year through!

Triptych di Amore

It is the color—the vibrant living color of this place—that will set me free, that will save me!

January 17, 1889 — He is here at last! Paul arrived by coach with a brace of baggage the likes of which I have never seen. He claims that he sold a painting in Paris just before he left, and had to wait for payment—thus his delay in arriving. We will work well together, of this I am sure. We will fight well together, of this I am also sure!

January 29, 1889 — I have been in this village more than a month and I still have not had one of their women! The southern girls are easily more beautiful than any of the northern peasant stock. Their faces are so finely angled, their eyes so big! They sit on their porches and in their sunny parlors sipping absinthe, and smiling at all the men who pass by. And yet they avoid me like a disease, and I dream of finding the prostitutes of this town. Always the whores for Vincent! Why must it always be this way for me?

February 18, 1889 — I had a terrible fight with Paul. We started drinking early in the day, and we ended up hurling insults, and finally our glasses, at each other. He is off at one of the cafes now, finding a woman, while I sit here with a pen in one hand, my prick in the other!

If I do not have a woman soon, I feel that I will explode like a cheap bomb. And yet I am painting like a madman already. To count up, I have painted ten gardens in ten days! It is nothing for me to spend fourteen hours a day at my easel. The colors are finally coming to life, and I can feel the energy of my body flood through my brush and light the colors of my palette!

I feel that I am painting well, and the thought comes to me that perhaps fucking and painting are incompatible, that a man cannot do both well, and must make a choice.

For me, the choice is already made! The women won't have me . . . not yet anyway.

February 22, 1889 — Paul is truly my friend. He has brought a young woman to meet me from the cafe where he drinks. She wanted to see my work, and she stayed to fuck me! What an experience! She was lean and young and full of energy. Such a rocking and a thumping—she, me, and my straw mattress! She has given me the inspiration and the element in my life which has been missing. Now I feel like I can paint forever. Just give me some tobacco, some drink, and an occasional woman, and I can be the artist of my dreams!

March 7, 1889 — Spring comes early to this part of France! Already the gardens are blooming with color and my palette is aswirl with inspiration. I have been learning to express the passions of humanity by means of reds and greens! There is a relationship between my colors and life itself! I can feel it and I know it! I am painting sunflowers because there is a special essence in the sunshine that these plants have captured, and capturing the flowers on canvas, I will thus capture that special essence of the sun!

March 9, 1889 — Paul and I share a studio where the light pours in like golden liquid. I am supremely happy here. I paint all day and spend my evenings in the cafes and brothels. The prostitutes are like sisters and friends to me. They do not reject me as an outcast because they are themselves outcasts. Yes, the whores give me my pleasure, but I long for a wife! I am filled with energy and the passion of all great art! Thank God for the wine which keeps me from becoming too crazy. When I take another drink, my concentration becomes more intense, my hand more sure, my colors more correct. Sometimes I believe that my painting can do nothing but improve because I have nothing left but my art. Sad? Yes. True? Unfortunately, yes.

Triptych di Amore

April 14, 1889 — Some days I am high as the birds which wheel and keen in the skies above my easel, and then suddenly I feel as though I belong with the white, eyeless worms beneath the flat rocks of the garden paths. My life is a jagged run of great joy and great pain. Sometimes I grow so tired of the starving conditions, the wretched life I choose to lead while I wait for the world to recognize me.

Am I truly crazy, as some say I am? Some of the village children have taken to waiting outside my studio window, only so that they might scream "madman!" when I come to the sill for a breath of air.

But my thoughts are this: I don't care if I am crazy—as long as I become that "artist of the future" which I spoke to Theo about.

April 23, 1889 — Today is the most glorious day of my life! My painting, *The Red Vine*, has been sold! Instead of working today, I have begun drinking as soon as I received the news, and I will no doubt drink up the profits of the sale within the next sunrise. But I care not!

May 3, 1889 — Today, Paul refused to eat at the same table as I because he claims I am a filthy pig and that he risks catching diseases by eating with me. Enraged, I threw my cup at his face and he struck me with his fist before storming off to the cafes. I fear we are incompatible, despite the wondrous atmosphere of this place, despite the stupendous number of canvases we have created here.

May 17, 1889 — I have often felt that if I did not have a woman I might freeze and turn to stone. I may never need feel that way again—Her name is Lyrica Rousseau and she entered my studio as though coming from a dream. To say that she is the most beautiful woman I have ever seen is such a silly cliché I am embarrassed to think in such terms. And yet it is true.

She was dressed like a woman to the manor born, a woman of social standing, education, and exquisite breeding. She told me she had come from Paris in search of artists, having heard that the truly talented have left the city for simpler climes. I smiled and told her that I was perhaps the finest artist in all of France, but no one yet knew that fact. I showed her my work and I am convinced that she was impressed with its vitality and utter newness. She even told me that she had seen nothing like it in all her days.

Pressing my good fortune (after all, one does not have an angel walk through his door every day!), I asked her where she would be going, and how long she planned to stay in Arles. To my surprise, she said that she lived by no man's schedule, and that she traveled freely in search of what she wanted. She said that it was possible she might be staying in Arles for a good while. I told her that there was only one good hotel in the village, and recommended that she stay there. She smiled at this, excused herself, and returned to her waiting carriage.

I walked to the door of the studio, watching her, trying to imagine what kind of perfect body might be hidden beneath the folds of her dress. I told her to visit me at her convenience, and to my shock and delight, she said that she would be doing so!

May 26, 1889 — Lyrica has come again! And again, she chose a time when she knew Gauguin would be out on one of his binges. She offered to pose for me, but the painting was never begun. As her clothes dropped away, I became overwhelmed with desire and a hardness in my prick I hadn't known since being fourteen years old!

To say that we fucked would be a blasphemy, a miscarriage to describe what truly took place. Locked together like a single organism, we aspired to the place of the gods. This woman, this Lyrica, is different, in an almost scary way. I had always thought that only men actually liked sex, and women merely tolerated our affliction and our hunger for it. But here is a woman who seems to like the sport as much as I!

Triptych di Amore

June 24, 1889 — With Mademoiselle Rousseau as my inspiration, I am painting with a furious, soul-burning energy. When I paint I am not conscious of myself anymore, and the images come to me as if in a dream. When I am painting like that, I know that I am creating beautiful art. Until I met this woman, only when I was painting did I ever feel that totally unleashed, totally free feeling of wanton fulfillment. But now my fucking is like my painting and I soar to the heights of my soul with her. She is an angel, this woman, and she tells me that she knows in her heart that I am a gifted painter, a great artist, and that someday the world will recognize my potent talent, my "special vision." That is her phrase: *my special vision*. She says that I see the world differently, that I "feel" the world differently . . . and that is why she comes to see me.

August 15, 1889 — My entries in this journal—what I have come to call my "secret" journal—have been more erratic lately. Still, I pour forth the letters to Theo as a way of resting and relaxing from the furious pace of my work, but there are things I do not tell him, that I can explain to no one, and those are the thoughts reserved for this separate ledger. Lyrica has been coming to see me less frequently, and when I ask her why, she only smiles. When I ask her where she goes when she is away from Arles, she only smiles. She is the most mysterious woman I have ever known, and she is easily the most self-assured, the most confident. I commented upon this once, and she laughed very musically, saying that she had learned how to act from the best teachers—men. For some reason, this threw me into a wildly depressive state, and I drank myself into a disgusting stupor after she had left my studio that day. I think that I had been entertaining crazy fantasies of marrying this independent woman! I think that I had become terribly possessive about her little "honeypot," and the thought of other men dallying about with her drove me into a frenzied state of mind. How silly of me to think that I could possess a woman so magnificent. I should consider myself fortunate to merely use her on the odd occasion!

September 10, 1889 — Lyrica visited me today. She has begun the curious habit of inspecting my work, my output of canvases, from one visit to the next. She seems overly concerned about the chronology of when they were completed, comparing the times to the times of her visits to me. She looked especially hard at a canvas of a row of green cypresses against a rose-colored sky and a crescent moon in pale lemon.

October 2, 1889 — The energy to paint fourteen hours a day is no longer in me. I find that I grow tired so quickly and that the visions and dreamy images of my work are not as clear. This bothers me and when I tell Paul he simply laughs. When I mention it to Lyrica, she only nods in silence, as though she understands perfectly.

October 27, 1889 — I am alone more and more. Paul is so disgusted with me, so angry and passionate all the time, that we can no longer talk. This morning it occurred to me that he has never met my Lyrica . . . it is uncanny how she has timed her visits to avoid him . . . and he has accused me of fantasizing the whole affair with this mystery woman. He claims that no one in the village has ever seen her come here, that no one knows of her, and that she probably exists only in my "demented" mind. How bizarre all this is becoming! Could it be that I have imagined such a woman? Could I have imagined such fucking? No, it is not possible—she is as real as I am! And yet the laughing jeers of Paul have set me to thinking that perhaps I am as crazy as everyone says.

November 23, 1889 — This is the worst day of my life, and I am very drunk as I try to pen these words. Lyrica has left me! A messenger delivered her note today: a terse, cold sentence which said that she must leave for Italy, and that she could see me no longer. I can't believe it! To neither see nor touch that incredible creature ever again! It is unthinkable, yet she states it so simply that there is a part of me which believes it totally. It is to laugh or cry. I don't know what to do. I know that I feel more sick and more troubled than I have ever felt. And if this is the pain of love, then I have finally felt it!

November 30, 1889 — She is truly gone. Of this I am certain. I have tried painting to soothe my pain and suffering, but there is something missing, and I know that I must struggle to regain it. I am tempted to tell Theo of this woman and her effect on me. I am tempted to hire men to investigate her past, to track her down. And perhaps I would do this if I had the funds to finance such a hunt. But alas, for me it is only a fantasy, a fairy tale in which I find her and bring her back to my studio forever. I find myself thinking of painting with very dark colors, with the bloodiest reds I have ever mixed, but I know not what to paint. And I am ill with a list of petty diseases. I cough up terrible gouts of mucous, and I shiver when there is bright sun on my skin. I have terrible fits at night when I lie in my bed in a sweat. I must start sleeping at longer stretches, must stop sitting up in my bed, staring at the moon while Paul grinds on through the night with nose-rattling snores.

December 19, 1889 — A month has passed and I am truly mad for her touch and the lingering smell of her cunt in my beard. My health continues to slide as I do not eat regularly, and I do not take care of what Paul calls my "most basic needs." But worse, I know I am truly mad. None of the colors look right anymore! My palette is a place of confusion and the colors of the oleanders and the rose-colored twilights come no longer to me on canvas. I thought the absence of her would be good for my painting, but I have seen little to cheer me. It occurs to me again that painting and fucking are not compatible. This fucking weakens the brain. If we really want to be potent males in our work, we must sometimes resign ourselves to not fucking much! There are times when my thinking seems to clear, when I do not hear the flies buzzing in my ears, when I can think clear thoughts and plan beautiful canvases. It is at those times that I know that she was bad for me, that her fucking was killing something in me in ways I can never explain. And then I think about this and I know that this also sounds crazy, and that I am probably so sick and so mad that it no longer matters what I think or what I feel.

January 15, 1890 — I feel so embarrassed for what has happened, and yet there is no way to show these feelings. After the argument with the whore, I still do not recall cutting my ear, or the first days in the hospital. Only Theo's face bending over me do I really remember. Upon returning to the studio, I learned that Paul had left, heading for Brittany, says Theo. I am tempted to say that I am happy he is gone, but that would be untrue. More truthful is to tell how lonely it has become without him. Even his quarrelsome nature is preferred to the silence. I don't even want to think of how much I miss the woman.

April 13, 1890 — The calendar says that it is April so I must believe it. I have lost track of the passing of the days and nights, and even the months. I have only recently broken my silence and written to Theo. I feel used up, like an old, ugly whore! I am mixing colors again, and I am seeing the colors of spring come back to this place with a wild and happy vengeance, but I am not painting good canvases.

May 16, 1890 — The world seems more cheerful if, when we wake up in the morning, we find that we are no longer alone, and that there is another human being beside us in the half dark. That's more cheerful than shelves of edifying books and the whitewashed walls of a church, I'd swear! And that companionship is something that the Fates have denied me. Lyrica is less than memory, like a half-remembered dream. I cannot imagine ever being happy in my life. Even the village is against me now, having the inspector jail me for being an incompetent. I have been in and out of the hospital so many times that I fear I am becoming a nuisance to everyone. It is only too true that heaps of painters go mad. I shall always be cracked, but it's all the same to me. When I become a nuisance to me, I will simply kill myself.

Scarpino, Sicily 1891

"This is the village of my ancestors!" Mauro Callagnia said proudly to her.

He was a tall, handsome boy of nineteen who literally bristled with energy and invention. Everything he touched or attempted became a natural ability under his hand. He was an expert horseman, a deadly archer and swordsman, an accomplished musician, poet, and painter. He had so much to give, he was like an unending fountain.

"It is so small and unimposing," she said as they drew their horses to a stop before the old wall and gate which marked the entrance into the small mountain village of Scarpino. Miles below them, huddled in the hazy cloak of twilight, lay the city of Palermo, the current home of Mauro's family.

Mauro smiled. "It is from such humble beginnings that many great things may come," he said.

She nodded, and looked carefully down the narrow streets ahead, then started to direct her mount toward the central avenue.

"Wait," said the boy who was already a man. "We should wait for the rest of the caravan, don't you think?"

She did not really wish to wait for Mauro's family, especially his father. She did not feel comfortable in the presence of the Duke. "Very well, Mauro. You are right."

LOVE IN VEIN

She looked back down the trail, which snaked back and forth across the hills, to see the remainder of their party slowly negotiating a narrow path. The line of horses carried men and women in gaily colored dresses and suits. Even in the failing light, she could see the mark of breeding and royalty in their carriage. Her young Mauro was the product of admirable bloodlines, and it was certainly no accident that he was so talented and gifted.

A minute passed in silence as Mauro's father, a Duke whose family title originated before the formation of the now defunct Kingdom of Two Sicilies, appeared over the nearby ridge. She noted that he was a hale man with great stamina and strength for his age. The Duke's face was creased from the years, but a fierce intellect raged behind his bright eyes. There lay a hard casting of determination in his features. The Duke carried a reputation as a man to be respected, and to be dealt with fairly.

Lyrica was forced to admit that, although she feared few men, she could possibly fear the Duke of the House of Callagnia.

"What took you so long, father?" Mauro smiled after his greeting.

"A slower horse, and not my age, if that's what you imply, my son!" The Duke turned and signaled to the rest of the family party. "Follow me, it is not far now!"

Mauro assumed the lead and led the procession down the central avenue of the village. It was a narrow street that leaned to the left and ascended the hill toward the small village church, whose spire rose above the low-slung houses like an aspiring dream.

As they approached the rectory, a moderately large residence beyond the church, she felt a twinge of apprehension. She had come this far because she had always been cautious, always watchful of the fears and superstitions of the humans. It was easy to become overconfident, and she had always tried to be vigilant against that failing. Of Mauro, she had no fear or distrust—he was so in love, so infatuated with the joys of the flesh, that he could never be a problem.

But there were others who were not so intoxicated. It was as though certain men—admittedly few through the ages—were immune to her powers of entrancement, and while she had only seen the man several times, she suspected that the Duke might be such a man.

And so, she thought with a sense of adventure and daring, perhaps it was a reckless thing to accompany this brilliant boy to his parents' anniversary dinner.

She would know soon.

The procession wound its way toward the rectory, and as the line of horses passed, many of the villagers appeared at windows and doors to have a look at the last of the village's *nobilia* in a time when nobility was a dying art form. She looked down at the people in their ragged clothes and their ragged faces, returning their stern expressions with looks of patronizing kindness and false friendliness. It was the haughty carriage that the peasants expected, and she gave it to them with little effort.

Finally they reached the rectory where they were greeted by two small boys, presumably acolytes who worked for the pastor. Everyone dismounted as the boys tended to the steeds, and faced a tall, wizened old priest who walked forward with open arms to greet the party.

"Welcome, my children," said the priest. "Come into my home. Dinner is almost prepared."

They entered the foyer to the stone and stucco rectory, and she was introduced to Pastor Mazzetti.

"Lyrica," said the Duke's wife, Dulcima, "I would like you to meet my mother's brother, my uncle, the Pastor Francesco Mazzetti!"

The old priest reached out and took her smooth white hand in his. His palm felt like the bark of an olive tree. He smiled and his runneled face looked as though it might crack like old leather. She smiled back and curtsied, but she could not avoid the intensity of his gaze. This was a man of great confidence and faith . . . and, therefore, power.

"I am pleased to make your acquaintance, signorina," said Mazzetti. "You should feel privileged to attend what has become a grand family tradition . . . "

"She is my guest tonight, uncle!" said young Mauro with a burst of pride as he cut into the conversation. "Is she not beautiful!?"

The old priest smiled, nodding. "Yes, nephew . . . she is that, and more, I am certain."

An old woman appeared in the doorway, which led deeper into the house, and nodded silently, catching Father Mazzetti's attention. He looked about at the assembled guests and brought his hands together in a practiced gesture. "And now the dinner is served. This way, everyone. . . ."

The anniversary dinner was indeed a wonderful affair. Seated at a long table headed up by Father Mazzetti were the Duke and his wife, her brother and his wife, their daughter Carmina, and of course Mauro and Lyrica. Mazzetti had arranged the chairs so that Lyrica was seated at his right hand—presumably the place of honor, but she was beginning to wonder what might be the true motivations of the priest. He kept looking at her throughout the dinner with intense, probing eyes.

After having glossed over the usual family pleasantries and toasts to good health and long life, the conversation about the table had drifted, inevitably, into politics. Lyrica knew this topic was not unusual among the noblemen of Italy because there were finally signs that the unending upheaval and unrest of the country might be nearing surcease. She listened to the banter with a halfhearted interest, while running her long fingernails up and down Mauro's thigh beneath the table.

". . . and I think the best thing that ever happened to us as Sicilians was getting rid of Premier Depretis," said the Duke as he reached for more wine from a crystal decanter.

"Of course, brother-in-law!" laughed his wife's sibling. "You belabor the obvious, don't you think? Since our new prime minister is a Sicilian, it is to be expected that he would look out for the interests of the Island!"

The Duke nodded. "Perhaps, but he must do it with some tact, with diplomacy, yes?"

"Francesco Crespi is no fool," said Father Mazzetti. "Let's not forget he fought with Garibaldi many years ago. He has made the ascent to power up the rear face of the mountain—he knows how difficult and delicate and lonely it can be at the top."

Lyrica watched the priest as he spoke. He seemed to be totally engaged in the conversation, and yet, she had the distinct impression that he was observing her, recording her every movement and reaction. Even though he appeared to be in his late sixties or early seventies, he seemed bright and strong. An interesting old man, she thought with a smile.

"Still," said the Duke. "I think Crespi's taking office is the most important thing to have happened to all of us since the beginning of the *Risorgimento!*"

The Duke's brother-in-law shook his head. "Some would say that Umberto the First's ascension to the throne is the real key to everything . . . . "

The Duke seemed to flush with a moment of anger. "That fool! Do you really think that the crown prince of Germany should be the King of Italy? It's time we throw out the house of Savoy once and for all!"

Father Mazzetti smiled. "Ah, me . . . the Duke will always be a headstrong man, a man of impulse and raw emotion."

Everyone laughed softly except the Duke.

"And what of it, uncle? My personality has served me well, has it not?"

The priest shrugged. "Perhaps," he said, "but you're starting to sound like Antonio Labiola."

The Duke appeared perplexed. "And who is he?"

"A professor at the University of Rome who has been teaching Marxism to his students."

"Marxism!" The Duke exploded with laughter. "Do you actually think that a nobleman like myself could ever espouse the writings of such a crackpot as Marx?"

"Why not?" Father Mazzetti said *sotto voce*. "You seemed to have embraced the socialism of Mazzini well enough."

"Oh, please!" said Dulcima, the Duke's wife. "Must we talk of politics endlessly?"

"I'll talk about what I please!" said the Duke.

Dulcima turned to the pastor. "Uncle, I fear you agitate him. You do this for your own amusement!"

The priest smiled. "I am an old man. . . . I need something for my amusement!"

Everyone laughed as the priest used the opportunity to gaze sharply and quickly at Lyrica. She could not escape the hard, cold aspect of his glance.

The moment was interrupted by the appearance of the pastor's cook, who began clearing away the main course plates and dishes with a clattering efficiency. The conversation at the table fragmented as though on cue into smaller one-on-one exchanges. The Duke seemed to be upset with his wife, while Dulcima's brother was making amusing small talk with his niece Carmina.

"My family is rather outspoken," said Mauro, leaning close and whispering in her ear.

"Don't sound so apologetic," she said absently, trying to cast unnoticed glances at the priest. She was feeling more and more uncomfortable, and she was thinking of ways she could handle it.

"I'm not being apologetic," said the boy.

"Oh, yes, you are!" She smiled and kissed his cheek.

Even that small gesture seemed to excite him and she could sense his desire pulsing from his body.

The cook reappeared with a tray of Sicilian pastries and a small urn of espresso. She placed it in the center of the table and everyone oohed and aahed appropriately.

"And now the dessert!" said Father Mazzetti clapping his

hands. Everyone smiled as he began to pass about the tray and the cook began pouring out small cups of the dark, sweet coffee.

The tray was passed to Lyrica, and she selected a cream and almond pasticceria. As she placed it on her plate, the cook offered her a small gold-rimmed porcelain cup of espresso. It was a delicate, exquisite piece of work, and she marveled at the relative opulence in which the priest lived when one considered the humble surroundings of the village.

Such were her idle thoughts as she sipped the thick dark liquid from the demitasse cup.

Drawing the porcelain away from her lips, she felt a stabbing pain in her stomach, and an almost instantaneous numbing sensation spreading outward from her head down into her limbs. It was a paralyzing effect, turning her to stone. Even her breathing seemed to be affected and she had the sensation of suffocating.

Poison!

The single thought pierced her like an arrow, and she glanced about the table as she began to straighten out like a plank and slide from her chair. She tried to cry out, but no sound would come. The power of the potion was strong indeed, obviously imbued with the priest's blessing to have any effect at all. She would need all of her cunning and strength to overcome it.

Everyone was talking at once at the table, and, as she slipped into a semicomatose state, she was only vaguely aware of the torrent of voices that swirled and eddied over her.

"My God! What's happened to her?" cried Mauro. She could feel his soft, gentle hands on her as he helped lower her to the floor.

"Let her be!" cried the priest in a sepulchral voice. "Stand back!"

The Duke had left his chair and was rushing to her side. "It's true, then?" he demanded of the priest.

"Father," said Mauro, "what is happening here? Of what do you speak?"

The priest advanced and huddled over her. She could see him through a filmy, gauzy aspect which had overtaken the light in the room. She was fighting off the effects of the poison, and her body was sending signals that she would be able to overcome it with time. She was thankful for that, but there was still a panic deep within the core of her being. A panic like a glowing coal that threatened to burst into flame in an instant.

"She failed the tests!" cried Father Mazzetti. "Stand back from the Demon! Stand back from the Possessed Creature that she is!"

"What!" cried Mauro. "Have you all gone mad?" He reached out and pushed at the old priest, who was leaning over, peering into Lyrica's glassine eyes.

Suddenly the Duke lashed out with his large hand and smacked Mauro in the face. The force of the blow knocked him back off his feet so that he went sprawling.

"Silence!" cried the Duke at his son. "You mewling pup! What do you know of this woman other than the fire of her loins!"

Mauro propped himself up on one elbow, stunned and confused. "Father, what you speak is madness! My mistress Lyrica might be, but she is no demon!"

"No, she is far worse!" cried Mazzetti, who now held a gold crucifix over her face. "Her food was laced with ground bitterroot . . . enough to choke a man, and she noticed it not! It is as the tales have told—a monster tastes not of man's food!"

The Duke moved to his son and held him in his arms. "My son, I am sorry for what I must do, but it is for the best."

"Oh, father!" The young boy sounded very panicked. "What are you going to do with her?!"

"We have suspected for a time that the young woman is possessed," said the Duke, as the rest of the dinner party gathered about to peer down at her in a ragged circle of faces. "And so we have brought her to the finest exorcist in Sicily—our own Father Mazzetti!"

"Bring her into the church!" commanded the old priest. "I must prepare myself. . . ."

Triptych di Amore

Lyrica could feel the effects of the poisons coursing through her supple body. Soon the effects would be lessened enough for her to effect a change. Soon, but not yet. And so she was powerless to stop them lifting her up from the cold stone floor and out into the night. The sky above the foothills was a brilliant midnight blue, laced with stars and frosted by the wind. They crossed a small courtyard, passed a fountain, and went into the sacristy entrance of the church.

Her vision was blurred, but she could still determine that the tough old priest had already assumed the mantle of his office, his silk raiments of the priesthood. He stood like a man posing for a sculptor or a painter, striking a posture of defiant strength.

"Take her out to the altar," he said as calmly as his voice would allow. Even in her distressed state of mind, Lyrica could detect the metallic scent of his fear. Fear was indeed the mindkiller, and if she could capitalize on Mazzetti's own fears and self-doubts, she still possessed a chance.

She was carried out of the sacristy and into the nave of the church, where the white marble altar lay surrounded by statues of the saints and several elaborate stained glass windows. As she was placed before the altar, the priest moved down beside her and anointed her forehead with oil. Her muscles were beginning to contract involuntarily. Either the effects of the poison were wearing off, or they were getting worse.

Suddenly there was a stinging sensation in her face, and after being so totally numb and paralyzed, she was ecstatic to feel even the faintest pain in her cheeks. Mazzetti had sprinkled holy water on her, and the droplets burned like acid. It stung, but it was such a sweet stinging.

She could see Mazzetti standing over her, holding up a gold crucifix. In a booming, echoing voice, he began speaking in Latin: "*In the name of the Father and the Son and the Holy Spirit, and by the power and authority granted to me by the Holy Mother Church and Pope Leo the Thirteenth, I invoke the rite of exorcism over this woman . . . .*"

Mazzetti continued droning on as Lyrica secretly smiled at him. His prayers were totally ineffectual; she wanted to cry out and laugh at him, and tell him what a fool he was. More feeling was returning to her cheeks, her limbs. Soon, she would show them that their silly poisons and potions had little real power over a being as great as she.

Yes, it was happening now. . . .

She could feel the power returning to her once-numbed body. In an instant, the juices of the changes were produced and shot through her soft tissues. She could feel her flesh hardening, flaking, and sloughing off, as she began the transformation to the True Form.

The Duke was the first to notice and he cried out in an uncharacteristic voice of alarm. "Father! Look! What does she become?"

"Oh, my God in Heaven!" yelled Mauro. "What are you doing to her! She's dying! Can't you see that she's dying?"

Father Mazzetti paused, placed the crucifix upon the altar.

"Silence!" he said quickly. "It is all right! Behold the power of the Lord!"

Suddenly, the priest turned and opened the small tabernacle atop the altar, bringing forth a small golden chalice. Slowly, and with great reverence, as he continued to mumble through the endless Latin prayers, Father Mazzetti reached into the chalice and produced a large, paper-thin wafer of unleavened bread. She knew it was the host, the Eucharist. Holding it carefully between thumb and forefinger, the priest placed the host inside a magnificent gold benediction mantle. It was a chalicelike object that held the Eucharist face-outward in a circular glass locket surrounded by delicate, radiant spires of gold. The cast beams were intended to suggest a great radiation of light from the central figure of the host, but in this case, it was not necessary.

As soon as the old priest turned to face his adversary, the Eucharist began to glow with white heat and light, a miniature sun in his hands. The shadows in the small village church were banished by the brilliant explosion of light. The golden benediction mantle became a torch so bright that no one dared look directly upon it.

Lyrica had almost finished the transformation and it progressed rapidly now. In the short moments of the priest's preparations she had assumed the changeling shape of the magnificent green serpent. She reveled in the return to her natural form, and writhed in ecstasy as the Duke and Mauro reeled back from the horror they now perceived. She moved quickly, arching up in her spine and dislocating the hinge of her jaws, unfurling her great hollow fangs. Cobralike, she reared up to face the foolish priest and his pyrotechnic show to impress the masses. Tightening her coils, she prepared to spring—

—and was stunned into immobility by a searing white wave of energy which hit her like the shock of a fiery explosion.

How foolish she had been! How wildly overconfident and arrogant! She had amused herself by walking proudly and defiantly into the lair of her natural enemy, and now he was proving to be her match . . . !

"Behold the beast!" cried Mazzetti. There was a collective, horrified gasp from the assembled dinner party; Carmina had swooned into the arms of her mother.

"My God!" cried out young Mauro, who fell to his knees, grasping the legs of his father in supplication for forgiveness and in thankfulness for seeing the true evil with which he had become involved.

Lyrica could see everything taking place with a deadly clarity, but at the same time she felt totally blinded, totally overwhelmed by the power and light emanating from the Eucharist. It was the first time in her very long life that she had ever encountered such a force, and she was truly shocked by its fury and total domination. Resisting with all her strength, she could do nothing, and as the priest approached her with the Eucharist, the blinding light felt as though it would sear the flesh from her bones. The pain became an intolerable wave, and she succumbed to its numbing paralysis, slipping into a terrible comalike state in which she was stingingly aware of everything around her, but completely and irrevocably powerless to react.

The priest reached out and touched her dry, scaling flesh. She tottered for an instant, then fell to the stone floor. Her coils remained stiff and tight in the grip of a rigor mortis–like power.

Moving to the altar, Father Mazzetti spoke again. "Lift the altar stone! Quickly now!"

"Father, what are you doing?" asked the Duke, as he moved with his son to fulfill the priest's request.

"Just do as I ask!" said Mazzetti, almost delirious over the show of power at his command.

Quickly, silently, Mauro and his father grasped the corners of the marble altar and heaved upward and away from the massive base. Lyrica lay frozen in constricted coils by their feet, watching and suddenly understanding what the priest intended. A shudder of abject horror rushed through her, and she wanted to scream, but no sound could ever come.

The two men eased the marble slab to the floor and looked up to face the priest.

"Take the beast and commend it herewith!" cried Mazzetti. He had a wild-eyed, prophet-in-the-desert look to his features. Mauro and the Duke moved rapidly, automatically. She could feel them as they hunched over, reaching out to wrap their fingers around her girth. The touch of their warm, soft flesh against her scaled coolness repulsed her, and a shudder passed through her. Unable to fight back against the blinding light of the Eucharist, she felt herself being lifted from the floor.

Up over the edge of the altar she was roughly carried. The droning Latin prayers of Mazzetti accompanied this, and despite her terror, she felt a spasm of utter hate wash through her. She vowed her vengeance against this old man who deceived her. She would punish him! He would regret his actions of this day!

Triptych di Amore

Now she was being dropped into the hollow center of the altar. Like a thick-walled casket vault, like a coffin, it accepted her with a dark, mute finality. She felt the cold stone against her flesh, colder even than the scales that protected her.

No! This could not be ... ! She fought against the paralysis which gripped, railed against the force of the Host, but her power was nothing compared to the awesome magic of the priest.

Looking up from her crypt, framed by its rectangular walls, she could see the streaming light of the Host still lacing her like a lethal radiation. She heard the grunting effort of the men as they lifted the capstone, an immense slab of white marble, and heaved it up to the edge of the altar.

"Enclose the beast called lamia!" cried out Mazzetti. "And the Lord shall entomb his Adversary forever!"

The sound of heavy stone, grinding, grating, sliding against heavier stone echoed through the hollow crypt of the altar. She cried out to them for mercy, but the sounds were only in her mind. She could do nothing but watch the rectangular slab slowly creep across the altar's topmost edges, sealing her within like a moldering corpse.

Except that there would be no moldering.

There would be no mindless, black oblivion here. No, she realized with a rising panic, with a thick column of terror rising up in her mind. Instead, she would be alive in this total darkness, in this state of eternal paralysis. She would be conscious of the nothingness that entombed her.

Forever.

The thought shot through her being with a searing, exquisitely painful reality.

No! The single word reverberated through her mind as she watched the last edge of light being constricted and finally pinched off as the slab slid into place. Stone met stone with a final resonant thud, leaving her in a place of total darkness, of a silence so deep and so profound that she felt she might go immediately mad. . . .

LOVE IN VEIN

Coda: Scarpino, Sicily 1944

The plane was a B-17, a bomber called the Flying Fortress. It had been coruscated by flak over Anzio and the navigator's instruments had been knocked out. The pilot, a twenty-six-year-old farmer's son from Kankakee, Illinois, named William Stoudt, had lost his bearings and was trying to pick up some landmarks by heading vaguely south from his target. He'd dropped his eggs just as some shrapnel ripped through his plane's underbelly, half-closing one of his bomb bay doors, and hanging up the last 500-pounder in his bomb-release rack.

As he struggled to get his crew home, they scurried about the tunnellike fuselage of the plane in a desperate effort to free the final bomb. Making a landing with 500 pounds of H.E. in your gut would be suicide and Captain Wild Bill Stoudt knew they were all doomed unless they could kick free of that fat boy with its tail fin hung up on the hinges of the bay door.

Waist gunner Sammy Sharpe from Brooklyn, New York, decided to be the hero. He unraveled his auxiliary parachute and tied his silks into the bulkhead. Always a daredevil, Sammy loved the challenge of dangling himself through the bomb bay 10,000 feet above the Sicilian mountainside. Inch by inch, he lowered himself down until his boot reached the jammed-up bay door and the twisted hinge. A good kick and one of two things would happen: the thin white metal of the bomb's fin would collapse and the payload would drop free, or it wouldn't and the bomb would probably detonate against the bay door.

Either way, the problem would be over.

Leather touched metal and Sammy Sharpe from East 24th Street (just up from Avenue R) smiled as he watched the last half-ton egg fade away. The B-17 had just passed over Palermo, so the bomb should land harmlessly in the mountains. Nothing down there for miles but a little village, and what were the odds . . . ?

Queen of
the Night

by
Gene Wolfe

"Queen of the Night," the ghouls called her, and, more frequently, "Her Highness."

Because they referred to meat in the state they preferred as "high," the usage had confused the boy when he was smaller. "Her Highness must see you." "Her Highness will never approve you." He had pictured one of them taller than any—although they were all tall—fragrant with decay, as they were.

He could not eat the putrid flesh they relished, as he and they had learned when he was still very small. For him, meat in summer could be not more than two days in the grave, and in the dry harsh heat at the end of August (when fevers raged and many were buried) even two days might be too long. Mostly he lived on food that the pious living offered to their dead: hot breads three times wrapped in clean cloths sewn with crosses and holy verses he could not read, and the boiled turnips and cabbages of the poor, these last wrapped once or twice or even five times in clean rags that were only rarely decorated with crude religious pictures executed in the red blood of beets.

He supplemented these foods with roots and stalks snatched from gardens by night, pears and cherries filched from orchards, and certain herbs and berries that he had discovered himself, though rarely with the fungi the ghouls enjoyed, which ofttimes made him ill.

"If Her Highness does not approve, will I die?" he asked Eeesheeea.

"She will approve."

"You may eat of me."

"Not dancing." Eeesheeea bowed her head and seemed a stone.

"I am too thin," the boy acknowledged. The stone did not reply.

They traveled; and no one, not even Beeetheeeor, could say when the queen would appear to judge him, or where. The spring floods brought low meat and easy, together with drowned cattle (which they disdained though the boy did not) and swine, which Neeeneeeaih claimed to relish.

Summer was the best time. Water from farms where all the living had died, they poured into healthful wells and even holy springs, although the latter was unlucky and rarely effective. So bold were they at times in summer that they were seen by moonlight, dancing as they feasted in clothing furnished by their meat: the dead wife's particolored kirtle (fouled now by groundwater and the ichors of decay) beneath her husband's rotted coat.

Autumn found them foolish and fond of jests, hiding in new-dug graves and violated mausoleums, and careless of the fading sun. It had been in autumn that they had found the boy, as Eeesheeea confided, feeding him as a prank, chortling when he vomited and leading him to waters that they hoped might hold the fever still. "When I'm bigger," he had boasted, "I'll be like you," but she had shaken her head.

Winter was the worst season, when the earth of even the freshest graves froze, and month-old meat wore flesh too hard to chew. The

Queen of the Night

boy had snared a hare, skinned it with his teeth, and was sucking the largest bone from a hind leg preparatory to cracking it. "Come with us," Beeetheeeor told him; and he did, flattered, walking alone (as it appeared) through the freezing winter night.

Beside the dark and half-ruinous church, the caretaker's cottage glowed with firelight; and candles stood guard at every window, save the shuttered window of the loft. "They sing," Eeesheeea hissed. Her ears were sharper even than the boy's. "Send back their song to them."

"I must hear it first," he told her, and cupped both ears.

> *The oracles are dumb,*
> *No voice or hideous hum*
> *Runs through the archèd roof in words deceiving:*
> *Apollo from his shrine*
> *Can no more divine*
> *With hollow shriek the steep of Delphos leaving.*
> *No trace or breathèd spell*
> *Inspires the pale-eyed priest from the prophetic cell.*

The boy grinned, and as the final note faded, replied:

> *The singers all are dumb,*
> *They voice their hideous hum*
> *Right through the windows wide themselves relieving,*
> *These puppies' worthless whine*
> *Can fright no folk of mine*
> *When o'er the haunted downs we come a-thieving,*
> *Our night-long dance and sprightly call*
> *Shall tire the pop-eyed beast from out the stall.*

Silence fell upon the cottage. Eeesheeea said, "That was better even than last time." And he, creeping closer to the caretaker's cottage, gloried in her praise.

At length a man's quavering voice ventured, "It's the Gray Neighbors in search of a steed."

A woman, "Isn't the White Lady curse enough?"

A boy, "Will they steal Maria?"

"The queen had been visiting them," Beeetheeeor explained. "That is why they have opened a grave for us."

Soon out came the caretaker, his wife, and their son, beating pans and calling out: *"No horse, no cow, no byre, no barn. But warn ye fair, 'twill soon be morn!"* Three times they marched sunwise around the cottage repeating this, their freezing breath a ghostly herald in the moonlight. Then the wife put a bowl of milk upon the step, with bread on one side and salt on the other. *"Bread for life and salt forever. These the bonds between us sever. Milk for mercy, milk for friend. Drink, and let thy mischief end!"*

The boy drank the milk greedily and ate the bread, too; but spit out the salt, angrily scattering it across the step. Then he climbed onto the roof, put his head down the chimney and howled like a wolf. When this evoked only a terrified silence, he peered over the edge of the roof, upside down into the loft through a chink in the shutter, where he saw a yellow-haired girl, much wasted, whose wide frightened eyes stared at nothing; his forefinger soon teased out the wooden bar, and he opened the shutter and swung inside to crouch next to her bed.

Slowly, she turned her head to look at him.

"Tell them iron will keep us out," he whispered, knowing it was what Beeetheeeor would want him to say. "Call to them."

The yellow-haired girl called, but her voice was without strength. When nobody came, the boy plucked an onion from a string of them hanging from the rafters and threw it down the ladder-hole into the fire, scattering sparks and embers over half the room, and hid under a heap of husks.

Soon the caretaker's wife mounted the ladder. "Maria," she inquired, "were the fairies up here?"

"One," the girl said. Her voice was less than the sigh of a leafless tree. The wife returned to the ladder-hole and called, "Johann, there was one up here troubling the child."

The caretaker, a spare man with a long sad face, climbed into the loft as well, with a tattered old black-letter Bible in one hand. "An ouph, Maria? With a red cap?"

The sick girl rolled her head across the pillow.

"With cobweb wings? An oak-man?"

She said nothing and stared at nothing, as before.

"Describe it."

"Here," the wife said, "I'll help her sit up."

"She'll be dead before the moon," muttered the boy to himself, peeping through the husks and noting how her bones poked the threadbare nightgown she wore. "And little enough for Eeesheeea."

"How looked it, child?" the caretaker asked. "Tell us."

"He. Thin. Dirty."

"Young, Maria? Was he young? Shivering?"

The sick girl nodded.

"A cauld lad." The caretaker shivered himself. "They start fires, they say. That must have been what he was trying to do. You have to leave them a warm coat to be rid of them."

"We've none to give," his wife protested.

"Iron," the sick girl whispered. "Iron will make him go."

Her father rubbed his chin. "It might. Iron charms them hence at childbirth, they say. Scissors open underneath the cradle."

When they had gone, the boy stood up. "That was kindly done," he told the sick girl. "We'll trouble you no more, I think." In the cottage below, he heard the clank of a pick-head against the blade of a spade. "I'll do you a favor, if I can."

"Go away," she told him.

"Sometimes I can grant three wishes," he said, and at the moment he almost believed it.

Her head rolled from side to side, as before. "The White Lady will come tonight, and I will die."

"Bar the window after I've left," he told her; but there was no indication that she had heard.

Outside, Reeezthorreee had taken the spade from the back door; Beeetheeeor was already at the reclosed grave, swinging the pick. "They dug this meat up again," Eeesheeea explained, "and broke the frost, though the ground is hard again at the top. They believed it was Her Highness."

Before long Beeetheeeor and Reeezthorreee cast aside the tools and dug with their claws as they always did, making the clods fly. There was no coffin, the boy saw when he peered into the grave, but a stake had been put through the meat to hold it.

"She comes," Eeesheeea whispered.

Until he heard the horses' hooves, the boy thought she meant only that Beeetheeeor was lifting the meat, as he was.

The clouds parted to show a black carriage racing across the plain, dropping from sight into a declivity, reappearing at the crest of the hill on the opposite side, and rattling across the Roman bridge over the frozen brook. "Her Highness will approve you this night," Eeesheeea assured him, her tone less confident than her words.

"Is that one of our carriages?" he inquired. She did not reply, and he ran to the road for a closer look.

When it drew up in front of the cottage, he saw that the coachman was one of the living, though he had never seen one with a face so savage or eyes so cruel. A groom scuttled off crablike to catch the boy by one arm. "Want him, ma'am? I got him for you!" Eeesheeea stood, and the groom hid behind his wild-eyed horses. A soft laugh came from the carriage.

"I'm all right," the boy told Eeesheeea. "I could've got away. You better eat before they finish it." Neeeneeeaih had emerged from a moon-shadow to join the feast.

"Her Highness has seen you," Eeesheeea told him. "I am here to speak for you."

The voice from the carriage murmured, "Come, my child. Let

me look more closely." He went to the window and peeped through it, but there was no one inside.

Eeesheeea said, "For seven summers he has been ours, Your Highness. We found and we claim him. If it please you, three more?"

Bright with lions, swords, and crested helms, the door of the carriage pushed the boy back.

In the moonlit silence that followed, he heard a shutter creak. The sick girl appeared at the window of the loft. A moment more, and she was crouching on the sill, then scrambling down the wall. Save that her eyes were open and staring, her expression was that of one who dreams, and would awaken if she could.

A slender figure in white stood beside the boy, without having come from anywhere. His first impression was of hair; it was black, and he had never seen a woman with so much, a somber aureole about her lined and bloodless face that stirred as if in a wind, though no wind blew.

Beeetheeeor, Reeezthorreee, and Neeeneeeaih were ranged behind Eeesheeea now. All knelt; seeing them, the boy knelt too. Eeesheeea raised her face and her hands, her eyes black with tears. "My head in surety for all he does. Have mercy on your slave, Your Highness! Just one summer more?"

The sick girl stood at his shoulder, swaying and trembling in her nightgown. Still on his knees, he put his arm about her waist and felt her febrile heat.

Coldly, the White Lady told Eeesheeea, "This is a child of the living, and already of age. It is time that he return to his own. I shall arrange it." Before she finished, the ghouls vanished as though they had never existed.

"Come with me freely," she said to the boy, "and I will show you wonders, man-child."

He looked about him. "Where's Eeesheeea?"

"Where she has always been."

He got to his feet. "This girl's ailing. I'd like to take her back inside."

"Their doors are barred," the White Lady told him, and her coachman laughed.

"Her mother and father will let her in if I knock."

"They sleep." The White Lady's face was as expressionless as a naked skull; the boy found himself wishing she would smile or frown—be impatient, prideful, or even angry.

"I'll pound on the door," he said. "I'll wake them up."

"Do."

He led the sick girl back to the cottage, asking whether she was all right, suggesting she might be cold, and at last pleading, "Won't you say something?"

Picking up the bowl that had held his milk, he rapped the door with it, and at once heard the rattle of the bar. "See," he told the sick girl, "they hadn't gone to sleep yet. You go back to bed and stay there."

The door opened, and the White Lady held the bar. She motioned to the sick girl, who went in and climbed the ladder to the loft.

"You're making her ill, aren't you?" the boy asked.

"I am breaking her bonds, one by one."

"Do you still want me to come with you? Promise you'll let her alone, and I will."

"For one year."

"Forever!" It seemed to the boy that they must surely wake the caretaker and his wife, but no one stirred.

"How long did you live among the ghouls?"

"We call them the People." He was sick with fear, but fought it with boyish stubbornness.

"How long?"

"I don't know. You heard what Eeesheeea said."

"How long? The truth."

"Nine years, I think."

The White Lady nodded slowly. "Go back to my coach. Get in."

The walk from the carriage to the cottage had been short; the walk from the cottage to the carriage seemed long indeed. The boy wanted to run, to hide among gravestones as he had so often, in so many such churchyards. He was free, he knew, and could do so if he chose; he knew, also, what the White Lady would do if he did.

The carriage door stood open; the coachman and the little, twisted groom watched him, grinning, as he put his bare foot on the iron step, stepped up, then stepped up again and into the coach.

It rocked ever so slightly on its leather springs, and the door swung shut and latched itself. Through the open window, he noted the earth Beeetheeeor and Reeezthorreee had scattered, black in the moonlight; the pick, the spade, and the stake that they had cast aside, and a few bones. *From the meat*, he told himself—but something in him turned it to *from the dead woman*. He was one of the living now, as she had been.

The coachman's whip cracked. The coach creaked and jolted into motion. He had never ridden in a coach before and, boylike, delighted in it, exhilarated by the novelty of effortless speed. There was a rug on the backward-facing seat opposite him; he unfolded it and covered himself with it as he sometimes had with stolen altar cloths, tucking it about him and telling himself that he must accustom himself to such comforts now, as befitted the living. He would wash when the ice broke, get a house of his own by whatever means houses were obtained.

As the carriage rattled across the Roman bridge, he grew conscious of something cold pressing against his right side. His fingers found nothing there, but the pressure continued, and even increased. Feeling again, he discovered that his ragged trousers had parted from waistband to knee.

"I am here," the White Lady said.

"I can't see you," he told her. Only silence answered. He tried to push her fingers away, but there were no fingers. "Don't do that," he said.

"Don't do that," she mocked him.

The rug slid from his lap to the floor.

"Freely," she said, "freely." And then, "You will never know another like me."

"I don't want to," he told her; and yet, he did.

"Kiss me." Hair and chill flesh moulded themselves upon his face. He kissed her, and from somewhere near the dark and swaying ceiling she laughed.

"You're cold."

"You are not. Lie down on the seat. I want to show you something."

Reluctantly he did so, and she loved and bit as though her teeth were within her loins.

"You see? You are a man."

"No." He shook his head. "No." He sat up again, and for a long while sat with his face in his hands. He was naked, though he could not remember how he had come to be, or what had become of his clothes.

After a time he covered his shame with the rug, and after a time still longer, began to enjoy the ride again. It seemed their horses could never tire, but galloped on forever through a night no sun would end. Looking out of the windows, he saw a dark castle upon a darker crag and pretended that he was its owner, a great lord—with a white charger—with medals on his chest—with a sword and a fur cloak. His wife would ride in a carriage like this, and he, swifter than the wind, would gallop before her to see that every lamp and cresset blazed, and that the servants had begun their dinner.

"Have you recovered?" the White Lady inquired. "You are young and should recover quickly."

When he looked at the window on her side of the coach, he could see her in the corner very faintly, as a traveler among mountains sees, and then does not see, a face in the profile of a cliff, or a silent traveler like himself in a standing stone. When he tried to look at her directly, she vanished, becoming a glimmer of moonlight on the leather seat. "Please don't," he said. "I don't want to. I want to go back to Eeesheeea."

Queen of the Night

She laughed—or perhaps it was only the tinkling of a bell on the neck of one of the sheep on the hill below the crag. "You shall. Eventually."

He would have opened the carriage door and thrown himself out, but the door would not open. He dived through the window instead.

And found himself in a deep, soft bed, with sheets and blankets and a puffy comforter over him. Each bedpost was a black candle, and all four candles were lit, sending up smoky flames as long as his forearm, about which the bats clinging to the arched vault above stirred and chittered in complaint. Something cold lay beside him, and for hours he dared not look.

"You were fatigued. I let you rest. Let us see if you are well rested."

He felt her fingers and smiled despite himself, trembling.

"Perhaps you would like food? I would."

"No," he said; and she kissed him on the lips, covering his eyes with her hand.

"Am I so cold? Do I seem a dead thing?" She warmed him between her thighs.

"No," he said again.

She laughed with delight, her laughter like church bells far away. "Nor am I. Do you recall what I taught you in the carriage? Here I lie. It is your turn."

He pressed himself to the face he could scarcely see, and she licked, and tore him with her teeth until her pillow was wet everywhere with his blood. It frightened and sickened him, and yet there was something beyond them both that shone like a gem, turning and beckoning to him—something he seemed about to grasp at each moment.

"These are the pleasures of Hell, you see, man-child. In Hell they are not punished by pain alone, because pain alone can never be punishment enough. Now do as I taught, and show me that you still live, and I as well." Her hands upon his hips directed his motions, and with each she grew more real, a living woman whose naked body rose from the blood-soaked sheet, bright as morning and white as alabaster. "For the blood is the life," she said.

He slept, and woke alone.

For days, it seemed, he lay dreaming. That he was in the castle on the crag, he knew. There were windows in every wall of the great domed bedchamber—a tower room, then, high above all the rest. So would he have chosen, he decided, could he choose. Black velvet drapes streaked with cobwebs closed each window; and though at times those drapes were drawn back so that he looked down upon the cottages of their peasants or out upon the sea, or up into that endless night through which the queen's carriage, somewhere, still thundered past stars white with anger or red with guilt, always he woke at last and found himself still in the great bed, with candles burning silently at its corners and never burning down, and the soft, stirring tester of bats overhead, bats who sometimes left their places to flutter aimlessly about the room or dart behind the drapes, never to be seen again.

By him, at least.

The White Lady returned, carrying a child of three, a girl with terrified eyes whose tears and struggles the long road had exhausted. The White Lady's countenance was smooth and glowed with health; her red lips smiled as a cat smiles, displaying sharply pointed white teeth. "Do you like me better thus, man-child? Have I not become beautiful for you?"

He nodded, unable to speak or to tear his eyes from her.

"You are not afraid?" She dropped the little girl on a chair, like a parcel.

"Please. Please hurry." He sat up, not bothering to conceal his nakedness.

"You will die. You have rested less than you imagine." Her hands were behind her, loosing her dress. "You have one more in you, possibly. Then death." The dress fell at her feet.

It seemed to the boy that his pounding heart would break his ribs.

Queen of the Night

"Look upon me, man-child." For a few seconds that seemed eternity to him, her camisole wrapped her marvelous, living hair like a turban. Raising her arms, she pirouetted before him. "I was old when first you met me, but I am young as you, now. Younger, with your youth."

Her body was above perfection, filling him with a hunger that consumed him until it could consume her. He sprang from the bed and rushed upon her.

Like mist she vanished. With her, the captured girl, the great bed with its flickering candles, and the vast bedchamber itself. Briefly he knew snow, and daylight beneath a low gray sky.

When he woke again, it was in a hard, narrow bed with one side against a rough plastered wall. He moaned and closed his eyes and sought to dream again, because it had been of her.

"You can't stay here," Johann the caretaker said when he was able to sit up and drink broth. "Don't you remember your own name?"

"I'm called 'the boy,'" the boy said. It was the name Eeesheeea had given him.

"I call him Jon," said fat Anna the caretaker's wife. It had been the name of their first child, born when she and the caretaker had been married less than a year.

"When will I get my bed back?" Robert the caretaker's son demanded.

"Tonight. He can sleep in front of the fire tonight, and tomorrow he'll have to go."

"Where?" the boy asked.

"Anywhere you want, as long as it isn't here." Johann the caretaker was silent a moment, rubbing his chin. "Go into the village. You must've come from there, and dozens of people are sure to know you."

The boy said, "I did?" though he wanted to say I did not.

"Certainly. You must've walked out here last night, the good God knows why, and fallen among the body snatchers. They hit you on the head and knocked the sense out of it, and stole your clothes."

Faintly—very faintly in the distance—the boy heard the jingle of harness and the rattle of the coach. "It snowed, didn't it?" he said. He was scarcely conscious that he spoke aloud. "That's why I can't hear the horses' hooves."

Anna the caretaker's wife went to the window. "Johann! It's the carriage from the schloss."

Her husband went out into the snow with his hat in his hand.

Sitting at the scarred but sturdy old table, propped on his elbows drinking soup, the boy heard a rough, sneering voice from beyond the front door of the cottage, and knew it for the coachman's, though he had never heard the coachman speak. The carriage, he promised himself, had come with a fur robe for him and a basket of hot food, pheasants and partridges (birds that he had snared for himself when he could) tucked beneath a clean white cloth. The carriage would carry him to the castle, where she would be waiting. They would kiss, tenderly at first.

The coachman's whip cracked, the harness creaked, and the wheels squeaked as the carriage lumbered away. Johann the caretaker opened the door again, stamped snow from his boots, and stepped inside.

"What is it?" his wife wanted to know.

"They—he . . . "

"Is it bad news?"

There came the softest of creakings from the loft; and the boy knew that Maria, the sick girl, had come to the ladder-hole to listen.

"I don't know." Johann the caretaker sat down, his hat still in his hand. "Perhaps it is. Perhaps not."

"Tell us!"

"He asked if we had anyone staying with us. I said only— only—"

"Jon."

"Only a lost boy I found in the snow."

Queen of the Night

No more broth could be got from the bowl with the spoon, and the boy did not like spoons anyway; he lifted the bowl to his lips and drank the last drops.

"And he—the coachman. There was no one in the coach."

"What did he say, Johann?"

"He said we were to keep him. Keep Jon."

Robert the caretaker's son asked, "Until summer?"

"Not until anything," his father told him. "Until he is a man, or until we are told something else to do with him."

He turned to the boy. "You will call me Master Caretaker, Jon. Is that understood? Otherwise there will be trouble."

Putting down the empty bowl, the boy nodded. "Yes, Master Caretaker. That is understood. There will be no trouble."

"And you will call my wife Madame Caretaker. Our son is Robert. Our daughter is Maria."

So it was settled. The boy called the caretaker's wife "Madame Caretaker" in the presence of her husband and children, and "Mama" when they were alone. The wounds he had suffered (from wild animals during the night, Mama said when she treated them) healed at last, although each left a black scar.

Spring came, and people talked of flooding on the river; the brook under the Roman bridge rose until it flowed across the roadway. With axe and pole, Johann the caretaker and the boy cleared the brush and uprooted trees that sought to dam it there, finding among them the corpse of a girl for whom they dug a shallow grave in the worst corner of the churchyard that kept filling with water.

Summer followed, decked with apple blossoms and loud with bees. Maria grew so strong that she left the loft to play in the sunlight, smiling at the boy with blue eyes that said, I know. He smiled back, and his eyes said, I know you do. But now and again, when the sun was setting and bats set out from the ruined mausoleum in the middle of the churchyard, the boy heard his own voice saying: "*Nine years, I think.*"

And the White Lady, Her Highness the Queen of the Night: *"Go back to my coach. Get in."*

She'll come for Maria, he told himself, and I'll be here waiting for her. Or, she'll come for Maria, and I'll run—help with a barge on the river, join the crew of a ship when the river reaches the sea, and go to Amerika.

Once he dreamt that he rose from his pallet by the hearth, and opening the shutter saw Eeesheeea, Beeetheeeor, and others dancing in the churchyard. Eeesheeea saw him at the window and waved to him; and though he could not quite make out her face, he knew that she smiled. Waking, he wept. But in time he came to understand that not all that is seen waking is real, nor is all that is seen in sleep false. Although he tried over and over to summon that dream again, it never recurred.

One afternoon at the end of summer, when the apples were ripe and the sheep on the downs were knitting themselves new coats, Johann the caretaker sat sighing on the doorstep, with the boy (who had helped him dig three graves that day, for the fever had waked) beside him.

"Jon," said Johann, "you're rich. You think you're poor, I suppose. It's very likely. You'd say you've got nothing. But you've got youth, which is the second greatest treasure in the world. And you've innocence. For a few years more you'll have that, and it's the greatest of all. A poor man can get rich. A rich man who's lost his money may get rich again, that happens, too. But when childhood's past, life's greatest treasure is gone forever. Nothing can replace it, Jon, or even reconcile you to its loss. There's no return to innocence, and beyond youth nothing but sorrow."

"Yes, Master Caretaker," Jon said. "I know. I know."

The Marriage

by
Steve Rasnic Tem and Melanie Tem

He had chosen her as his mate because of her ability to renew her emotions again and again, however thoroughly he might deplete her. Even after long periods of hysterical grieving, she would come to him and he would be surprised by her ability to smile, to love, to rage, and to endure serious pain. From the start he had known, of course, that it could not continue forever, for she, like all the others, was mortal, and sooner or later would die. He had thought that most likely he would kill her with his need, all the more ferocious because it would not be satisfied, and then he would be forced to find someone else or to content himself entirely with strangers.

Not that the variously flavored emotions of strangers lacked attraction, not that the surge and substance of their bodies were any less sweet, but even he liked someone familiar to come home to.

She knew, of course, of his predilections, what he did with his days and most of his nights. Sometimes she would request a particular detail, worrying the painful morsel in order to expand her passion in interesting ways.

"We all need our daily tickle and rub," the guy next door was fond of declaring coarsely. He wouldn't have been so cheerful about it if he'd known about certain late-night and midafternoon visits to his sad-looking wife and his brittle but equally sad-looking daughters.

Not that *he* had been the cause of any of this sadness. The neighbor himself, with his anger and his appetites, was sufficient cause for any degree of sadness. He had only found the well and chosen to drink there. Taken a taste of the family's miseries by way of blood and vaginal secretions. And—when he finally got to the paternal source—by way of semen.

But the passions of that particular family, the passions of all the mundane sorts he met, sorted through, and tasted each day, paled in comparison with those of his wife. For this part of his life, for the last eighty-four human years, she was by far the most intense person he had met.

Just now, on her deathbed, she was in considerable pain, and her pain was his for the taking. Nearing a hundred in human years, her body was frail, the pain very close to both the surface of the flesh and the marrow of the bone, and he could have sucked it out of her with scarcely any effort, relieving both her and himself in a single easy act.

Instead, he lingered. He teased. He kissed her gently, his lips and teeth closed, all over her aged body, while she moaned and writhed under him in the titillated passion of her suffering. He bared his penis, entered her dry vagina, and probed, curious whether he could increase either her agony or his arousal, seeing that he could. She cried out, begged him. He waited as long as he thought he dared, then drew the pain out of her and into him in one swift current.

She was spent, crumpled against him like a used paper sack. He was, as always, disappointed. He should have waited longer. She could have held more suffering for him. She could have given him more.

The Marriage

So he left her, though she tried feebly to hold him back, and in a bar full of dark music and dim light although it was midafternoon he came, without warning or foreplay, upon a woman who almost at once asked him to tell her he loved her. Readily he took her away from the eyes of that place, out onto hot asphalt and into heady automotive perfumes, where he professed his love for her with perfect, borrowed sincerity. She nodded, licked her lips. "Bite me," he whispered. "No, there." He experienced only a distant discomfort, no true pain, as the tiny mouth-shaped ovals of skin disappeared from his arm.

"Now, my turn," she insisted, too eagerly. She did not care that he had not received pleasure. She did not feel for him.

So he took too much from her too quickly, gorged himself on the pain he had spared her, a mercy which she did not deserve. "Love me," he urged, and shook her. But by now she could feel no more than he could, so he left her in the parking lot and went back home.

Tonight his wife was afraid of dying. She was not always so. Sometimes she approached death with a giddy sort of readiness that he found insubstantial, difficult to hold on to, and utterly unsatisfying, like spun sugar. At other times she seemed not to be aware at all that the end of her life was near.

But tonight she was profoundly frightened, and fear was among the sensations he savored most. He surrounded her with arms and legs, tongue and teeth, anxious for the fullness of her fear to descend upon them both, and when it would not come fast enough he found himself nibbling at her dry skin, licking every orifice for any available secretion. She'd been incontinent for years, and to allay any suspicions he had accepted the doctors' prescriptions for catheters and adult diapers, but of course he would never apply such ugly contraptions to her flesh, insisting instead to clean her in his own way, and to keep her clean with his appetites, several times each day.

Tonight he lay in their marriage bed with her in his arms, waiting for her fear to ripen, and he reflected that, although it went without saying that he did not love her, he would indeed be sorry when she was gone.

Which was not to say that she was or ever had been enough for him. Nothing was ever enough, no one could keep him full. Strangers had provided him with some memorable experiences, however. Vivid enough that even in his long life they might make an impression he could dessert on. Just last week, was it, or last month:

"You don't have to tell me you love me," the man with the crooked teeth had assured him magnanimously.

"Maybe I will anyway," he'd said with a borrowed feminine smile.

"You will," the man had agreed, stroking his woman's cheek, gliding a hand down under the lacy collar and pulling away the blouse, unhooking the satiny brassiere to expose his woman's nipples.

He'd wrapped his female arms around the man, who had assumed, no doubt, that the scratches in his back were being made by long scarlet fingernails mining for passion when in fact the fingertips themselves were sharpening and lengthening as his famished body and soul realized the imminence of a meal. "Love me," he'd begged the man in his breathy female voice, with his woman's shortness of breath, and pushed himself into him until skin interpenetrated. Disoriented by his own paltry lust, the man had perhaps thought this some strange undergarment when actually it was a thin layer of his own skin peeling away. The man kissed, sucked, thrust, struggling to remove all real and imagined barriers between him and the object of his desire, all the while causing himself to bleed. Ultimately, it was pain which made the man's erection rise, fear that thrust itself past his labia, lubricated by the man's free-flowing blood as they writhed together. The man's passionate desperation probed and scraped until tidal spasms of horror washed both their minds clean, so that they could feel nothing, for once again he had taken and used it all.

But he always came back to her, and she was always waiting for him, welcoming. Willing, eager, often frantic for him to siphon off the emotions that were too much for her and never enough for him.

The Marriage

"Hold me," she pleaded now. Thinned and cracked with age, it was still the importuning and caressing voice that he had been hearing for what now seemed like such a long time but would reveal itself, once she had died, as only the most fleeting instant of his interminable existence. "Take it. Take the fear. Death is a natural part of life. Everybody dies. Everybody has always died. I don't want to be afraid."

Through her toothless kiss she spat in a hot stream into his throat the acrid roiling broth of her terror. Though she was more than willing, and he was expert, and their give-and-take had been the core of their marriage for more than eight decades, it took a deliciously long time for him to get it all. By the time they had both achieved a transitory calm, he was already not thinking much of her anymore but of his next foray.

Rather recently he'd discovered the accessible pleasures of hospital emergency rooms. Even the most commonplace passions were magnified within familes, and in an emergency room a family was opened and left bleeding, especially when one of its children was hurt or ill, dead or nearly so. He would go again tonight, when his wife was asleep. He could tell by the way she breathed against his shoulder that she was nearly asleep now, and his mouth began to water in anticipation of what this night was likely to bring.

"Noooo!" The mother wailed her denial. That sort of hysteria was filling, to be sure, but hard on the finer nerves if taken by mouth, so he'd developed a method of taking it in through the nostrils. He'd dallied pleasantly with images to describe the particular odor of frenzied despair: Vaguely, it smelled like a child's soiled shirt, and also like the kind of sunlight that can be trapped only in a child's hair.

He'd seen the teenage daughter, the older sister, hovering around the edges of the knot made by the rest of the family. She obviously wanted to be part of the high drama of grief, but—so typical of her age—could not quite permit herself to join them. Her grief was tinged with embarrassment at her mother's noise, with resentment over having lost the center of attention, with fear that her father might grieve himself insane.

Eventually the daughter detached herself from the palsied fist of pain which the other brother, sister, father, mother had become, and sought out a quiet dark corner. Where he waited, had been waiting for more than an hour.

"Everybody's dying," she said softly to the wall, as though she knew he was there. Her tongue played with sadness as though it were prey, a mouse that might escape the damp chamber of her mouth. Inhaling deeply, he immediately knew that her vagina was moist, and he stepped into her smell. He then allowed her to smell him. He heard her pulse quicken. He felt his spirit soar, then, and change.

Via his own and her desire and shadow and lament, he willed buttons and fasteners to fade, fabric and elastic to dissolve. As he pressed against her he momentarily permitted her to see him, encouraged her youthful fantasies and her senses engorged by shock to create the bare-skinned youth of him, the long and impossibly thick black hair that became a creature all its own, and the dark penis down there in the shadows, because she wanted only a glimpse.

At that moment she began to weep, not so much a child's cry as the cry of a child departing, and the depth of it actually surprised him, made him gasp. He was quickly engulfed in this young woman's exploding emotions, gliding into the turmoil of her, feeling himself alive in the orgiastic brevity of his taking, taking, until she was irrevocably emptied and he, however fleetingly, was filled.

When he returned to their marriage bed he found his wife still asleep. Comatose. Her withered face looked blank, stripped. Perhaps she was dead. He held his breath to listen for hers. He peered at her, laid his ear against her hollow chest. She was not dead.

He slid his arm from under her shoulders and crept out of their room, out of their house. He would leave her for a while, and then he would return to take whatever else she had for him in the last hours of her life.

The Marriage

This time in another emergency room he waited afterwards, and was gratified that he had thought to do so. Numbly, this other teenaged girl rejoined her family, her body spent, her eyes glazed. They would think perhaps that sorrow had overtaken her, and after a few hours there would be speculation that drugs were the cause, and the passions so exhibited would have been as nectar to him, and only after days or months had passed would they suspect that something was dangerously amiss. That she had given away her ability to feel.

The parents' despair would then be doubled. They would brood over how they had considered the adolescent daughter selfish. They would berate themselves for not understanding how desperately attached she'd been to her little brother, how fervently attached she was to them. They would try their best to reach her, then, but she would be beyond them.

At still another emergency room vigil it was the father he determined to stalk and court. The father welcomed him, grasped him in a savage embrace, wanted to kill him. The father's rage was a sweet surprise that lasted well into the morning hours, and so he was late getting home.

This time his wife did not respond to him at all when, already wincing from the pangs which he had learned to term "hunger," he presented himself at her bedside. Her eyes, nostrils, mouth gaped, but it was obvious that she neither saw, smelled, nor tasted him. Her fingers clawed, but she was not touching him.

He knew her, though. She was his mate, his wife, his companion for this stretch of his endless life. Since she'd been a headstrong beauty of fifteen, renowned for her intensity and reputed to be untamable, she had belonged to him. She had loved him beyond all others. She had given him everything she had, countless times, and replenished herself in order to give him more. She would not fail him now. He knew how to take what was his.

He pulled her to him. Her body and mind were flaccid, but she was not dead, for he could feel her heartbeat and her faint rattling breath. He kissed her, bit into her, but she gave him nothing.

He entered her. At the surface and for many layers under the surface there was nothing—no fear, no pain, no passion, no love for him.

Trembling with hunger and with the anticipation of an even greater hunger—starvation, famine—to come, he thrust deeper into her with nails and teeth and penis. So deep, distant and all but closed to him, was *something*. Joy, he thought. Profound peace. But he could not reach it.

She died in his arms. Reluctant to let her go, he lay there for a few minutes with the emptied body. "More," he pleaded. He stroked the creviced face. "I am not finished with you. I have not had enough. I need more." He lifted her in his arms and shook her. Her head lolled back across his forearm but her throat was motionless, did not pulse. Her lips hung slack but did not part for him. She had given him all she had, and it was not nearly sufficient.

Eventually he sighed and rose. Wearily he prepared himself to go out again, wondering whether he would find another mate as good for him as she had been. As he shut and locked the door of their home behind him, it came to him that he had loved her. He was shocked and—for a few, brief astonishing moments—full.

In
This Soul of
a Woman

by
Charles de Lint

—◆—

If I were a man, I can't imagine it would have turned out this way. I will say no more except what I have in my mind and that is that you will find the spirit of Caesar in this soul of a woman.

—from the letters of Artemisia Gentileschi
(1593–c. 1652)

1

—⁓—

"**E**ddie wants to see you."

"What's he want?" Nita asked. "Another blowjob?"

"Probably. I think he's tired of the new girl."

"Well, fuck Eddie. And fuck you, too."

"Christ, Nita. You on the rag or what? I'm just passing along a message."

Nita didn't turn to look at Jennifer. She stared instead at her reflection in the mirror, trying to find even one familiar feature under the makeup. Even her eyes were wrong, surrounded by a thick crust of black eye shadow, the irises hidden behind tinted red contacts. From beyond the dressing room came the thumping bass line of whatever David Lee Roth song Candy used in her act. That meant she had ten minutes before she was up again. Lilith, Mistress of the Night. Black leather and lace over Gothic-pale skin, the only spots of colour being the red of her eyes, her lips, and the lining of her cape. Nita's gaze dropped from her reflection to the nine-foot-long whip that lay coiled like a snake on the table in front of her.

"Fuck this," she said.

The dressing room smelled of cigarettes and beer and cheap perfume, which just about summed up her life. She swept her arm across the top of the table and sent everything flying. Whip and makeup containers. A glass, half-full of whiskey. Cigarettes, lighter, and the ashtray with butts spilling out of it. A small bottle filled with uppers. The crash of breaking glass was loud in the confined quarters of the dressing room.

Jennifer shook her head. "I'm not cleaning that shit up," she said.

Nita looked up from the mess she'd made. The rush of utter freedom she'd felt clearing the tabletop had vanished almost as quickly as it had come.

"So who asked you to?" she asked.

Jennifer pulled a chair over from one of the other tables and sat down beside her. "You want to talk about it?"

Nita bit back a sharp retort. Jennifer wasn't her friend—she didn't have any friends—but unlike 99.9 percent of the world, Jennifer had always treated her decently. Nita looked away, wishing she hadn't sent her shot of whiskey flying off the table with everything else.

"Last time I was up, my ex's old man was in the audience," she said.

"So?"

"So the only way I could keep my visitation rights with Amanda was by promising I'd get a straight job."

Jennifer nodded, understanding. "The old bad influence line."

"Like she's old enough to know or even care what her old lady does for a living." Nita was really missing that drink now. "It's so fucking unfair. I mean, it's okay for this freak to come into a strip joint with his buddies and have himself a good time, but my working here's the bad influence. Like we even want to be here."

"I don't mind that much," Jennifer said. "It beats hooking."

"You know what I mean. He's going to run straight to a judge and have them pull my visiting rights."

"That sucks," Jennifer agreed. She leaned forward and gave Nita a quick hug. "But you gotta hang in there, Nita. At least we've got jobs."

"I know."

"And you'd better go see Eddie or maybe you won't even have that."

Nita shook her head. "I can't do it. I can't even go out on the stage again tonight."

"But . . . " Jennifer began, then she sighed. "Never mind. We'll figure out a way to cover for you."

"And Eddie?"

Jennifer stood up and tugged down on the hem of her miniskirt. "That's one you're going to owe me, girl."

2

—⚬—

When Nita stepped out the back door of Chic Cheeks in her street clothes, all that remained of her stage persona was the shock of jet black hair that fell halfway down her back in a cascade of natural curls. She was wearing faded blue jeans that were tucked into cowboy boots. The jeans had a hole in the left knee through which showed the black fabric of her body stocking. On top of it was a checked flannel shirt, buttoned halfway up, the tails hanging loose. Her purse was a small khaki knapsack that she'd picked up at the Army Surplus over on Yoors Street. Her stage makeup was washed off except for a hint of eyeshadow and a dab of lipstick.

She knew she looked about as different from Lilith in her

leathers and lace as could be imagined, so Nita was surprised to be recognized when she stepped out into the alleyway behind the club.

"Lilith?"

Nita paused to light a cigarette, studying the woman through a wreath of blue-grey smoke. The stranger was dressed the way Nita knew the club's customers imagined the dancers dressed offstage: short, spike-heeled boots; black stockings and miniskirt; a jean vest open enough to show more than a hint of a black lace bra. She wore less makeup than Nita had on at the moment, but then her fine-boned features didn't need it. Her hair was so blond it was almost white. It was cut punky and seemed to glow in the light cast from a nearby streetlamp.

"Who wants to know?" Nita finally asked.

"Does it matter?"

Nita shrugged and took another drag from her cigarette.

"I saw you dancing," the woman went on. "You're really something."

Now she got it. "Look," Nita said. "I don't date customers and—no offense—but I don't swing your way. You should go back inside and ask for Candy. She's always looking to make a little something on the side and I don't think she much cares what you've got between your legs, just so long as you can pay."

"I'm not looking for a hooker."

"So what are you looking for?"

"Someone to talk to. I recognized a kindred soul in you."

The way she said it made Nita sigh. She'd heard this about a hundred times before.

"Everybody thinks we're dancing just for them," she said, "but you know, we're not even thinking about you sitting out there. We're just trying to get through the night."

"So you don't feel a thing?"

"Okay, so maybe I get a little buzz from the attention, but it doesn't mean I want to fuck you."

"I told you. That's not what I'm looking for."

In This Soul of a Woman

"Yeah, yeah. I know." Nita ground her cigarette out under the heel of her boot. "You just want to talk. Well, you picked the wrong person. I'm not having a good night and, to tell you the truth, I'm not all that interesting anyway. All the guys figure women with my job are going to be special—you know, real exotic or something—but as soon as you go out on a date with somebody they figure out pretty quick that we're just as boring and fucked up as anybody else."

"But when you're on the stage," the woman said. "It's different then, isn't it? You feed on what they give you."

Nita gave her an odd look. "What're you getting at?"

"Why don't we go for a drink somewhere and talk about it?" the woman said. She looked around the alleyway. "There's got to be better places than this to have a conversation."

Nita hesitated for a moment, then shrugged. "Sure. Why not? It's not like I've got anything else to do. Where did you have in mind?"

"Why don't we simply walk until we happen upon a place that appeals to us?"

Nita lit another cigarette before she fell in step with the woman.

"My name's not Lilith," she said.

"I know." The woman stopped and turned to face her. "That's my grandmother's name."

Like people couldn't share the same name, Nita thought. Weird.

"She used to call me Imogen," the woman added.

She offered her hand, so Nita shook it and introduced herself. Imogen's grip was strong, her skin surprisingly cool and smooth to the touch. Shaking hands with her was like holding onto a hand made of porcelain. Imogen switched her grip on Nita's hand, shifting from her right to her left, and set off down the alleyway again. Nita started to pull free, but then decided she liked the feel of that smooth cool skin against her own and let it slide.

"What does 'Nita' mean?" Imogen asked.

"I don't know. Who says it's supposed to mean anything?"

"All names mean something."

"So what does your name mean?"

"'Granddaughter.'"

Nita laughed.

"What do you find so humourous?"

Nita flicked her cigarette against the nearest wall which it struck in a shower of sparks. "Sounds to me like your grandmother just found a fancy way of not giving you a name."

"Perhaps she had to," Imogen said. "After all, names have power."

"Now what's that supposed to mean?" Nita asked.

Imogen didn't answer. She came to an abrupt halt and then Nita saw what had distracted her. They'd been walking towards the far entrance of the alley and were now only a half-dozen yards from its mouth. Just ahead lay the bright lights of Palm Street. Unfortunately, blocking their way were three men. Two Anglos and a Hispanic. Not yet falling drunk, but well on the way. Palm Street was as busy as ever but Nita knew that in this part of the city, at this time of night, she and Imogen might as well have been on the other side of the world for all the help they could expect to get from the steady stream of pedestrians walking by the mouth of the alley.

"Mmm-mmm. Looking good," one of the three men said.

"But the thing is," added one of his companions, "I've just got to know. When you're fucking, which one's pretending to be the guy?"

Drunken laughter erupted from all three of them.

Imogen let go of Nita's hand. She was probably scared, Nita thought. Nita didn't blame her. She'd be scared herself if it wasn't for the fact that she'd come to a point in her life where she just didn't give a shit anymore. Reaching into one of the front pockets of her jeans, she pulled out a switchblade. When she thumbed the button on the side of the handle, it opened with an evil-sounding *snick*.

"Oh, *conchita*," the Hispanic said, shaking his head in mock sorrow. "We were just going to have some fun with you, but now there's got to be some pain."

In This Soul of a Woman

He stepped forward, the Anglos flanking him, one on either side. Before Nita could decide which of them was going to get the knife, Imogen moved to meet them. What happened next didn't seem to make any sense at all. It looked to Nita that Imogen picked up the first by his face, thumb on one temple, fingers on the other, and simply pitched him over her shoulder, back behind them, deeper into the alley. The second she took out with a blow to the throat that dropped him on the spot. The third tried to bolt, but she grabbed his arm and wrenched it up behind his back until Nita heard the bone snap. He was still screaming from the pain when Imogen grabbed his head and snapped his neck with a sudden twist.

Imogen held the dead man for a long moment, staring into his face as though she wanted to memorize his features, then she let him fall to the pavement. Nita stared at the body, at the way it lay so still on the ground in front of them. Her gaze went to the other two assailants. They lay just as unmoving. One moment there had been three half-drunk men about to assault them and in the next they were all dead.

"What—" Nita had to clear her throat. "What the fuck did you do to them?"

Imogen didn't even seem to be breathing hard. "It's a . . . a kind of judo," she said.

Nita looked at her companion, but it was hard to make out her features in the poor light. She seemed to be smiling, her teeth flashing as white as did her hair. Nita slowly closed up her knife and stowed it back in her jeans.

"Judo," Nita repeated slowly.

Imogen nodded. "Come on," she said, offering Nita her hand again.

Nita hesitated. She lit a cigarette with trembling fingers and took a long drag before she eased her way around the dead man at her feet to take Imogen's hand. The porcelain coolness calmed her, quieting the rapid drum of her pulse.

"Let's get that drink," Imogen said.

"Yeah," Nita said. "I think I could really use a shot right about now."

3

They ended up in Fajita Joe's, a Mexican bar on Palm Street with a terrace overlooking Fitzhenry Park. The place catered primarily to yuppies and normally Nita wouldn't have been caught dead in it, but by the time they were walking by its front door she would have gone in anywhere just to get a drink to steady her jangled nerves. They took a table on the terrace at Imogen's insistence—"I like to feel the night air," she explained. Nita gulped her first shot and immediately ordered a second whiskey, double, on the rocks. With another cigarette lit and the whiskey to sip, she finally started to relax.

"So tell me about yourself," Imogen said.

Nita shook her head. "There's nothing to tell. I'm just a loser—same as you've got to be if the only way you can find someone to have a drink with you is by hanging out around back of places like Chic Cheeks." Then she thought of the three men in the alley. "'Course, the way you took out those freaks ... those moves weren't the moves of any loser."

"Forget about them," Imogen said. "Tell me why you're so sad."

Nita shook her head. "I'm not sad," she said, lighting up another cigarette. "I'm just fucked up. The only thing I'm good at is running away. When the going gets tough, I'm gone. My whole life, that's the way I deal with the shit."

"And the dancing doesn't help?"

"Give me a break. That's not dancing—it's shaking your ass in a

250

meat market. Maybe some of the girls've convinced themselves they're in show business, but I'm not that far out of touch with reality."

"But you still get something from it, don't you?"

Nita butted out her cigarette. "I'll tell you the truth, I always wanted to be up on a stage, but I can't sing and I can't play a guitar and the only way I can dance is doing a bump 'n' grind. When you've got no talent, your options get limited real fast."

"Everyone has a talent."

"Yeah, well, mine's for fucking up. I work with women who are dancing to put themselves through college, single mothers who're feeding their families, a writer who's supporting herself until she can sell her first book. The only reason I'm dancing is that I couldn't make that kind of money doing anything else except hooking and I'm not that hard up yet."

"Perhaps you've set your sights too high," Imogen said. "It's hard to attain goals when they seem utterly beyond your reach. You might consider concentrating on smaller successes and then work your way up from them."

"Yeah? Like what?"

Imogen shrugged. "Breathing's a talent."

"Oh, right. And so's waking up in the morning."

"Feel this," Imogen said.

She caught Nita's wrist and started to bring it towards her chest.

"Hey!" Nita said, embarrassed. "I told you I'm not like that."

She was sure everybody on the terrace was staring at them, but when she tried to pull free, she couldn't move her hand. She might as well have been trying to move the building under them. Imogen brought Nita's palm through the open front of her jean vest and laid it against the cool smooth skin between her breasts. In the light cast from the terrace lanterns, her eyes gleamed like a cat's caught in a car's headlights.

"What do you feel?" Imogen asked.

"Look, why don't you . . . "

Just get out of my face, was what Nita was going to say, except as her palm remained on Imogen's skin, she suddenly realized—

"You . . . you're not breathing," she said.

Imogen released Nita's wrist. Nita rubbed at the welt that the grip of Imogen's fingers had left on her skin.

"I'm sorry," Imogen said. "I didn't mean to hurt you."

"How can you not breathe?"

Imogen smiled. "It's a talent I don't have," she said.

This was seriously strange, Nita thought. She was way, way out of her depth.

"So," she began. She had to stop to clear her throat. Her mouth felt as though it was coated with dry dust. She took a gulp of whiskey and fumbled another cigarette out of her package. "So what are you?" she finally managed.

Imogen shrugged. "Immortal. Undead."

That moment in the alley flashed in Nita's mind. The three men, dispatched so quickly and Imogen not even out of breath. The viselike strength of her fingers. The weird gleam in her eyes. The cool touch of her skin. The fact that she really didn't breathe.

Nita tried to light her cigarette, but her hand shook too much. She flinched when Imogen reached out to steady it, but then accepted the help. She drew the smoke in deeply, held it, exhaled. Took another drag.

"Okay," she said. "So what do you want from me?"

"No more than I told you earlier: company."

"Company."

Imogen nodded. "When the sun rises this morning, I'm going to die. I just didn't want to die alone."

"You want me to die with you?"

"Not at all. I just want you to be there when I do. I've lived this hidden life of mine for too long. Nobody knows me. Nobody cares about me. I thought you'd understand."

"Understand what?"

"I just want to be remembered."

"This is too weird," Nita said. "I mean, you don't look sick or anything."

Like I'd know, Nita added to herself.

"I'm not sick. I'm tired." Imogen gave a small laugh that held no humour. "I'm always amazed at how humans strive so desperately to prolong their lives. If you only knew . . . "

Nita thought about her own life and imagined it going on forever.

"I think I see where you're coming from," she said.

"It's not so bad at first—when you outlive your first set of friends and lovers. But it's harder the next time, and harder still each time after that, because you start anticipating the end, their deaths, from the first moment you meet them. So you stop having friends, you stop taking lovers, only to find it's no easier being alone."

"But aren't there . . . others like you around?" Nita asked.

"They're not exactly the sort of people I care to know. I'm not exactly the sort of person I care to know. We're monsters, Nita. We're not the romantic creatures of myth that your fictions perpetuate. We're parasites, surviving only by killing you."

She shook her head. "I look around and all I see is meat. All I smell is blood—some diseased, and not fit for consumption, it's true, but the rest . . . "

"So how do I smell?" Nita wanted to know.

Imogen smiled. "Very good—though not as good as you did when those men attacked us in the alley earlier. Adrenaline adds a spice that smells like hot peppers and chili."

The new turn their conversation had taken made Nita feel too much like a potential meal.

"If your life's so shitty," she asked, "why've you waited until now to put an end to it?"

"My existence is monstrous," Imogen told her. "But it's also seductive. We are so powerful. I hate what I am at the same time as I exult in my existence. Nothing can harm us but sunlight."

Nita shivered. "What about the rest of it?" she asked, thinking

253

of the dozens of late-night movies she'd watched. "You know—the running water, the garlic and the crosses?"

"Only sunlight."

"So tomorrow morning you're just going to sit in the sun?"

Imogen nodded. "And die. With you by my side to wish my spirit safe-journey and to remember me when I'm gone."

It was so odd. There was no question in Nita's mind but that Imogen was exactly what she said she was. The strange thing was how readily she accepted it. But accepting it and watching Imogen die were two different things. The endings of all those late-night movies went tumbling through her in all their grotesque glory.

"I don't know if I can do it," Nita said.

Imogen's eyebrows rose questioningly.

"I'm not real good with gross shit," Nita explained. "You know—what's going to happen to you when the sunlight touches you."

"Nothing will happen," Imogen assured her. "It's not like in the films. I'll simply stop living, that's all."

"Oh."

"Have you finished your drink?" Imogen asked. "I'd like to go for a last walk in the park."

4

—🜊—

Fitzhenry Park was probably the last place Nita would go for a walk at this time of night, but remembering how easily Imogen had dealt with their attackers in the alley behind the club, she felt safe doing so tonight. Walking hand in hand, they seemed to have the footpaths to themselves. As they got deeper inside the park, all sense of the city surrounding them vanished. They could have been a thousand miles away, a thousand years away from this time and place. The moon was still working its way up to its first quarter—a silvery sickle hanging up among the stars that came and went from view depending on the foliage of the trees lining the path.

Nita kept stealing glances at her companion whenever there was enough light. She looked so normal. But that was how it always was, wasn't it? The faces people put on when they went out into the world could hide anything. All you ever knew about somebody was what they cared to show you. Nita normally didn't have much interest in anyone, but she found herself wanting to know everything she could about Imogen.

"You told me you live a hidden life," she said, "but the way you look seems to me would turn more heads than let you keep a low profile."

"I dress like this to attract my prey. Since I must feed, I prefer to do so on those the world can do better without."

Makes sense, Nita thought. She wondered if she should introduce Imogen to Eddie back at the club.

"How often do you have to . . . feed?" she asked.

"Too often." Imogen glanced at her. "The least we can get by on is once a week."

"Oh."

"I've been fasting," Imogen went on. "Preparing for tonight. I wanted to be as weak as possible for when the moment comes."

If Imogen was weak at the moment, Nita couldn't imagine what she'd be like at full strength. She wasn't sure if she was being more observant, or if her companion had lowered her guard now that they were more familiar with each other's company, but Imogen radiated a power and charisma unlike anyone Nita had ever met before.

"You don't seem weak to me," she said.

Imogen came to a stop and drew Nita over to a nearby bench. When they sat down, she laid her arm across Nita's shoulder and looked her directly in the face.

"It doesn't matter how weak or hurt we feel," she said. "We have to be strong in here." Her free hand rose up to touch her chest. "We have to project that strength or those around us will simply take advantage of us. We can take no pride in being a victim—we belittle not only ourselves, but all women, if we allow that to happen to us without protest. You must stand up for yourself. You must always stand up for yourself and your sisters. I want you to remember that as you go on with your life. Never give in, never give up."

"But you're giving up."

Imogen shook her head. "Don't equate the two. What I am doing is taking the next step on a journey that I should have completed three hundred years ago. I am not surrendering. I am hoping to kill the monster that I let myself become and finally move on."

Imogen looked away then. She shifted her position slightly, settling her back against the bench. After a few moments, she leaned her head against Nita's.

"What do you think it's like when you die?" Nita asked. "Do you think everything's just over, or do we, you know, go on somewhere?"

"I think we go on."

"What'll you miss the most?"

Imogen shrugged. "What would you miss if you were in my position?"

"Nothing."

"Not even your daughter?"

Nita didn't even bother to ask how Imogen knew about Amanda.

"You've got to understand," she said. "I love her. And it makes me feel good to know that something I was a part of making isn't fucked up. But it makes me feel even better knowing that she's going to be raised properly. That she'll be given all the chances I never had. I didn't want her to grow up to be like me."

"But you still visit her."

Nita nodded. "Once she's old enough to understand what I am, I'll stop."

If not sooner. If John's old man didn't get the judge to revoke her visitation rights because of what he'd seen her doing tonight.

"It's getting late," Imogen said. She stood up, drawing Nita to her feet.

"Where're we going?"

"To my apartment."

5

—m—

To call it an apartment was a bit of a misnomer. It turned out that Imogen owned the penthouse on top of the Brighton Hotel, overlooking the harbour. The only time Nita had ever seen a place this fancy was in the movies. While Imogen went to get her a drink, she walked slowly around the immense living room, trailing her hand along the polished wood tables and the back of a chesterfield that would seat five people comfortably. There was even a baby grand in one corner. She finally ended up at the glass doors leading out onto a balcony where she saw two images superimposed over each other: a view of the lake and Wolf Island in the distance, and one of herself standing at the window with the living room behind her, Imogen walking towards her with a brandy glass in each hand.

Nita turned to accept the brandy. Imogen touched her glass against Nita's and then they both drank.

"Why'd you pick me?" Nita asked.

"The name on the flyer outside the club first caught my eye," Imogen said. "Then, when I began to study your life, I realized that we are much the same. I was like you, before the change—deadened by the ennui of my life, feeding on the admiration of those who courted my favour much the same as you do with those who come to watch you dance. It's not such a great leap from using their base interest as a kind of sustenance to taking it from their flesh and blood."

Nita couldn't think of anything to say in response to that, so she took another sip of her brandy.

"I want you to have this when I'm gone," Imogen went on.

"Have what?"

Imogen made a languid movement with her arm that encompassed the penthouse. "This place. Everything I have. I've already made the arrangements for everything to be transferred into your name—barring unforeseen difficulties, the transaction will be completed tomorrow at noon."

"But—"

"I have amassed a considerable fortune over the years, Nita. I want it to go to you. It will give you a chance to make a new start with your life."

Nita shook her head. "I don't think it'd work out."

She'd won a thousand dollars in a lotto once. She'd planned to do all sorts of sensible things with it, from taking some development courses to better herself to simply saving it. Instead, she'd partied so hearty over the space of one weekend she'd almost put herself in the hospital. The only reason she hadn't ended up in emergency was that everybody else that weekend had been too wasted to help her. She still didn't know how she'd managed to survive.

"It'd just make me fuck up big-time," she said.

Imogen nodded—not so much in acceptance of what she was saying, Nita realized, as to indicate that she was listening.

"I have to admit that I haven't been entirely honest with you," Imogen said. "What we're about to embark upon when the sun rises could be very dangerous to you."

"I . . . don't understand."

"I won't die the instant the sunlight strikes me," Imogen said. "It will take a few minutes—enough time for the beast inside me to rise. If it can feed immediately and get out of the sun, it will survive."

"You mean you'd . . . eat me?"

In This Soul of a Woman

"It's not something I would do, given a choice. But the survival instinct is very strong."

Nita knew about that. She'd tried to kill herself three times to date—deliberately, that is. Twice with pills, once with a razor blade. It was astonishing how much she'd wanted to survive, once it seemed she had no choice but to die.

"I will fight that need," Imogen told her. "It's why I've been fasting. To make the beast weak. But I can't guarantee your safety."

Nita filled in the silence that followed by lighting a cigarette.

"Understand," Imogen said. "It's not what I want. I don't normally have conversations with my meals any more than you would with a hamburger you're about to eat. I truly believe that it's time for me to put the monster to rest and to go on. Long past time. But the beast doesn't agree."

"You've tried this before, haven't you?" Nita asked.

Imogen nodded.

"What happened?"

"I'm still here," Imogen said.

Nita shivered. She silently finished her cigarette, then butted it out in an ornate silver ashtray.

"I'll understand if you feel you must leave," Imogen said.

"You'd let me go—even with everything I now know?"

Imogen gave her a sad smile. "Who'd believe you?"

Nita lit another cigarette. She was surprised to see that her hands weren't even shaking.

"No," she said. "I'll do it. But not for the money or this place."

"It will still be in your name," Imogen said.

Unspoken between them lay the words: *if you survive the dawn.*

Nita shrugged. "Whatever."

Imogen hesitated, then it seemed she had to ask. "Is it that you care so little about your life?"

"No," Nita said. "No matter how bad shit gets, whenever it comes down to the crunch, I always surprise myself at how much I want to live."

"Then why will you see this through?"

Nita smiled. "Because of you. Because of what you said about us having to be strong and stand up for each other. I won't say I'm not scared, 'cause I am, but . . . " She turned to the glass doors that led out onto the balcony. "I guess it's time, huh? We better get to it before I bail on you."

She put down the glass and butted out her cigarette after taking a last drag. Imogen stepped forward. She brushed Nita's cheek with her lips, then hand in hand they went out onto the balcony to meet the dawn.

The
Alchemy of
the Throat

by
Brian Hodge

—⁓—

M

y mutilation was accomplished when I was a child of seven. I no longer remember myself any other way.

A recollection of such an act must be buried deep within, but beyond me, lost as I was to a drugged haze. Even so, when I dwell upon it, the event becomes as vivid as only imagination can make it. It must have been very much like this:

Those to whom my parents sold me plied me with sweets or trinkets, winning my trust until they got me to the conservatory hidden in the Sicilian countryside. And until they got me into the cutting room. Having rendered me insensible, they pulled my pants to my ankles, then held me flat atop a table that was as sterile as they could make it. Hands would have briefly held the little boy's penis back toward my stomach, while another pair applied the knife to the soft parts below. My scrotum would have been opened swiftly, slit like a small plum and its contents cut out, unwanted pulp. I imagine some snaggletoothed mongrel being tossed these warm and bloody grapes, although there's no reason to believe that actually happened. It distinguishes it for me, though, and that's enough.

Once they were through, my empty sac would have been sewn shut, or the incision simply cauterized. As I grew, the useless and barren scrotum withered to nothing, the excess reabsorbed by my body, leaving nothing behind but the puckered ridge of scar that curves back between my thighs.

It was done for the sake of music, of course, just as it was done centuries ago. In Italy, some traditions date back so far they have become institutions with lives of their own, and to argue against them must be like trying to argue with God.

And when traditions must go underground to survive, it sets them in stone harder than granite.

To the world at large, the castrati sopranos are a vestige of centuries past. I know better, can sing a different tale with a voice that those who trained me told me surpassed even that of an angel. And training me, and others like me, is their life's purpose, to preserve that which most believe lost to the past.

One of the maestros who taught me the vocal arts was fond of saying that a true castrato is born, not made.

It was several years before I knew what he meant by that.

I was twenty when sent away from the conservatory. My training was complete, my education beyond the arts comprehensive, and my voice honed and polished for thirteen years, an instrument on which a small fortune had been lavished.

An even greater fortune purchased it outright.

While our voices, our songs, were a part of daily life, once each year the maestros opened the conservatory to those whose wealth was so fabulous that nothing in the world was denied them. From across the globe they would fly to Palermo; then a small fleet of hired cars would sweep across the Sicilian countryside to converge upon our ancient edifice of stone and tiles. When rested and dined, they would fill the velvety purple seats in our auditorium, and we would take the stage—the castrati, from whom our lives of birth had been stolen, in their place substituted a regimen that we came to embrace as we came of age because it was the only choice left to us. The outside world no longer existed for us, as we were no longer made for it.

So with our audience waiting, a small orchestra would take up its instruments, and we would sing in voices high and sweet and powerful, voices that could plunge even angels into despair over being denied them. Operas by Scarlatti, arias by Verdi, liturgies that had once rung out in the Sistine Chapel for the pleasure of popes . . . music penned for throats just such as ours. Voices whose beauty had always been unearthly—a soprano's range driven by the power of a male chest—but never more so than now, with so few privileged to hear it.

As we performed, solos were taken by older castrati, those in their late teens whose days at the conservatory were drawing to a close. Librettos had been distributed to the audience so they might know who was who, with ample margins left for notetaking.

After the performance, we would mingle over wine and baroque chamber music with our potential benefactors, so they might get to know us up close, and pay us the adoration we had been awaiting for years. We craved it like starving puppies, lapped it up for hours. They would fly home then.

And within another day or two, the silent auction began.

His name was Julius, and when I learned he had offered top bid for me, I did recall him: a man of slight build and a slouching elegance when he sat, with the refined and light-skinned features of northern Italy. His blond hair he wore gathered back in a short limp ponytail, and his eyes I especially remembered as watchful and smoky gray.

I felt a distinct relief; Julius had seemed kind, even respectful. Many of the boys I had grown up with would be making their new homes with leering old men whose money could purchase only the thinnest veneer of refinement. In my room, a week before all the financial and travel arrangements would be completed, I remember feeling quite lucky.

He sent men in his employ to meet me in Palermo, and take me over from the conservatory's escorts, and back I went with them to southern Italy, just outside of Capua. He lived in a huge old villa, a rambling fortress of cool marble worn smooth by centuries and laced with ivy. The gardens had gone to riot, choked with flowers that needed better tending, a colorful bedlam out of which rose crumbling statues of old Roman gods and goddesses, heroes and heroines. Fountains splashed with greenish water, in which frolicked frozen nymphs and satyrs.

It possessed an ageless beauty, and I, the castrato Giovanni, was but its newest fixture.

"It originally belonged to a Roman senator, as a secondary home," Julius explained as he gave me the tour. "I've had it restored, and remodeled to accommodate modern conveniences, but beyond that, I've tried not to tamper with the feel of the place. I'm mostly content to know *he* walked here . . . whoever the fat old sybarite was. It's my joke upon him, and that has to be enough. By now I can't help but realize it can never be much of a triumph."

I found it an odd thing to say, and frowned, as if there had to be more that he wasn't telling me. I realized Julius was older than I'd thought at the conservatory, small lines cut around his mouth and his eyes. Perhaps it was the harshness of the sun. At my puzzlement, Julius waved his hand in the air, dismissive.

"You'll understand, in time."

I nodded, as if this made perfect sense. It was what my kind had been taught to do; we knew so little of the world beyond the conservatory. Our education was broad, so that we would be well equipped to converse with our benefactors. But what had we really seen, experienced? *So* little. We'd been born into poverty, every one of us, a salvation to our parents when we displayed precocious talent for song. But all we'd done was exchange the limitations of poverty for a cloistered life as carved throwbacks to an earlier century.

Capua, and life with a new master, was an entirely new world to me. My first night under Julius's roof, I huddled in a corner of my room, hugging my arms about my body as it trembled, as tears ran freely. And where were the friends of my youth this night, my brothers, lovers, cut by the same cruel blade? Did they miss me as much as I missed them? I would never see them again, never know their fates. It seemed a deeper loss than that left between my legs. I'd not felt orphaned since I was seven years old, but this night it was as if my family had died to me all over again.

I was roused by a late-night knock at the door. I splashed my face with water from a bowl before answering. In the doorway stood Francesca, the short, compact old woman who, as near as I could tell, ran the daily business of the house for Julius. She cooked for him, supervised the cleaning by maids who came in from town, had seemed terribly unfriendly to me when we were first introduced and looked no kinder tonight. Her whitening hair she wore pulled back in a severe knot; her eyes were as even as an executioner's, and nearly as warm.

"He's ready for you now."

I blinked stupidly. I'd not been told to expect a summons.

"In his bedchamber." Francesca glared, impatient. "A *song?* Or did the maestros cut away a portion of your brain, too?"

"I'm sorry," I said. "I—I . . . " Oh, what a terrible impression I was making on my first day here. I grabbed a towel to dry my face, then let her lead me to where Julius lay, awaiting some lullaby to ease him to sleep.

As I paced the cool stone floors, I thought of those who had, in centuries past, performed similar duties. History's most famous castrato, an eighteenth-century Neapolitan known as Farinelli, conquered the stages of Europe, but gave up his career at the age of thirty-two to serve as nightingale to the court of King Philip V of Spain. Summoned by the queen, Farinelli first roused the king from a somber depression that confined him to bed, refusing to bathe, and afterward, for ten years sang the same four arias every night at Philip's bedtime.

Our voices can work magic; this too is old tradition.

Francesca tapped once at Julius's door, opened it, shut it after me without following. It seemed a vast room, dominated by a bed in which Julius's slim form was nearly lost. Soft moonlight spilled through the windows, dappling the room with shadows and a blue luster. Approaching the bed, I felt a peculiar power steal over me. This was what I was meant for. Julius may have been the master, but once I opened my mouth, *I* would be the one in control.

Our eyes met in the gloom, each of us expectant. Lying there, he seemed many things to me, most of them contradictions. Julius was ageless and ancient, child and crone, a cruel sodomite and a tender saint.

"Is there some special song you have in mind?" I asked.

He shook his head against its pillows, the silky blond hair unbound and glowing with moonlight. "Whatever you like."

I discarded all the music I knew for the stage; it might have been beautiful enough, but did not seem appropriate for a lullaby. Instead I lifted my voice with music intended to glorify something higher, written for the throats of young boys, with sweet innocent voices. What I lacked in innocence, I could more than compensate for in feeling. Through "L'abondance Cibavit" and "Alleluia," "Pange Lingua" and "Ave Verum," my voice rang warmly off the stone walls, cocooned us with its strange presence, turned Julius's room into a sanctuary.

I gazed at him as the notes lifted, soared, watching as he lay with eyes closed, soaking in every nuance. He was a sponge, taking in all that poured from my throat, my soul. His brow would furrow, then relax; beneath the sheets his body would flex taut, then sink with exhaustive splendor.

Every singer hopes for such an audience: one who listens so raptly, riding the crest of every note, until it no longer feels as if the song is being shaped by the singer at all. It felt instead that the music lay within me, perfect and whole, as pure as it had been imagined by its composer as he set it to paper, and Julius was pulling it from me as he might reel in a rope. I lost myself, floating among the notes, until the music was finished.

Silence, for many moments. Then:

"Splendid, Giovanni," he whispered. "Absolutely splendid."

I smiled, wondering if he could even see it. My entire worth was tied to his response. "More?"

"Soon. Sit, would you?" He kicked once beneath the sheets, indicated a spot near the foot of the bed.

I sat, wondering if Julius expected my favors to be physical as well as musical, and if so, if the seduction would begin this very first night. Castrati were strange creatures indeed, alluring to many women and to no few men, as well, even men who had never loved another of their own kind. Our hair was thick and lustrous, our skin soft and smooth, our faces never touched by a razor. We were androgynes whose service to either sex was limited only by our inclinations, and certainly I, with dark curls hanging to my shoulders and a bit of the brown-eyed, olive-skinned look of a peasant girl, broke no traditions.

"When you sing that type of music," said Julius, "I can close my eyes and picture a cathedral full of boys in robes, who trust their priests and believe every word that crosses their own young lips. Their faith is still . . . intact. Then I open my eyes and I see you, and I know that intact doesn't necessarily mean inviolable. Is your faith the same as theirs, Giovanni?"

I was not expecting this, but welcomed it over desperate advances. "When I was their age, it was, probably. But I'm older now, and I know how many lies are told to children. So my faith lies in the beauty of the notes, not the meaning of the words. The words are immaterial to me now. I could sing of degradation, and the music would sound just as beautiful."

"Latin has that insulating effect, doesn't it?" Julius said, and we both laughed. "Keep your faith in beauty, then, and it'll always be well placed. I suspect beauty is one of the few things that's always there to sustain us whenever we need it."

I nodded, thinking of the young castrati—whose sacrifice was irreversible—who had lost their voices to impinging manhood just the same, to be left with nothing. The knife was no guarantee. In the old times they became voice teachers, composers, musicians, or let themselves be destroyed by their own despair. And today? They disappeared from the conservatory, quietly; last seen at supper, and absent from the breakfast table. None of the maestros ever said what happened to them. None of us dared ask. *There but for the grace of God went I,* some would think while staring at a boy's empty chair, but none of us truly believed that God's mercy had anything to do with it. How could infinite mercy be so . . . random?

"More, now, I think," said Julius, motioning me to stand.

So again I sang, and by the time I finished for the night, I could swear that those lines on Julius's face, which earlier seemed so prominent, had now faded away to all but nothing.

I settled in over the next weeks, and it felt like home, at least as much a home as the conservatory had ever felt. Francesca grew no warmer toward me, but to Julius I took a steadily growing liking. I couldn't have asked for a more appreciative audience, and after mornings, when he attended to his investments, he would shed this cloak of obligations and we might often talk for hours of more timeless things: of music and art, of beauty and souls. He was endlessly curious about my vocal training, was deliriously happy to hang over my shoulder as I sat at the harpsichord and demonstrated exercises the maestros had used to shape us from our raw childish ore. Sometimes it felt as if Julius were digging into me, pawing about in some dogged search for answers that had always eluded him.

"Did you have hopes of being a singer once?" I asked him.

"No. Oh no. There are voices, and there are ears. I've never mistaken my place in the arrangement. Still," and he shrugged, memories seeming to swell behind his eyes like forgotten sorrows, "to be one of those few voices worth listening to seems to me to be a holy thing. You make yourself sacred by what you've done with your voice. The rest of us? We just absorb it, and know we'll never see or hear anything that pure emerging from ourselves."

"You're discounting yourself." And why did I care to salve his feelings? He had, after all, paid money for me, my life. "Voices need those ears. You may love us, but we *need* you. What choir sings to itself?"

"So we both have a hold on the other, then." He seemed happy with the truce, although perhaps I shouldn't have been so quick to confess a need for something he could so easily withhold. A turned back, a deaf ear, could make my life miserable.

"Some friends will be coming here next week, and I'd like you to prepare a recital for them." Julius's eyes hazed over, a deeper gray, and he seemed so deliberately cryptic as he gave me a thin smile, a smile that hinted at all the things I didn't yet know about him. He could have hidden lifetimes behind that smile. "Oh, they'll love *you.*"

The days passed, a countdown toward some event that I knew nothing about, and Julius refused to tell me more. I believe he sensed my apprehension, and attempted to alleviate it by diverting me with a plump girl he brought in from the countryside. Women were a pleasure all but unknown to me, and while she warmed my bed without making note of my scars, my heart wasn't really in it.

Then she was gone, and that same day Julius kindly dismissed Francesca for the better part of a week. He sent her away by train to visit her family and, if it was possible to read anything at all from her stern countenance, she was glad to be going. I'd not even thought of her as having family, wondering if instead she hadn't one day stepped alive out of Julius's gardens from among the ranks of old statues, stone-faced and unyielding.

I began to truly fear for whatever Julius was planning. What could be so grandiose or ghastly that even Francesca would not be allowed to set her flinty eyes upon it? She knew my secrets, of course, and proved trustworthy with them. What could send her off with an expression of relief? And had she sent my way the merest glance of sympathy when leaving, or had that been imagination?

I again knew the same drops I used to sweat my first year at the conservatory, upon hearing footsteps approach my room in the night, wondering what else they might be coming to cut away. The villa seemed huge, a barren museum that rang coldly with my feeble attempts to give it the life of song.

And then it was suddenly, the next nightfall, home to some two dozen others. They overran it like a Mongol horde, spilling both wine and blood in their wake, and wherever they came from, it couldn't have been far enough away once they were gone.

They were men and they were women, in appearance, but in personae they seemed both more and less. They were all the baser appetites given flesh to house them, mouths with which to consume, throats with which to swallow. They couldn't all have come from the same place, so different were they. Some may have come down from Rome, others from Paris, still others from London . . . and beyond. One brown-skinned man had the wide features and dusty ringlets of hair of an aboriginal Australian; he laughed at my expression, said he had run very fast to arrive on time.

"You're teasing me," I said desperately, "*aren't* you?"

"Fast traveling, boy"—he winked—"it's a state of mind as well as place." Then he laughed with even greater uproar.

They wore lace or leather or furs, black and carmine, royal purple and deepest blue. They sprawled arrogantly about as if they were drunken aristocrats, or chased each other in carnal frenzy; a few of the more enthusiastic began coupling almost immediately, pounding their bodies together with a bruising hunger before their clothes were half-shed. Noise was constant, their din augmented by a chamber orchestra whose musicians were blind, every one of them, as they played from memory, without need of a conductor. Violins screeched as if played by Paganini at his most devilish, with terrifying runs at the strings that could make fingers bleed; sweat poured as violin bows sawed with feverish intensity. They played as if to slow down would mean to die.

I watched from a corner, not even daring to move until Julius came up to me with a radiant and feral smile.

"You're frightened," he said.

"And you wouldn't be, if our positions were reversed?" I shut my eyes but found it worse, what imagination conjured from sound alone. "Who are they? How do you know these people? I know my life has been a sheltered one, but . . . but *this*. . . ?"

"More things in heaven and on earth, than are dreamt of in your philosophy." Julius put his hands on my shoulders until I stopped trembling. I stared into the smooth chiseled planes of his face, stared with a thousand questions, and he gazed back with eyes that could never have grown so deep within a single lifetime. He was everything to me in that moment—benefactor and father, brother and protector. "You'll not be harmed, I promise you that. No matter what happens here, you'll not be harmed."

I wanted to fall into his arms, have him enfold me and make that promise again and again. What pathetic creatures we modern castrati were, so dependent on just one other. And when they died, would we be buried alive with them, like servants entombed in the pyramids with their pharaohs?

I looked beyond Julius's shoulder to a fresco covering the far wall, a vineyard where peasants of old Italy pressed succulent grapes into wine. Before it, two swarthy men hoisted a thin dirty fellow up by the ankles—I've no idea where he came from—and as he screamed weakly, they opened his throat with their fingernails. A half dozen of the guests scrambled beneath the flow, catching it with laughing mouths that seemed obscenely eager.

"Those two are old friends from Lebanon," Julius said. "I've known them a long, long time. And her?" He motioned elsewhere to a limber woman with near-translucent skin and serpentine hair that fell past her waist. As she lay contorted on the floor, her mouth opened wide to receive the issue of four men who ejaculated in rapid succession. She writhed, swallowed, rubbed the spatterings across her face until her tongue could lick them away.

"She's one of the Sisters of the Trinity. The sperm-eater." Julius gestured back toward the dying man, where a near-identical woman wallowed bare-breasted in blood, partaking of her own feast. "And she's another. The third one's around here somewhere, the flesh-eater. When they've not fed for some time? It's said there's nothing left of a man but bones, cracked open and sucked dry."

I wanted to cry, to crawl to the coast and swim the rest of the way back to the conservatory. There I'd known a world of safe routine, what to expect. Here outside of Capua, with Julius? It now felt as if I'd awakened in some Hell even Dante had ignored.

"These people here," I whispered. "You . . . you're one of them?"

He looked pained for a moment, took me gently by the hand, as if there was so much he wished to say, yet feared I would never listen to it all. Could never accept. "In most ways . . . I am. But think of yourself for a moment. You come from a secret school for boys who've lost their manhood. You each bear identical scars. But are each of you the same?"

I shook my head—of course we weren't.

Julius clasped my hand harder. "And neither are we."

"What *are* you, then, at the core?"

He smiled, a smile of ice and gray skies. "We're the damned. A few of them, at least. But we've chosen to make the most of it."

I let my gaze wander through this festival of grotesqueries. Drinkers of blood, eaters of flesh and sperm; insatiable satyrs whose arousal made the statues of their mythical brethren in the garden seem models of temperance; carnivores of marrow and spirit. They were beasts and in them I could see a horrible beauty.

The Alchemy of the Throat

They reveled in their bacchanal, recognizing no law but their own appetites.

As one who had spent the last thirteen years taking for granted the law of the knife, and what it had done to me, I couldn't help but feel a longing for such freedom.

But what of Julius? He seemed at one with them . . . but in my weeks here, I'd never witnessed a single indulgence like this. What was his ambrosia?

"Don't be afraid of them. Oh, a few may sniff you, or lick you, but they'll just be teasing. They wouldn't dare try anything more." Julius cupped my cheek. "You may even learn a thing or two from someone." He winked slyly. "Stranger things have happened in this house."

He left me to myself, and their questionable mercies, for a fearfully long time. I wondered from room to room but said nothing to anyone, for I believed they must all have lived nearly forever, and must be far wiser than I, in their ways. In their presence I felt like a dullard smart enough only to recognize his limitations, wandering down a hall peopled with the likes of Mozart and Einstein, Tesla and Shakespeare.

Julius later gathered everyone together and had me sing, and I thought it some miracle that I, in the small amphitheater beside the gardens, managed to hold their attention for over two hours. With Vivaldi I let my voice soar, let it sweep and fall, trill and sustain notes for a minute or longer. At my finale, the crowd of them erupted with applause and a cry that adoring audiences of old would bestow upon those deemed most worthy:

"*Viva il coltello!*" they shouted. "*Viva il coltello!*"

Long live the knife.

They descended on me, all ravenous smiles, and upon Julius as well, as my benefactor. He beamed, rosy-cheeked as a child; I'd never seen him more vibrant. He swept me into his arms, told me how happy he was with my performance. Another one tomorrow night, perhaps? I could not deny him.

LOVE IN VEIN

They seemed to accept me as one of them, the self-proclaimed damned, and to me it felt proper. Wasn't I damned as well, never to have a normal life, yet born in an age when I could no longer share my voice with an adoring world? I was as out of time as any of them.

The delirium continued, as if all had been inspired by the sound of my voice. I surrendered myself to Lilah, the third dark-eyed Sister of the Trinity, as she pressed herself against me and murmured what a shame she'd not been present for my castration, so she might've eaten of its fruits.

"They were fed to a dog," I told her as she drew my pants down, to rub a soft insistent palm at the empty space between my thighs.

"Such a delicacy—what a fortunate dog." She laid me back and lowered her head, hypnotizing with her tongue. "I can still smell where they were. I so love the taste of scars."

Little bites, she took. Little nips that all but devoured, and once I opened my eyes to see Julius gazing down upon us. What surprise his smooth face showed; then, right before his expression changed, he turned his back.

I wondered what it would have shown next.

On the revels went, the rest of the night, another day. Early the third day the great central room radiated with a quick blast that sent heat and light even through the adjoining rooms. A ferocious cheer arose from the heart of the villa, and I roused from a floor-bound stupor. Sticky with wine, encrusted with semen, I don't suppose I was self-aware enough to wonder what I'd come to until I staggered about to investigate this newest party trick. I could hear the clinking of chains amid a chatter of excited voices.

I stood in the doorway, unsteady, squinting in at some fading radiance. Most of Julius's guests were already here, milling before the frescoes, or anchoring chains that someone explained to me had been forged from an iron trellis stolen from the Bastille. All the sufferings it had heard, been saturated with? Chains forged from such iron could hold anything. A wise precaution.

The Alchemy of the Throat

What they held was like nothing I had ever seen.

"What *is* that?" I asked.

"The conjurings, boy. They *worked*," the Australian said. "You didn't hear them in here, all last night?

"No . . . "

"Right hard work. Well sod me, I didn't think they could do it." As he laughed, his long dusty curls jiggled.

What they'd captured had to have come from some other realm. Human in appearance, yet better, idealized, a master template from which all things human might have been cast. Its flesh like a translucent veil, it was beyond gender, elements of both male and female in a face I thought pitiful for its obvious terror. Matted and twitching beneath the chains were tattered membranes that might have resembled wings, if floating in some liquid plasm.

It chittered in no language I had ever heard, but, oh, such a voice. I wondered what its songs would sound like.

"An angel?" I guessed.

Julius heard me, left his companions to secure the final chains. He looked me up and down, the condition of me; what a fallen state I must have presented.

"Higher than an angel if you believe the myths of hierarchy," Julius said. "We've done this before, but it's the first time we've nabbed one of the Ophanim. They're said to inhabit a region that begins to take on substance and form as we know it. Where heaven meets earth . . . and can be corrupted." Julius swept his hair back from his forehead, mopped away sweat. What a portrait of bitter triumph he made. "But I think they're all just as confused there as most are here. Why shouldn't the centuries and millennia have driven them insane as well, and long before any of us were ever conceived? If there is a heaven, I think by now it must be the asylum of a mad universe."

The Australian clapped Julius on the shoulder. "We'll keep trying, mate. Someday we'll nab us a Seraphim, and maybe then we'll know more."

Julius said nothing as he returned to the spot where the Ophanim lay, with limbs bound and tugged wide, one side of its glorious face pressed into the floor. Its sides heaved like a dog panting its last breath while the car that hit it speeds heedlessly into the distance. Its cobalt eyes gazed farther than any of us could hope to see, and despite the pity I felt for it, I had to wonder if Julius hadn't been correct: *Suppose it really is insane?* Was it a protector? Or might it have toyed with our lives for sport, another time?

Julius left his worn and dirty clothes in a heap, approached the Ophanim. As master of the estate, I surmised, it was his right to be first.

Fleshy veils and membranes were parted, and the rest cheered as Julius mounted the Ophanim from behind. He thrust into it like a man who has stored away lifetimes' worth of fury. I turned away, wondering if everyone would have a go, debauching the divine, or what they thought divine, or what was, simply, close enough.

"If we consent to send you back," Julius told the Ophanim, through clenched teeth, "then share with your boss your newfound passions . . . and I daresay you'll find yourself his better."

It began to cry then—but from pain or from knowledge?—and at last I knew the sound of its song.

The party ended, as all parties must, the guest gone, only rubble left to mark their passing. The villa's new silence seemed an eerie presence, foreign. As Julius recovered by sleeping the next day through, I walked from room to room, feeling the echoes left by his friends. Even the Ophanim was gone, the floor where it had lain now stained with a film like mother-of-pearl that I couldn't quite scrape up with my fingers.

I drew a bath for myself, soaked in hot sudsing water until I drowsed against the side of the tub, drifting through dreams in which I was confused over what I should do next: mourn the death of the last of my innocence, or celebrate my rebirth as a wanton decadent. Rage, rage, against the loss of something I could never keep.

The Alchemy of the Throat

When I awoke, the water still warm in the tub, I found Julius seated on the porcelain rim. Tousled blond hair straggling along his stubbled jaw, he smiled with a weary gratitude.

"You're still here," he said. "When I went to bed, I wondered if you would be. Or if you'd be gone when I awoke."

"How far could I get? I have nothing of my own. You could've tracked me down without much trouble." I shrugged. "And the only people I know would've provided no refuge. They'd've returned me to you."

He would have none of it. "You could've left if you wanted. The world is big enough for anyone who wants to start life over."

I drew a long breath, let trickles of water pour from my hands over my chest. "Then I must not have wanted to."

Julius smiled. "It's important to me that you don't consider yourself a prisoner here."

"A prisoner? No." I shook my head. "But I do consider myself ignorant. These past four days I saw more than most see in a lifetime. But I still don't understand it."

Julius lowered a hand into the tub, stirring the water at my feet. "No, I don't suppose you do." His hand came to rest grasping my foot, now pruned from the bath. My toes stroked his palm. "My friends, those I've known longest . . . we're not very often in need of explaining ourselves."

I swept aside mounds of suds and bared myself to Julius—my dessicated groin, the huge scar that defined me. "I'm like very few men, Julius, but I was made by the hands of others, and their knife. So I want to know: What made *you?*"

After a brief struggle with himself, Julius seemed resigned to telling. He refused to meet my gaze, staring instead down into the water. "I must've been much like you at birth. Having nothing. Less than nothing, for myself . . . nothing but obligations. I was born a slave forty-five years after some say Jesus of Nazareth was born. Twelve years after they say he died. I sympathize with him, you know. I can personally vouch for the cruelty of ancient Rome.

279

"I would've been a few years older than you when I pledged my life to fighting under the leadership of a man I never saw at more than a distance. A man I never met. A man whose rebellion against Rome began with himself and his fellow gladiators, and soon encompassed tens of thousands of us."

"Spartacus," I whispered, feeling a stab of pity. The revolt of Spartacus had been a noble thing, but it had also been doomed. Who could have marched against the might of Imperial Rome?

"I was captured in the final battle with the legionnaires—they saved enough of us to set an example for anyone we may have inspired. They reserved the same punishment for rebellious slaves and political insurgents, and we were both. Six thousand of us and they crucified us all, lined the Appian Way with us, from Rome to here, to Capua. Imagine . . . a gauntlet of defeated, crucified men stretching for more than two hundred kilometers. Imagine hanging there between heaven and earth, lashed to your cross, listening as the men you fought beside moaned their lives away in the distance. Listening to the sound of death on the wind. *Listening.* For hours, at first. Then for days.

"I don't know how it happened to me. All I know is that the deeper my despair took me, the more strength I seemed to take from the moans of those I was outliving. I know that I prayed, but my faith in the god we'd trusted for our victory was gone, so I prayed to whatever might listen, without caring what it was. Maybe something did. Or maybe it was something inside me and me alone, that hated so deeply and wanted so badly to live that it took the only thing left as its fuel to keep me alive: the things I could hear. The beautiful as well as the terrible. I fed on the deaths of my fellow slaves, until they all were gone, as far as the ear could hear. After that, I fed on the songs of birds. I hung there for nine days before the Romans grew so terrified of me laughing at them and cursing them that a centurion ordered me taken down and released. He begged me to

forgive them. They thought they might have mistakenly crucified a minor god. I still find the irony in that very appealing."

"What power you must have had over them," I said.

"I told the centurion that forgiveness would be granted if he
would fall on his sword in atonement." Julius smiled. "He did it at
once. I listened to the death rattle in his chest, and it was as invig-
orating as a full night's sleep.

"But I was never the same after that. Something inside me had
changed forever. Whether it was a gain or a loss, I was never able to
decide. But instead of looking at the world, from then on I was
forced to *hear* it. I can drink so deeply of everything from the sound
of wars to violins, it becomes part of me, sustains me. I hear colors,
I hear smells. I hear the need in a bird that sings for a mate, and I
hear the bland evil monotony in the machines of a factory. I hear
things most people could, but never do, because they never take
time to close their eyes and listen."

I wondered what such a life would be like, drawing sustenance
from the world's ticking clockwork . . . no distinction between its
ugliness and its beauty. They told us in the conservatory that one
could behold no greater grandeur than what ears would admit—
even the sight of a celestial choir would diminish in comparison to
its song—and this was why we castrati were so special, anointed.
As Julius had said, we made ourselves sacred by our voices. Did
some of that grace seep into him, through the act of listening?

Perhaps this was why Julius had brought me here. Such sounds
as war, as children screaming in an inferno, might have kept him
alive, but might they not also have slowly poisoned him without
some antidote to soothe their distilled misery?

Julius's hand slid higher, to my knee. "You were wrong about one
thing, not long ago. You said that those of us lucky enough to hear
you may love the sound of your voices, but that the *need* was yours.
The need to be heard. But I need you more than you can ever know.
You keep me young. Since you came, I've felt more whole than I
have in a very long time. Against the years, *you* are my tonic."

"Then why did you chance driving me away with the past four days?"

"Before I came to depend on you any deeper, I had to know if you would stay. And I had to know what I could endure to keep you. When I found you with Lilah? I didn't know until then that I still could feel the pain of jealousy." His eyes began to drift closed. "Or maybe all I wanted was to dirty you up, turn you into something closer to what I am, and the rest of us." He laughed.

"How strange, all of us coming together the way we do. But we're proof that, if you live long enough, no matter how aberrant you may be, you'll eventually find you're not completely alone."

Alone. I dwelt upon the word, its implications like the tolling of a funeral bell. Was anyone more alone than a castrato who had grown up with others like himself, only to be separated from them forever? How outcast must he be that he felt grateful for being accepted by those who bled and milked those weaker than they, who sodomized angels?

But if being part of the normal world meant spending my days with those who might point and mock me for what I was, who would think me their lesser for what I had lost, I wanted no part of it.

Was it this rejection of convention that gave the damned their defiant lusts? *If this is what the world has made me,* they seemed to be saying, *then let it live with the consequences.*

I smiled at Julius, handed him a slippery cake of soap.

"You smell like a pile of dirty bedsheets in a brothel," I said.

His laughter rang from the tiles. "However would you recognize that smell?"

"I have imagination, don't I?"

He joined me in the tub, and we filled it to overflowing with fresh hot water, curling into its depths and into one another. We soaped each other with great slick lathers, and when we kissed for the very first time, for me it was like being devoured by a creature made of time, beyond time. His mouth might engulf me whole in a way that Lilah's never could.

And when he sculpted me so that I rested on my knees with my elbows propped on the rim of the tub, and took me as he had the Ophanim, a wet shuddering pressure bearing down upon my back, I discovered that Julius understood tenderness as thoroughly as he understood the intricacies of infernal pain.

I had to wonder what Francesca thought when she returned. Her flat gaze couldn't help but pick up on that which already seemed obvious to me in the mirror: I was different, it would show in my face. I had seen Julius's life as it really was, had tasted of it . . . and had been seduced by its exotic flavors.

I would sometimes catch Francesca watching me over the months that followed, when she wasn't away on what were again explained as family visits. Happy months for me, secure beneath Julius's wing as he himself was buoyed by my songs, and the hours seemed too short, filled as they were with wine and music, art and talk, the sacred and profane. And always, the sweaty delights of the flesh. I thought of those first few clumsy couplings at the conservatory, the way many of us had turned to one another in the absence of girls. A mouth was a mouth, the voice of a lover in an ear no less welcome for its male timbre. But they'd been boys; I had loved boys. Julius had had centuries to perfect the art of being the man he was.

Perhaps Francesca resented the way I was no longer a simple acquisition of her master, having instead become someone he truly cherished. Someone who could give her orders as well.

But when I awoke one day to discover I had sung so much my throat felt like a raw scrape, and lay weak and feverish beneath the covers, Francesca was there to feed me warm broth and sips of a lemon and honey mixture. Her stern face let me know that I was to finish every drop; her veined hands looked stronger than iron, the hands of a woman who has borne countless burdens, and is all the stronger for their weight and the bruises they left.

"He's terrified of you losing your voice, you know," she told me. "It would be more than he could bear now, I think."

"It's just strain, and a virus." My speaking voice was a lame whisper. "I'll be good as new in a week."

She forced more broth down me. "I'm sure you will. But you'll lose it one day. The years *will* take their toll."

Living as we did for our music, this was the one tragedy that castrati did not want to think about. At the conservatory we had heard a recording of the last great castrato the world at large had been blessed to know. Alessandro Moreschi had, as an old man, still been singing at the dawn of the twentieth century, when recording technology was in its infancy. He'd been the only castrato of old ever recorded, and in listening, we, his grandsons under the knife, could spot the ravages of time. In this we could hear our own futures.

"I'll be dead by the time that happens," Francesca said. "But where will that leave Julius? The same place he's been too many times, too many times."

"But he's lived so long," I whispered. "If two thousand years isn't time enough to learn to deal with it, what is?"

Francesca smacked the spoon into the empty bowl. "Of course Julius can deal with your loss. He found you when he needed you, didn't he? He can find another. But he'll hurt. How he will hurt."

"After so long, he's not beyond pain?"

"He lives," Francesca said, very simply. "And life is pain. You learned that lesson when you were a boy." And then, of all the things I never expected from her, came the most unexpected. She smiled so disarmingly I might not have recognized her on a Capua road. "But enough talk. Rest. Rest that lovely voice of yours. And then, when you are well? There's something I wish to show you."

•   •   •

The Alchemy of the Throat

Julius doted on me during my days of recovery, sitting at my bedside. He chatted amiably, but it was just that: pleasantries with which to pass time, meant to build a wall around the fears of loss that for the first time seemed real. The honeymoon was over. I might be accepted by his immortal friends, but I could never be one of them. Perhaps this was what angered them most, caused them to rage so defiantly against a sterile heaven that would never accept them. They knew they were stuck with one another for the ages, that mortal friends and lovers, their life spans like those of goldfish, would always be dying on them.

"How many were there before me?" I asked him one afternoon, the sky beyond the window the cold rainy gray of early winter.

He looked genuinely surprised I would ask this. "Why should it matter?"

"Because it does."

Julius nodded. "Many. There have been many. But if you want numbers . . . "

"No." I shook my head. "Were there other castrati?"

"One other, years ago. Beginning in the late thirties." Fine lines creased his forehead. "I met Mussolini at that recital. He was getting his own, imagine that." Julius met my eyes, seemed to read my mind, and that which seemed to me as important as it was pointless. "Of the two, yours is the better voice."

"Did you love him?"

"I needed him. Just as I needed them all. Men and women and castrati alike. What a choir all of you would have made, if you'd lived the same lifetime." Julius's hands found my bedsheets, idly began to twist them into knotted cables as his voice grew ever more husky. "I *needed* them, the same as I need you . . . because the world I hear is a world that's screaming, and those screams are my meat . . . and if I don't have a voice like yours around me, then I just might lose what's left of my mind. So I use you up until your throat is a dry husk, and I cast you aside and go on to the next. So you tell me, Vanni: Where in that process do you think there's any room for love?"

"Where?" I echoed, with Mona Lisa's smile. Knowing as only a trained musician can how music's beauty is best defined not by its notes, but by its rests. "In the silence."

But I was sure that Julius already knew.

Viruses burn themselves out, fevers cool, throats lose their rough edges. I was on my feet again and happy to be alive.

Francesca remained true to her word, waiting until late one morning when Julius was engrossed in paperwork and a conference call on the vast holdings he'd accumulated over his centuries. She led me out the back of the villa, past the amphitheater, through the gardens where statues now stood like lords over their withered flowers, with brittle stems and brown blossoms. I could crush one in my hand, grind it to a powdery spice of sweet decay, let it sift to the ground . . . and the frozen old gods would silently approve with their stone eyes.

"There's no reason for you to have known this," she told me, "but there has always been a Francesca in Julius's house."

"Always? For two thousand. . . ?"

"Well, for many generations. To me that *is* always—at my age, especially. Before me, my mother; before her, my grandmother; her mother before her . . . for many generations a Francesca. A legacy from mother to daughter, passed along with the name. Through wars and bad times as well as good, our family has been well cared for by Julius's generosity, and we've been proud to serve him." She looked to the cold sky with such sadness that I wanted to hold her, in spite of how I still wasn't sure I actually liked her. "But no more. All that? It's about to come to its end. I birthed no daughters. No sons, either. I will be the last Francesca."

Our long coats snapping loosely in the wind, she led me to a building that lay beyond the gardens, a squat marble hall half-swallowed by ivy. I'd been curious about it in the beginning, but it had always seemed unused, as forgotten as the gods one had to pass to get here. Francesca unlocked its heavy door with an iron key, and we stepped into its dim interior. It looked no more complicated inside than it had from out, just a simple length of hall, its air musty and brittle with the chill that only marble walls can hold.

When my eyes grew used to the gloom, I made out the rows of vaults lining the far wall, the older ones sealed with engraved stone slabs, newer ones adorned with lettered brass plates. The dead slept here, dozens of them, and I had never known.

"His nightingales," said Francesca. "Julius claims he can still hear them, when he tries very hard, but I've never heard a thing. If it gives him comfort, though. . . "

I walked before the nearest stone facings, running my fingers over the names, dates . . . touching them as if I too could hear their songs arising from their pillows of rock. These singers who must have been magnificent.

Francesca took me by the hand, led me down the row until halting before one tomb with a marker that I first thought was freshly polished, so bright was the brass. Only when I saw the name did I realize that it had had no time yet to tarnish:

GIOVANNI PETRELLI

That there were no dates meant nothing. It's still a fright to be shown your own grave.

"To my knowledge, this is the first time Julius has prepared a vault far before it's needed," said Francesca. "*He* needs it. He comes out here often, to remind himself that you too will someday leave him. Just . . . as I soon will."

I slowly turned away from the sight of my name to face her.

"I'm dying, Vanni. Soon. Much too soon. I have things growing inside me." She had a narrow smile for my shocked expression. "All my 'family trips'? Doctors. Julius doesn't know yet, and I expect he won't hear it from you, no? And I ask one other thing: I can guess what you must think of me. But don't think me a cold old woman because I never tried to know you better. It wasn't you I was trying to avoid . . . just the need to say good-bye someday."

"It's too late," I told her, and we stood in the chill gloom, huddled within our coats as we dared one another to care, to feel, to reach out for a touch of warmth against whatever awaited us one day. I was drawn to look once more at my brass name. "Why? Why show me this?"

Sighing, Francesca drew herself very straight, tall as she could stand. Her gaze lingered on the crypt wall, and I noticed that her tight bun of hair was beginning to fray.

"All things end," she said. "My life, yours, your voice . . . my family . . . empires. All things. Except for Julius. He goes on. But I believe he goes on because he fears what may come next. If it's painful, he will hate it. And if it's too loving, I think he will hate it all the more. Even so, I think he would like to find out, if only he had the courage. And someone to find out with. To grow old and die with. We can endure a lot, if we're not alone."

As she must have been. Poor Francesca—she might never have spoken from any greater personal experience.

"How much would you sacrifice to live out the rest of your days as a normal man?" she said.

"I'm not the one to ask. Even though something wonderful did come of it . . . what was taken from me is gone forever." *And it was fed to a dog . . . wasn't that right?*

Her narrow smile reappeared. "But if you *could* trade your voice for what they cut away, would you?"

It forced me to think. *Would* I relinquish that seraphic voice for the chance to be all its creation had denied me? A husband and father; a grandfather? The greater part of me rejected it, for that life was so very commonplace. Yet it was exotic, too, for it was something I could never, ever achieve.

"I don't know," I told her.

"I believe Julius would. I believe he's ready. At long last, he's ready."

The Alchemy of the Throat

"But how? Julius is . . . what he is. As you say, he goes on."

"All things end," she said once more. "When they seem not to, the trick is to find the sacrifice. And"—her smile began to broaden—"the heart to love enough to look for it."

She died two months later, when winter seemed its coldest, its wettest. She died with us at her side, not so far gone that she didn't know we were there, although I wasn't fooled. Francesca died alone, just the same. But she died well, her eyes open to the final minute, with spirit enough to extend either an open hand or a clenched fist to whatever met her beyond life's lacy black veil, depending on whether she liked it or not.

I hoped to meet her again someday, when my turn came. But not *too* soon.

"No Francesca," said Julius, the day after she was buried. He stood in the doorway to the kitchen that was nothing like the one she'd kept, filled now with dirty utensils and strong whiffs of food past its prime. "I'd forgotten what that was like. There was always a Francesca."

"Always?"

His back to me, his short ponytail tangled upon one shoulder, Julius nodded. "As good as always." When he turned in the doorway, I saw that he was crying, slow tears rolling down cheeks that had never seemed sharper. "I never told her foremothers to pass that name down through the generations. They just did it. All on their own. I think it must have been a kindness to me, so that when one died, or grew too ill to continue working, it would be all the easier to welcome the next. I'd always know whom to expect."

"Is that such a good thing?"

Julius bit his lip before shrugging his slumped shoulders. "I don't know anymore. Francescas come and Francescas go. I could know their name a hundred years before they got here; that, and one other thing: that someday they would die. I always knew to expect that much . . . and still, I was never ready when it happened."

We lived in silence for the rest of the day, except for those lone moments when the winter wind blew especially hard, shifting course for a time, coming from the brittle gardens and the crypt beyond. On the wind seemed carried the songs of ages past, sung by dead throats, and we would look at each other, Julius and I, as if daring the other not to hear it.

And I knew that those things we find most beautiful are made so by the brief span of their lives.

He had me sing for him that night, as most nights. Not so different from my very first night here, only now I did not retire to my own room once the song's last breath was loosed. Julius lay down first, the lights off throughout the villa, the room bathed in a soft glow of candles on which our bed seemed to float like a raft.

I climbed onto the bed, knelt just behind him, the top of his head barely aligned between my parted knees. We had grown to favor the lullabies this way, because I could look down and see the full effect my voice was having on his body, and Julius could, in turn, gaze up to see me rising above him, like an angel, or a gargoyle.

I kept my fists closed, as I had for the past few minutes. And had I known when Francesca died that I would be singing Julius his final lullaby in a few nights? I must have. I only now wish I had sung one to her as she lay dying, something to carry with her into that blackest night.

I would not let her down now, for she too had loved Julius, as if the mother of an ancient son, a son handed down through generations of mothers.

A son she had finally entrusted to his lover.

"Make it beautiful," Julius whispered from below me, gray eyes sad and trusting in the candles' glow. "And make it mourn the lost."

"Yes," I whispered, and emptied my right hand long enough to stroke the silken blond hair away from his forehead. The back of my hand caught a tear as it fell—but then why not mourn for myself? We would both be making sacrifices this night.

Then I sang, sang as I never before had, every note balanced on the edge of heartbreak. Long, slow, sustained notes of infinite sadness, Cherubini's *Requiem in C Minor*. It was music to mourn the passing of anything, everything, from a friend to an age. All things end, for all things must, the beautiful most of all.

And when the requiem was finished, I opened my hands, gripped their contents with trembling fingers. I bowed my head, deeply, so that I could kiss Julius on unsuspecting lips.

"I love you," I told him, so that he might, in years to come, think of it as the last thing he heard.

And then I plunged the nails into his ears, one through each eardrum, weeping but secure in the knowledge it was the only way. He screamed, he convulsed, but I held tight to those steel shafts, worked them like swabs, so that there could be nothing left of any membrane to grow back together. Only when I felt that deafness was assured, permanent, did I pull them free, hurling them across the room. Only I could hear the chime they made against the wall.

Julius was doubled in agony, his body perfect in the yellow-orange glow, and I looked, looked enough to last me a lifetime; I would never again see him any younger than he was this night. When would it begin, his descent into years that could never be turned back? When would I look upon him and see age needling its lines into his flesh, like scrimshaw carved into fine old ivory?

I did not know. But I would be there.

I fell beside him, my hand upon his hard shoulder while I spilled apologies he could never hear, and he pushed me away. I retreated to the edge of that vast bed, curled onto my side—and was Francesca watching from somewhere, proud?

After a time, Julius draped himself over my bare back; I felt the slow drip of his blood along my spine. Soon, our breathing fell into sync, and I looked to the years ahead with a fear that he might come to hate me, if he didn't already. I imagined Julius strangling me in my sleep, as even now his hand reached over and around me, fingers lingering upon my lips before loosely clenching over my throat. But he bore no harder, as if all he wanted was to hold on to the one dear thing he would forever be denied.

I knew the feeling.

I had lost my audience of one.

But if I could not be heard, there was always love to fall back on, and tonight, at least, love seemed surer by far.

Love Me Forever

by
Mike Baker

"**O**h baby, you're the best, the absolute best," the man moaned as the woman who lay atop him traced tiny circles on his chest with her tongue.

"Uh-huh," she said distractedly. Ceasing her licking, she nibbled playfully on the man's nipple.

"Really, baby, I mean it. I've never been with anyone like you before." The woman's tongue was in motion again, moving down the man's chest to his stomach, where it darted in and out of his navel. The pleasure was so great that he found it difficult to think, much less talk.

"Really?" the woman asked, the barest hint of mockery evident in her voice.

"Yeah, you're . . . oh, that feels great . . . you're one of a kind, baby."

The woman raised her head and made eye contact. Her violet eyes twinkled. "I know," she purred.

Then she lowered her head and did things to the man which no one had ever done before.

Deep in the heart of the city, in an area most people avoided at all costs, three college students flashed their IDs, paid the over-priced cover charge, and entered Inferno, the city's newest and hippest nightclub.

Mark, the tallest of the trio—a huge, strapping young man who looked every inch the football star that he was—was the first to speak after they entered. "Chet, you bastard, why didn't you tell me about this place sooner," he said as they shoved their way through the wall-to-wall mass of milling, babbling, trendier-than-thou flesh. "It's great."

"I told you, I only found it myself last week," Chet, who was almost as tall as Mark, but much leaner, replied.

"That's no excuse."

"Shut up, Mark." Chet turned to the model–handsome young man who stood to his left. "Hey, Peter," he said. "What do you think of this place? Is it cool, or what?"

"Never before have my eyes beheld such a vast array of delectable beauties, dear friend Chet."

Mark's face twisted up in a grimace of disgust. "Peter," he grumbled.

"Yes, Mark?"

"Talk like a normal person."

Peter flashed a gleaming white, perfect-toothed smile. "Never."

She waded through the sea of blackness, approaching the neon-stained concrete shore. Nearby, a fair-sized crowd milled about the entrance to the nightclub, waiting to be judged fit to enter.

Standing in the shadows, she studied the people in line, observing how they laughed and chatted with each other, pretending that they were having a good time while their feet grew sore and their bodies froze in the chill night air.

Love Me Forever

The disgust she felt toward the clubgoers gnawed at her. She loathed their dullness and their pretty dreams. Merely being near them made her skin crawl. It was beneath one of her kind, but she had to do it in order to survive; without human contact, she would surely die.

Stepping out of the shadows, she scanned the crowd, searching for just the right person. Noticing her gaze, and her beauty, men smiled and winked while women scowled and muttered disparaging comments to each other.

Not finding what she desired outside, she cut to the front of line, paid the doorman with a smile, and entered Inferno.

"Hey, dude," Mark said to Chet. He and his buddy had positioned themselves in a corner of the club which offered a prime view of the dance floor.

"There's no one here by that name, Mark."

"Sorry," Mark said, not sounding like he meant it. "Hey, Chet."

"That's much better. Yes, Mark?"

"Check out the dweeb."

"I see quite a few, Mark."

"There. The one dancing by himself." Possessing limited social graces, Mark raised his arm and pointed. "He's next to the fat chick with the bad dye job. See him?"

Chet scanned the crowd, spotted the person in question. "Yep," he replied, snickering condescendingly. "Looks like he's on 'ludes or something."

"No shit. If it weren't packed so tight out there, he'd probably pitch over on his face."

"No doubt," Chet said, nodding his head. "He's such a fashion plate."

"Yeah, those pants clash really well with that shirt."

"I wish I could dress like that."

"You do."

"Look who's talking here," Chet shot back. "Mr. if-I-wear-my-underwear-for-three-days-I-won't-have-to-do-laundry-as-often himself."

Peter, carrying three bottles of beer, shoved his way through the throng by Chet's side. "My dear friends," he announced, extending bottles toward the arguing pair. "The beer is here."

Mark snatched a bottle out of Peter's hand. "What took you so long?"

"En route to the bar I was waylaid by an attractive young nymphet who seemed rather taken by, as she so eloquently put it, my rad looks."

"Where is she?" Mark asked. "What happened?"

"Nothing." Savoring the moment—there were few things he enjoyed more than stringing Mark along—Peter smiled, then took a swallow of his beer. "She still prowls, searching for prey."

"What?" A look of confusion had crept onto Mark's face. It was an expression which could often be found there. "You mean to tell me you dumped her?"

Nodding his head, Peter sipped his beer.

Mark was aghast. "Why?"

"Because, friend Mark, she had to wear lead shoes to keep from bouncing about on the ceiling."

Chet chuckled. Mark looked even more confused. "What?" he asked.

"I think he's trying to say that she was an airhead," Chet offered. "Right, Peter?"

"Absolutely correct, friend Chet."

"I don't care if she's dumb or not," Mark said. "As long as she's cute, and stacked, nothin' else matters." He drained the remainder of his beer in one swallow, then belched.

Peter grimaced at the display of crudeness, which was something he'd come to expect from Mark; his friend had a knack for making rude bodily noises, especially in crowded places. "She wasn't your type," he told Mark. "She was able to see her own feet."

Love Me Forever

Anger flared in Mark's eyes. "Are you saying that I like fat chicks?" he snarled. "Cuz if you are, you're wrong. Just because I went out with Wanda—"

"A rather rotund girl, if you ask me," Peter interjected.

"I wasn't asking you, pretty boy. And you leave Wanda alone."

Peter smiled. "I wouldn't dream of touching her."

Face flushing red with fury, Mark tightened his grip on the empty bottle. "You know," he said, his voice low and menacing. "If you weren't my best friend's roommate, I'd knock your teeth right down your throat."

"Hey, kids," Chet said, stepping between the two. "Check out what just walked in the door. Is that a babe, or what?"

The instant she entered the club, she knew she'd made a mistake. A warning buzzer went off in her head, an instinct that had saved her life many times before, that she trusted implicitly. She realized it had been a mistake not to change before coming here. Now she was stuck, since she couldn't change in front of all these people.

Violet eyes scanned the room, taking in all the details. In one corner she spotted some prospects: two jock types and an extremely handsome boy with the fires of intelligence in his eyes. Each was young and strong; she could sense the power within them all the way across the club. Deep inside her, the need called. Becoming aroused, she licked her lips hungrily.

Hoping for a swift entrapment, she smiled at the trio. Over the years she'd learned that while the old were easier to attract, the young were much more satisfying; their minds were still full of hopes and dreams and their bodies filled with power and life. They weren't yet broken and bowed, worn down by life.

That's why she only visited college towns; they were so full of life.

On the dance floor, the young man with the clashing shirt and pants saw her. Weeping with joy, he stopped dancing and stared. "Baby," he cried. "I've missed you so much."

Hearing the sobbing man's cry, she quickly glanced in his direction, then turned away. Fool, she thought, mentally kicking herself. *You should have known that he'd return here hoping to find you again.*

The young man shoved his way through the dancers toward her. "Baby, I need you," he sobbed. "Don't go."

One of the displaced dancers grabbed the young man's arm. "Watch it, geek," he snarled. "Where the fuck do you think you're going in such a hurry?"

"Let me go!" the young man cried, struggling to break free. "I need her!"

Sneering, the dancer punched the young man in the face, snapping his head to the side. Blood flowed from the young man's nose.

"Please," the young man pleaded through crimson-stained lips. "I have to get to her. I need her."

"Fuck that."

The dancer's next blow struck the young man's stomach. Clutching himself, he fell to his knees on the blood-spattered dance floor.

Emerging from where they'd been watching the incident with a great degree of amusement, a pair of burly bouncers headed for the dance floor.

Taking advantage of the confusion, she slipped out the door, diving back into the sea of blackness that is the night. *Work before play*, she thought as she effortlessly moved through the darkness. *You have unfinished business to take care of.*

On the dance floor, the young man began to scream, his cries the plaintive, desperate wail of a lost soul.

Around him, people looked away, not wanting to get involved.

Muscular arms lifted the young man off of the dance floor, pulling him toward the doorway. As he was dragged through the crowd, the young man ceased his cries, returning to sobbing quietly instead.

As he was tossed out onto the neon-stained concrete, harsh-sounding voices informed the young man that he was no longer welcome in Inferno.

Love Me Forever

The blood in the young man's mouth tasted coppery. It made him feel ill, but he didn't care; she was gone and that was all that mattered in his life.

Eyes blank, face bloody, the young man pulled himself to his feet and shambled off into the night. "Baby," he muttered to himself. "Baby."

A seductive voice floated out of the darkness of an alley and caressed the young man's ear. "Yes, my love," it said. "I'm here."

The young man froze in his tracks. "Baby?"

"Yes, my love."

The young man stepped into the alley, following the sound of her voice. And suddenly there she was, stepping out of the shadows, her hands behind her back.

"Baby, I need you," the young man said. Reaching up, he ran his hands through her long black hair. His green eyes peered longingly into her violet ones. "I can't live without you."

"I know." With the speed of a striking snake, she lashed out with the broken bottle she'd been holding behind her back, slashing the young man's throat. The glass sliced through flesh, severing his jugular vein. "I know."

The young man clutched his throat, trying in vain to hold back the fountain of blood which was spraying from it. Weakened by blood loss, he fell.

She watched, devoid of emotion, as the young man bled to death by her feet. Until he died, his expression had remained constant: confused, hurt, but loving nonetheless.

The young man's death meant nothing to her; she'd taken all she'd needed from him already. He existed merely to satisfy her needs and, having done that, his life had been forfeit. By killing him she'd done him a favor; now he no longer had to endure the soul-numbing agony of his boring existence.

Having no fear of being traced by her fingerprints, she dropped the broken bottle beside the body. Then, changing as she moved, she headed back toward Inferno.

After all, the night was still young, and she had a trio of young gentlemen to meet.

"You know, when I first saw you at the club, I thought you were the most beautiful thing I'd ever seen. Just like Michelle Pfeiffer, only sexier."

"Thank you."

"I'd have never thought you'd have chosen me; girls usually don't."

"Really?"

"Yeah. Anyway, I'm glad you're here. You're special."

"I know."

"And you've got the most beautiful violet eyes I've ever seen."

In the next room, Peter listened to the sounds of passion which drifted through the paper-thin wall. Curling up into a ball, he pulled his pillow over his head and cried himself to sleep.

Mark was in middle of a wonderful dream featuring the girls from the latest *Sports Illustrated* swimsuit video when his phone started to ring. "Fuck," he muttered as reality shattered his nocturnal fantasy. Snatching up the receiver, he snarled, "What ya want?" into it.

"Mark, it's me, Peter." Silence. "Mark, are you there?"

"Yeah."

"I'm sorry if I woke you, Mark. But you see, there's something wrong with Chet and—"

"What!" Wide-awake now, Mark slid over on his bed until he was sitting on its edge. "What happened?"

"It's, uh, kind of hard to explain. You've got to come see him, Mark. Maybe you can help him."

"I'm on my way," Mark said. He grabbed the shirt he'd worn the night before off of the chair he'd tossed it on when he'd gone to sleep. "Don't do anything until I get there, you hear."

Love Me Forever

Hanging up the phone before Peter had a chance to respond, Mark hurriedly dressed. As he did, all he could think about was Chet. The two of them had been the best of buddies ever since their freshman year of high school, where they'd first played football together. They were inseparable, pals forever, as close as two guys could be and not be fags. If anybody had hurt Chet, Mark intended to make them pay.

Mark was letting himself into the on-campus housing unit Chet and Peter shared less than five minutes later.

"I'm glad you came," Peter said as Mark closed the front door behind himself.

As he entered the room, Mark gave Peter a quick once-over: He was unshaven, had dark bags under his eyes, and his hair stuck out in a dozen different directions simultaneously. Seeing Peter like this gave Mark a warm feeling inside; it was reassuring to know that even pretty boys looked like shit when they crawled out of bed in the morning.

"Where is he?" Mark asked.

"In his room."

"Then what are we waiting for," Mark grumbled. Storming past Peter, he crossed the room and pushed open the door to Chet's room.

"I hope he's okay," Peter said as he followed Mark into the room.

Glancing over his shoulder, Mark saw the look of genuine concern on Peter's face. *Pretty boy's got a crush on Chet*, he thought. *Shit, I ought to slap him around some for even thinkin' thoughts like that about my buddy.*

Restraining himself—if there was one thing Mark hated, it was fags—Mark looked down at his friend. Chet, wearing nothing but pale blue bikini briefs and a wistful smile, lay atop a bed which had quite obviously been used for more than just sleeping in the recent past. "Hey, Chet," Mark said with forced cheerfulness. "How ya doin', dude."

"She's so beautiful," Chet said, his voice barely above a whisper.

Mark leaned over the bed so that he could hear his friend better. "What?" he asked. "Who ya talkin' about?"

"She's so beautiful, and she came home with me."

Peter crossed the room, moving to Mark's side. "That's all he talks about," he said. "I came in a half hour ago to tell him that he had a phone call and he told me the same thing. He won't talk about anything else."

"Fuckin' weird." Frowning, Mark scratched his head. "Shit, man, I don't know what to do."

"Me, either. That's why I called you."

Mark's face lit up as an idea hit him. "Where's that chick he scored last night?" he asked Peter. "Maybe she knows what's wrong with him."

"I haven't seen her since we got home," Peter replied. "She must have left while I was sleeping."

"The bitch probably dosed him," Mark stated. "Nailed him with some bad shit, then cut out when he started actin' weird."

Peter ran a hand through his tousled hair. "You think that's what happened?"

"Yeah," Mark said, nodding his head as if he were agreeing with his own statement. "It had to be that."

"She's beautiful," Chet said. "So beautiful."

"I've got a buddy who's been thinkin' about gettin' into med school," Mark told Peter. "If anybody can help us, he can. You stay here while I'm gone. Make sure he doesn't wander off or something."

"She'll be back soon," Chet continued, totally oblivious to his friends' presence. "I know she will. She loves me; that's why she came home with me."

Looking down at Chet, Peter shook his head sadly. "I hope your friend can help, Mark," he said. "I really do."

Mark was so caught up in his own thoughts as he hurried across campus to his friend's dorm complex that he didn't see the short, buxom brunette who stepped out from behind a stand of trees until he collided with her, knocking her, and her armload of books, to the ground.

Shit, Mark thought. *As if I didn't have enough to worry about already.* "Sorry," he said, reaching down to help the girl who lay by his feet. "I guess I wasn't watching where I was going."

Much to Mark's surprise, the girl wasn't angry. And she was a looker, to boot, a ten on his personal scale. The girl had a model's face, just the right amount of meat on her bones, and, to top it all off, a great set of knockers. Mark, to put it mildly, was in heaven.

Flashing a perfect smile, her violet eyes atwinkle, the girl took Mark's outstretched hand. "Don't worry about it," she said. There was a provocative lilt to her voice, a hint of pleasures to come. "It was my fault."

Deciding that Chet could wait a little longer—Peter was watching him, so he'd be okay—Mark helped the girl to her feet.

Chet dozed off shortly after Mark left. Not wanting to leave his friend alone, Peter grabbed a chair from Chet's cluttered desk and settled down to watch over him.

The knock on the door caught Peter by surprise. Starting, he sat bolt upright in the chair.

Hoping that the sudden noise hadn't woken Chet, Peter shot to his feet and hurried from the room. As he crossed the tiny square which the student housing pamphlets referred to as a "spacious living room," there came a second knock, louder and more insistent this time.

Wondering why Mark didn't just let himself in—he had his own key, for Christ's sake—Peter opened the front door.

Standing on the front porch was a stunningly attractive woman with long, luxuriant red hair.

Stepping out onto the porch, Peter pulled the door closed behind himself. "Can I help you?" he asked the woman.

"I'm sorry to bother you," the woman said. Like Bacall in her prime, circa *The Big Sleep* and *Key Largo*, she had a voice which was deep, gravelly, and very, very sexy. "I'm looking for Peter Whaley. I was told that he lives here."

His expression deadpan, Peter nodded his head. "I do."

"Mark Andrews sent me," the woman purred. "He told me to tell you that he's going to be late."

"Thanks for passing on the message," Peter said, his voice as cold as a winter morning.

Raising her hand, the woman touched Peter's cheek with her fingertips. "Mark didn't tell me that you were so cute," she said as she traced the line of his cheekbone.

Peter stepped away from the woman, moving so that his back was pressed against the door. "I've got to be going," he told her as he reached for the doorknob. "I'm in the middle of something right now."

White teeth gleaming, violet eyes aglow with passion, the woman moved in closer to Peter. Her firm, perfectly rounded breasts pressed up against his chest, pinning him to the door. "Don't you find me attractive, Peter?" she asked.

"Not particularly," Peter replied.

The woman stepped backward, away from Peter. "All real men find me attractive," she told him. "Chet did. Mark, too. They were *real* men, Peter, unlike you." Her perfect lips twisted into a cruel sneer. "But then, you're not a *real* man, are you Peter?"

Peter's face flushed red with anger. Eyes blazing, he glared at the woman. "Who the fuck do you think you are?" he demanded.

"Whoever I want to be," the woman replied, smiling mockingly as she did. Then her face began to shift, to flow like quicksilver. Constantly moving and changing, a steady stream of faces flowed before Peter's startled eyes. All were beautiful, and each had the same violet eyes.

Peter's face drained of all color. He grasped the doorknob with a trembling hand.

As swiftly as it had begun, the flow of faces ceased. Her features once again the same as they had been before, the woman fixed Peter with a cold stare. "Good-bye, Peter," she said. "We'll meet again someday. Maybe tomorrow, or next week, or even a month from now; you'll never know until it's too late."

Pushing open the door, Peter retreated into the safety of his house, slamming the door on the woman's mocking laughter as he did.

In the other room, Chet stirred. "She's beautiful," he whispered. "So beautiful."

The weeks which followed were pure hell for Peter. Chet withdrew deeper into himself. No outside stimulus, not even food, could hold his attention; he just stared off into space, mumbling about how beautiful she was and crying.

Distraught over his friend's rapidly worsening condition, as well as the sudden disappearance of Mark, Peter finally broke down and called the school's doctors who, in turn, summoned Chet's parents. They arrived the next day to take their son home where, they said, he would be treated by "real" doctors.

Even though they never said anything to him about it, Peter sensed that Chet's parents blamed him for their son's condition. The few times he had met them before they had been warm and friendly; now they were cold and distant, their eyes filled with barely concealed loathing.

Two days after Chet was taken away, Mark reappeared. According to the reports Peter read in the papers, and the gossip he heard around campus, Mark walked into the cafeteria in the student union during the lunch hour rush, headed for the center of the room, climbed up onto a table, placed the barrel of a .38 Special in his mouth, and calmly pulled the trigger.

Numerous eyewitnesses quoted Mark's last words as being, "I love you, baby. I can't live without you."

Mark hadn't left a suicide note, so the circumstances surrounding his death were shrouded in mystery. Nonetheless, Peter knew what, or to be more specific, who, had driven Mark to end his life. The only thing was, he couldn't tell anyone; if he went to the police, they'd just dismiss him as some crackpot.

Peter's schoolwork began to suffer. He couldn't concentrate in class; every time he started to lose himself in a lecture, he felt violet eyes watching him. Any laughter he heard was directed at him. Hauntingly familiar faces peered out of crowds, jeering at him as he hurried past.

One day three weeks after Mark's death, Peter was in the school library halfheartedly attempting to work on a paper he knew he would probably never finish on time when a pretty blond girl sat down in the chair across from him. Smiling shyly, she placed her books on the table. "Excuse me," she said, her voice hesitant. "I don't know if you recognize me or not, but my name's Jennifer and I'm in Brit Lit with you. I was wondering if you could help me with yesterday's assignment; it's got me baffled."

The sound of the girl's voice roused Peter, who had been staring, half-asleep from exhaustion, at the textbook which lay before him. "Whuh," he muttered as he slowly raised his black-ringed, blood-shot eyes.

When he saw the girl's pale violet eyes, Peter screamed.

A shocked look on her face, the girl half rose out of her chair. Throughout the library, heads turned and eyes stared.

"Keep away from me!" Peter yelled. Pushing away from the table, he shot to his feet. His chair fell to the floor behind him with a loud crash.

"Are you okay?" the girl asked. She reached out for Peter, who stood, trembling with fear, across from her. "Do you want me to get a doctor?"

Like a deer which has caught the scent of the hunter stalking it, Peter bolted the instant the girl's hand moved toward him. Abandoning his books and papers, he sprinted for the nearest exit.

As he approached the doorway and freedom, Peter glanced back over his shoulder to see if the girl was following him. He caught a glimpse of her, a concerned look on her face, gathering up his belongings. Then he ran into something and blacked out.

Peter awoke in an unfamiliar room. He lay fully dressed on a large, comfortable bed. Peering down at him was a handsome young male face, one with dark, brooding good looks: a cross between a young Al Pacino and Richard Gere.

"Welcome back to the land of the living," the young man said. His voice was warm and friendly, his blue eyes full of kindness and humor.

"What . . . what happened?" Peter asked. His words came out slurred, as though he'd had too much to drink. He felt weak and tired and had difficulty concentrating. "Who are you?"

"You had some sort of fit in the library," the young man said. "You were running for the door when you ran into me."

Peter's face flushed. "I'm sorry," he stammered, feeling like a total idiot.

The young man smiled. It was warm and open, without a hint of malice. "Forget about it," he said. "We all have bad days."

"Where am I?" Peter asked.

"My apartment," the young man replied. "After the collision, they dragged you and me to the campus doctor's office. You were really out of it—the doctor said you were suffering from exhaustion—so they pumped you full of drugs to help you sleep."

Peter nodded his head; that explained why he felt so groggy.

"Anyway," the young man continued, "they didn't want to send you to the hospital, you weren't sick enough for that, and they couldn't keep you because of some lame insurance thing that I didn't understand, so I volunteered to take you home and watch over you until you woke up."

Peter's limbs felt like lead. He fought to keep his eyes open, to stay awake. "Why?" he asked.

"It's kind of my fault you got hurt," the young man told him, an embarrassed look on his face. "If I'd been paying more attention to where I was going, then maybe you wouldn't have run into me."

"It's not your fault," Peter mumbled. Unable to keep his eyes open any longer, he let them close. "What . . . what's your name?"

"Robert." The young man took Peter's hand, held it between his. "Sleep," he said. "You need it."

"I'm so glad I ran into you last week," Peter said as he led Robert into his bedroom. "I appreciate you taking the time to help me with my problems."

"No problem," Robert replied.

Pulling Robert close, Peter kissed him long and passionately. When he broke off the kiss, his heart was pounding like a jack-hammer in his chest. "I want to repay you for all your kindness," he said, pulling off his shirt as he did. "But first I have to make a quick trip to the bathroom."

Robert let his eyes play over Peter's torso, scanning every inch of his smooth, muscular chest and flat abdomen. "I'll be waiting," he said, smiling.

"I won't be long."

Robert sat on the edge of Peter's bed as the bathroom door closed. Reaching up, he popped the blue contact lenses out of his eyes and tossed them to the floor, where they were soon buried beneath a pile of clothing.

Turning off the bedside light, Robert sprawled on the bed, a satisfied smile on his face. It had been so long since he'd toyed with his prey that he'd forgotten how exhilarating the thrill of the chase could be.

The bathroom door opened. A band of light flowed from the doorway, illuminating both the bed and the naked figure upon it. "You've got a beautiful body," Peter said.

There was an edge to Peter's voice which made Robert wary. *Something is wrong here*, he thought. "I try to make myself as beautiful as possible," he said, squinting his hungry violet eyes, peering at his latest lover.

Love Me Forever

Peter was standing in the open doorway, backlit by the bathroom light, a revolver clasped tightly in his hands. "Miss me?" he asked.

Drawing upon over a century of experience, Robert altered his face so that it showed surprise and shock. "Peter," he gasped. "What are you doing?"

"Cut the crap," Peter snapped. "I know who you are."

In the blink of an eye, all traces of expression vanished from Robert's face. "How?" he asked.

"I've known all along," Peter told him. "Right from the start. You were too perfect, too good to be true. Nobody's that benevolent, that kindhearted, not even fucking Mother Teresa."

Robert sat up, swung his legs over the edge of the bed. "You don't want to do this, Peter," he said, his voice calm and reasonable. "I can give you pleasure the likes of which you've only dreamed of."

Sweat broke out on Peter's brow. His hands began to tremble.

"I can be whoever you desire," Robert said as he slowly rose to his feet. His features shifted, changed. Tom Cruise, Jeff Stryker, Luke Perry, Robert Smith, and a host of others passed before Peter's eyes. "Anyone."

The weight of the gun seemed to increase with each passing second. Holding it up, keeping it aimed at the figure standing before him, took all of Peter's rapidly fading strength.

"Let me satisfy your every need," the figure said. Smiling, arms outstretched, it stepped toward Peter, becoming a double for Chet as it did.

Deep in his heart, Peter had always known that his love for Chet was a futile one. It would never have worked, was never meant to be; if they'd become lovers, it would never have lasted, would have destroyed their friendship in the process. That didn't stop Peter from dreaming, though. Without dreams, what use was life?

"I need you, Peter," the Chet-figure said. Its penis stiffened, grew erect. "I want you."

Fighting back tears, Peter squeezed the trigger. The gun roared, bucking in his hands.

Eyes wide with shock, the Chet-figure stumbled backward, a gaping hole in its stomach. No blood flowed from the wound. It was empty inside, hollow, a void waiting to be filled.

Hands clutched to its wound, the Chet-figure slumped down beside the bed. As it did, its features flickered, popping in and out like a television set with faulty reception. One instant it was Chet, healthy, tanned and muscular, the next a scrawny, pale, sexless creature with a smooth, hairless head, twin slashes for a nose, a lampreylike mouth lined with saw-edged teeth, and large, pain-filled violet eyes.

Shaking from the effort, the strain showing on its face, the creature erected the Chet-facade once again. Raising its head, a hurt look on its face, it peered up at Peter. "I love you," it croaked. "Hold me, Peter. I don't want to die alone."

Tears streaming down his face, Peter raised the gun, aiming it at the ruggedly handsome face he had once secretly desired. "You don't know what love is," he said.

Then he pulled the trigger.

—And
the Horses
Hiss
at Midnight

by
A. R. Morlan

"Sure you've heard of *that* one," Mona the Tattooed Girl told me as she slipped her vine-covered fingers into my shirtfront. In the busy near-silence of the approaching nightfall, I heard one of the buttons give way and softly roll off into the trampled grass behind the midway, the sound all but lost in the swell of crickets and the distant tire-kisses on the highway far beyond.

Tracing the swell of one halter-trapped breast with my left hand, as my right wound around her bat-and-vine-encircled waist, I whispered once again, "No, I've never heard of snakes hiding in carousel horses. . . ."

Another of my shirt buttons was liberated from the surrounding fabric before Mona replied, "But they do . . . it's only the people who don't believe who say it's untrue. The people who don't dare believe"—another pair of fingers sliding down my chest, another button rolling off to be forever lost in the litter-flecked grass—"and the people who are *afraid* to believe. . . ."

"Why would they hide in wood?" My right hand slid downward, to her needle-embroidered belt with the navel buckle, lingering at that delicate indentation before seeking the softer, far deeper indentation below.

Mona's lips brushed against my chest a moment before she spoke against my skin. "Not in the wood itself . . . they hide in the cracks in the wood, the places hidden by the shadows and contours of the horse's surface . . . places you don't normally look. But just because they aren't seen, doesn't mean they aren't *there*." The last was almost muffled by my own quickly rising chest. My breath was coming in hitches. I let my hand wander across her back to fumble with the knotted ties of her halter as I asked her, "But why be there if no one sees them? What's the point in living just to hide?"

The Tattooed Girl's eyes glittered in the almost-full moonlight; her lipstick shone near-black against her small white teeth as she stared at me in the darkness. *"What's the point*— That's like saying what's the point in me getting all of these"—she used her button-popping hand to point to her embellished breasts and flatly decorated torso—"if I don't walk around all but naked all the time . . . which I *don't*," she added defensively, and for a moment, I feared I'd lost my chance with her, the chance I'd been all but praying for since I'd first seen her earlier that evening, standing on her small stage in the Fabulous Freaks tent on the midway.

The "Freaks" part may have been something of a misnomer; the best this carnival could come up with was the ubiquitous Headless Woman sitting light bulb–surmounted in her wooden chair, the parabolic mirror which hid her head *almost* flawlessly set up and lit, along with a merely anorexic-looking Thin Man and mediocre sword-swallower (he used no sword thicker than a good-sized shish kebab holder). But "Fabulous" more than applied to the spotlit Mona the Tattooed Girl. I thought, upon seeing her, that the word should've been forever reserved for her alone.

— And the Horses Hiss at Midnight

Spread-wing bats flapped with each languid exhalation and inhalation, all but flitting from bloody thorn to moon-kissed leaf. Kudzu vines seemed to grow upon her red-tipped fingers, winding and spreading over and around her knuckles, growing more dense by the second. The arabesques encircling her arms and neck crept up onto the bare sides of her head, touching the roots of her shaggy dyed-blond mohawk before winding upon themselves and snake-trailing down her spine, down to the low-slung waistband of her high-cut shorts. Sylphids and shaggy satyrs chased each other down and around her thighs, around each rose-touched knee, and spiraled down her calves to her flatly braceleted ankles. Below the links of yellow gold sunk into her flesh, branching thinner chains of ink and imagination, leading down to her red-tipped toes. Only her face was free of permanent embellishment; her kohl-lined green eyes and glittering carmine lips had been decorated by her own hand. But the color in her cheeks which bloomed and flushed when she read my silently mouthed *Will you make love to me?* was perhaps the most wonderful, thrilling adornment on her entire ornamented body. . . .

And more wonderful still, she was waiting for average, unadorned *me* after the carny wound down, after the wooden carousel horses did their last prance and canter before resting still and frozen in the moonlight. Taking my sweating, naked-looking fingers in her own cool vine-wound ones, she led me to a place of undisturbed grass and near-silence, her long mythic legs scissoring beside me. . .but before we could undress, before the promised lovemaking could begin, she'd whispered a strange thing about the horses, and the hidden snakes—

Hoping to recapture her ardor, or whatever it was that made an exquisite being like her blush and then mouth "Yes" to my request for sex (was it my use of the word "love" that had swayed her, or did she find my mundane exterior somehow exotic in its ordinariness?), I reached up and caressed the smooth side of her head, then moved my fingers and thumb close to her eyes, her lips, and said, "All right, all right, so they live *to* hide . . . maybe they want to, or like to?"

That brought back her smile, made her dancing eyes glitter. "Yesss," she said in a rush of warm air against my gently probing fingers, "that's what they like best of all . . . the coming out *after* hiding. . . ." Closing her eyes until her lashes cast fluttery crescents across her upper cheeks, she reached behind her and undid her halter ties herself, but allowed me the honor and pleasure of removing the twin triangles of black fabric. Revealed in the moonlight, her nipples and breasts cast small shadows on her flesh; both fleshy protrusions were decorated right up to the very tips of the nipples with petal after layered petal—each breast was a full-blown chrysanthemum surrounded by curling rings of leaves.

Closing my eyes for a moment, I could almost feel the individual petals beneath my delicately tracing fingers, but Mona reached up and thumbed both my eyes open, then let her forefingers linger on my temples. Rubbing them gently, she whispered, "Time for botany later . . . they wait until they're being ridden, before coming out, y'know," she went on dreamily, as she moved her hands down my cheeks and neck, her flesh gliding smoothly, like slick leaves, until she'd reached my chest, and nipples.

Circling my flesh with her thumbs, Mona shifted slightly below me as if trying to squirm out of her cutoffs without touching them with her hands, as she went on in that same lazy yet succinct voice, "It's best when there's a child, or a woman on the horse . . . that's when the snakes slither out of the cracks, one by one, and inch by inch, and when there's a little bit of silence between the notes of the carousel, they start to hiss . . . maybe one at first, then a couple of them, hiss *hiss* . . . and while they're doing that, they undulate, maybe touching the rider's calf, or a kneecap . . . whatever's exposed, whatever's unsus*pecting*—"

Finally taking her nonverbal hint, I reached down and began to undo the buttons under the fly of her cutoffs, wanting to pop the buttons off as she had done to me, but still afraid to be so rough, so obvious. This was her place, her world, and I didn't know who might come running should she cry out or worse.

— And the Horses Hiss at Midnight

"—and maybe at first they think it's a bug, or some part of their clothes that's loose and flapping, but then, when the snake's little tongue does that slow flicker and snap-back, *then* the rider knows . . . and *then* the rider hears the hissing for what it is, but the ride is going 'round, y'know? It can't stop . . . there's no emergency brake on a merry-go-round," she added with this little chuckle that never reached her staring eyes. Mona waited until my fingers had freed the last of the buttons before wrapping both arms around my back and whispering in my ear, "So the rider just goes 'round and 'round, while the snakes slither up and around their little knees and feet, hissing and waving, enjoying the ride . . . and all the rider can do is grab hold of the pole and scream against the music . . . and the ride goes so fast, no one else can see the snakes . . . 'specially not the other people on the ride, the ones whose snakes are hiding for now—"

Hitching my fingers into her waistband, I waited until Mona arched her back slightly before tugging down the shorts. Once they were past her hips, her knees, she wiggled until they could be kicked off her body with her lower legs . . . and as she was busy freeing herself of the cutoffs, she relaxed her grip on my body just enough so that I could get a good moonlit look at what was tattooed beneath the place where her shorts had been—

That she was bare down there was a given; hadn't she told me earlier that she was going to get rid of her mohawk, add more snaking swirls and geometric designs on her very skull? But I had to blink my eyes a few times to register what I saw tattooed on and around her gently mounded mons and swollen labia—the second set of carmine lips and sharply outlined, tattoo-crosshatch-shadowed teeth surrounding her lower set of lips, the colored twin curve of the faux carmine-inked lips glistening, as if she'd just licked them moist. I reached down to probe and caress that second waiting mouth, but what I felt only confused me more. The lips seemed to pucker against my flesh, as if to kiss my fingertips, while just beneath them I felt the hardness and rounded smoothness of teeth—some of them sharply pointed. I longed to probe deeper, to touch her hidden depths and moist inner pools, but to do so, I'd have to risk passing those teeth. Something as dangerous as it was unexpected . . . yet something enticing, because it *was* so out of the ordinary.

I started to speak, to question, but Mona shook her head, the thick swath of silvery curls in the middle rippling against the grassy ground under her skull. "Ride's started," she whispered, "No emergency brake, remember?" Wrapping her legs around me, trapping my swelling organ against my undershorts, Mona snaked her right arm down my back and dug her thumb under my waistband until she could pull my jeans and underwear down close to my hips, then lower . . . and she hugged me against her as the snap and zipper let go, and the last of the entrapping, protective fabric pulled free of my lower body. She was hissing in my ear, "I won't bite it *off* . . . but don't be surprised if you feel a tiny pinch down there . . . remember the snakes, how they love to flick their tongues. And the snakes only come out when the ride's going 'round, so be ready to get off once the music's over. . . ."

I could have left her then, before it began, but no other ride at this carnival promised so much, even as it so openly threatened me. Even the horses with their hidden snakes seemed tame in comparison with what Mona was offering me, and me alone—

—and so as she pulled me closer and deeper, I felt a brief, slick hardness as I slid into her. The ridges of the longest, sharpest teeth barely grazed my incoming flesh, but true to her word, those teeth never bore down on me. She began to hum softly, a lilting drone that swelled in my ear . . . and I never got to ask her what the consequences of lingering too long in that tightly warm elastic-walled mouth might be once that melody reached its unexpected end, for the ride had indeed begun, and since there was no stopping, I felt compelled to keep up my own dizzying rhythm while my own lips explored her face and

breasts, even as her nether lips explored and sucked deeply on
my own imprisoned flesh.

Perhaps she sensed the throbbing in my lower back, a pain
barely perceptible through my steadily growing orgasmic haze. Perhaps she sensed the gradual slowing up of the rhythm between us, a
union of motion matched to her melodious murmuring. Perhaps . . .
she sensed that the snakes longed to be hidden once more. Pushing
me up and safely out of her, she abruptly stopped the song, just as I
felt a teasing, yet definite nip close to the base of my now slippery
organ (accompanied by a deep sucking pull on the pinched flesh).
The heretofore melody-masked sound of crickets and highway
movement came flooding back against my eardrums. Like a snake
shedding its skin, my member shrank and rested as if satisfied
against my now-dangling testicles. A glistening black pearl-like
drop of blood welled up from the spot where I'd been bitten. *Ride's
over, time to get off.* And like the stilled-in-motion carousel horses,
Mona's sated set of faux tattooed lips grew flatter and less detailed
as they and the teeth below sank back into a pool of inky color and
detail against her still moist flesh. Soon only a fine dribble of her
own saliva-like juices remained near the natural pucker of her
labial lips, as if waiting for a good-bye kiss. . . .

I don't know if she comprehended my last caresses, my last lingering, tongue-probing kisses above and below; only by the slight
rise and fall of her nightmare-bloom bedecked rib cage and
breasts could I tell she was even alive. Her flushed eyelids were
closed, but whether she slept or whether she was merely reliving
recent pleasures, recent meals, in the darkened confines of her
mind, I could not tell. She was just silent.

But . . . what *was* there to say, or to ask? I doubted she'd answer
any of my questions, even if she could. Even if she knew, telling
would only spoil her dark, exotic magic for me. Like probing tiny
cracks and crevices of the carousel horses for hidden snakes
before the music and the motion began . . . or like pulling aside

her clothing *before* she'd mouthed that magical "Yes" of assent. To have done that would've spoiled the surprise, ruined that pleasure which comes with the gradual revelation *after* hiding and hinting. I could never ask her which came first, the snakes with their teasing tongues, or the tattooed lips and barely grazing teeth, for both were as intertwined as they were unique, one forming the echo to the other's sound, or the shadow to the form. . . . Enough that she'd shared *her* own hidden "snakes" with me . . . and had asked so little in payment for the ride.

I gathered up my clothes and threw them on, alternately peeking at her supine form and quickly looking elsewhere. Beyond, the rest of the carnies were busy taking apart the rides, the booths, and talking softly among themselves. None of them noticed me (or if they did, they knew better than to acknowledge my unoffical presence, perhaps remembering Mona's other rides, and other riders) as I darted, buttonless shirt flapping, through the last remainders of the midway, a rider perhaps *too* ordinary for comment despite what Mona had revealed—and done—to me.

The bite on my now-covered flesh still stung almost pleasantly with each step, even though *I* still seemed to be unchanged. I wondered if one of the carnies would come to fetch Mona from her sated slumber before morning came, provided someone *had* noticed us out there. But as I passed the carousel, its painted mounts air-suspended, hooved legs caught in midarc, I realized that my passing in Mona's domain hadn't gone entirely unnoticed—nor had my small payment for the ride left me unaltered, or *ordinary:*

Emerging from its hiding place for one daring, riderless second, a snake hissed at me from one of the suspended horses. . . .

Elixir

by
Elizabeth Engstrom

H

aving been born with defective cones in the retinas of his eyes, Simon could not tell what color the prostitute's garter belt was, only that it was one of those tear-away kinds. It gave a satisfying amount of resistance before the Velcro ripped apart and he held the bit of cloth in his hands. He unhooked her hose, then pushed her breasts out of the top of her bra and suckled them.

She felt so good to him.

Her skin was young and tight, smooth and flawless.

He flipped her over onto her belly and brought her hips up to him and rubbed against her. He liked the way her loose breasts filled his hands.

"What's this?" he asked as his fingers found a lump on her ribcage, inches under her right breast.

"Nothing," she said, and she jerked from under that touch.

The last thing Simon needed was a lumpy prostitute. He felt his magnificent erection deflate. He turned her over and held her down with one hand. It was a definite lump.

"It's nothing," she whined, but he held her still to feel it. He'd gone to medical school for two years before they found out he was subnormal, could only see black and white, and invited him to take up some other profession. The veterinary school had no problem with his disability, but he had never been able to quench his thirst for human anatomy and human medicine.

God, he wished he could have a normal life, normal sex with a normal girlfriend. No. Not him. He had to pay for his sex. Always had, always would. And what did it get him? Lumps.

He touched it and it hardened.

She bucked under him, trying to throw him off. "Leave it alone," she said.

He took a tighter grip on her, noticing with wry humor that his erection was coming back. He didn't know if it was the anomaly or the wrestling that did it. He held her still and palpated the lump. It grew and became hard.

"It's a nipple," he whispered, and his erection thrummed. He slid inside her, gratified by the little sigh that escaped her. Then he moved slowly, one hand fingering one fine young breast, one hand toying with the odd little nipple. Life was indeed grand.

He pushed her away and looked down at her in the dim light of his bedroom. Beads of sweat stood out on her upper lip. Strands of hair stuck to her forehead and temple. He didn't think he'd ever really aroused a woman before. Her nipples were hard—he turned her and looked—all three of them. He touched the one, the strange one, gave it a gentle squeeze, and a drop of liquid appeared.

His erection grew to what felt twice its normal size.

He rubbed his penis on her leg and took the little nipple in his mouth. He sucked and drew in a tangy little taste. It tasted like . . . tasted like something fresh, something from his childhood. An experimental taste . . . He couldn't quite recall . . .

Elixir

He sat up, savoring the flavor, trying to remember, trying to remember.

She touched his arm. He looked at her, at her young face, at her shimmering eyes. He looked at the geometric pattern in the sheets, and it looked different. He didn't recognize it. Everything was different. Everything seemed to be more sharply defined, as if he had suddenly discovered a new depth of perception.

Colors! He was seeing colors! He closed his eyes and rubbed them, thinking as he did so, that it was the logical cartoon thing for him to do, but when he opened his eyes again, the colors were still there.

Colors everywhere!

His erection gone, his lust forgotten, he leaped out of bed and turned on the light. He grabbed his bathrobe. It was absolutely beautiful. "What color is this?" he asked.

"Kind of a teal," she said.

"Teal," he repeated. He picked up a book. "And this?"

"Red," she began to smile.

"And this?"

"Brown."

"This?"

"Green."

"This green too?"

She nodded.

"And this?"

"That has more yellow in it."

"Yellow?"

She looked around, saw a shirt hanging on the hook in his open closet. "Yellow," she said and pointed.

"Yellow," he said with reverence, and he went over and took the shirt out of the closet. It was the most beautiful thing he had ever seen. He put it on and then went into the bathroom. He turned on the light. "Ha!" he shouted. "My eyes are green. My bathroom is blue. My towels are . . . . " He brought them into the room.

"Orange," she said.

"Orange! Ha!" He went around the room, touching things he'd seen thousands of time before, but always in black-and-white. He'd never known color before, never. He was overwhelmed with the profusion of colors, with the subtleties. He looked at the oiled wood in an oak barstool for a full five minutes. He opened all the cabinets and was shocked with the colors on the packages. The pictures, the paintings on his walls . . .

Eventually, he remembered the girl in the other room. He went back to her. She was sitting up, smoking a cigarette. Her bra and the discarded garter belt were both red. She smiled at him. "I can't believe this," he said. "I've never seen color before. Never. It's uncanny. Suddenly, I can see! I can see!"

She smiled, a slow, amazed smile. "So," she said, taking a long pull on her smoke. "You're the one."

"The one?"

"The one my mama told me about." She shook her head, stubbed out the cigarette. "Amazing. Fucking amazing."

Simon looked at her, but he had no patience for her. "I don't know what you're talking about," he said.

"Doesn't matter." She put on her garter belt, pulled her flagging stockings back up and fastened them. "I'll leave you to your colors." She slipped into her dress, then held out her hand. "Twenty."

He fumbled for his pants, then fumbled some more in his pockets. He pulled out two bills and looked at them. "They're beautiful," he said.

"Yeah," she said, then took them from him. She opened her purse, stuffed the money inside, then took her lipstick out. "Do ya like red?"

"Yes," he said.

"Good." She wrote her phone number on his mirror.

Simon couldn't believe the diversity of nature. He almost wrecked his car (white with tan interior) driving to work. The world was so green. He marveled at his receptionist (redhead with dark green eyeshadow and pink lipstick), at his waiting room (green walls, green floor, green plants, green draperies, brown chairs), at the colors of the drugs and their labels that he'd seen every day for years upon years. But most of all, he was stunned by the colors of the animals that came through his door.

The first patient was a yellow and black and white cat with the deepest yellowish-green eyes he'd ever seen. He couldn't stop gushing about how beautiful the cat was. At first the owner was pleased, but as Simon kept petting the cat, staring into its eyes, the owner began to shield her pet from him. Finally she picked up the cat and held her protectively. Simon looked up and the woman regarded him with suspicion.

Simon realized he'd better be careful.

The next was a weimaraner. He couldn't figure out what color it was. When the owner left with her dog, he called the receptionist in and asked her what color that dog had been. "Sort of liver-colored, I guess," she said, and suddenly Simon couldn't wait to do surgery to see what colors lay inside the critters.

Oddly enough, the rich red color of the blood at the first pressure of the scalpel made his stomach turn. He had never been squeamish before, but then he had never seen the color of blood before.

He was astonished at the colors inside the dog he was spaying. He loved it. He wanted to poke about in there all day, he wanted to open her up wide and look at the lungs, at the heart, at the brain.

Self-restraint came hard. But he made his way through the day.

What a marvelous day.

It wasn't until almost a week later that he took the time to wonder why he could suddenly see colors. It took him almost a week to begin to take the new sight for granted, to have the time to wonder about such things.

It took a week. About as long as his new sight lasted.

At first he noticed that the blood had turned gray.

And then he noticed that all the cats were gray.

And then he noticed that his yellow shirt was gray.

He began to hyperventilate, and had to go for a walk. By the time he got back, the whole world was gray again.

He bought a bottle of wine on the way home to keep him company. Black-and-white company. All that he deserved.

He poured a glass of the gray liquid and sat in his gray chair in his gray living room and drank. He could see the bedroom mirror through the door. He could see her phone number, written in black, on his mirror.

He drank until he couldn't stomach any more, then lay down on his bed and fell into a restless sleep.

He dreamed in color. Fabulous Technicolor images swept through his psyche for hours. He saw himself in his dream, gaping at the kaleidoscopic images.

When he awoke, he tasted it. Her elixir. He needed more.

Agitated, he called his receptionist and had her cancel his appointments for the day. He needed to think. He needed to plan.

He paced the room, the hooker's phone number burned into his deformed retinas. He needed to call her. He needed her.

He hated needing her. He felt like a junkie.

She could use him. She had something he wanted, something he needed, and she could blackmail him, she could use that against him. There was no telling what price an unscrupulous prostitute would put on such a personal, rare drug.

He would pay it, whatever it was.

Or would he? Was there a limit? After all, he had lived for almost forty years without seeing colors, and now, after one week, he was ready to sell his soul to have color sight?

It didn't make sense.

Of course it made sense. He wanted it simply because it was glorious to have, and because for the first time he felt equal with everybody else. He felt normal. He knew that nobody could tell by looking at him that he was different, but he *felt* different. He knew. He could tell. And when he had proper sight, he didn't feel inferior anymore. He'd always lived feeling lower, slimier, less worthy. It took nothing for Simon to tell himself over and over what a worm he was, and believe it.

But that was stupid. He might *feel* inferior, but he *wasn't* inferior.

He had to have his color sight back. It was the one thing, the *one* thing that made him normal. Absolutely normal. Above ground and on a par with everybody else.

He picked up the phone. And then put it back. He had to have a plan first. He had to know exactly how much he would pay.

He paced into the night, growing ever more agitated.

He called the office and left a message on the service for the receptionist to cancel his appointments for the next day, too.

Then he sat down and let reality flow over him. The idea that he'd had in the back of his mind, that one idea, that bad idea he hadn't let come forth. It now cloaked his mind like a mildewed blanket.

He wouldn't pay anything for her. He would have her, hold her, keep her. He would be in control of this situation. He was tired of being on the ends of everybody else's strings. First his parents, and then the idiots at the medical school. Then his veterinary professors. Then his clients. It was as if he had no balls.

But now *he* would be in control. For once.

His penis pushed against his pants as it began to swell. He went to the clinic to gather up a few things he needed.

Then he called her.

No sooner had she walked in the door, then he had her on the floor, ripping at her clothes. As he was doing it, he wondered at his behavior, this was so unlike him, but he was so eager, so anxious, so desperate . . .

And she liked it. She liked it a lot.

Ahhh. The fluid coated his tongue like oil, and when he finished reveling in its odd flavor, he opened his eyes to spectacular color.

He grabbed her hand and pulled her along to the bedroom.

When he was finished, they lay together, she smoking a cigarette, he trying to memorize the nuance of every color, shade, hue, and tone within eyeshot.

"What's your name?" he asked.

"Alexandria."

"Will you marry me?"

She snorted and got up off the bed, gathering her clothes.

He lay calmly, watching her dress. She frowned at him, and showed him the torn seam in her blouse. He'd ripped the button off her skirt, too, and broken its zipper.

She walked over to his side of the bed and stood looking down at him, her long, smooth legs within reach. He reached. She backed away. "Twenty," she said, "plus another twenty for the clothes."

"Marry me, Alexandria."

"No way."

"Please?"

"Why?"

"I have to have you."

"You know my number."

"That's not good enough," he said.

"Tough. Give me my money."

"I'm begging you."

"Simon," she said, her eyes earnest. "Your color sight doesn't come from me."

He opened the headboard and withdrew a syringe. Before she could react, he grabbed her and shoved the needle deep into her butt. He pushed the plunger and a full dose of animal tranquilizer entered her bloodstream. She stumbled from him, and made it through the living room to the door.

He caught her before she fell, and carried her back to the bedroom.

He spent an hour removing her clothes. He looked at all the colors in her faded denim miniskirt, inside and out. He investigated all the details of her panties, her blouse, her underwire bra. He inspected her from pink-polished toenails, up through bronzed legs, to reddish blond pubic hair, across tan lines to her lovely breasts, the freckles across her chest that matched the ones on her nose, the remnants of red lipstick, and her hair, reddish blond, like down below. She was long and lean, and he liked her lines.

He touched a nipple and it shrank like the sea anemones he'd seen at the aquarium. He touched the other one. It did the same. Then he touched the little strange one, and it too, acted like the others.

He squeezed it, but no fluid came out. He suckled it, but got nothing. He covered her with a blanket and waited for her to waken.

She slept for two days.

He monitored her vital signs with growing dread. After the first day he was certain he had killed her—induced an irreversible coma. *You jerk*, he said to himself. *You lowlife. You worm.*

Eventually, she moaned, and turned over, and her eyelids fluttered.

He was so grateful, he cried.

He dressed her in his bathrobe and made her some soup. After she had eaten, and her headache subsided somewhat, he got her up and walked her around the apartment until she felt better. He apologized over and over, but she seemed to have no memory of why she was still there.

He seized upon the opportunity and convinced her that she had merely fallen ill, and he had nursed her back to health.

"How long have I been here?"

"Two days."

"Two days! I have to call my mother."

He handed her the phone. She dialed with pale fingers.

"Hi, Mom, it's Alexandria. I'll call back later." She hung up. "Machine," she said.

She's reasonable, Simon thought. *Surely I can reason with her.* "Alexandria," he said. "We need to talk."

"About what?" She was looking better by the moment.

"I need you. I want to have you with me. All the time."

"You mean like live together?"

"Yes."

"I don't think so."

"Why not?"

"I don't even know you."

He got off the bed, onto his knees, and took her hands in his. "Listen. It's through you that I've found life. I've become whole. Without you, I'm nothing. I *need* you. I've got to have you."

She pulled his bathrobe tighter around her. "You're scaring me," she said. "I think I better go home."

"No. Please don't. Please stay with me. I beg you."

She got up to leave and he hit her with the needle again. This time, the dosage was right.

When she became unconscious enough, he rigged up an IV, dripping an ever-so-slight mixture, just enough to keep her subdued. He strapped her to the bed, and when she was secure, he showered, shaved, and went to work.

When he returned home, she was in much the same state. He stood looking at her half-lidded eyes, and the pulsing began again in his loins. His dreams of being a doctor flew through his mind. With her, he could be a doctor. He could go back to medical school. Then he would be more than equal. Then, maybe, he would even be a little bit superior for a change.

He walked over to her, and saw the dark circles under her eyes. He saw the gumminess at the corners of her mouth. The nipple stayed dry.

Over the next few days, he kept her in a catatonic state, but the reality was this: Alexandria's elixir was a product of her arousal, and as long as she was sedated, she would secrete no milk of the gods for him.

Defeated, watching the colors slide into shaded halftones, he took the IV out of her arm, put a bandage over the bruise. He felt even lower now that his last-chance experiment had failed. How long would he have kept her there? Weeks? Months? Years? What had he been thinking? His actions were criminal, were monstrous. He was a slimeball. He should be shot. At the very least, he didn't deserve her. Didn't deserve her youth, her body, her devotion, her . . . her elixir.

He untied her and lay down next to her. She put an arm around him, a heavy, unwieldy arm, and he held her close, crying into her hair, ashamed to the very roots of his soul at what he'd done.

But his self-recriminations hadn't diminished his excitement, and as soon as she began to respond, he was out of his pants and into her, his hand toying with that odd little nipple. With her half-conscious arousal, it oozed and oozed, and Simon lapped it up like a puppy.

Once a week. That's all she would agree to.

Every Monday night at eight o'clock. Every Monday night he waited for her, fear keeping his bowels in a clutch. What if she'd been killed during the previous week? Found somebody to love and moved to Memphis or something?

But every Monday night at eight o'clock, she showed up.

She squealed as he grabbed her in a bear hug and whirled her to the bedroom, where he would tease her until that sweet little gland began to overflow, and then he'd make love to her. He would beg her to marry him and she would laugh him off.

One Monday night he begged her to have his child, and that got a different kind of a laugh. She dressed and left, and Simon lay on his new, wildly colorful bedspread, and thought about that. She could be convinced to have his child, he realized. Then they would be bonded together forever. He went to work on it.

The following week, they lay together on his bed after having some of the best sex of Simon's life. She was smoking, staring at the ceiling; he was toying with her delicate ear.

"Make you a deal," she said.

"Hmmm?"

"I'll have this baby for you on one condition."

He waited.

"If it has the gift, you must give it up and let my mother and me raise it."

"The gift?"

"You know," she said, and he knew what she meant. She meant the nipple. The elixir. The breast from heaven.

This was something he hadn't considered. What if the baby did have it? Wouldn't that be a perfect, loyal, lifetime source?

You pervert, he thought. *You snake. You would suck your own child's breast?* He was disgusted with himself, especially since he knew he could.

"You would live with me throughout your pregnancy?"

"I could."

"And after?"

"We'd have to see."

"And if the baby didn't have the gift?"

"We'd have to see."

"Okay," he said simply, and the deal was struck.

She moved in the next day. Simon came home from work and found her waiting for him in his bedroom. She grabbed him by the tie and pulled him to the bed. Her hungry mouth moved over his while her hands deftly unbuckled his belt, unzipped his pants, and pulled his clothes to his knees.

With a ferocity he'd never seen in her, she threw him onto the bed and straddled him, lowering herself slowly, carefully, hotly, deliciously down onto him.

He closed his eyes. This was too good.

He looked up at her, and her eyes were closed. She was concentrating. A drop of clear fluid sparkled on the tip of her third nipple, beckoning him, tantalizing him. He touched it, then licked his finger. Oh, God, this was good.

She began to move, her inner muscles fluttering like butterflies, like birds, like bats, and then it felt as if her womb extended its lips and sucked the semen from him as through a straw. He came so hard, so fast, there was no time to relish the feeling. In one long agonizing spurt, he was finished.

She put both hands on her belly and smiled a quiet, secretive smile. She nodded. "Done," she whispered, and rolled off him, falling into a deep sleep with one leg still thrown over his wrinkling pants.

The next day, the supernumerary nipple dried up and became little more than a little discolored lump on her rib cage.

Alexandria was pregnant.

He went to work and when he came home there was usually a home-cooked meal waiting for him. She seemed to enjoy playing house as much as he did, until his color sight faded back to black-and-white. Then he grew irritable and grumpy.

She blossomed and grew round and plump, rosy and giggly.

He glared at her.

She laughed at him.

He counted the days. They proceeded with infuriating slowness. Nine months of black-and-white. After having color sight for so long he felt seriously handicapped. And bitter. Totally and absolutely inferior. Useless. Worthless.

She used that. She spent all his money on baby things. She seemed to favor pink, referred to the baby as "she," and when he questioned her about it, she said that her mother had pronounced the child "the one."

"The one?"

"Perfection," she said.

A girl. That news was the only encouraging thing in his life, since he had no intention of giving any girl child of his to this prostitute and her weird mother.

Early one morning, after a restless night, when Alexandria's belly was hard, swollen and veined, a knock came on the apartment door. Simon wrapped his bathrobe around himself and opened the door.

A hawkish little woman brushed past him, throwing her damp coat and wet umbrella onto his new red-and-yellow sofa that had been gray to him since the day it was delivered.

"Excuse me," he said.

"Make tea," she said to him, and walked directly into the bedroom. He followed her in.

"Mama," Alexandria said, then frowned as a contraction worked its way through her.

"Your mother?" Simon said. It was inconceivable that this lovely, soft creature could be the product of this hardened, wrinkled, gray thing with rodent teeth and glittering eyes.

"Tea," she said again, then crossed her arms until Simon left the room.

He brought back three cups of herbal tea on a tray as another, harder contraction pulled on Alexandria.

"Want me to call the doctor? Should we be getting to a hospital?"

"No doctor," the woman said. "No hospital. We'll take care of this right here." She looked at her watch. "And soon." She pulled a bottle from her bag and poured some thick black liquid into Alexandria's tea. "Drink up, Alexandria." She turned back to Simon. "Leave."

"Leave? No way. This is my child, and I'll be here for her birth."

"This is not your child, you ninny. This is *our* child. Get out of here."

Alexandria gasped and clutched with pain.

Simon's stomach seized. He hated to see anyone in pain, especially Alexandria.

"I have pain medication," he said. "Alexandria, do you want something for the pain?"

"Nothing," the woman said.

"I'm asking *Alexandria*," Simon said, feeling a test of wills boiling up, and feeling equal to the task. He'd throw this old woman right through the window if he had to, and he'd take Alexandria to the hospital.

Elixir

The woman stood up and faced Simon. "I'm telling you that we know better than you do how to handle this. She can have nothing for pain. Now leave this room."

"And *I'm* telling *you* that this is *my* house and *my* child and if you aren't a little more reasonable and considerate, I will ask *you* to leave."

She stared at him.

"I'll call the authorities," he said.

"You don't know what you do," she said. "You don't know what you do."

"I've had medical training."

"You see yourself as unworthy," the woman said. "Therefore, you are. You endanger this child."

Alexandria wailed.

The woman whipped up the sheets and Simon saw the baby's head crown between Alexandria's legs.

"Get towels," the old woman hissed. "Lots of towels."

"Mama . . . "

"It's coming," her mother said, and pushed Simon toward the door.

He came back just as the baby's head came out. Its little cheeks were fat and full, but dark-colored. Very dark.

"One more," the old woman said, and with a heart-wrenching grunt from Alexandria, her mother pulled the baby out by the arm. "A girl," she said.

Simon dropped the towels on the floor. "Does she have it?" he asked.

"She's not breathing," the mother said, then held the baby up by one foot.

"Make her breathe, Mama," Alexandria begged.

"Does she have it?" Simon asked. "Let me see."

"*Get out of here,*" the mother said, as she put two fingers in the baby's mouth and wiped out something thick. She whacked the child on the butt, but there was no response.

"Let me see," Simon said, he was too eager, too anxious, he couldn't stand it.

The mother put her mouth over the child's and sucked, then blew in little puffs. She listened to the chest, but there was sadness in her eyes. "There is no life," she said, and straightened up, looking far older than she had when she walked in.

Alexandria sat up, wailing, reaching for the dead baby that was still connected to her by its umbilicus.

Simon picked up the warm, slippery little thing. Under its right nipple was another nipple, tiny but erect, and what looked like a tiny breast beneath it. He pushed on it gently with his thumb. Liquid.

He kissed the child on the forehead, on one fat little cheek, and then he put his lips to the nipple and sucked.

"No!" the mother yelled.

"No!" Alexandria screamed.

But with a little pop, it opened, and a bitter liquid gushed into his mouth and down his throat. He swallowed before he could react. It must have looked like black pus, he thought, as he winced and spit and thrust the cooling child at its mother.

Both Alexandria and the woman watched him.

He wiped his tongue on one of the towels, but the taste was oily and wouldn't go away.

The mother slapped her moist, smelly palm against his eyes. "*As thou seeist thyself*," she hissed at him.

"Worm," Alexandria whispered.

Simon knew he was beneath contempt, and his sight faded, faded, faded.

The next time Simon awoke, he didn't know if it was day or night. His house was absolutely silent.

He felt his eyelids. His eyes were open, but he saw nothing. He stared into nothing and wondered what had happened. He must have passed out.

Then he noticed a flickering movement out of the corner of his right eye. He sat up in bed and turned his head to the right. Something slipped past his vision. Something white?

Something in the house?

Heart pounding, he lay awake, unseeing eyes open wide, afraid, wondering.

And then he saw something right directly in front of him. It wasn't completely dark. He wasn't totally blind. He tried to focus on it, but it was too close, it was too close. He waved his hands in front of his face; nothing there, *he was still in his bed, but what was he seeing?*

He buried the back of his head in his pillow, then threw the pillow on the floor, but that didn't seem to help. He was still too close. It wouldn't focus.

Then, with a force of will, he moved backward in his mind, and the object retreated.

Black shiny tunnel wall. Moist. Damp. Close. Earth. He could smell it. He could taste it.

What the fuck?

And then, as a white grub dragged a bit of a green leaf past him and the root he was hiding behind, he knew. He knew that his life had been colorless before Alexandria, and that he deserved his new sight. He had acted abysmally, sinfully, beyond all respectable behavior, but he wished she had just blinded him instead.

"As thou seeist thyself," the old woman had said. He was a worm, always had been, always would be, and he knew exactly what that leaf tasted like. Tangy. Fresh. Like Alexandria's elixir.

The
Gift of
Neptune

by
Danielle Willis

How does one compose an epitaph for a mermaid?

They called her the Gift of Neptune and she gave good head. At night you could hear the dry scrape of her scales against the straw as she shifted about in her cage. I was in the cage next to her and could watch her. Her face was smooth, white and lunar with enormous black eyes and pale lips. She smelled vaguely saline and there were always flies buzzing around the desiccated bulk of her great fish's tail. She slapped at them and moaned.

I would have liked to befriend her but she was mortally afraid of me, as were the other freaks. They called me the Thorned Rose and I gave dangerous head. Men would dare each other to have me go down on them and I would make a halfhearted attempt to be gentle but did not always succeed. My mouth was cold and sharp and I raked in more business as a spectacle than as a whore. No other traveling curiosity show had a genuine vampire, despite which fact they treated me quite miserably and treated her even worse. Freaks were freaks, no matter how rare or valuable. We were always sick, underfed, and jostled over miles of rough terrain every day so that inbred peasants could poke sticks at us through the bars of our cages or fuck us for a few coins extra.

We were fantastic and dismal and none more so than she. She cried and swore to herself in her strange tongue and huddled in a corner of her cage, clutching her moth-eaten rag of a shawl around her bare torso. They sometimes beat her for her modesty, and would pull the shawl off during exhibition hours and splash water on her to make her scales glisten. She coughed bloody phlegm and her nose ran constantly.

I watched her. My ribs being pelted with dirt clods, I would let my eyes wander over to her. My mouth full of some yokel's cock, I would stare at her and imagine her life underwater, grin at my tormenters and imagine them drowned. Sometimes, seeing her in the same position, I would bite down and cause much screaming and merriment, after which the owner would beat the piss out of me.

The owner's name was Graf and he was a very stupid white man with no teeth. Since he couldn't chew, all he ate was a thin, lumpy gruel that made him ill-tempered and flatulent, and since he was a sadistic bastard, he made everyone else eat it as well. His wife cooked it up in foul-smelling vats and slopped it in congealed gray ladlefuls into the rude wooden bowls for which he constantly reminded us to be grateful. "I could have you eating out of troughs like pigs," he'd say as he sauntered along the shabby row of cages, "so count yourselves fortunate." He knew I lived entirely on rat blood but saw to it that I got my portion anyway, just so he could shriek at me for dumping it through the privy hole when I thought he wasn't looking. I often fantasized about ripping his throat out.

His wife was a frail, straw-colored wench of a woman who was dying of something or other. They had an idiot albino son he planned to use as soon as the wife was safely in her grave. He would torment her with this eventuality whenever she was too sick to fix him his gruel. The boy was harmless enough, but had the rather repulsive habit of constantly stretching his penis until it looked as though he were going to pull it out by the roots, at which point he would let it snap back. The noise it made always reduced him to hysterical giggling. Graf beat him savagely whenever his wife wasn't looking.

The only thing that made my existence halfway tolerable was having the cage next to the Gift of Neptune. I would lie there in my filthy straw cursing the fact that I frightened her and that I couldn't speak her language. She was the only genuine nonhuman freak in the show. Graf had acquired her in a scabby little coastal hamlet littered with fish heads and the bleached bones of sea serpents. Two pulpy-faced sailors pulled her in flopping in a net, her scales glistening blue-and-green in the sunlight. They'd thrown in a wine barrel of salt water as part of the bargain, but Graf abandoned it by the side of the road after a few days because it leaked. She deteriorated quickly after that. Her scales dried out and turned the color of calluses, and she lapsed into a state of semiconscious delirium. Despite this, she was easily the most popular exhibit of the lot of us.

The other freaks were an unremarkable assortment of dwarves, hunchbacks, pinheads, harelips, and other genetic prodigies common in those days of poor medicine and rampant inbreeding. What made this particular freak show unique was that it doubled as a whorehouse. Men have always been willing to fuck anything with an orifice and never was this trait more pronounced than amongst the brain-damaged peasantry of medieval Europe. After a hard day of toiling in the wheat fields of some equally brain-damaged noble, there was nothing the average serf would rather do than down a couple pints of ale and go have some cross-eyed microcephalic with a wooden leg give him a blow job.

The only one of us that didn't have to whore in a cage was the dwarf Gustav. He had begun his stay at the freak show as part of the perennial "Bugger a Dwarf" exhibit, but soon endeared him-

self to Graf by poking his fellows' eyes out with a fork. Since
Gustav could also juggle and tell lewd stories, Graf made him his
personal assistant. He was the bane of my existence, always
squeezing his fat turnip of a face between the bars of my cage
and hissing "Rat-Catcher Rat-Catcher" in a piercing falsetto
whine that never failed to curdle my innards. Once I lobbed my
bowl at his head and bloodied his nose. Of course he went
screaming to Graf, but the broken bones were well worth the satisfaction of watching the wretched creature do a stubby-legged
jig clutching his nose and howling an accompaniment. There was
very little else available in the way of entertainment.

In the end, the Gift of Neptune no longer flinched when I
reached through the bars of her cage to stroke her hair while she
conversed with herself through lips that cracked and bled with
her incessant raving. I brushed my fingers across her mouth for a
taste of her blood, which was oily and rancid and made me so ill
I lay trembling in my filthy straw hallucinating swollen fish
bloating belly-up in chamber pots, only dimly aware of the rats
scurrying across my legs and the hateful dwarf prodding my legs
with his sharpened stick, shrilling threats to report me to Graf if I
did not immediately rouse myself and dispatch the emboldened
rodents. I was too far gone to show any evidence of pain, so after
a while the revolting little pustule grew weary of me and went to
torment the carrion hound. I could hear it snarling while the
dream fish burst and overflowed the chamber pots with their brilliant intestines.

I woke to the dry rattle of the Gift of Neptune's breathing. She
was lying on her stomach with her tail twisted at a strange angle
beneath her, as if she had tried to shift positions and collapsed
halfway through the endeavor. I struggled to my hands and knees
and crawled over to the partition between our cages, reached
through and took hold of her crescent-shaped tail fin. It cracked in
my grip and came away in brittle, iridescent flakes as I pulled her

straight. She was still raving to herself but now her voice was gone and her lips writhed in silence, the corners of her mouth caked with dried blood. I remembered the taste of it and nearly retched.

Seeing me awake, the dwarf scuttled over.

"You've been slacking long enough," he squeaked. "We'll be overrun if you keep this up. Aren't you hungry? Look, there's a fat one now."

"Where?"

"Eating out of your bowl. Are you blind?"

"I don't see it. Show me where it is, I'm famished."

"Stupid leech, must I do your work for you?"

He thrust his arm through the bars to point it out and I seized him by his hair and held him in place while I slit his throat with my nails. I caught a few spurts in my mouth before I unfastened his key belt and unlocked my cage and the Gift of Neptune's. A great pounding and bellowing went up along the row. I tossed the key belt to the werewolf, then gathered the Gift of Neptune up in my arms and hurried to the clearing where the horses were tethered. We rode off into the forest on Graf's prize dapple mare, the shouts and curses growing dim behind us.

After we put what I thought was a safe distance between ourselves and the freak show, I slowed the mare to a walk. Although her flanks were lathered with foam, she fought being reined in. Her eyes rolled with fear and she shied at the slightest crackle in the underbrush.

Presently we came to a shallow stream, which we followed for a few miles until it turned into a pool. I laid the Gift of Neptune in the shallows and let the water wash over her. She floated listlessly just below the surface, the frilled slits beneath her ears pulsing feebly.

From Hunger

by
Wayne Allen Sallee

"**H**urt me," I told her. "Rip the skin open at my temples."

"You'll still kill me," she said.

"Yes." I agreed. "But it will be easier if you tear my skin now."

That's how many of the conversations with my victim began. It ended with the moaning.

My moaning, because I was into s&m big time.

Or so I thought. Until I met Veda Daanse.

Then it was a whole new skin game.

One of the better points about being a vampire is that I get to fly around naked. When I was alive, before I met the girl with the smile from dark nowhere, it got to be that the only way I could get myself into a state of sexual arousal was if I or my partner—real or on glossy magazine print—had been in a state of public exhibition. That usually did the trick, but if I still couldn't get it hard, I had to cause myself some pain and discomfort, yet come short of self-mutilation.

When I fly around nude, I can usually hook my dangling penis against a cornice in one of the north shore buildings. Or swing low among the town houses in the Kenmore corridor and bounce my nuts off the pointed tips of the wrought iron fences encircling the properties.

That really gets the bloodlust going.

In both cases stated above, I'd chalk my idiosyncrasies up to the job I had until the chick bloodsucker forced me into an early retirement. Vampire cops are strictly from hunger and late-night syndication. I had been a thirtysomething homicide dick working the gay and lez bars along North Halsted toward the end. And I had no doubt that there was such a thing as a vampire, though I hate the fact that the world needs so badly to romanticize them.

There is nothing moral about killing anybody for the sake of sating one's own thirsts and lusts; that is tantamount to Ted Bundy wanting us to place the blame of his murderous spree on the publishers of the adult, glossy magazines that I choose to have safe sex with. Barry Cook said it best back in '56, after being questioned on dismembering Judith Mae Anderson. He said that he had an urge. Simple as that.

Vampires have urges, the other ones out there that remind me of Bundy and Richard Speck and Larry Eyler. But myself, I needed to survive. I hate having to lamely justify it, but that's the spot I was put into. It's all from hunger that I do it.

So the swooping down on people like the ultimate raincoat exhibitionist sans raincoat is a cool thing, but when that doesn't do the trick, how the hell does one cause pain to himself to help retain an erection when he can't even feel pain? I had to discover ways. Hell, I had eternity, assumedly.

The public romanticizes vampires too much, but it is true that there is more to it than just the bleeding and the feeding. I still like the sucking and the fucking and the jerking off, too. Too much blood in me, I fart and belch as good as the rest of the living when they've eaten too much junk food.

From Hunger

I just don't get what the thrill is for young kids to go gothic and do everything short of worship Satan. It is like what I said about the killers—and I admit there are followers of scuzbags like the Night Stalker chuckmeat out in California—and how I compare them with the vampire ideal. Myself, I'd be much more sympathetic to a werewolf, if there is such an animal, because I think of their particular suffering the same way I do that of an alcoholic. I can't help but feel sorry for them in the way they are so utterly controlled by something they cannot change. The werewolves, I mean. Lon Chaney in the film, begging to be locked up. Only an infinitesimal number of the alkie cops I know abuse anyone but the dregs of our criminal community, and that's the truth. Maybe the gothics don't see the struggle because alcohol and drugs make them feel the immortality they crave.

The reason I knew about the vampires and their existence had its roots in a case I dealt with several years back. It was the summer and fall of '91 and there were several sudden deaths in a prominent gay bar under the el at Roscoe and Halsted. The Glory Hole, it's called. One of the first to have an attraction called a "grab bag," which would be best likened to the blind pigs of Prohibition days. Instead of illegal hooch and gambling, the gay bars (and presumably the dykeholes, too) had embarked on a thing where a patron could go into a darkened room way in back. In some cases, down stairwells. Naked men in chaps or crotchless Spandex would be hovering like wallflowers, discernible by neon hoops worn like bracelets or neon pins inserted in the penis or bicep.

(It is this, as well as seeing the lezzies wearing earrings in their temples or sewing their gash shut—I'd see the latter in lockup or hear the stories from the backups—that started me in on the No Pain No Gain aspect of my lovemaking.)

Yeah, I suppose it's hard to swallow, no pun intended. I lost my sex drive completely over the course of those weeks. The kicker was when I came across a stash we found in the apartment of a well-known Chicago news anchor, which also happened to serve as a backdoor buddy's fuck pad. Back room at the Wellington Hotel, a big box of magazines. Bootleg out of Farmingdale, Long Island, a stroke mag to end all stroke mags: HUSKS. Burn victims in erotic positions. Paralytics sixty-nining. Double limb amputees doing it doggy-style. My erection was so big, my ejaculate so strong, I was disgusted at myself. How could I be aroused at such atrocities?

"It was midsummer," I told Veda the very first night she asked about my attitudes toward kinky sex, vampire-style. "I was able to hose down my pants in the shower down the hall, deal with them being sticky-dry for the rest of my shift."

"Isn't nothing wrong with having thoughts about a book like that," Veda Daanse whispered, licking her fangs as I licked her nipples, her saliva running down her Nordic breast to mix with mine. "It isn't like they were being tortured."

"But I feel like I'm torturing my own victims for my own inadequacies at attaining the bloodlust . . . "

"Oh, I wouldn't call it torture, baby," she told me. "Their deaths were quick and painless. All you made them do was struggle a little. We all struggled when we were alive . . . "

I had told Veda everything. About my descent into the minor s&m dens, the endless bars, the one joint on Eugenie where I met the perfect date. The girl with the smile from dark nowhere and a snatch that beckoned with sanguine anticipation. I swallowed it and she swallowed me, never even getting to the point of finding a cheap dive on Belmont and a bed she could handcuff me to; no, it was suck, fuck, out of luck. Fangs in the neck, you know the drill.

In the back seat of a '93 Taurus.

The worst part about it, she only led me on with the kink bit so that she could get at my blood. The hell with these romantic soap opera/rock star/Beverly Hell 90210 vampires you see on the bestseller lists. This one was a damn bloodsucking killer, yet she couldn't believe I wanted someone to inflict pain on me! I never saw the undead bitch again. Just up and left without a simple by-your-leave (a gothic vampire phrase, that last part, huh?).

Well, it was bad enough that I found myself with a pair of fangs and a face as pasty as Drew Barrymore's in that Amy Fisher made-for-TV flick. Hell, I'll save you all that virgin vampire ennui crap. The idea of being undead was secondary to the fact that I still had my sado-masochistic tendencies.

As above, so below. Yeah, right. Just like the days before the change, when I'd find it so hard to get an erection, nights that I'd masturbate with futility so hard that the skin would break and bleed when I finally got a blue-veiner of any worth, now it was the same, except that I needed to get the taste. The bloodlust. Wanted to give someone the crimson kiss. Sanguine sex. All those phrases that filled pages of cheap vampire novels the way phrases like "boxing the clown" and "revving the Viking Pontiac" appeared in the s&m books in my hall closet.

It didn't just suck. It *blew*.

I knew what I'd become; I understood that I'd have to kill. But it wasn't the scent or smell that got me going into a frenzy. There had to be pain on my part. Physical pain, like the things I begged my first victim to do as told at the beginning of my narrative.

Gouge into my temples with blood-red lacquered fingernails. Tear open my lower lip so that it hung down like a deflated balloon. I had begged this from every one of the undead wannabes from the Division Street singles bars to the clotted neon dives beneath the elevated tracks on Belmont, windowless joints where fourteen-year-olds hung out wearing crotchless leather pants and black overcoats, listening to teenage death songs.

Show them what the hunger was really like when taken to the extremes. Like a warlord's lackey in Mogadishu forcing a captured airman to read some trash statement on camera before blowing a hole in the back of his head, my requests were as insane. Did the kid in the bomber jacket from Ludington, Michigan, ever think he would die in the desert reading a maniac's bible? Hell, how many rape/murders did I handle as a cop where the victim's last words equated to *just tell me what to do and let me live?* (The killers would always talk about it, either in lockup or at trial.)

Within months I had degenerated to the point that I could no longer get the bloodlust simply by having my skin torn and shredded. I forced a girl in Bucktown to try and bite off two of my fingers before I broke her neck.

No. Forced is not a pathetic enough word.

Requested might do it. At the very least, I wasn't pleading yet.

Veda and I in bed in the abandoned factory on Goose Island. She was a damn exciting lay and was into more than a little experimenting. I am handcuffed to her bed. She has taken a dog muzzle I reshaped and placed it on my face snugly so that my lower eyelids are pulled down over my cheekbones.

I try to squeeze my eyes tightly into focus, like gun turrets, and the simple pain excites me greatly. My eyes dry out quickly and the light from the lone bulb in the hallway burns me.

Veda is nude and luxurious to watch. Even before she begins to play with herself, putting four fingers up her cunt and jamming her thumb into her pelvic bone, I am already erect with the anticipation of what she will do to me.

With her free hand, she takes a plastic gun, one that squirts high-powered streams of water. It is filled with formaldehyde.

She aims at my eyes. Blows me a kiss with fingers that glisten with her come.

With Veda, I did not have to beg.

Seven months into my new eternity, I started moving my killing ground farther west, past the housing projects and into the part of Chicago where art galleries sprang to trendy, two-dimensional life from the husks of converted factory lofts. It was here that I met Veda Daanse.

The place was called Indulgence. First of the new strip bars to return to Chicago after a decade-long ban; I was a rookie walking the

From Hunger

State Street mall beat back when Joe DiLionardi, along with the Cook County Sheriff's Offices instituted Operation: Angel. A modern day Eliot Ness, the cops under his command had effectively shut down every major prostitution house in the downtown district. The fact that Robin Gecht and the Korkoralis brothers were serving up the breasts of street whores for devil worship had little to do with things. Truth was, there was a mayoral election the next spring.

Come the summer of '93, there was riverboat and casino gambling in all of Chicago and its collar counties, and "topless dance halls" such as Indulgence and The ToyHouse emerged from the cracked husks of long-empty buildings in the River West area. Forbidden fruit behind stucco walls painted in pastel colors.

If I had still been human and driving around in my old beater Pontiac Sunbird, I might've circled for an hour looking for the place. Indulgence was housed in a nondescript building on Blackhawk and Kingsbury, white stucco, red neon, a maroon rococo roof with rain dancing off of it the first night I flew over.

I perched atop a water tower for an abandoned paint factory and watched the men walk in, arriving in cabs or limousines. Three hours later, in the false dawn, I was still there, watching the women leave. In the time between, I had flown through one of the air ducts to check the activity on the inside. I had to remain in the shape of a bat because my clothes would not rematerialize after I had shrunk so small. It's not like all us vampires are tight with some guy like Reed Richards of The Fantastic Four, and have Spandex outfits made of unstable molecules.

The place was disco meets industrial, with most of the music that the girls table-danced to being heavy metal and rockabilly. Because they served alcohol, full nudity was not allowed; the girls wore g-strings and rubbed latex over the nipples that quickly bubbled in the stage lights. On a few of the women, the result reminded me of the antiskid things one might have on the bottom of a shower stall.

I watched over three dozen women making their rounds, some with fine blond hair on their backs like gold dust, others with black manes that hid everything but their eyes, lips, and intent. A few of the girls wore dog collars; others dressed like drum majorettes.

None excited me in the least. The bloodlust was not there, though I was in need of a kill. I felt as frustrated as some of the chinless wonders sitting at the tables below, imagining their sex with women named Mercedes or Ballou while they stuck their tongue between their teeth and lower lip as if exploring for food. When times were this bad, I broke into blood banks and felt like some pathetic drunk. And burdened with the guilt of someone who masturbates his dick purple.

I watched the women leaving near 5:00 A.M. The rain had stopped, the sky a bluish-grey, like in a rock video. In a last-ditch effort, I had rolled naked in the muddy water of the rooftop and tried to look feral as I imagined Mercedes or one of the others clawing at me, their rubberized breasts bouncing in their final moments of life.

While I was standing up above, I saw a blond woman I hadn't recognized from within walk by, alone and defiant. She was wearing black boots and a matching raincoat.

She raised her head and looked directly at me, the dawn at my back, my pubic hair matted and dark. She opened the sash on her raincoat and I saw an almost white thatch and the sharp line of her pelvic bone. I felt myself harden as she smiled and crossed the railroad tracks.

Behind the abandoned factory, I watched her strip, out of sight from everyone else. Her skin was almost as white as her teeth, her hair a frosted blond. I wasn't certain if I was imagining that her lips looked too blue to be lipsticked. The hair that reached up from her pussy to her navel was the texture of miniature snowflakes.

Incredibly, I stared as she metamorphed into the purest white cat and pranced off as if following a ball of twine, her clothing rolled up and stashed beyond a broken window.

I hurried into my own clothing, holding back my desire. I had barely taken flight when I ejaculated into my jeans.

From Hunger

That was how I had first seen Veda Daanse. An innocent tease, I let her love me and become corrupted by me, as well.

An innocent tease, the way an employee of a major nationwide strip joint chain is expected to portray oneself. In the months we were together, Veda never knew of my sado-masochistic tendencies. Not until the very end.

She never handcuffed me and shot my eye sockets full of formaldehyde and hydrochloric acid, never sewed my tongue to the inside of my cheek. Those were all my private fantasies of her, albeit slightly different than those of the men at Indulgence, watching the women dancing while they probed their mouths with their tongues, thinking of the most proper witty comment.

I remembered the desperate thoughts from my days as a cop. My days among the living. Yessir, becoming a vampire has also done wonders for my writing skills. I could've used this speed when I was typing my F.I. reports in triplicate.

Veda's body hasn't even been reduced to slack skin on bone and here I am on, what?, page thirteen. A regular speed demon.

And when I'm done writing this, bringing it all to the present, well . . .

I'm doing myself up next.

I followed her through the streets of River West, across Goose Island to a cul-de-sac by the Kennedy Expressway. Willard Court had mock-brick buildings on only one side of the street the farther north it wound. The two-story flats along its west side were rented to artists and other self-employed individuals, including drug dealers. The east side of the street was devoid of houses and littered with burnt husks of cars. Before she jumped up to one of the shattered wrecks, an old Delta 88, I watched in awe as her cat-form successfully dodged across eight lanes of interstate traffic. This, after strutting along past the warehouse, allowing me to stare up the crack of her ass as if she were in her human form.

LOVE IN VEIN

I landed in front of the Delta 88; it had probably been maroon once. The cat perched on the hood and stared at me with, what's that word, aloofness? Blinked several times, sniffed the air.

Then simply walked on by me like the girl from Eugenie Street, the girl with the smile from dark nowhere, padded on by me with my dirty clothes and my pubic hair matted to a wet spot on my trousers with her tail swaying in the light of a summer's dawn. I was thinking "What the hell?" when she nudged her snout against a brown door halfway up the street. It opened easily and she disappeared inside.

A moment later, the door swung open full. She was there in her human form, nude with no one to see but me, the cars speeding along on the expressway eight feet below as if their drunken, overtired drivers were also vampires trying to race away the sun's cancers.

She kept the door open, hand on the inner knob, allowing me to stare at her nakedness. It was no longer just a flash of the pubes from a distance, it was everything. She looked almost Nordic. I thought this even before being told her name. Blond hair frosted near-white, though I didn't know which was the true color. Cut in a pageboy bob. Her face was all soft angles and she had a slight cleft in her chin, enhancing her bluish lips and eyes the color of chipped ice, her smile tight and turned down as if she were trying to look drop-dead sexy for the first time.

Her nipples were large for her breasts and I followed the shadows all the way down her flat stomach until I reached the downy mane of her pussy. Her legs were set apart and I longed for a look at her ass, because I knew I'd be able to see her pubic hair between her legs. As light as it was, it was full and sleek.

"You think I was going to change out there?" she said to me, her voice like a breeze. She had a slight accent that matched any of the Slavic languages spoken in the neighborhoods that side of the expressway. I suspicioned that she had lived there, in that neighborhood, before being bitten.

"What?" I mumbled back, probably drooling.

From Hunger

"I mean, it's a bad neighborhood, y'know?" She smiled and I saw her tiny sharp fangs.

"But you're a shape-shifter, a vampire like me."

"Actually, I like to think of myself as a simple little hatcheck girl who maybe lets men follow her home sometimes," she said without moving away from the door. "So are you coming in, Sherlock, or what?"

I walked in, the door slamming shut behind me.

"You're my first vampire," she said as she moved closer to me. Her breath smelled like springwater and I could hear my own blood rushing in my ears. "I mean, since the one I brought home who bit me and turned me into this." She did a little pirouette; I found myself correct in how I thought the view of her fatal ass would be.

The small talk continued as the light from between the slatted blinds crept across the room. All it really did was make me tired, the way the change to daylight savings time affects so many people. Veda told me her full name, telling me that there was some Norwegian in her blood, though her surviving line was from some country that had Alps in it. She asked me to get out of my clothes as she placed a cassette of Alannah Myles on the stereo.

We danced, nuzzled, and finally fucked in her back room in an oaken coffin that doubled as an ironing board when darkness came around again.

In my fevered dreams, Veda was everything I had always wanted, always needed, in a partner. The way she had let me approach her was so brazen it reminded me of my beat copper days at the Halsted Street bars. The casual abandon with which men and women chose their partners.

Back before there was such a thing as AIDS, which begat complimentary condoms with your drinks at the finer gay establishments, most of the homosexual action occurred around Clark and Kinzie. The gays, lezzies, and punkers slummed in dives like O'Banion's and Passport. There were no dark rooms in the back; it was mostly people of the same sex giving each other neck hickeys while teenagers danced to The Culture Club and Dexy's Midnight Runners.

I had been approached by many young girls, my youthful appearance garnering me the club detail in the first place, and I had always turned them down. They had shaved their head and pierced their eyelids. Years later, it was new detail, and men in leather who did the same body modifications approached me with similar offers of satisfaction.

It was then that I had become desensitized, although I am in no way homophobic. But I found pain to be an outlet for my self-gratification. I liked it, the first time experimenting by backing naked into a hot iron while I stroked myself.

It became my only release, the way I now wanted Veda to be my release. When I woke, she was curled up knees to elbows, and I could see her pubic hair like a thin line of trees between two pale hills. The coffin more than accommodated us.

I watched her and thought how easy it would be to hurt her, like so many of the lovers I watched in the bars, empty vessels dressed in biker gear or three-piece suits satisfied to watch women wearing latex so that they all looked like the Stepford Wives.

I couldn't hurt her, and I couldn't ask of her to hurt me. I could only imagine it, the way I would imagine mounting her in my bat-form, my small claws embedded in her inner thighs, my tongue snaking far up her into her cunt until she begged for release.

Shutting it out of my mind when she awoke, stretching like the playful cat she imagined herself to be.

Veda and I had no formal commitment toward each other, though I became more than just a casual lover for her. I did want more—to me the idea of commitment is about as romantic as a vampire tale can get—but she had her work. Hard work and no prey, huh? No, it wasn't like that. She did go out with others, although they were all one-night stands, of course. She did like me, but not enough to spend more than one day a week in my arms, one night a week fucking my nuts off. And gone from beside me as soon as the sun went down, all through the summer and autumn.

It was like that in my human days, when I met a lady cop or a neighbor I liked. No one wanted commitments, but they'd end up dating the guys who would abuse them most. Maybe that's the only reason the women from my human days even dated me, because they saw some effeminate quality within my clever banter and shoulder shrugs. Maybe they saw the willingness for self-abuse just below my skin level . . .

I didn't think this to be the case with Veda, but being without her was making me crazy. When she was out hunting someone else, I turned again to my deviations.

"Where did you get these scars?" Veda asked me the twelfth time we spent together. She had not noticed them in the candlelight. Telling me of the week's kills, every man of which deserved it, she said without derision. Talking about it like it was her regular business conversation, that she worked behind a desk and not from street level, jumping up to claw out the eyes of her men before killing them quickly.

I watched her one night. I had to, hoping it would excite me more than anything else. She followed someone who had laid some lines on her at Indulgence, then cursed her indifference toward him. Cursed her most graphically, thereby damning himself in the process.

She took a cab in her human form, following his own Mercedes 450 SL. Tipped the cabbie twenty dollars because he followed the Mercedes all the way to the far north side, Veda then shape-shifted into her feline form, jumped the guy and imbedded her cat fangs in his neck, her claws digging into his ears all the while.

Not knowing I had watched, she told me all this, all the things he had called her, how it made everything all right by her way of thinking.

Then feeling my scars when she nuzzled against my skin.

"How did you get the scars?" she asked again.

I silently cursed myself for the way I made everything all right. By my way of thinking.

LOVE IN VEIN

I had broken into Alexis Snavely's Medicinal Emporium, a place the cops were always one step short of busting, at the corner of Wabansia and Damen. Stole myself a collagen derivative that the Reverend, as he liked to call himself, had created under the auspices of some medical practicioner's license he had procured along with a notary public's license in Richmond, Virginia.

It was an absorbable hemostat, and I knew how to use it in all the wrong ways. I also brought several other items back with me to the house on Willard Court.

I spent one evening slicing away with a straight razor. Not hesitation marks; these were down to the bone. Of course, there was little blood. I had not pierced my heart.

I even strophed the blade against my inner forearm, causing wet tears of blood, like bad shaving nicks along a jawline.

Satisfied, I injected the collagen, before the accelerated nature of my body could allow the skin to close. The technique caused fault lines—technically, wound dehiscence—just beneath skin level that caused the skin to scar ever so slightly.

I hadn't expected the scars to be there three nights later when I saw Veda.

I felt that honesty in our relationship was important, and I wanted badly to tell Veda what I had done to myself. I tried leading into it by talking about the low-level thugs she encountered at Indulgence, the difficulties I had in not being around her every night.

And while I was trying to answer, Veda took it perhaps to mean something else. She went into the kitchen area to fix herself a drink. There was dead silence in the rooms.

Too late, I remembered the strychnine that Snavely kept stored in bottles of white zinfandel.

I hadn't thought about the strychnine when Veda came back into the room, passing a wall mirror. I watched the dimples in her butt as she bent to sit cross-legged in front of me.

"Well?" she cocked her head. I tried to look sheepish.

I told her that I had tried experimenting morphing into a new form, that I was tired of perching on rooftops. I said that I had misjudged the size of the beast I had become and got caught in an electrified fence.

Veda had started to sip at the glass, threw her head back in laughter, swallowing the drink whole. The stuff foamed out of her nose and we both started laughing. Then she made a high, keening sound. After the foam stopped, we both stared down at bone cartilage on the wooden floor.

Veda fell over, her spine arching in constriction, and I knew what had happened. I could do nothing at all. She could not talk, but her eyes told me that there was only surprise, no distrust or denial in her gaze toward me.

She was only an innocent tease, one who knew nothing about being physically hurt. All she had ever been dealt before was verbal insults. God forgive me.

I knew she wanted to morph into a cat, but was unable. Her hands were claws when she reached for my embrace. She fought it for full minutes before the blood came. It trickled from her nose and the corners of her eyes, like a weepy girl beneath red neon. The floor felt sticky beneath me then, and I looked down. Thick blood was pouring from Veda's cunt and rectum, her once-downy pubes looking like a dirty burr that had adhered to her crotch.

I know that there was talk between us but it's gone from my mind at this time. She coughed up great gouts of crimson before dying in my arms without ever knowing that it was I who had killed her.

Veda Daanse died the way she did because she was a vampire.

A human could not have survived the initial effects of the strychnine poisoning. The next level is something called DIC.

Disseminated Intravascular Coagulation, it says in the book I brought back with me from Snavely's. All plasma has this protein that will interact with calcium and cause a rejection of convulsions. Veda experienced massive DIC in her small blood vessels, and she was killed by hemorrhagic tissue necrosis.

The book also mentioned puncture sites of invasive procedures. I thought of my collagen injections.

And I also thought of my own depraved way to end my existence once and forever.

I am hanging upside down from the Casablanca-style ceiling fan, long dormant and dusty. There is an enema bag shoved up my rectum and I am seconds away from shooting my asshole full of strychnine. The most vulnerable organ is the anus, and anuric renal failure would allow it to work through my system faster. I can finish up these last few lines, toss the notebook in the corner with the medical manual and the other crap.

Veda's remains are below me. Her crotch and nipples are the color of gangrene. I loved her so.

I will start the fan revolving slowly as I let the screw on the enema bag loose. My blood should burst through every single wound I made that was affected by the collagen. That's about seventy punctures in all, not counting the eyes and mouth, my ass and dick. I'll be a fountain of blood, fuck the romanticism of it all.

I wonder when the cops will find us? Veda's employers will never report her missing; that kind of thing doesn't happen. Maybe drug dealers will come across us. Think it was a satanic thing.

I made sure I was hanging loosely, though. I want to have the strength to fall when I know the end is truly here, that I might fall down into Veda's dead arms, allowing our bodies to explode in one final embrace of gas and pus and blood.

A tale of two pathetic vampires who had great sex together, one who knew too much about the world, the other who knew too little.

All those who feel any kind of pity out of all of this are from hunger themselves.

A
Slow Red
Whisper of
Sand

by
Robert Devereaux

When you realize that what love is all about is heartbreak, you're all right. But if you think it's about fulfillment, happiness, satisfaction, union, all of that stuff, you're in for even more heartbreak. . . .

Romantic love keeps the world dead.

—*James Hillman*

Young willing pussy stuck on beautiful slinky moist-crotched bodies, tan, lithe, lubricious if superficial to a fault—that's what had drawn him to L.A. They were no-brainers all, into the new kink if given half a shove and enough nose candy to blame their natural prurience on. A set of cuffs, a fashionable ceiling bolt, a butt plug set to placehold for his cock, and the laying on of lashes at breasts and buttocks sufficiently rough to recall fathers trying to whip sense into them—these made them happy and tenderized them for the unexpected descent and feeding of himself and his wives. Drain the life out of them, watch tans blanch, hear screams dwindle to swoons as they swung limp and bloodless from their manacles: all prelude to a suck-and-blow multifucked frenzy with Flopsy, Mopsy, and Cottontail.

That's why he was caught short at the first sight of Esme. He'd just scoped out the hopeful couchbait, a fast eyeflick over the crowd, and was in the process of taking in the cheesy paper lanterns and

cheesier Hawaiian piped-in music—*enjoying* actually the fake long-
ings it miasma'd over the beautiful people—when his eyes slanted
downward and fixed on undying love. She strode easily, her simple
dress swaying with unaffected rhythms, an intoxication of blood and
bone beneath. Made him hesitate. Him, who had lived long ages and
had long ago learned smooth means for attaining any desire. Her
walk exuded confidence born of contentment. She floated, he could
tell, above the petty needs of the empty smilers she threaded
through, past the refreshment tables, along the pool, embracing their
beefy host like family—Ah, she was!—and moving on.

This raven-haired beauty, black fall breaking at her shoulders, had
stuff and substance. Rare integrity shone from her eyes, a commodity
lacking mostwheres he went but especially here, where dreams or
drugs guided the will-less through lives bereft of all but surface meaning. She saw him, glanced aside, was approaching a pocket of isolation
concaved between two chattering drink-holding groups, one of which
would quite soon, surely, notice her and open up to draw her in.

He began his approach.

Her brother'd latched on to show business, nothing in the world
reaching out and grabbing him in particular, so settling for a sinecure
with Dad at the studio. But Esme had always been deep in books,
found odd friends, cast an eye of bemused puzzlement on the sun-liq-
uid dealings, the impressionless series of prettymates her father rou-
tinely passed through the house—in one day, out the next—to be
replaced by another passing show. Back from Denver for a few days,
say hello, remind herself of what she didn't in the least miss. Breezing
through the party seemed a bare sacrifice, no skin broken; but it
pleased her father, for who knew what reason, immensely. She didn't
even have to stay for long. Pop in, pop out, like one of Dad's slinky
bedmates. But superficial obviously pleased him, and she knew that
their relationship—from his looks, his drawing her aside at surprising
moments to confide this or that—went much deeper than most; so she
gave him this one tiny thing of surface whenever she stopped home,

knowing it in some small measure pleased him, provided a conversational stopgap for the streams of nodding ghosts going by, Proud Daddy a role he loved to play, a role Esme loved watching him play.

She slowed toward the diving board, chubby Ed Partch with his flab-arms angled out of a Hawaiian shirt to hold a fistful of drink and with his mouth flapping to delight (as he seemed to hope) the underlings he spoke to. About to backtravel to avoid him, she sensed movement at a pool angle. Advancing in a familiar way, and yet not quite so taggable as that, was the dark loner she'd glanced at. A weird mix to him. Belonged and didn't. Thirties was her offhand guess. Not an actor, but handsome and intriguing enough to be one. In the business, but not of it. Blood hunger rode in his eyes—a lawyer, Esme supposed. Let him do his damnedest to seduce her, his intent obvious from a series of fumbled and skilled but rarely successful tries from either sex to bed her over the years; she'd wear him down until he wised up and fixed on other prey.

Not quite a smile there, not blank. When would this deep odd man deliver his line? Still he came on, totally an easy assault, more an envelopment, an assurance, words needless not tainting the air. Then he was beside her, a hand touching hers. She took it, a smooth warm grip from him and from her in response. "I'm not sure I—"

"Your name?" Soft velvet voice, a faint aroma which hinted vaguely of frankincense. An impression of ancient knowing came to her, impossible, surely, in this muscular young man.

"Esme." Her voice blushed in falter.

"Esme," he said, both a repeating and the opening of a new question. "It's time. Are you ready?"

Ready to leave the party, ready to go with him where he said, ready to climax at the slightest touch, ready to abandon completely her life in Denver—all of that was in his question, this man whose name she didn't yet know but who made her feel so good just by looking at her; and her answer, absurd but true, was yes. "I'm ready," she said, and she followed his strong dark form knifing through the crowd, windblown streamers of chat falling away to either side as they went. In the car, his car, no memory of her entry there, his hand rode up under her dress, fingers at her bikinis, beneath the lace, moistening up and down her labia, deepening, dipping in, swirling at her clit, touch at flash-point sizzling up an orgasm, moaning unbelievably into his mouth—and by the time her body reconstituted, a smooth fast road was zooming beneath them, she was belted in, he drove dark and shadowed within caressing distance, and Esme had never felt more blessedly safe and secure in all her life.

Brad resented Esme. She had an in with Dad, clearly his preferred child, and this despite the fact that Esme, long gone to Denver, only dropped in once or twice a year and barely showed herself even then. More than that, she had no trouble in the love department, sleek breasty lure with that long straight shiny black hair of hers. *Always* the guys were hitting on her, just like in high school, a look, a snag, bingo, they were wrapped tight as pigs in a blanket about her finger. Sure, he had the beginnings of a paunch (but only when he bent at the waist), and yes, a surly god had given him a bunchy sort of face; but he had lots to offer the right girl—correction, the right girls—and he was tired of watching turned-off bimbos suddenly turn *on* at hearing who his father was, cash registers hot and flashing in their eyes. He'd fucked 'em. Got off as they acted their way toward pretend orgasms. Christ, who wouldn't? But it was like humping tinsel. Just a little bit hotter than porn flicks, but no less impersonal.

Personal. Real. That's what he needed.

So he turned to the personals ads, found someone who pushed a few buttons. Mmm, redhead yes. Non-addict? No problem. No fatties? He'd sit up straight, and besides, he'd seen lots worse lardbellies than him—like his daddy for one. Looking for someone spiritual and sensitive; he qualified most definitely, having read *Out On a Limb* once or twice. Worth the 900-number charges—besides which he had his own personal phone, so he wouldn't have to wonder who'd think he was into phone sex.

A Slow Red Whisper of Sand

He dialed, listened to her message, Janice her name, fell into the depth of Janice's voice: "Hello, I'm in my mid-thirties, I have long red hair, I'm fit and trim, one child who lives with his father. Oh yeah, yes, my name's Janice. I'm an established professional and I expect you to be too. I'm looking for someone in good shape, honest and open with his feelings, at least five-ten. No facial hair. Someone who has wide cultural interests and who is a good listener but can hold up his end of things. There should be a depth to your thoughts, a kind caring quality in your voice, a breezy independence that isn't afraid to begin and sustain an intimate relationship."

There was a little more, about leaving a message. A demon said, "Leave one now," drowning out the angel whose advice was to write something down first, then call back. So he punched in the leave-a-message choice. One minute? Christ, you couldn't say anything in a minute!

The phone beeped at him, a prompt.

"Um, hello, my name is Brad. Short for Bradley. My work is profes-sional, and I really like your voice. Hair color is vaguely brown, I'm thirty-eight, hazel eyes, not a bad body. I like to sit around and chat, and I think I have a lot to offer the right person. And Janice (that's a pretty name, by the way) maybe you're that right person and maybe I'm right for you. Hope so anyway. Umm, let's see, what else: I could use a caring person and you sure sound that, and I'm ready for a direct, open, honest one-to-one relationship and then we can see where things want to go from there." Suddenly he remembered the minute and man-aged to slip in his phone number before the final beep cut him off.

He hung up, stared at his pork-hand on the receiver, picked up the newspaper and read over her ad again. Then he tilted the mini-blinds upward. He fancied he could see her, a surge of curves, a sweet face, shiny red waterfall of hair sweeping down upon white freckled shoul-ders. His hand rustled up whip-whip-whip three Kleenex from the box by his bed, pastel blue, weren't making them as strong as they used to, used to take just two and now the paper, as he wiped clean, would stick annoyingly to his dicktip. A minor matter. He laid them neatly square on the bedspread and had his shorts and Jockeys down about his knees in no time, positioning himself so he wouldn't overshoot. Then he stared at her ad again, moving, moving, whispering her name, Janice, and conjuring him and her and that hot babe his dad had practically fucked by pool edge yesterday, an amazing threesome right here on his bed, the smell of the bedspread mingling with the aroma of pussy and the lovely feel of twin lips twining up and down his manhood.

Janice weeded out four callers at once, those with a tad much eagerness for red hair, or the bozo who liked to go four-wheeling (she had no idea what four-wheeling was, but she saw huge-tired trucks colliding under floodlights and x'd him out), or the ones whose words laid a cold hand on her brain stem for reasons Janice couldn't figure. Of the ones remaining, she felt drawn to this Brad character the most. Boyish and firm, a little bit awkward, sincere in tone as far as she could tell. He wasn't ideal. None of them were. But he'd do for a start, meet him at least and check him out, let her bullshit detector do the rest.

He lifted on the third ring. "This is Brad." Solid rock, a no-nonsense directness that had its appeal.

"Hello. It's Janice. From the personals?"

He fumbled and she liked that too: "Oh, yes, hello, Janice. Thanks for calling, I mean, well, that sounds like a sign-off or something, which I hope it isn't. Ummmm, so you liked what I had to say?"

"What you said, how you said it." Janice could hear the amusement in her voice, but she felt relaxed, not put upon by some macho with a psychic wall, and that seemed a promising thing to feel about Brad.

"So would you like to meet?" Too eager? Maybe, but this meeting through ads wasn't exactly the natural thing to be doing. She gave him the benefit of the doubt.

"One thing I forgot to mention. No smokers. You're not a smoker, are you?" Damn, he was going to be a four-pack-a-dayer, a type-A loser with a cellular phone glued to his ear in some high-demand profession, heart pounding and hurtling him toward an early grave.

"Filthy stuff," came his answer. "You know, I tried it a total of once, just to see, you know, a long time ago cuz I figured why not, see what the big deal is. I guess there was some vague buzz there, but no great appeal, and it looked weird in the mirror. So that was that."

"Good," she said, relieved. "I left that out of the ad and then kicked myself. I guess it was so obvious, my mind just skimmed over it."

"Pretty kicking, I bet."

"Excuse me?"

"The kick, pretty legs—oh nothing, a backhanded and ham-fisted compliment, never mind, forget I said it." His stammering had an endearing quality to it; not mealy, not in the least. His voice felt like suede leather stitched over steel, very indrawing and comforting.

She laughed. "It's forgotten. And I *do* have pretty legs, not that it's any of *your* beeswax."

"Of course not." He'd picked right up on her flirty tone and batted it right back, good as he got.

"So let's meet," she said, and after he'd proposed a dinner date at a swank restaurant, she countered with her standard frozen-yogurt-in-the-mall offering. It was well lit, populous, and ideal for quick, diplomatic thank-yous and good-byes if the chemistry proved, in those first five minutes, to be absurdly wrong.

He ended, more confident than he'd begun, on a joke. When she cradled the receiver, she felt hearth-warm in an odd full-tummied sort of way. Spirits lifted after a day of feeling like nobody special, the same old dusty mopers surrounding her at work. On impulse, she dialed the free number and skipped to Brad's response, listening to it in silence, stilling her fancies, playing it over again, the real human being behind the fumbles now engaging her more fully. Could she hear her one-and-only in his voice? If she listened past the wine-fruity baritone, could she see and feel her soul mate pining to get through?

•   •   •

LOVE IN VEIN

When he drove up to his beachfront home, their faces were pressed like kitten faces to the front window. Once they'd been human, once borne a touch of rare uniqueness, a thing that had singled each one out. But fetching-time was long gone for them, that time teetering between human and undead, when their teeth had not yet turned to hollow fangs and their nips and clits and labia had not yet gone razor-sharp and as blood-receptive as leeches.

"All this is yours?" She was used to opulence—that he knew. But it was the privacy of the drive in, and how proximate the ocean waves pounded, that clearly impressed her.

"The world meets my needs," he said.

She drew to him, felt him below, that enticing pulse in his eyes drawing her. "I'm not usually so bold."

"It's something to learn." He accepted Esme's kiss, warm press and lick and withdrawal. "Come inside." Hard to believe her uniqueness was subject to vanishment. But he'd seen it with the three inside and countless times in ages past. Esme's turning he vowed to prolong, resisting the end of fetching-time for an eternity if he could.

The door swung open at his touch. They stood at the edge of the hallway, their faces raptored on Esme. Mopsy had two fingers inside Cottontail's pussy, and Flopsy, at their left, worked at pleasing herself. Dried bloodspray from past climaxes rhubarbed their inner thighs, and their vulvas glistened red and wet with arousal.

"Pay them no heed," he suggested. Then, raising his arms and advancing toward them, he intoned in the ancient language of his forebears the words to keep them off. At the instant he began, they hobblefooted backward over the blood-spattered oak floor, torn between pure need and the impelling power of his injunction.

In the past, Esme had shown restraint in initiating, in accepting, sexual advances—much more so, she thought, than most of her generation. It had paid off too. Close scrapes with near intimacy, because she'd deflected them, had kept her wounds superficial when bad choices revealed themselves.

A Slow Red Whisper of Sand

But with *him* (names didn't matter), that foolish not-quite-yet coyness dropped away. Odd feeling. Completely in control and yet not like herself at all, the trappings of ponderous convention having been cast off like a thick fur coat she hadn't known she was wearing.

Esme gestured. "Who are these—?"

"My wives," he said. And that was all right. Still more startling, *they* were all right with her, these lynx-eyed creatures from a world of nightmare. Esme saw them, yes, for the red-crusted fright-hags they were, but could not deny their allure, not deny the staying power of eyes that comforted and caressed nor the sensual craving these three had set going in her heart and soul. Then abruptly he appeared in front of her, gazed a wounded longing into her eyes, crouched, never breaking that gaze, brought his right arm up under her dress, bunching it upward like the spooned-away crust of a custard, until his biceps saddled snug against her crotch, his hand splayed on the small of her back, and he lifted Esme straight into the ocean-rich air and walked with her, eyes locked upon hers, through a high arch into a faintly metallic-smelling room bathed in candlelight and awash with pillows.

In lowering her, steadying her torso with his strong left hand, he drew her lips downward to his, obliterating melt of flesh upon flesh, and his right arm slid by moist lace until his warm fingers cupped her cunt through cloth and fondled her so beautifully that her briefs clung like sodden terry cloth against bare skin. She came like that, moaning into his mouth, feeling the odd dentition against her tongue but not caring, not at all, not even the sting of lipcut where he moved slightly there and left numbness behind like mosquito puffiness.

"Love me," she whispered into his ear, and his whole body felt so good, shaped against hers as his hands undid her dress at the back. But wait, it was a frontbuttoner, and yet his fingers parted cloth along her spine as if it were Velcro'd on, a gentle controlled ripping and rending that bared her shoulders and her breasts, soft red-tipped lovelies he blessed with his mouth. A stinging there too but it only drove her excitation higher, like breath taut from the sudden thorn-prick of a sweetheart rose.

LOVE IN VEIN

And then she was naked and his clothing too was gone and she touched his penis, thimble-hard it seemed just at the very tip, just about the slit of his warm rubbery cap of cock. But he brushed away her hand, and laid her upon soft pillows, and mounted her, easing in deeply, quickly, amazingly, she was so moistly receptive, so needy for his flesh. She reached up and hugged him fiercely, moving to his long slow thrusts. Then orgasm claimed her again, at her G-spot an incredible spread of goodness, and his love stayed hard and beautiful in her sight, dark and muscular and young and ancient all at once. She was still pulsing beneath him, still moist with fucksweat. "I want to make you come," she said, her yoni moving about him yearningly like the idle sway of a belly dancer winding down.

But he stopped her, held her hipbones in both hands, a thick bible thumbed open by a god, and drove as deep as he could inside her, his head turned aside. "You'll feel a tiny sting," he said, apology and promise in his voice.

Then she did.

It began very small, a burning sensation deep in her vagina, the front wall where his cocktip rested. Then it widened, a needle of pain (flashback to the bedclawing of arterial blood being drawn from an arm); but she embraced the small agony of it, seeing the radiance in her lover's eyes, feeling how turned on by it he was. He was drawing something, a deep strength from her, and she gave it with all her will. Gold touched her. The ability to give him such pleasure seemed miraculous, made her want to cry for joy. And then, his excitation becoming audible, the pain suddenly ceased, and he was again thrusting, past the odd puffiness he'd left, back and forth against it, massaging it to distraction with his cocktip. He seized her and in his coming she heard the wounds of ages crying forth; and hearing them, she sobbed uncontrollably, cradling him and comforting him in the locked cling of their bodies.

Brad found the mall, one he'd been to just after its opening a few years back. Plant theme. Skylights, glass elevators with golden

A Slow Red Whisper of Sand

Christmas lights down the sides. A jaunt up a steep escalator and he spied the yogurt place, its blue-and-pink plastic motif managing miraculously not to be garish but somehow tasteful. Not close enough yet, this Janice possibility hidden from him, if she was there at all. He checked the time, ten minutes late and damned if she wasn't going to ding him for it.

Then he saw her. *Had* to be her. Brilliant puffs of red hair on her head and a long luxurious fall down to an antic flip at the shoulder blades. A slight, slender girl, her tight ass perky on the pink plastic chair. She arced her neck, saw him, knew it was him, gave a wave. Oh dear Jesus, he thought; she was cute and snazzy and sweet, and she had seen him and not immediately cut him cold.

Careful, don't trip on anything. He was moving, the butt, the petite strain on her blouse front, coming round to sit opposite her, her full reddened lips, collagen not an impossibility there but he suspected hers were natural and, as he glanced across them, he ran his tongue in fancy along the inviting rip in her mouth. "Janice, right?"

"You must be Brad." No hand offered; handshake'd be gauche, uncool. Tight waist. Must work out, jog, clingy leotard and a rainbow sweatband about that pillow-perfect tumble of crimson hair.

"Pleased to meet you," Brad said.

"Pleased to meet *you*," she echoed. "I recommend the coconut custard, dusted with carob shavings. Like a full helping of Breyer's without the consequences."

No fool, he had it. Pleasantries passed between him and this beguiling stranger. Nice eyes. Beautiful eyes. By god, what was the world coming to that such a kissable darling felt it necessary to place an ad in the personals column? He'd been hoping for a cut above average, no dog at any rate—but Janice was sheer wonder, a moving target and a devastation waiting to befall. Don't get too close to her, he cautioned. She's being polite, leading to the letdown at the end, nice time but we're not right for one another— meaning you're too ugly, you've got hair on your ears, the thought of touching you revolts me.

381

But he could play pretend as long as she cared to do the same; and he decided to enjoy himself, be natural and forthcoming, take her in, all the way in. And later that night, alone in bed, he could replay those images, replay her words, her smiles—and have her six ways from Sunday, courtesy of the Kimberly-Clark Corporation and his expert groin-shift and stifle-come, developed through decades of practice, upon the sheets.

Janice appraised him. No Redford, no Costner, but no Quasimodo either. He seemed, what, *comforting* as he went on, spooning up yogurt, talking about his managerial work at the studio. Didn't seem overdressed or too casual. A cologne (she usually hated scent on a man) both vague and pleasing buoyed his words.

He skimmed a melt of yogurt onto the spoon as Janice leaned forward, elbowing the table. "Does it bother you, meeting me through the ad?" Of course Brad would say no, but, beyond that, the answers to this question were often revealing.

"Not at all," he said. "It's refreshing. You supply a what-you're-looking-for list, give some kind of essence of you. I look it over, maybe I'm not a match in all the particulars, like that 'very handsome' stuff, now I'm not exactly—"

"I *like* the way you look."

"Well thanks. Okay, maybe that was a bad choice cuz I'm decent enough I guess, and you, by the way, are sweet as honey on the eyes—"

That was touching. She could sense his appreciation of her, a deep non-surface directness that warmed her and startled her. He was human. Not at all pushy or leering the way some clueless guys were. It was subtle, the bond forming between them, but it existed and felt good.

"—but anyway, we get to turn over this distillation of who you are and what you want, examine it, peek around it and play with it. I guess we use it as a base, a kind of nucleus, for whatever comes after."

Janice smiled. "I was pretty careful, wording it to screen out the riffraff. If you don't say no addicts, a nice loaded word, they come flooding in." She told him a few of her horror stories, that time with seamless Henry, a tiger in bed (she left that part out) and seemingly all hatches battened down in his head—then the dependence on her coming clearer, Chinese fingercuffs holding harder to her the more insistently she tried to pull loose. Brad's reaction was warm and commiserating and endearing.

Too soon, the hour was over.

"Let me ask you something," he said.

She said sure.

"I'll bet men, maybe all of them, say I'll call you, even if they're not going to. Well I *do* want to call you but only if you want me to. Do you want me to?"

She did. Oh my, did she ever. "Yes, please, Brad," she said. "I'd like that."

He smiled and rose and said good-bye, ambling off. A total fix on him, craning to see this engaging man shrink along the upper mall walkway, then vanish slice by slice, diagonal escalator cuts taking him down. There was going to be sex, and soon. And with luck, there would be love.

When he returned from dropping her off, the three of them, in the moonlit driveup, crowded his car, not daring to smear it with their touch. Once they had, each in her turn, been special to him. Now they were raw convenience alone, to be fed upon as they had fed upon fresh victims, to be fucked in the sweet mire of total animal abandon, a surge of blood-come pumped into one or another orifice or showered hot and bisque-pink upon breast or face.

He got out, pinged shut the car door. Esme wouldn't leave his thoughts, the lingering taste of her liquids, a depth to their intimacy he'd never known before.

Plump bellies on the bitches: feverish feed tonight and more drained victims found tomorrow. Mopsy gurgled a question, and Flopsy topped her unintelligible words with a higher-pitched repetition: "Why no feed?"

Cottontail emerged between the two, her wanton brown hair greasy and clumped with gore. Her neck appeared—an illusion of her single-minded desire—to telescope toward him. Her lips touched his and she disgorged an upchucked gout of blood, fear-tainted but sustaining. She left off her kiss, chin-dribble, and said, "The cream-skinned one. The black-haired one. We smelled her, we heard the pulse in her wrists, we felt her breath on the air."

He thumbed the outer nipples of the bookended beasts and felt them prick and draw from razor tips. "Esme will not be drained. Mild pulls only, and *her* feeding must be shallow as well."

"She's joining us?" The bloodsmear was so thick, it cracked when she smiled, night parch of desert sands. An eagerness obscene and enveloping filled her question.

"Twilight state," he replied, thumbs tingling at the drainage. Their areolae pulsed like cockheads. "Forever on edge, not to be turned."

Cottontail felt herself, bloodcunt gleam, with a red hand. She fin-gered a wet aromatic smear across his upper lip, stiffening him below. "We want to indulge. Refined platelets. Not the alley druggy stuff out there."

"Must fuck," Mopsy gurgled, tugging at his belt.

"Must fuck," Topsy echoed, zippering down, shredding his briefs so fiercely she furrowed taut hipskin.

He unstuck his thumbs, licked them, pointed. "She's mine. You won't touch her unless I'm here." He uptugged his shirt and tossed it aside. Tight toned torso—sipped varietals at many bedsides, care-fully chosen, keeping him young and fit. That, and the simple fact of his by-birth origins, never human, never blindly fed upon to turn him, had, he believed, kept him from devolving.

The blood was up in him. Bitches looked sweet, felt like wet bestial insistence, writhing upon him, reddening him, drawing him onto the moonlit lawn. Surf pounding in the near distance, they leaned right-ward—a mutual baring of necks—into a fourway suck. Esme would never do this. No, she would join him on his nightly ventures, sip where he sipped, lightly, savoringly. But he'd keep this breed of creature around for heavy rutting, for the red wet hot fuck of it. His back hit chill grass, and he had a quick image of bloat-belly above, Flopsy, before her blood-quim gaped to his feasting and his hard-on pulsed to the pierce of six fangs, drawing blood at its tip from the palate of whichever one mouthed down over his cockhead. His hands, fumbling, found the greasy gapes of wet yoni, felt labial cuts plantlash across his fingers and begin to draw there as he fondled Flopsy and Mopsy, left and right.

Esme, ever Esme, on his mind. She'd watch him, glad at his rough pleasures; and maybe, at times in a measured way, he'd draw her in, restraining the creatures circling her refinement, commanding, holding off, savoring in turn her pleasure in the sweet excesses of multifuck; then, at last, turning the trio out and knowing again the delicate wonders of his and Esme's private intimacies.

Flopsy's clit cut into his tongue, and then she came sprays of bloodfuck across his face. The hot wash of it, fevered and chaotic, drove him murderous with lust and he sucked and sucked at her vulva, whitening it (could it be seen) faster than her replenishing at his cock rereddened it. But control returned, and he unpussied his mouth for new breaths of ocean air. And the foursome writhed anew, seeking another apt position for bloodlust à *quatre*.

Later, he ordered Mopsy to fetch the toys.

Esme's father, the belly of a bear engreened beneath his polo shirt, stopped her the next morning. He squired on one arm a big-bosomed blonde, looking lost and wincing at the sunlight.

"You okay?" he asked, unsure what had halted him.

"I'm fine." Esme's words were cotton-soft.

"You're not . . . Esme, are you in love?" He gave a mock frown, enfolded in a grin.

"Me, Dad?" she said. "Practical me?"

"'At's my girl." Dad slow-rounded a fist-tap on her shoulder. "Put that Frank bastard out of your mind"—her three-year disaster of a marriage—"take your pleasure as it comes, and let the world go hang." Bimboing along, he bellowed back: "Make yourself at home, blow off frigging Denver for eternity—and bring the boyfriend by sometime, okay?"

Denver. Her flight left in three hours. She didn't care. Let her tickets expire; let them wonder at work, a world off, what had become of her; let the utilities shut down, her neighbors fret, her landlord key open and clean out and rerent the place. She couldn't recall them, not their names and only faintly their faces. What was *real*, what kept form and focus, was the soft warm shiver he had blessed so many places on and inside her body with. What was *real* were his face and hands, his lips and his sharp-tipped arousal. And the alluring aircloy of his dripping wives, those sucklovely eyes, those kissable faces pasted like pink round petals on the wet bark of night.

All day, she idled. The timelessness of a cloudless day became her timelessness. From south along the coast, she felt desire, his, her own, a desire which deepened as day waned. She wandered the estate, alone, feeling for a frightening time such loneliness as she hadn't felt since just past college; and as she wandered, the tingle inside her vagina, walled a long finger's length within, grew so intense that she came just thinking about his penis there piercing her, drawing sustenance from her. Her southward longing picked up sharply as the sun set, and, before she realized it, she stood outside the garage, thumbed it up, backed out the sleek Maserati, and somehow managed in her state—half-cloudy, half-aroused—to negotiate sufficient freeway to find the coast road, his private drive, a gate yielding obediently open for her, and his seacoast home.

He stood there, waiting, naked, erect. Esme started a grasp toward the door, but he held up his hand, rounded the bumper, bent to her window. "Undress," he said.

"In here?"

Eyes hot with love, he nodded.

"Where are your wives?"

As if in answer, they loomed up out of the darkness, before the windshield and wrapped to her right. His look seemed to darken, but then his eyes returned to her and a smile once more grazed his lips. "I'll watch."

She complied, easy at first with blouse buttons, but then struggling in the small space, her shoulders hurting as the blouse resisted removal and her breasts arched out and up. Unbelted the skirt, shimmied out of it, his eyes a comfort, theirs both a menace and a turn-on, whose glare steamed into her and made her mind blaze. When blue lace was all she wore, she slowed down, angled toward him, put a finger inside herself, licked it as he watched, then in idle ease drew her panties down and off.

The door clicked. Before her? Behind her? No cold air rushed in, but she felt nails singe down her back and she saw his face surge forward and felt the flaypain ease away in instant heal. And then the night came around her like black wool and the house unmouthed to scoop them in, the walls dimly fired with candlelight, tiny torch go-by, go-by. She was coming beautiful comes in his arms, doing nothing, touching nothing nor being touched, just feeling his voluptuous enwrapment and the close earthy breaths of his women wraithing nearby. Their rhythm shifted, stairs pumping, the creatures' feet slapping like thongs of whip on stone steps.

A warm room, no windows. Iron bolts in the ceiling, which seemed so low one might have to stoop to pass. The soft bedding met her, a slight backburn at how swiftly he set her down. Who was she? She couldn't remember and it didn't matter. They grabbed her wrists, one each, hot as collie paws, the ones he called Flopsy and Mopsy, and had her pinned in *(first contact)* their grip. He plunged his face into her heat so ferociously it seemed he would bury his head, jaw first, inside her right up to the neck. At her temples, the third wife's hands clamped and caressed. Could wrists and temples be sex organs? She couldn't see their restraints, but she could sense as solidly as brick that they wanted desperately to feast upon her and that a muzzle had been placed upon their slavering jaws. At her yoni, open freely for him, he kissed and licked and stung and sucked, sharp pangs again but then quickly numbed and covered with kisses. She loved the contrast of iced pain and warm gentle loving. Then he had her clit between his lips and (he wasn't going to) yes, he was, he needled her there, fast and gone and puffed taut with need, building, building, until she released her climax upon his swirling tongue, head back and thrashing, looking into the hot wet eyes of the three and coming more feverishly for what she saw there.

Her complexity and her boobs, that's what Brad liked about Janice. He couldn't believe how quickly things had progressed. A week ago, the yogurt shop; then that sweet evening above-the-waisting in his car (a throwback to the ineptitudes of high school days but sure and skilled this time); and now, watching her reach for coffee and measure it into her coffeemaker, they were very close to fucking. Her complexity and her tits and her pussy—soon that more complete appreciation of her would be his.

Wanting to touch her, he rose from the kitchen table and came up behind her. They were smalltalking, her fire of hair filamenting down against her gray jogging outfit. He hugged her close, turned her, kissed her. That lovely lip aroma again. She'd made monogamy noises over yogurt. But Janice was complex, persuadable surely once she'd had a taste of his prowess. Tired of being alone and longing to find a soulmate, that's what she'd said; he thought it might become a stumbling block, but that was a discussion best kept until his bedroom skills made him indispensable and her definition of relationship malleated accordingly. She could be primary. She was certainly delicious enough for that. They'd catch at Dad's dregs, snag and shack up with one or two at a time, console them, lick them, share their perfect bodies in sensual writhe, then send them on their way. Janice with him at the core, drawing luscious bi-babes into their bed, maybe eventually latching onto a permanent third. It could happen, it really could.

He felt her perfect back under the jogging top, drew about and thumbed her nipples. Nice subtle inbreath from her. "Don't you want your coffee?" she teased.

A Slow Red Whisper of Sand

On the edge of her soft full lips, he gave his reply in kisses: "I want . . . honey . . . cream . . . lots of cream . . . lots of honey." He eased his left hand under the elastic at her waist, no underwear, just taut expanse of skin, and a thrill of hair, and moisture grooving down at his fingertip. She seized up, grinding her mouth hard upon his, her hips in slow rotation slick on his finger.

Her hand brushed him, pressed him, the lizard scales of his jeans preventing direct touch.

Kiss broken. "Let's go to bed," he said, thick with lust at her ear. He retrieved his finger, licked it, and went with her out of the kitchen, tugged along like a mom leading her child. Zesty package, this Janice—a fitting start to his harem, and her body tasted of sunshine.

Janice felt snugly smothered in warm assertive flesh atop her bedspread. Undressing her, he showed gratifying awe in word, in kiss, in caress. They felt good together no matter what he did—and eventually what she did. Brad proved a fanatical oralist. She'd never known there were so many orgasms to be licked from her in so short a time.

Curiously, after a while, for all the waves of sheer pleasure that washed over her, he began to seem not quite human, too consumed with technique. But then their being together was still so new, there was still so much yet to be learned. And in between comings, the snuggling was so sweet and the words shared so soft and loving.

Yet one theme, even as his chin rhythmed up and down upon her yoni hair and his nose tipped into her vulva, in recurrent whisper played in her head: He's nowhere close to being exclusive, nowhere close to monogamy, as distant from commitment as Pluto is from the sun. But was that a truth absolute, or an illusion born of her insecurities? She felt—or did she—the beginning of something precious between them, something that perhaps would be blessed and nurtured by the very intimacies she now allowed.

She liked his ideas and his wit and his warmth. The riches he'd revealed tonight were a nice surprise. But a rich man was no substitute for a devoted one, and Janice, fingers on the warm tiller of his rod, felt that Brad was poised to declare his devotion—if not tonight then soon. When he did, she'd be ready.

She arched back upon her pillows, feeling his tongue in quivery swirl drive her heavenward again. "Oh, Brad," she said, "I want you inside me." And he was off her, in floorward dive, digging excitedly in his pants pockets, a square finally in his hand, that cellophane crinkle she'd heard subliminally whenever he moved or sat, a rib-tipped Trojan torn free at last and hastily rolled on. The glow radiated from her, the need, the need, and then he warmed her again, filling her rushingly beautifully full.

A week had passed. He'd allowed them a taste of her under stringent restrictions. And he'd let her lick wide redness, careful to hold open the razored labia and avoid the needling clit—until her face came away like a baby's covered in beet juice, cuts savory on her face where Esme had accidentally brushed past a labial edge.

But now, during their fiveway, he noted with alarm a change in her: Her clit tongued no longer soft and sweet but bore the beginnings of a crust; and her labial splay, once as yielding as the meat of a clam, now sprawled upon his face with all the hardness of wooden spoon edges. In his fingers, her nipples felt more like thimbles than the erasers she'd previously hardened up into.

At once he insisted her off his face and ordered his three wives, their hunger terrible even in restraint, out of the playroom.

"But why?" she asked him, and in answer he only drew her close to a flame and held her head tight in his hands and gazed fiercely into her eyes, as deep as he could go. No turn, not yet, but teetering precariously close. From that moment, he kept the wives away, forbade her to drink his bloody seed no matter how much she demanded it, moved into the stimulus of pain to match the upped ante of need she showed. He chained her up, hanging stretched and hot in her animal gorgeousness from the bolt. And he whipped open welts, across her buttocks and elsewhere, which then he plowed with the thin-strawed suck of his fangs, a tiny draw of blood only. But no longer—no, not until crusted nips and clit softened again and her labia lay like moist warm babyhands against his mouth—would he allow her lips to touch bitchmeat nor to suck at a vein he opened nor to take in orally the pink surge of his love.

And she did soften in her holy parts somewhat; but a hostile glaze covered her lovedeep eyes. Unnoticeable if unsought—and he didn't confront her for fear of sparking it into flame—but there or not, the passion, once whole, now had a rent in it. And it tore at him, as later, bent to drink from dozing forms, he could not escape the image of Esme in her new guise.

The following night, a need seized her. She went to a health bar, ordered Green Drink—a shit-vile concoction of celery and spinach leaves—and sipping it lightly, she seduced, first with her eyes then with her words, a needy dork who looked shy and wounded but took the bait. Up in his room, he ouched away from chest-to-chest embrace. To her steamy entreaties, though, he allowed her to suck him passably hard and then, above his need-a-condom protests, to pussy down upon her work and clamp tight when the need welled up in her.

"Hey, wait," he said. "That hurts."

Esme smiled and relaxed, then dug into his shaft more deeply than before, trying for blood. A scratch, a strain of suck—and a tingle thrilled her pussy at its first lip-taste of indrawn life. She could feel the pull, a sunlamp radiating groin-deep as her labia capillaried blood.

But the dork pushed her off him as best he could, and his cock scraped against her edges pulling out, more cunt-shudder overwhelming her into the most delicious orgasm of her young life. When she dwindled down to his reedy pleas for her to go, pathetic whine as he held out her clothing, he no longer mattered. Esme dressed and left, feeling the look of triumph on her face.

She'd show *him*.

There was no summoning this time. But she drove down the coast anyway, feeling a tantalizing something fill the air; and when she pulled up, hardly able to wooze out from the bloodlust pulsing in her loins, his trio of wives were standing there, bent like hothouse plants, waiting.

It had been a lovely dinner, sitting close to her as the waiter brought one choice Italian dish after another, finishing things off with cannoli that seemed to come from heaven. Brad had needed to touch her thigh and her hand, easing down to hold his there. She spoke of her friends, her family, her colleagues; and he in turn told her about his kid sister Esme and his lascivious dad, hoping Janice would get the hint, from his tone, that multiple partners was foremost on his own want list. Didn't dwell on it, a tad too early for that; he passed on to other things, but he saw no blip of disapproval on her face, if anything an unreadable sparkle in her eye that *might* signal interest. Soon (fondling her between fucks, he thought) he'd broach the subject, talk of his past experiences, hope she'd had some of her own—and off they'd go.

But on the drive back to her place, God knows how it came to happen, she smoothly segued into a statement that after years of dating she wanted monogamy, and that, with her, it was all or nothing. Beat. Beat. He let silence fill the car, humming, pretending needful interest in the traffic patterns; and then the conversation turned in new directions, ones more blithely handled. Near her home, a warm hand fondled above his nape. "Your hair's so soft," she said, and Brad knew things were all right again.

He held her close as they walked toward her door, an insistent crave in his voice when he murmured how much he wanted to have her, what sweet undressing there would be. By God, if he were a one-woman man, this would be the one for him. She opened the door, her hand went to the light switch, he stopped her hand. "Not just yet," he said and he turned her and kissed her and reached under her dress, the apartment door still open onto the night, to ardently fondle her buttocks and strip her raw naked and lickable, down upon his knees and rustling the fabric upward to get at her moist treasure.

Too bad about Brad. More than repulsed, Janice felt sad. He was a fine man, with much to draw her love. But he was also yet another lover not ready for commitment, a bit of chaff in the wind, restless, blown by the next new breeze where his lust's caprice dictated.

Well, she'd show him what he was about to miss. His clear unreadiness to embrace only her—his silence in the car—did nothing to diminish his ardor in bed nor did she suddenly hate or revile him. Sad case. She'd turn it on for him, be more uninhibited than ever, let the memory of her flesh burn into his brain, feeding his future regret. Happiness now, sorrow hereafter. That's what she decided to aim for. Hers, his, theirs.

She pushed him down on his back, a sudden surge from her orgasm. She was rough; the springs jounced as he hit the mattress. Then, straddling his skull, she boneground her open pussy onto his mouth and helped herself to a big serving of hard cock. In went its head, an inch of shaft hot and pushing upward, another, another. Gag reflex, an ache of stretched lips, gotta get past it, a little click at the back of the throat, there it was, and she lipped a wide few inches more until his ballhair tickled her nose. "Oh, Jesus," he gasped around her squished crush of cunt, men loved this shit, and she undicked her throat, shafted down *again* past the click, once more, once more, hurrying him, feeling the pulse and throb of his cock and carrying him all the way onward into the peak moment from which he would, she hoped, forever after tumble into regret.

His loss. She drank deep, draining him, regretting, knowing she'd too suffer; but his would last longer, poor fool, and when he woke to his folly, she'd have moved on, seeking the one-woman man she knew was waiting for her.

Perhaps it was the rich creaminess in the one he met that night, the surge of sweater-fill, perfectly embodied desire, top to toe; or perhaps it was his home trouble, a trio of wives tired of denial no matter how ruthlessly he tried (once Esme'd left) to compensate with knifeplay and the sinking of sharp stakes near the heart. Whatever the reason, he urged the wheat-blond Bekka back to her condo, where he tongue-fucked her into realms of bliss, and then drained her an albino white, supercharged beyond bloat by the beauty of her dying whimpers.

Tonight he wouldn't summon Esme. And tonight at his arrival home, the fourway equation of his household would change. They'd know. They'd smell Bekka's rich offering on him. And they'd know he hadn't shared as he'd done so many times before. Time to ditch them, time to shove the stakes clean through and behead them, time to concentrate exclusively on Esme.

Esme. He geared the low-lying BMW and roared out on the road. She'd stay forever in that special state, half-alive, half-undead. Through the ages, he'd adore her and pamper her, savoring the fine lacings of her blood, being her primary fucktoy as he was hers, bringing her along to witness his engorgings and sharing-in-sex the best of the alluring ladies he found to feed his needs.

He thought of his wives, how once they'd been loving and capable of being loved. But that evanescent state of bliss had vanished under his greed, too swift the turning of them, too fast the imbibing of their lives, until they had turned into needy things of mere sex whose names he'd long forgotten. There was use in depravity, and his lust enjoyed could not be gainsaid. But there was also use in paring a strayward life to the bone and starting anew, in tossing off the detritus of mates gone sour.

He threaded through glaring lights and moving metal, eager to reach home, to clean house, to subsume his bride and sweep her into eternity with him.

The night was warm and the surfpound beckoned. Esme suffered the three to strip her where she stood, a button popping off between bloody fingers that shredded and tore her blouse asunder. Taut elastic wired against one thigh and snapped free; then more viciously upon the other. No clothing blocked the salty breeze, only hands everywhere, touching her, turning her on. Then they lifted her, need heavy about them, and carried her around the house out to the moonlit shore.

Dune flora whipped past their ankles, and their feet sank and slipped, making their movement toward the sea an amble. Then they stopped, eased her down, connected deep and triangular the moment her back touched the dark sand, soft savage mouths touching her here, here, here. Stings far deeper than he had dared *thrilled* her, the blood gone from her in a faster slipstream. She gasped and weakened at their taking, at the satisfaction of their need. Then they sheathed their tips and moved to tongues merely, two at her nipples, one at her yoni. Hard sizzled harder, so taut her erectile flesh that it felt bone-like, toothlike, against their ardent tongueswirls.

And then, her hands groping crumblefists of sand, an outward press of arousal turned suddenly inward, needling at tongues, drawing blood, the liquid flowing beautifully into her breasts and past the nerve ends in her clit. So wild it drove her, that she thought she might pass out or explode. These three beloveds were licking her, exciting her, feeding her, turning her, painting hot gold upon her inner heat.

"More," she said, "more."

But Flopsy left off suddenly below, mouth gone. The sands shifted softly as she moved. Esme reached a gritty hand to herself, cut it against labia, then more gingerly touched the blood fingers to them, drew in her own blood to feel there a new self-love discovered, wounded to feed her puffed organ's cravings. Then Flopsy was at her head in straddle, kneeling, hunkering down. Using an inverted V of fingers, she held herself open and lowered the moist meat to Esme's lips. Her tipped clit was covered, labial razor edges parted and splayed outward in harmlessness as aromatic exudate plashed upon Esme's mouth. Moonlit pink waited, and the turning Esme bared her teeth, and touched the tips to blood-flesh, arcing them an inch deep upward, the suck coming natural to her, hot womanblood tracing an intimate path through mutated nerve and pulpwork.

She'd show *him,* came the thought. But she couldn't, for the life of her, recall who he was. There was only a moon glimpsed past moving thigh, and the high distant cry of sea gulls, and a fourway imbibing of lifeblood—her own below, these three giving at mouth and breast to get back later, and all of it driving her into a dreamy, delicious frenzy unending.

Brad had blown something but he had no idea what. No calls came back from Janice. Or when they did, she placed them at hours she knew he wouldn't be there, her voice all alien suddenly, not soft at all, on the tape—this or that reason, blah blah blah, we'll talk soon.

His work became posturing, not that he'd been so fine a manager before. Focus came hard or not at all. Finally he caught her—out of her interminable string of meetings, not traveling to hell and back on business.

Her phone greeting, a real voice this time.

"Hi, it's Brad."

"Oh, hi," a dull tarnish, the polish suddenly off her professional voice.

"Is this a good time to talk?"

"Well, actually no, I—"

"Look, I won't take much time," he said. "It's just, well, it's just that things were going so well, and all of a sudden they're not."

"Ah," she said, decision there. Pause. Then a shift in tone: "I like you." Acting again. "I really do. But there isn't enough there to build anything on, anything—um—long lasting I mean."

"But I—"

"I need something deeper than you can give me."

"If you'd just let—"

"I'm sorry, Brad," she said, "please . . . there's no point in calling again. All right?"

His head felt woozy.

"All right?" she said again.

A Slow Red Whisper of Sand

"Yes, Janice, if that's the way—"

"Bye, then." And she was gone.

Janice cradled the receiver, feeling, despite how in charge she'd seemed, completely at a loss. What if she'd misread him? What if he really *were* the one? Stiffness, her phone arm tight under crimped cloth. She relaxed it, withdrew her hand, wiped the palm on her left thigh.

She swore under her breath.

Air change at the entrance to her cube. Looking up, she saw Gene Ryman, chubby guy, nice, standing there. He had been about to say something, noticed her startle, her demeanor. He waved a hand. "I'll come back," he said, a shift already in his body.

"Give me five, Gene," she said. "I'll drop by."

"No problem," his voice fading down the aisle.

Damn these open cubicles, some bastard's brainchild, constant distractions and no privacy at all. The impulse to call him back struck, punch up his number, go with him somewhere for lunch, talk it through, be open, frank, not a bent truth nor a screen between them. That was the way to build a relationship. All the books said so.

Ah, but in her gut—and gut feel was all—Janice knew she'd done the right thing. Not done it right, she still needed to work on that; but Brad had rightly been dumped, of that there could be—yes, but there *were*, goddamn it, there *were* doubts. Big ugly ones around her tight prissy center of certainty. Life's a bitch and then she whelps. So Gene had once said, and he'd been right.

She lifted the receiver, jabbed three buttons, got a glitch in her fingers and hit the wrong fourth. Again in its cradle. No. No. She felt the tension in her spine, eased back in the desk chair. Take a deep breath, forget him, get up, go talk to Gene, get her dithering mind back on track. That was the way, let Brad stay dead.

Palming the nape of her neck, Janice rose. Somebody paged someone she didn't know over the intercom. Drained was how she felt, bloodless, heartless. But she'd get by that soon enough.

Life went on. So would she.

Long before he saw the curved chrome and burgundy of her Maserati etched across the dark doorway of his house, he sensed Esme's presence, felt the sting of grief in his heart, a spreading outward, a plague. He passed into the house, oblivious to odd shapes and corridors, grabbing up the sex toys and going out the back way, down to the flop of figures on the shore. Silvered in moonlight, they dug and sucked in sensual frenzy, roiling like bloody seethes of fish in a ketch. Entwinement. Kickups of sand at the periphery. The four were interlocked to maximize contact of nip and clit, fangs and labia, with the blood-yield of exposed flesh.

As he approached, Mopsy raised her cranberried lips, her eyes to his. "You mad?" Her gaze fell to the tools. He covered his grief. When her eyes rose again, it found a convincing mask of lust. Mopsy leered through drips of gore, an alluring frog-blink.

"You mad?" Flopsy's echo. "Must fuck." She it was who found most delight in the stake and now her eyes grew wide with a sharp upratchet of anticipation.

He laid down mallet and stakes and scimitar, tore off his clothing, saw Cottontail's dream-lidded eyes drunk at the savory inner thigh of his beloved. Her head seemed a bloated wart grown dark and cancerous, fanged onto it and sucking, her paramour's thighskin punctured and puffed.

And Esme, dear Esme. His throat bamboo'd with tubed wood. She was arched, pressing a full-breasted nipple to Flopsy's neck, the bloodsuck overspill idling red runnels down the white of her breastmeat. Her teeth were sunk to inch-depth in splayed cunt, and crusted clit needled into her cheek. But Esme's eyes, as he retrieved the tools to draw near—these, with their filled canyons of depth, the articulated peaks of love leveled and made brutish, these tore at his heart. She was gone, turned, become just one more monomaniacal wife.

He let them draw him down, embroiling in their flesh feast, sucking, being sucked, hands everywhere, spreading the sting of tooth and cocktip wherever they touched, and taking the needle and knife of needy womanlove wherever a connection flared. But in his mind was mayhem. And when he brandished the toys and sank stake into breastskin, so that their lips steamed in delight at the pain the nearer he drew to their hearts, he, tormented to his depths, met the near-orgasm in Flopsy's and Mopsy's eyes and drove home the sharpened rosewood, swing-pound with the mallet, here and here. Cottontail backed off, unpeeling from the gore stickings of torso-to-torso, suddener and suddener in the moonlight, oh-no upon her face and then a turn and arrowshoot along the shore. The staked ones on the sand moved in thrash, arcs of red urine upshot and spattering as big gouts of black blood bubbled and burst from their anuses. Rise of scimitar, a smiting, another, and their shrieking heads dropped sharply off, washed in a gush of neckblood. For all their twitching, they were gone, silent, becoming fodder for the earth.

Esme waited, confused, looking at him, looking away, her eyes, her hands, her mouth groping the air for a love suddenly gone. He took up the last stake and went to her eager arms. Through smears of blood he could still smell her subtle aroma as he kissed her, her fresh sunlight and buttercup scent. He fed her fangs through his tongue and took lipblood and tongueblood from her, one drop, another drop, tasting wife-taint and turning there. He wanted to break right then into tears, but he steeled himself as an impoverished hand found his penis and stroked it hard and fed wristblood to its tip. The stake rose, the chocolate tip dimpled the streaked perfection of her breast, drew a hollow of flesh inward, straining, straining, breaking—a short sharp thrust deep through, twisting it, turning it, not needing the mallet for her, just the determination of his love, the deep penetration of solid rosewood invading the pulsing chambers of her heart.

Esme fell back, trying to pull it out, but he batted her hands away, found the scimitar, swung with a misaimed gouge to the shoulder, then swept clean through, her body seeming to topple like children's blocks out from under a head that went straight down. Then, stroking himself, he broke down, falling to his knees. He held her head close to her yoni, kissing her lifeless lips, cutting his mouth on her urine-stenched labia, back and forth between them, loving Esme, refusing to believe she was gone. Then back upon his knees he sat, pressing her severed head upon his cock, sucking throatblood, brainblood, and keening at the moon until there was no blood left. He rubbed that sweet flesh raw, up and down, faster, faster. Then he shot his red seed deep into her and she wept ruddy tears from eyes and mouth, gobbing his naked thighs with the thick liquid of sadness and remorse.

For a time, he considered waiting for the sun to arc up behind him as he stared out at the sea; but finally he rose, found a spade, and buried these three—bodies here, heads there—raking sand over the dunes of burial. Later or perhaps another night, he'd hunt down Cottontail, give her eternal rest. Her scent was still strong in his nose and she would be easy to find. Or maybe he would let her go. But for now, for him, it was nearly time to sleep, a first long daytime of lying there, dreaming about Esme, a first long daytime without her.

Brad was amazed at how drained he felt, whole cities leveled and left in rubble inside him. Through rancorous meetings, and the soulless razzle of pitched ideas in his office, and the black-ballooning of turnedforty Harrison Sanford—through all the pointless scurryings to and fro, Brad filled his usual pointless role. Jabber jabber, she said to him (this one, that one, who cared). And rumblety rumblety, he shot back, knowing by force of habit what in hell to say and being astounded beyond words when whoever it was nodded and sway-hipped from his office.

He cut out at three and hit the bars, his favorites, usually in rotation day by day, now sequential all in one evening. He saved the one with the sorriest cast for the end, smoky haze, lots of solitary heads hunched over dark tables, a sudden belt-back, the reflective glint of glass moving, red circles glowing at the pull of mouths. Joker tending bar, tall walrus-eyed fucker, had seen him dozens of times, never acknowledged it, never said shit beyond a name-it and a that'll-be-x-dollars.

Brad named it. He named it often. And Janice, more beautiful than he thought possible, hovered and hazed and hurt him. All or nothing, she'd said; and now she'd gone and chosen—or had *he?*—nothing. Dumped him. Sucked out his love (Jesus, he'd never realized truly how much she'd come to mean in so short a time) and left him to think on might-have-beens. It was gone. *She* was gone. Sprockets once yanked backward couldn't be rereeled.

Staring at last into a dreg, sloshing it, he thought suddenly of the ocean. A sad patch of rocks and breaking waves came to mind, a skull-numbing convention he escaped from once in Redondo Beach to find late-afternoon privacy and feel the sunset deepen that moment's melancholy. The place called him now. He paid his tab, avoiding the eyes of the bartender, and left.

Hit the road.

His car door slammed in the empty restaurant parking lot, a shatter of the peace but then gone, and the cry of gulls washed in again. He rounded the darkened building, a scrunch of sand against the blacktop, then the softness and unsteadiness of the dunes. A curved paring of beach. At his back swept a soft swish of cars, but mostly he was isolated enough to drop his cool and let hopelessness in. Moon glimmer touched him, chilled him, brought loneliness welling up and sobs. Amid the diamond glitter of moon on sea there glinted red teasings, a sheen of hair, hers.

He paid them little heed—the call of gulls, a crush of nearby tires, the rustle of dune growth in quick puffs of breeze. So, when suddenly a bulked figure appeared to his right, close but gazing out to sea, not at all giving off danger vibes, it caught him unawares. The man wore a leather jacket, was tall and muscular, and his long black hair he'd bound up in a ponytail. His gloved hand held a cigarette.

Reaching into a pocket, the leather creaking, he pulled out a flat-tened pack. "Want one?" he asked.

On Brad's left now, he noticed two more men, younger and far-ther off but still nearby, talking to one another, ignoring him. Same leather. On the back of the one with blond hair, a cherry red BLUDSUKKAHS was emblazoned. "No thanks, I don't smoke." Ordinarily he'd be alarmed. But there were times when you just didn't give a fuck, when a touch of low-down funk made you and the world one. If you looked a lion in the eye and didn't flinch, they said, he wouldn't attack you.

"Your call." Nice friendly manner. He pocketed the smokes. "Peaceful place here."

"Kinda soothing." Brad heard distant murmurs behind him. Didn't fucking matter. Even young toughs could use a break from whatever mayhem they'd been about. And he'd established a rapport with their leader. Pair of rejects they were, taking comfort from the sea.

"The world don't give a shit," the guy said, eyes on a restless car-pet of silver and red and blue.

"You got that right." They were getting on. He saw the two at the left wander closer, both thin, one of them gawkier now and younger than the other; they ignored him. The blond one, the older hood with pockmarks on his face, called to Brad's new friend: "Hey, Michael, Joey here he needs a match. You got some?"

"Think so." Calm voice, comforting. And he reached in and caught a matchbook, raising it between two fingers like a flag. Then there was a quick dash in the sand and the two on the left surged inward, their bodies violating his space as if it didn't matter; and there flew new rush of sand behind him, voices coming in and hands assaulting him, his arms yanked back and bound, oily cloth whip-drawn across his mouth and tied so tight it felt as if calipers had been clamped to his face and were digging for bone.

Brad struggled. He was falling, backward into rough arms. They blanketed him, rolling him, his nose striking a smack of sand, then onward until he was on his back and they duct-taped the blanket tight about him and moved off like triumphant calf-ropers. The leader cowled over him, a new edge opening inside his eyes. "Life," he said, "it just gets tougher, don't it?"

The blond one said, "Fuckin' Joey, no *way* he's ready for this. He's gonna pee his fuckin' pants."

A higher-pitched voice piped up: "Lick my shit if I *ain't*." The tone of it sank Brad's heart. He'd thought, in those first moments of being subdued, that he'd escape with bruises, a bone broken, a shaved head maybe. Beyond that, his mind had refused to go.

Now he knew better.

"Prove it, you little fuck," the blond one said. "I think this guy needs a smoke real bad." A challenge, one Brad didn't understand.

Then Joey flurried about like a scrawny rooster from one hood to the next. He came back to Brad with two long glowing cigarettes, dragged to enflame the tips, blew the smoke out the side of his mouth like it was a curse. And then the cigarettes were one in each hand and coming down closer and closer to his face, not stopping, the heat and the glow on *on ON*, eyelids closed against them, struggles to turn his head, avert it—but the toughs held him still and the searing tips bit, burned, kept burning deeper and deeper, blinded him without mercy over gagged screams.

Then Brad was lifted and hauled, yanked in jangle by many hands, and tossed into the back of a pickup truck, a slammed right hip and shoulder, the knock of metal at his right temple as the bare platform of the truck came up to stun him. The motor gunned into life. A crazy turn. It shot out into the surge of cars, zooming hard like it was late and time was running out.

Before long, they stopped.

Holding a glass of iced tea, mint perfect, he paused by the pool in the midmorning sun. Deep breath of still, moneyed air. Bliss. His left hand idly rubbed his lemon belly, the fine weave sensual beneath his fingers. Green and yellow were good colors, most of the off-reds way too faggy somehow for his tastes.

Milly, over the hill now at fifty—funny, how women, even the sleek ones like Milly, aged less gracefully than men—rumbled out the breakfast cart. Steam off scrambled eggs as she lifted the silver cover. "Juice this morning is orange or cranberry or grape," she said.

"Mix 'em."

She gave him her once-cute grimace. "Come on."

"Humor me. A third of a swig of each."

Milly didn't move.

"You only live once," he said. "Gotta eat the whole enchilada while you can."

"Your funeral." As Milly poured the concoction, the kids occurred to him, a vague feeling of absence. "Where is Esme? And Brad? Haven't seen 'em for days."

"The cars are gone, the one she was using, Brad's as well." She shrugged. "Tooling around?"

"Brad maybe, blowing off his frigging job. But Esme she wouldn't do that, she'd tell me. Maybe we should put out some feelers, call around."

"You want me to?"

He sipped his drink, cringing it down.

Just then, the French doors opened. Orchestrated by good old Darren again, he'd have to give the canny fucker a raise: Three killer bitches, bikini bottoms only, made their sexy way through the sun-glow, perfect boobs lightly bouncing. High heels, matching their tri-angles of cloth, clicked on concrete. Tall blonde, pert brunette, a short platinum dandelion puff atop the third.

Heartmelt.

They sang and strutted to Darren's silly song. Gave him enough time to size them up, watch their big red lips O'ing around words, as soon they'd O around his cock.

"Very nice," he said, and they smiled. "I just love to check hair color right about now." He gestured toward their crotches, a magician's flick. Darren having primed them, at once they tugged at the string ties, whipped the fluorescent triangles off and away.

He moved, glass still in hand, to them. No perfume. He'd made sure of that. He wanted to smell the life from that perfect flesh unmediated by manufactured scent. The left one was high school prom-queen stuff. "A two-tone," he said, touching her dark private hair, gripping it like a squeezed Brillo pad. "I like two-tones." The next one was shaved and squeaky smooth, swooning in a fetching way when he fingered her, parted the lips, admired the smooth moist pink. But the third girl—platinum above, platinum below, and a face that could melt diamonds—she gave such pleasure from her whole body that he sensed possibilities in her. She excited him sexually, yes; but there was far more than that, *far* more, that just might harden the mind cocks of movie audiences coast to coast.

He touched her silver-white softness of private hair and felt blessed. Her eyes, if she was acting, showed it not in the slightest. All he saw were subtle shadings of pleasure as he fondled her and moved finger-deep, finger-tight, inside her—shadings a camera would see and caress and pass along to needful men sitting in darkness.

"I do believe," he said, holding eye contact with an angel in heat, not looking at the others, "that it's time I gave you three lovelies something to suck on."

And that time it was indeed.

Inevitably, eternally, under the sun.